THE SHAPESHIFTERS

Stefan Spjut

Translated from the Swedish by Susan Beard

Mariner Books
Houghton Mifflin Harcourt
Boston New York

First published with the title *Stallo* in 2012 by Albert Bonniers Förlag, Sweden
First published in Great Britain in 2015 by Faber & Faber Limited

www.hmhco.com

Library of Congress Cataloging-in-Publication Data is available.
ISBN 978-0-544-08408-7

Map by Don Larson/Mapping Specialists, Ltd.

Printed in the United States of America
DOC 10 9 8 7 6 5 4 3 2 1

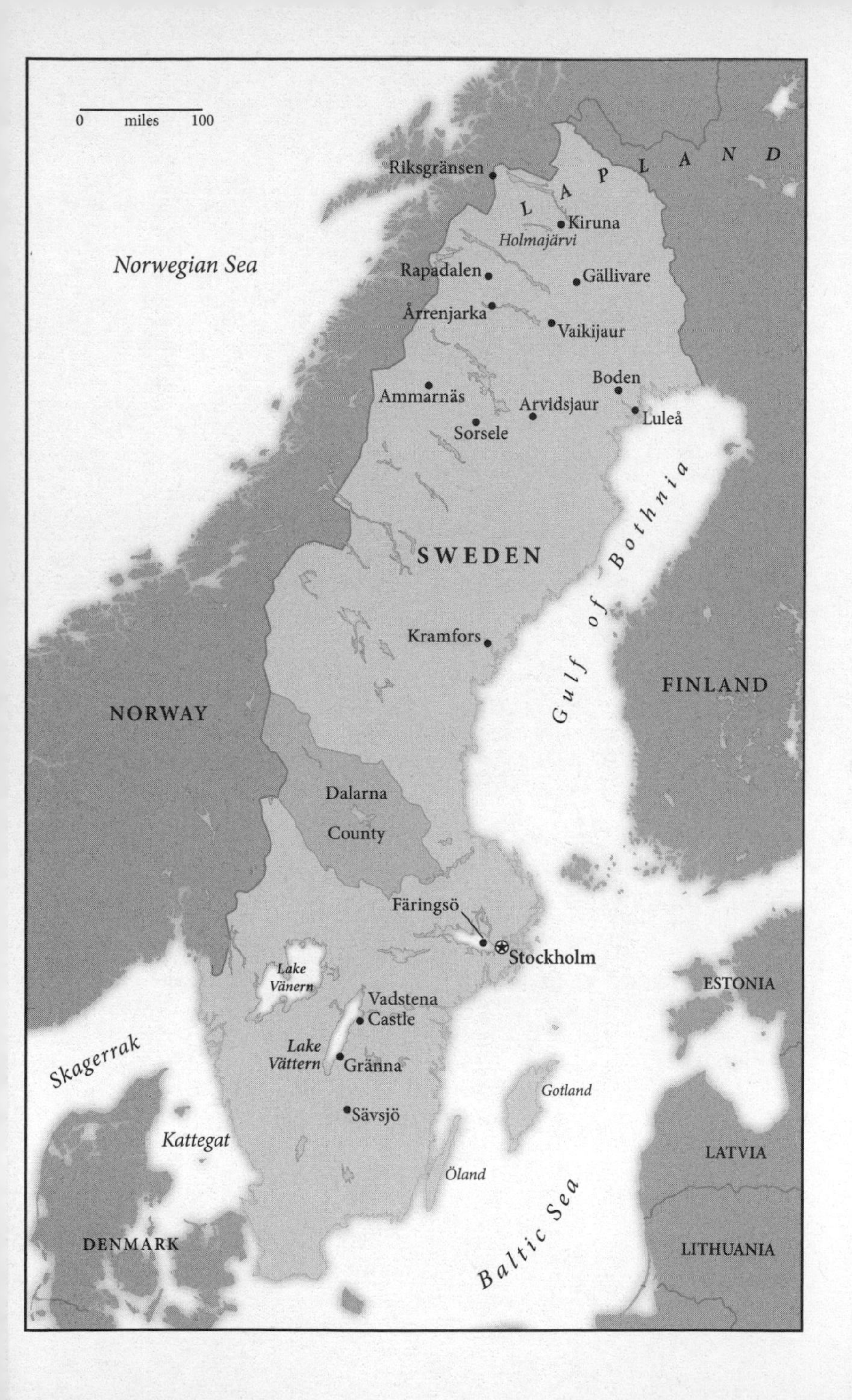
0 miles 100
Norwegian Sea
L A P L A N D
Riksgränsen
Kiruna
Holmajärvi
Rapadalen
Gällivare
Årrenjarka
Vaikijaur
Boden
Ammarnäs
Arvidsjaur
Luleå
Sorsele
SWEDEN
Gulf of Bothnia
Kramfors
FINLAND
NORWAY
Dalarna
County
Färingsö
Stockholm
ESTONIA
Lake Vänern
Vadstena
Castle
Lake Vättern
Gränna
Skagerrak
Gotland
Sävsjö
Kattegat
LATVIA
Öland
Baltic Sea
DENMARK
LITHUANIA

The worm glued to the tarmac is as long as a snake. No, longer. It reaches all the way to the grass verge beside the main road. The boy's eyes follow the slimy ribbon and notice that it stretches across the ditch and curls into the belly of a grey animal. A badger. Dead but still looking. Its eyes are black glass and one paw has stiffened in a wave.

The car door opens and his mother calls, but he cannot tear himself away from the animal.

Then she gets out.

She stands beside the boy. Wrinkles her nose so her glasses ride up.

'It's been run over,' she says.

'But why does it look like that?'

'Those are intestines. A bird pulled them out. Or some other animal.'

He wants to know which bird, which animal.

'Come on now,' she says.

'But I haven't peed yet.'

'Well, do it then.'

He presses his cheek against the window but the pine trees are so tall he can hardly see where they end. His knees are gripping a large Fanta bottle and from time to time he blows into the neck.

The glass is warm and the last few mouthfuls have also been warm. They have been driving for almost three hours, and he has never travelled for such a long time in a car before.

When they stop he does not understand that they have arrived, because they are right in the middle of the forest. There is no sign of a cabin. Only trees.

'Are we there?' he asks.

His mother sits motionless for a while, lost in her thoughts, before pulling the key from the ignition and climbing out. She opens his door.

It is as if the mosquitoes have been waiting for him. They come from all directions and land on him in such a teeming mass that his legs look mottled. He makes no attempt to brush them away but instead stiffens and lets out a plaintive yell.

His mother heaves the bag onto the bonnet and finds a bath towel, which she wraps around him like a cape. After she has tied it round his neck she starts running, with the bag in one hand and the plastic carrier from the supermarket in the other. She leaves a kind of furrow behind her in the long grass. She is wearing a short-sleeved top in green velour, and an oblong-shaped sweat mark is spreading out between her shoulder blades. Her flared jeans flap around her ankles.

He follows after her and the little figures in his backpack rattle inside their plastic box. He holds the shoulder strap with one hand and uses the other to grip the towel to stop it from flying away. Running is difficult and soon his mother's back disappears in the dense greenery in front of him. He calls out to her to wait, but she carries on, calling over her shoulder for him to hurry up.

The ferns have formed tight, thick clumps, and beyond them the fir trees tower above the pitch-black ground. All around him the spiky stalks of the grass hum and tick with insects, and his cloak flies behind him as he runs.

The forest is a silent reflection on the windowpanes. Pine cones, thin twigs and drifts of old pine needles are piled up on the metal roof. The fir trees sway high above against a sky that has grown pale.

His mother has reached the door. Pulling a face she leans forwards, feeling under a windowsill.

'Oh, please,' she says, bending up the metal and forcing her fingers underneath while blowing puffs of air to each side to keep the mosquitoes away.

The boy has untied the towel and pulled it up over his head like a headscarf. He spins around in pirouettes and his trainers thump on the veranda. Grass has grown up in places between the planks, and he stamps it under his feet. There is an ashtray filled with water resting on the wooden railing, and a fly is floating on the surface. Or could it be a beetle? All he can see are crooked legs sticking out. But when he looks closer he notices more insects. The water is thick with them. It looks like a disgusting soup, the kind witches make.

His mother has knelt down and is trying to look under the windowsill.

'I don't believe it,' she says.

Then she starts hunting in the grass below the window.

The boy watches her for a while. Then he tries the door handle.

'Mummy,' he says, 'it's open.'

She pushes him in front of her, lifts in their luggage and slams the door shut behind them. The boy stands in front of a wall hanging of dark swirls and hard, staring eyes and he wonders what it is supposed to be. An owl? Then he gets another push from the hand holding the plastic bag. The bag is cold from the milk cartons at the bottom.

'In with you then!'

The words leave his mother's mouth and seem to fasten in something inside, a web left behind by the silence that has reigned for so long inside the cabin. The boy feels it and is hesitant. He would prefer to stand where he is for a while.

'Go in!'

With wary eyes he walks inside and looks around.

The walls are covered in unpainted pine panelling below and woven wallpaper above. Small pictures and copper pans hang here and there. Through a door he sees a bunk bed with fringed bedspreads. He peers in. The room is very small. Beside the bed is a stool with a book on top of it. Outside the window stands a tree. Its pointed leaves almost touch the windowpane.

He lays his rucksack on the kitchen table, unzips it and takes out the plastic box. It is an old ice cream container with BIG PACK written on a wrinkled label on the lid. Carefully he pulls off the elastic band because he knows it might snap, then tips the figures out onto the table. The ones that came free in boxes of biscuits are all tangled up as if to show they belong together. He also has Smurfs. A hippopotamus with a gaping mouth. A gorilla beating its chest. A galloping horse unable to stand up. A man who is sitting down. He is blue all over, even his head.

Opposite the wood-burning stove is a little sofa, and he sits down on it with a Smurf in each hand. A floor lamp with a pleated shade leans over him. There is no light bulb in it, only a gaping hole. They have borrowed the cabin from someone his mother works with, and the boy wonders why the owner has not put in a bulb. Perhaps for the same reason that there is no television.

He runs his hands over the sofa's upholstery, which is mustard yellow and knobbly. He knows if you play about wildly in a sofa like this you can burn yourself.

There is a small kitchen area, and he walks over to look. The fridge is so small he has to bend down to open it. It is empty inside; no light comes on and it does not even feel cold. He has to push the door firmly to make sure it stays shut. The wall above the draining board has the same cork covering as the floor – reddish brown with a hexagonal pattern.

There is a string of plastic garlic hanging from a nail. He points at it and asks if he can take it down, and she says he can. By climbing on a stool he can get onto the draining board and reach the garlic. Not that he can do much with it, but it is only pretend anyway. He pinches the stiff plastic leaves, testing to see how well they are attached, while his mother walks around opening cupboards and drawers. She opens the fridge too, and shuts it again.

The boy says there is floor on the walls.

'Yes,' she sighs. 'And walls on the floor.'

His mother brings in flowers, a large bunch, which she pushes into a vase and places on the table. They have a powerful, spicy fragrance and are called camomile. The boy notices that the white petals are covered in tiny, tiny insects, but she tells him not to mind. Some of them fall like snow onto the table, and so that he can see them against the grain of the wood he has to lower his head and look closely. The creatures are in a hurry and know exactly where they want to go. He tries to stop them and make them change direction, but he fails.

'Do you know how small these insects are?' he says.

'I'm sure they're minutely small.'

'They are so small they die when I touch them.'

Later that evening they lie on the bunk bed under a quilt patterned with huge fantasy flowers and spiralling stems. They have fitted an insect screen to the window and the whole cabin echoes to the chirping of grasshoppers.

'Listen,' she whispers, her lips against his hair. 'It sounds as if they are indoors, don't you think? As if they are here, in the cabin, playing for us. Under the bed perhaps?'

The boy nods and asks about the shielings she had been talking about in the car.

'Where are they?'

'In the forest.'

'Can we go there?'

'Perhaps.'

'Can we?'

'We'll see.'

In the early morning the rain comes and does not stop. The raindrops are hitting the ashtray on the veranda rail so hard that the water looks as if it is boiling. Now the witch is cooking her soup, he thinks. The wooden seat of his chair is cold and he crouches on it, pulling his sweatshirt over his knees. He is waiting for breakfast. Once more he asks about the huts. Are they far away?

'We'll do it another day,' she says.

He protests loudly and is told they have no rain clothes with them. That disappoints him and he complains. He has his boots, after all. He whines until she strokes his hair.

She looks at him, her thick, shiny brown fringe falling over her large glasses. Her forehead is completely hidden.

They eat cold rosehip soup and bread spread with margarine.

'Boring sandwiches,' she says.

'When-it's-pouring sandwiches,' he replies.

Afterwards they play cards, Beggar My Neighbour. He is an expert at Beggar My Neighbour. You have to be especially careful when you lift your card in case the other person sees it. His mother does not understand that. She sits with her chin resting heavily on her hand, studying the cards that she turns up – she does not stand a chance. The boy triumphs again and again, slapping his palm hard on the tabletop and giggling every time he wins a pile of cards.

Finally she gives up, moves away from the table and curls up with a book on the little sofa. In her bag she has a whole pile of books. She rests her feet on the armrest and curls her toes. Her nails are squares of red varnish. She is wearing a chain around her neck, and as she reads she slides the pendant backwards and forwards, making a rasping noise. There is no point now in trying to talk to her. He knows that only too well.

The wood burner is a cavern and he puts his little figures in there, kneeling down and making the doors creak, and then shouting in a high-pitched voice. The stove is a prison and the figures hate being shut in. It is terrifying in there, dark and with only ash to eat. But they have only themselves to blame! Goofy tries to escape but is caught near the log basket and returned to the sooty cell, howling in protest.

His mother smiles at him.

He dislikes that, so he keeps quiet.

*

Towards afternoon the rain stops, and he gets excited. Now they can go out and look for the shielings! But his mother shakes her head. She says it is still raining in the forest. The trees will be dripping with water and it will be wet everywhere.

'We'll be drenched in no time,' she says, turning the page.

Then she says:

'You can go out on your own and play, can't you?'

He can.

He rolls mosquito repellent on his forehead and chin and over his hands, all the way out to the fingers. Even on his sleeves and the front of his jeans, just to be sure. Then he puts on his boots, pulls up the hood of his sweatshirt, opens the door and shuts it quickly.

The plot is not large, more like a little glade in the forest, and he has soon explored it. The door of the woodshed is open, and inside a grey ball is hovering. A wasp nest. It looks uninhabited, but he does not dare take a closer look.

The silence brought on by the rain is still hanging over the forest. From the top of the steep glistening wall of pine trees come isolated, experimental trills. He walks slowly along the trail, his face upturned, trying to catch a glimpse of the birds, but the trees reveal nothing moving within them. They have secrets.

The forest drops, drips and dribbles. Plips and plops. The glossy, weighted vegetation shines. He feels as if it is coming towards him like the big wet brushes that spin against the windows in the car wash. Here and there are streamers of pinky red. Those flowers are called fox's brush, he knows that. The name is not difficult to remember.

He is thinking he might reach the car soon, that the

chocolate-brown lacquer will flash among the trees. He is not sure what he will do there. Perhaps look at it, peer through one of the windows and then go back.

But then he catches sight of a ditch. The water is completely green, so the bottom is hidden, but it does not look deep. He wonders where the ditch is going and decides to follow it, stumbling over ground made bumpy by tussocks of grass. He tries as far as possible not to put his feet where it looks hollow and risky. With detours and small leaps from stumps to rocks he makes his way forwards. His ears are covered by his hood, so he cannot hear much, but the sounds come mainly from cones and twigs cracking beneath his boots and the wind slowly moving between the wet trees.

A shieling is an unpainted wooden shack – that much he knows, at least. Nobody lives there, but in the old days, long ago, animals lived there. *Alone.*

A house with animals. What would such a house look like? Has it got windows? If so, do the animals stand inside looking out, feeling bored? It was a strange thing to imagine. He is sure animals often feel bored, that they are so used to being bored they never even think how bored they are.

Occasionally the ditch disappears behind some impenetrable undergrowth and spiky clusters of reeds with long leaves. The grass swishes against his boots, and his trousers have gone dark at the front because of the water. It chills his thighs. His mother was right and he wonders if he should turn back.

Then he spots the footbridge and changes his mind.

A couple of dark tree trunks with planks nailed across them.

Is it a bridge to the shieling? Do the animals walk across this bridge?

He stands there with cold legs, hesitating a while.

The water beneath has a pea-green skin. It looks poisonous. A pine cone is floating in it. He could end up like that if he is not careful. He knows that. Someone floating, immobile, face down. Someone drowned.

Holding onto the rail he walks across the bridge. His mother's lips mouth a warning inside him, but he is already on his way into the sea of grass waiting on the other side. It is so tall that he disappears in it. When the wind blows the leaves bend and brush against each other. They become waves that whisper.

He can be just like an animal in the grass. A shrew, perhaps. Nothing is visible apart from strips of green slicing against each other. Holding his hands out in front of him he uses them to part the rustling reeds. This is what it is like for the shrew. Exactly like this.

The boy walks further and further out on the moss.

When he sees water in front of his feet he immediately steps to the side. He does not like the boggy feel of it. From time to time his boots gets stuck, as if the ground is sucking them down. It scares him, and after almost stepping out of one boot he has had enough and turns back. But instead of going back to the wooden bridge he cuts diagonally across the moss and wanders in among some birches he has spotted, and soon the forest is closing in around him.

Now he is walking on a carpet made of spongy moss. It is soft to walk on. It seems to want to spread everywhere and has even crept up the tree trunks. It covers the stones too, making them all as round as each other. He likes the look of that.

The branches fan out above him like a roof, so he does not feel any rain, and the wind that combed the gigantic grass cannot find its way in here.

He looks into the forest.

It is perfectly silent. It is actually odd how quiet it is. Nothing is moving, not even the small leaves on the bushes or the tops of the grass.

There is not much space between the trees. Narrow slits of light and that is all, it seems.

On the ground there is a lot to explore. There are dead things left lying about, a tree that has split open and whose insides are bright red, like meat, and just beyond it a rotted birch trunk that has fallen apart. Scaly shards of bark surround it. He digs the toe of his boot into the birch and presses carefully. It is soft right through.

Another tree trunk is dotted with yellow saucer shapes that look like ears. He tries to count them because there are so very many – how many ears can you actually have? – but he loses count when the mosquitoes fly into his face.

A hollow stump looks like a cauldron among the blueberry branches. A crown of moss surrounds the cavity. He looks down into the stump but there is nothing particularly interesting inside it, only dampness and pine needles stuck together in clumps. He would like to put his hand in and feel down to the bottom – perhaps a mouse is sleeping there – but he does not really dare.

Far, far inside the forest a bird flies soundlessly from one tree to the next, as if drawing a line between the trunks. The boy can see it out of the corner of his eye. He stands up and walks on, singing a little and talking to himself in a soft, jokey voice. His mother has told him there is nothing to fear in the forest, so he is not particularly afraid. No wolves, no bears, nothing that wants to eat him. Apart from the mosquitoes.

Still, when the roots of an overturned tree loom above him his stomach lurches because he almost imagines it is an old man standing there waiting for him. A man who will not move out of the way.

After a while he plucks up enough courage to approach the fallen tree. The underside is a mass of twisted roots, and on the ground is a gaping void, covered in bracken. It is black between the fronds, unpredictable and very deep. Someone lives down there, he is sure. A badger, perhaps. Badgers are underground creatures, piggy-eyed and bad-tempered. They only come out at night to nose around and whisper.

As he stands there, peering down into the bowl below the roots, he hears a crack.

Small furtive footsteps, very close.

Quickly he tugs at his hat so that he can see properly.

His eyes wander between the columns of pines. Someone was there, he is convinced of that.

He takes a little step sideways, at the same time craning his neck to see what is behind the upturned roots. He hardly dares to look.

A movement. A streak of grey fur.

That is what he sees.

And then he runs.

Runs away towards the light where the forest thins out.

Undergrowth and branches whip against his boots.

He follows the forest edge, tripping and stumbling his way forwards.

Not until he has staggered out onto the trail does he dare to stop and look around. He beats at the mosquitoes circling his face. His fear seems to have made them even more excited.

*

His mother is sitting curled up on the sofa with her book, and when he comes in through the doorway she looks up at him with a sharp little crease between her eyes. She has folded the book so that she can hold it in one hand. Around the fingers of the other she is twisting her chain. It digs into the skin of her neck.

She asks where he has been, and when she notices how wet he is she puts the book aside and helps him take off his jacket. His hair is standing on end in damp little tufts and his jumper has ridden up over his stomach in wrinkles, but he hurries to pull it down as he tells her. That he has seen an *animal*.

'What kind of animal?'

'An animal!'

She twists off his boots roughly and finds his socks squashed up, the toes wringing wet. His feet have turned red. 'Oh, Magnus,' she sighs.

To get his jeans off he has to lie down while she pulls and tugs at the legs because the wet fabric has glued itself to him. The boy thumps his head against the floor, and that makes them laugh.

'Let go!' she shouts.

'I can't,' he giggles.

Finally he has to stand up and stamp the trousers off instead. She picks up the jeans and asks him if he has been swimming. He didn't go near the pool, did he?

In the bag, which is open on the floor, he finds a pair of dry underpants patterned with roaring hot rods and motorbikes, and after he has put them on he climbs up onto the sofa and buries himself under the sleeping bag. The zipper is a track of cold steel teeth against his thigh and he changes position to avoid the feel of it on his skin. The knobbly sofa fabric is rough against his legs and it is warm where his mother has been sitting.

He hears his mother rustling behind the log basket, stuffing wads of newspaper into his boots and hanging up his clothes on the chairs around the table.

He wants to tell her about the animal. That it was grey.

'But what *kind* of animal was it?'

He sits with his mouth open for a while as he thinks.

'I think it could have been a lynx.'

His mother shakes her head. 'I don't think so.'

'A wolf then?'

'It was probably a bird. It generally is a bird.'

'No. It wasn't a bird. Birds don't have fur.'

She has come to sit beside him. With her index finger she lifts a thick lock of hair from his forehead. He stares out through the window and is still in the forest.

'It was an animal, Mum.'

She nods.

It has started to rain again, and soon it is thundering on the roof.

The fox's-brush flowers down by the path are lying on the ground after the downpour. Everything is flattened and changed and glistening moistly. It is still raining slightly and now a wind has started to blow. It can be seen in the swaying pines and the other trees that flicker and reflect the light, and every so often small gusts of wind hurl handfuls of raindrops at the windowpanes.

Groups of dead insects have collected on the windowsill. They have crawled close together to die – flies, mostly, but also wasps grown brittle. A butterfly with closed wings. It has shut itself up like a book. It would not look dead otherwise because it has kept all its colours. He asks his mother what the butterfly is called, but she does not know.

'A peacock butterfly, perhaps. Or a small tortoiseshell. I don't know . . .'

He reaches for the little box made of bark that is standing on the table. He knows it is empty but looks inside anyway. Something ought to be kept in it, but he does not know what.

Then he has an idea. He picks up the folded butterfly and lays it in the box. He takes great care, and when he has replaced the lid he shakes the little box to hear the butterfly inside.

Darkness has deepened in the forest, and around the glass lamp beside the door moths are flitting about. They rustle against the illuminated globe, entranced. It looks as if they want to get inside. His mother reads to him from one of his comics. In the middle of a speech bubble she stops because the boy has lifted his head from her arm and is looking open-mouthed at the window.

'I heard something!'

His mother raises herself up on one elbow and also listens. The grasshoppers are making their rasping sound, and the shadows under the bunk bed make her face pale and turn her eyes into dark pockets. A gap has opened between her lips.

Then she sinks down again.

'It's nothing.'

The boy does not want to believe her. He jumps down to the floor and pulls aside the towel hanging as a curtain at the window. He rests his hand on the mosquito mesh and cranes his neck, looking down the path.

'It sounded like something was walking out there. Something big.'

His mother has laid her head on the pillow.

'It was nothing,' she says.

So he wriggles down under the quilt again.

Lies there alert.

Listening.

'Shall I carry on reading?'

He sniffs and nods.

Afterwards, when they have turned off the light, they hear a faint rustling on the roof.

The rain is falling softly. As if practising.

He can hear a mosquito moving about the room, but it seems unable to find its way to the bed. It goes quiet from time to time. He thinks it is waiting.

'Mum,' he says, but he can hear from her breathing that she is already asleep.

After flicking through the comics and looking at the pictures on the last page that show what the next comic will be about, he wanders into the main room.

Outside the window he sees a movement. His mother is standing out there, her hair a shining curtain in the morning light. She is bending over something.

When he pushes open the door she instantly straightens up.

'What are you doing?' he asks.

She is wearing a thick jacket. One of her hands is stuffed inside a large gardening glove.

'I think there might be a bat around here somewhere,' she says. 'A dead one.'

'Is there really?' he asks, and moves closer.

They help each other to look, and he is the one who finds it.

The little animal is suspended in the grass. It does not have the weight to slide down so it stays there, trapped, like a brown leaf. He has never seen a bat before. To think they could be so small. A long and oddly curved claw is sticking out from the wing, and his mother pinches hold of it. The skin opens out, a net of folds and wrinkles, criss-crossed by fine veins. The abnormally large eyelids are covered with the same sheer, ancient-looking skin.

'It's got a ring,' he says.

She holds up the bat and the thin wing turns pink as it is hit by the sunlight. A tiny silver ring shines in one ear.

She touches it gently with her index finger.

'Why has it got a ring?'

'I don't know,' she says, reflectively.

She has taken hold of the ring and is studying it closely.

'It must be marked in some way . . .'

'Why is the bat dead?'

His mother does not reply, so he asks again.

'Why is it dead, Mum?'

'It collided with me in the night,' she says, letting go of the ring. 'I went out to pee and it flew at me. Here.'

She puts her fingers on her temple.

'I expect it got confused by my nightdress,' she says. 'They're attracted by light colours. It fastened in my hair and I snatched it out and threw it away from me. Right against that wall. That killed it. It's so tiny. I didn't mean it to die, I just wanted to get it away from me.'

She twitches her hand and the bat bobs up and down.

'Do you want us to bury it?'

The boy leans up close to the ugly little snout. Deeply set in the crumpled face are black eyes like beads. The teeth sticking out of its mouth are like shards of glass.

He shakes his head.

'Sure?'

He nods.

His mother walks over the grass and throws the bat into the nettles growing like a green sea on the other side of the wooden fence. Then she cranks water out of the pump and rinses her hands, and as she walks towards the boy she smiles, drying her hands on her nightdress, which is hanging down below the old jacket.

They eat breakfast outside, in sunshine that makes them squint their eyes. They have to make the most of it, says his mother, laying out a bedspread. The grass is so stiff that it makes the bedspread stand up in peaks, and together they stamp them down to make it flat and comfortable to sit on. The mosquitoes that are flying around in the morning sun are no bother. There are so few and they do not seem to know what they want.

They have a loaf of white bread and a tube of cod roe spread. They munch, looking at each other. He is crouching and she is sitting cross-legged with the sun falling like a banner across her legs. Between bites she tells him that his grandmother was not affected by the mosquitoes because one day when she was out picking blueberries she was bitten so terribly that she lost her way and went down with a fever. Ever since that day she had been immune and was never bothered by mosquitoes in the slightest.

'But what about bats?' he wants to know. 'Can you be immune to them too?'

She explains that bats do not suck blood.

'It's only in stories,' says the boy. 'Isn't it?'

'Yes. And not in Sweden.'

She wipes away a blob of the cod roe spread from her upper lip with a fingertip.

'Bats here only eat old butterflies and things like that,' she says.

That information disappoints the boy. He has seen for himself that bats have sharp teeth. Like needles. He thinks it is likely they *can* drink blood, if they want to.

'Yes,' she says. 'If they are really hungry.'

'Then perhaps you are immune now, Mummy.'

'Except it didn't bite me.'

'But think if it had!'

'Yes,' she says, nodding with her mouth full of bread. 'Well then, maybe I am.'

There is a beach on the nearby lake, and now that the sun is motionless in the sky and beating down they decide to go swimming and then do some shopping. They pack their swimming things and a mask in a canvas bag and hurry down the path. The boy carries his bathrobe and flaps it about. He allows the mosquitoes to get up close before he hits them.

The sun has been baking the car for hours and a strong smell of upholstery and overheated rubber hits him as he climbs into the back seat. It is so burning hot that he has to sit on his bathrobe, crouching like a monkey.

It is not far to the beach and he is surprised when after only a short while they pull up in a gravel car park. Pine cones crunch under their feet as they follow the path down towards the water.

Alders with large shiny leaves hang down over the jetty and entangle themselves in the reeds. The boy and his mother are alone, but someone has been there recently because in the grass on the lakeside is a glittering pile of shells. All the shells are tiny and fragile. The boy does not dare to touch them. He does not want to spoil anything.

The water has a strange red colour which he tries to collect in his cupped hands, but the red does not come up with the water. It is only in the lake, which is not actually a lake but part of the Dal River, his mother tells him, as she sits on the jetty with a towel draped around her shoulders and her hand like a sun visor above her glasses.

Using a stick he dredges up dripping seaweed, which he collects in a pile. It is a silent game. The only sound is the water trickling back into the lake. From time to time the sun shines through patches of wispy cloud. Later he tries the swimming mask, seeing the undulating gravel on the lake bed. Something is swimming there, a tiny fish. He tries to catch it in his mask but it darts away.

The shop is located in an old wooden building with empty advertisement boards on the walls and sun-bleached awnings. It looks shut but his mother says it is not. There are steps up to the door and the metal railing is encrusted with rust. His mother is walking quickly. She is in a hurry all of a sudden.

They both fill the basket, the boy putting in a Falu sausage which he thinks they should have for dinner. He goes to fetch milk cartons too, but they are difficult to find because they do not look like the ones at home.

In the queue for the checkout they stand behind an old woman who is buying a bottle of elderflower cordial, and his mother lays her hand on his head, feeling how his hair has begun to dry and stand up from his scalp.

'Was it nice to go swimming?' she asks, but he does not answer. He is engrossed in the comic he has been allowed to buy, guessing what it says in the speech bubbles.

With both hands he hauls the heavy paper carrier bag up the veranda steps and in through the door, which he quickly closes behind him. The air has turned warm in the cabin and he can hear an insect buzzing against one of the windows. He puts the bag down by the fridge, takes out a carton of milk and opens the door. And recoils.

It is lying there on the rack, next to the tube of cod roe spread.

Small, shaggy and greyish-brown, with crumpled wings drawn up tight to its body, its head like a shrunken dog. Strange cupped ears.

He races out so fast the hood of his bathrobe falls down.

His mother is on her way back from the outside toilet. She is carrying a folded newspaper and looks at him in surprise.

Panting and shrieking, he tells her what is in the fridge. But she refuses to believe him. Without a word she walks ahead of him into the cabin.

She stares at the bat and is suddenly angry. She says, 'What the hell . . .?' and blames him. He is the one who has put it there.

Then he bursts into tears, and when she realises that he is distraught and the crying stems from anger, she crouches down in front of him. She asks him if he is sure it was not him.

'Yes, honest!'

He rubs his tear-filled eyes with the palms of his hands and sniffs.

'Well then,' she says, 'someone's playing a joke on us, that's all.'

She tears off a sheet of kitchen roll and uses it to pick up the bat, then walks outside and throws it from the same place, this time hurling it far in among the trees. The paper falls away and floats like a leaf to the ground.

Then she goes in and gets the fridge rack and stands with it under the pump, scrubbing it with a washing-up brush. The boy asks if there is blood on the rack, but she does not answer.

The pine needles which have collected in the folds of the tarpaulin fall off in huge slabs as they uncover the lawnmower. Spread over the hood is a layer of flattened cardboard boxes. When the boy lifts them off, the earwigs race around like brown sparks.

'What are they doing? What are they doing?' he shouts, excited and alarmed at the same time.

His mother shakes the handle, and when she hears the splashing in the petrol tank she pulls the starter cord. After a couple of attempts she straightens up, grimacing at the sun.

The boy scratches his cheek where he has a row of mosquito bites.

When the motor finally starts with a rattle he runs out of the way and sits on the veranda. He covers his ears with his hands and watches as she forces the machine through the overgrown grass. It is a struggle. The motor keeps stopping. It growls and then falls silent. He squints. The sun has wedged itself between the tree trunks and is shining directly at him now. She crouches down to clear out the clippings from under the hood. He studies his kneecaps and the downy hairs shining on them. Where there was once a scab the skin has turned light red and is slightly raised and there might be a scar, so his mother has said. He presses his thumb against the redness and then immediately starts scratching his calves until he breaks the skin. He has been careful to shut the door of the cabin, but the mosquitoes come in anyway. It is worst on his calves and ankles – they really feast there while he is asleep. After that they go and sit on the wallpaper and the ceiling and no one knows they are there until night comes. Then they let go and drop down.

'Magnus!'

His mother is half standing and pointing to the edge of the forest diagonally behind the cabin, where the brush-like branches of the trees weave together and make everything dark. What is she pointing at?

At first he can see nothing, but then he notices that something is moving, and the next second a grey head sticks out. Knobbly ears, pointing backwards, and whiskers hanging straight down from its mouth like long strings of saliva. A matted, flattened forehead turned towards them.

'Can you see?' she shouts. 'Can you see the hare?'

It feels exciting having a forest animal on the doorstep, exciting that it wants to be with them, and because they do not want to frighten it they go indoors. Cutting the grass can wait. There is no rush, and perhaps it has its young in the grass? Baby hares so small that they are rabbits?

His mother opens a can of vegetable soup and heats it up on the stove, while the boy sits glued to the window, giving reports about where the hare is and what it is doing. Not that there is much to report. Its jaws move from time to time but mostly it sits looking straight ahead.

When they are sitting with the soup bowls in front of them, blowing on their soup, he asks her who put the bat in the fridge.

She does not know.

Is it the man they borrowed the cabin from?

'It was just someone,' she says quietly, moving her spoon among the steaming pieces of vegetable. 'Someone who walked past in the forest and saw us throw away the bat. There are lots of people here, fishing and camping. It's just someone having a joke.'

Does she think it is a good joke?

'No,' she replies. 'I don't think so.'

'Neither do I,' he says to his plate.

They play cards.

'Snap!' he yells, and shuffles the cards with the blue chequered pattern on the back. His mother rests her elbows on the table and pretends to be annoyed. He likes that.

She is wearing a strappy top with horizontal stripes. The skin shines on her jutting collarbones, and the outside of her upper arms are sunburned. You can see where the towel covered her. It has left a line.

When she wants to stop playing he becomes sulky and tries to play cards on his own, but it is not the same. He finds a fountain pen and scribbles in some of the comics, on the white spaces between the squares. Then he draws on his knuckles, mainly to see if it works, but the ink rubs off.

It is only when he looks to see if the hare is still there that he catches sight of the fox. It is standing at the bottom of the path, staring with round, shiny yellow eyes at the window.

The boy leaps up and shouts out loud.

'Come here! Quick!'

His mother puts down her book and walks to the window.

'Well, look at that,' she says, leaning forwards and resting her cheek against the boy's.

In silence they study the fox for a few moments, until she says:

'It knows there has been a hare around here. The smell stays in the grass for a long time. It thinks the hare is here somewhere.'

'It is,' he says. 'It's there!'

He points and she cranes her neck, seeing that the boy is right. The hare is like a dark-grey patch behind the tufts of grass beside the woodshed.

'I'm sure it's all right,' she says. 'It'll get away, you'll see.'

The fox has opened his ears so they stand like two scoops on top of his head. He directs his black nose towards the hare.

'Now he can sense it,' she says. 'The trail.'

Behind the dipped back and skinny dog's body, with ribs defined like bars, the fox's tail projects like a grey and bushy burden. The corners of its mouth point downwards. The animal starts to creep closer, edging forwards with its head to the ground. The quick, slender legs are dark at the front, as if it has stepped in a forest pool.

The boy feels a whispering breath against his hair.

'It smells very strange because we've been out there too, so he can't find the hare.'

But he can.

The fox walks in a straight line to the pair of long ears that are sticking up out of the grass. The two animals regard each other for an instant and then the fox sits down, immediately next to the hare. And there they sit, beside each other in the grass, their eyes directed at the cabin.

'It looks like they're friends!'

The idea of the hare and the fox being friends makes the boy's mother crane her head forwards. Her eyes are staring behind the lenses of her glasses.

Finally it becomes too much for her and she slaps the palm of her hand against the pane of glass. The boy, who has climbed onto the table, jumps at the sound. She slaps the window again and then thumps it with her fist, making the glass rattle.

'Don't do that!' he wails.

But the animals are not scared by the sound.

They merely sit there.

His mother fetches a couple of saucepans from the kitchen, but on her way to the door she exchanges one of them for the axe.

The animals jerk when the door flies open and the woman comes out onto the step. They move apart slightly but they do not run away. She calls to the boy to stay inside, but he disobeys her. He pads out behind her. He also wants to see.

There is a clang, cling, clang! as the axe hits the saucepan.

Stamping her feet, she strides forwards.

The fox stands up and runs a short distance away, looking at her over its shoulder. Its legs are bent and its chest is down in the grass. Its ears fold back, its nose wrinkles and its lips curl. The sight of the yellow teeth dripping with saliva brings his mother to a halt, but only for an instant, because she then rushes towards them waving the axe. The fox slinks away between the fence posts and disappears.

But the hare sits as if nailed to the spot. It looks as if it is forcing its skinny shanks to be still. It is shuddering and gaping, and yellow shards of teeth are visible in its sloping lower jaw. Its ears are black-tipped and ragged.

Not until she is standing directly over it does the hare leap aside, remarkably elongated. It runs in a loop around them, coming so close to the boy that he cries out. After that it rushes off, like a shudder in the grass.

His mother is breathing heavily through her nose. Her forehead and cheekbones are oily with sweat and her nostrils are shiny. Her lips are pressed tightly together.

The boy inundates her with questions. What he wants to know most of all is why she chased the animals away. Instead of answering she shoves him ahead of her into the cabin, and when they are inside she locks the door.

'There was something wrong with them,' she says, cutting up his sausage. It surprises him that she is cutting up his food because she is always nagging him to do it himself. 'They were sick. Do you understand?'

Her voice sounds tense and her gaze keeps wandering to the window. She has not put any food on her plate yet. It is shiny, and empty apart from some scratches. There are still flickers of sunlight in the grass down at the bottom of the path, but below the trees everything has become black and intertwined.

After a moment she leans forwards, staring at him.

'Do you want to go home?'

The boy has stuffed his mouth full of macaroni.

He eats and looks at her.

'Do you?' he asks, reaching for his glass of milk.

Then she snorts and small wrinkly lines form round her eyes.

He should have gone to bed ages ago, but it seems she has forgotten all about him as he sits by the wood burner. The cork flooring where he is sitting is scattered with splinters of wood and small strips torn from a newspaper. He has pulled up one leg and is resting his chin on his kneecap. The little figures are lined up. He is planning some kind of competition.

His mother has remained at the table, looking out through the window. She has turned to stone over there, her back hunched and her elbows resting on the tabletop, which is why he jumps when she suddenly stands up. The chair scrapes the floor, almost toppling over behind her.

The boy stares.

'What is it?' he asks.

But she does not reply. She just continues staring out of the window.

He walks up to her.

'Is it the fox?' he asks.

She has cupped her hands against the glass and is breathing hard.

'Mummy!'

He tries to climb up on the table, but she pushes him back down. She does it so roughly that he almost falls backwards.

'No!' she says.

He is not sad. But he is angry.

All he wants is to see what she is seeing.

He makes another attempt to get to the window, and when she stands in his way he runs towards the door.

'Magnus!'

She screams at the top of her lungs, a pleading howl that makes her voice crack. She tries to grab hold of him and knocks the kitchen table with her hip.

But he has already run outside.

He is already gone.

Because the first news picture of Magnus Brodin, carried in the *Gefle Dagblad* on 24 July 1978, takes up over four columns, there is no need to read the headline to realise that something bad has happened to the boy. That's always the case when a large face appears in the paper.

This picture was the only one to be published. A black and white passport photo, probably taken in one of those little booths you have to feed with coins. His hair is unusually thick and cut bluntly across his forehead. He isn't looking at the camera but down to the side, and he looks a little uncertain, almost afraid, I think. You'd like to imagine that a sliver of fate would show in his eyes. A dark glimmer.

Another news photo shows two men in grass up to their waists. They are wearing white short-sleeved shirts with epaulettes. Pilot sunglasses, bushy sideburns. One of them is carrying a black briefcase, and it looks odd, a case like that out in the forest.

The caption tells us they are inspectors in the forensics division of the Falun police force. They look puzzled.

You could say it's a photo that speaks volumes.

At first the newspapers said Magnus had been kidnapped, but a couple of days later they weren't so sure.

Magnus's mother, Mona Brodin, insisted that a giant had come out of the forest and taken her child, and despite the fact that the Falun police inspectors found proof that oddly enough appeared to support her statements – footprints of an unprecedented size and depth had been found in the vicinity of the cabin – no particular importance was attached to the unlikely details of her testimony. People preferred to think that the boy had been kidnapped by a taller-than-average man who, in the eyes of the terrified mother, had grown to incredible proportions. A man who had then melted back into the pitch-black fir trees from which he had so threateningly materialised that July evening.

Or had the trail come from someone not connected with the case? And if so, what had happened to the boy?

Mona Brodin's credibility was reduced to practically zero as a result of two things: the prescription for Librium in her handbag and the fact that she continually spoke about the forest animals. She insisted she had seen a hare and a fox showing no indication of their natural enmity on the same day the boy disappeared. It was as demented as it was irrelevant. It didn't appear in the newspaper.

Could medication have caused a hallucination? Was there no kidnapper? Could she have taken the boy's life *herself*? These questions, especially the latter, lay like a repulsive slime over the story. The dreadful event became merely a tragedy, and when the newspapers ceased to write about Magnus it was almost as if he had disappeared for a second time.

The newspaper clippings have been cut out neatly, if not to say obsessively so. It could have been Sven holding the scissors, but I think it was Barbro. After sitting hunched over the newspaper cuttings for goodness knows how many hours I hardly dare say anything about my recollection of Magnus Brodin's disappearance, which, in the beginning at least, caused such a sensation in the press and on radio and TV. *The media,* as we call it now. A jigsaw puzzle of yellowing strips of paper with columns of text and grainy photographs of helicopters, policemen and desolate forest roads has eclipsed the almost transparently vague memories I once had.

Going back step by step in my mind just won't work. It's like trying to scrape one layer of paint off another. His face is there like a blurred stain. I know I thought the whole story was particularly nasty. First, that a kid could be abducted like that by an unknown person in Sweden, and then it didn't make it any less nasty when it appeared his mother might have killed him.

There is no end to the times I have dug for premonitions.

Premonitions of *evil.*

That summer I was carrying Susso, and even if I have no particular memory of it, I'm sure that on occasions I must have cupped my hands over my stomach when I saw Magnus's face in the newspaper. Shouldn't I have felt then that my unborn child's destiny was linked to that boy's? Shouldn't I have felt a shudder go through my body?

SUNDAY 12 DECEMBER 2004

She drove through intervals of snow, particles streaming fast in the beams of the headlights, sputtering against the windscreen in waves. At times they came in such a mass that she had to lean over the steering wheel, wrinkling her eyebrows. The wipers squealed at full speed but made little difference.

Even when there was a break in the snow showers Susso could not relax. Billows of snow whipped across the road, whirling ceaselessly from one side to the other, and threatened to swirl up and blind her at any moment. If she met an oncoming truck or was overtaken, she became enclosed in a white chamber for one, two, possibly three seconds at the worst. In those moments she held her breath, clenched her hands on the steering wheel and exhaled abrupt obscenities from between her clenched teeth.

But at least it was still light.

She picked up her mobile from the seat and checked the time.

Surely she would be there soon? She tried to think when she had last seen a road sign.

Just before Jokkmokk she turned off to the right and onto a road that wound alongside the lakes which led away towards Kvikkjokk and the horizon with its undulating fells. Under its streaks of frost a brown sign indicated that this was the way to Sarek

National Park. The only way. An ancient route, she knew that. Linnaeus had walked it once. Or had he ridden along it?

She soon saw the name, surrounded by a tangle of birch branches. White lettering on a blue background: VAIKIJAUR. On top of the sign an undulating ridge of snow. Between the trees she saw the white sphere of the lake.

She slowed down, put the car into second gear and leaned over the wheel, letting her gaze wander between the houses scattered on either side of the road.

Advent stars in the windows, light strings spiralling around naked branches. Council rubbish bins of green plastic frozen solid in snow drifts. Grey satellite dishes on gable walls. Snow-clearing tools lined up on porches: scrapers, shovels, long-handled brushes. Every household had the same collection.

Someone had hung out a claret-red blouse on a coat hanger that moved in the wind. That was the closest thing to a human being she saw.

She zigzagged slowly down the road so that she could read what was written on the letter boxes. Åke and Maud Kvickström. Thomas . . .

She drove on like that, squinting her eyes to read. Many boxes were covered in snow, but she thought she might strike lucky, and fairly soon she spotted the name, written by hand on an old metal lid. Mickelsson.

The house looked weighed down by the snow clinging to the roof in bulging drifts. The land around it sloped down towards a lake, and on the far side it was just possible to discern spinneys of stunted birches in a grainy mist. Was it snowing over there?

She pulled up behind the car that was parked in the driveway and switched off the engine, but sat where she was for a while, looking at the house. She felt paralysed by sudden doubt brought on by the silence.

On the kitchen windowsill, seven glowing lights of an Advent candleholder, shining in a pointed arch. A ladder of flimsy metal leaning against the roof, on every rung a lip of snow.

To announce her arrival she slammed the car door shut. With her eyes on her mobile she walked towards the house up the narrow pathway cleared of snow. A wreath decorated with bows hung on the door, which opened before she had time to knock. Raising her eyebrows in surprise she took a step backwards, grabbing hold of the handrail.

In the hall stood a thin woman. Her light-grey hair was abruptly cut just below her ears. Underneath her long knitted waistcoat she wore a blouse with meandering embroidery around the neck. She was pressing her left hand to her chest. It looked as if she was in pain.

'Are you Edit?'

The old woman nodded.

'Susso Myrén,' said Susso, reaching out her hand.

After they had greeted each other Edit backed into the hall. Susso took off her boots but kept her jacket on. She might be leaving very soon. That usually became obvious pretty quickly. The only lighting in the kitchen came from the electric Advent candles, so it was quite dark, and chilly as well. The refrigerator hummed loudly, on its last legs by the sound of it. Stuck on the door were vouchers, a handwritten receipt and a lottery scratch card. On the wall a collection of trays hung in a wide embroidered band. There were crocheted Christmas decorations, small paintings in various shapes and sizes, a calendar with notes written in neat lettering. Standing in the sink was a fuchsia in its plastic flowerpot and on the table was a newspaper, *Norrbottens-Kuriren.*

'Do you live here alone?' asked Susso, pulling up her belt and straightening her jeans.

Edit had clamped her mouth together so tightly that her pink lips had disappeared.

'It's lovely here,' said Susso, pulling aside the cotton curtain and looking up the road. 'In the village.'

A sharp, vertical line appeared between Edit's eyes, as if someone had struck her with a chisel. She was troubled and had no time for small talk. That was perfectly obvious.

'How . . .' she said in a thin voice that faded away. She placed her hand on one of the copper discs covering the hotplates on the stove. It slipped sideways and she moved it back into place.

Susso drew out a chair and sat down at the table. She pushed aside the newspaper and took her notepad and a ballpoint pen from her jacket pocket, not because she wanted to write anything in particular but mainly to get straight to the point. There was a click when she pressed the pen but it would not work. It had probably frozen solid. Looking around she found a pencil lying on the table and picked it up.

She looked encouragingly at Edit, who was fiddling with a button on the sleeve of her blouse. The lines on each side of the old woman's mouth were deeply etched, as if it required deep concentration to fiddle with that button.

'Shall I show you where it was? Where I saw him?'

It had been snowing all morning. It fell and fell in thick masses, and Seved sat at the kitchen table seeing nothing else. The slopes of the stubbly pine-covered mountain had faded into white and the wire netting of the dog enclosure was so clogged up that it was impossible to see what was going on in there. The dogs usually sat staring silently ahead when the nights had been long.

He leaned across and widened the opening in the curtains so that he could see the upturned Volvo 240 out in the yard. The snow had covered the undercarriage in such a thick layer that it was hard to see any of the components apart from the hump of the silencer.

As soon as he had drunk his coffee he would go out and try to turn the car upright. Make an attempt, at least. Most of the damage had already been done so there was no immediate hurry, but he did not like it being upside down. Although Ejvor did not seem to mind. From time to time a sticky little sound came from her direction as she licked the tip of her index finger and thumb and turned the pages of the newspaper. Apart from that the only sound was the hum of the heater.

Above the double doors of the barn, beside a row of reindeer antlers growing out of the wall, a huge lamp was mounted on a curved metal pole. Many years ago he and Börje had plundered a lamp from a pole brought down by the wind along the road to Nalovardo. Börje made sure the lamp was switched off during the day because it drew a lot of power. But it was on now. That said something about how stressed Börje must have been when he set off. Snowflakes lit up as they floated past the lamp, and Seved was staring at these slowly descending sparks when Ejvor put down the newspaper.

'Don't I get a cup?' she asked.

'I didn't think you wanted one,' he said, and pushed back his chair.

'I could have a small one.'

He took down a cup and saucer from the cupboard above the draining board, placed it in front of her on the table and poured. From the shiny silver spout came coffee and spiralling steam.

'That's enough,' she said, raising her hand.

He sat down and cradled his cup.

Now was a good time to talk to her. It seemed she was not in too much of a bad mood.

In a confused memory from the early-morning hours he remembered hearing a diesel engine idling for what seemed like an eternity. Car doors slamming. Börje's loud commands, Signe's muttering. A dog barking.

There was a clock on the wall above the Christmas decoration with little dancing elves that Ejvor had put up, and when he looked he saw it was getting on for eleven.

He cleared his throat.

'When did they go?'

Ejvor sipped her coffee, then put her cup down gently on the saucer, like she always did, so there was no sound.

'Yes, when was it? They went for the Isuzu too,' she said. 'Not upside down but on its side, so I think it must have been about seven by the time they left.'

'They made a hell of a noise. It was about three, I think.'

She turned the pages of the paper and then put it down on the table, looking at him.

'And one of the dogs,' she said. 'That small bitch. They had fun with her, throwing her up onto the barn roof. She just stood there, barking and barking, and couldn't get down, and Börje and I were too frightened to go outside, so she was up there for at least a couple of hours, poor little mite. She was scared out of her wits.'

Seved leaned forwards to look at the far end of the barn roof. Naturally there was no trace left of the dog, at least nothing that could be seen from this distance.

'They've never done that before, have they? Had a go at the dogs?'

Ejvor licked her finger and turned a page before answering.

'Once, in the seventies,' she said. 'They got into the enclosure and killed every single dog. Tore them to shreds, as if they wanted to find out how many pieces you can split a dog into. It looked like a slaughterhouse when I came out in the morning. Eleven dogs, and three of them pups. I cried like a baby when I saw it.'

It took a while for Seved to absorb what she had told him – she had told him! – and he felt his mouth go dry.

'You never said.'

'Well, it's so unusual.'

She did not want to say more. Sharp lines had stitched her lips together. But even so he tried.

'Why? What caused it?'

'It was all four of them that time. They got each other worked up. We had to separate them after that.'

'Because of what happened with the dogs?'

Her eyes scanned the pages.

'Among other things.'

Seved pushed the chair aside and leaned against the window, pulling aside the light-blue viscose curtain that reached all the way to the floor.

Directly opposite the barn was the building they called Hybblet. It looked like an old toilet block, and that is what it was, in a way. It had white fibre cement cladding, and with the roof covered in snow the place seemed to dissolve and recede until the only clear features were the door and the dark window frames, and the plastic pipes protruding like yellow elephant trunks taped to the base of the drainpipe. On the gable end was a satellite dish, but of course there was no television – Börje had attached it there to make the house look like any other house. Presumably that had been Lennart's idea.

On the front porch stood a pile of empty blue plastic storage boxes beside a row of black sacks, filled to the top. Flattened cardboard boxes poked out of one. The snow had blown in and settled in the folds of the sacks.

'Have you been cleaning up?'

When there was no answer he turned round and looked at Ejvor's face. It showed no expression. That meant it was her.

'When did you do it?'

'This morning.'

'But we weren't supposed to clean up. We were meant to wait.'

She put down the paper. She even stood up.

'Well, it won't make things any better if it's filthy in there, that's for sure!'

She spat out the words without looking at him, as if they had sprung from a suppressed rage, and Seved accepted them in silence. He knew she was not angry with him, but that was not the point. If he continued, if he reminded her once again what Lennart had said, then she would take her anger out on him, and he wanted to avoid that at all costs.

But it was already too late because she had gone out into the hall. The outer door opened and he heard her swear. He knew one of the hares was taking the brunt.

Seved finished his coffee, which by now was cold. He felt incredibly tired. His eyes fastened on the back page of the newspaper, a copy of *Västerbottens-Kuriren* that had to be at least a week old. There was an advertisement in red letters, which to him appeared as meaningless shapes.

You sleep well after a beating, Börje usually said.

At night he could only lie there, glancing every few minutes at the clock radio, because he knew when it usually kicked off. As soon as he thought he heard something he would hold his breath. That was the worst thing. Waiting for it to start. Because some nights nothing happened.

They plodded through snow a metre deep. Susso glanced towards the ice. The bottom of a boat, pulled up on the shore, stood out like a sky-blue sliver against a field of white so flat it was impossible to distinguish the shoreline. In the distance she could make out a mountain, but it could just as easily have been a patch of dark sky. A cold wind was blowing up from the lake and it stung her cheeks.

Edit pointed towards some leaning birch trees.

'There,' she said. 'At the edge. That's where he stood.'

Susso continued walking until she reached the trees Edit had pointed out. It was such a struggle to walk through the deep snow that she had to swing her arms to keep her balance.

'Here?' she asked, turning round, one hand on her hat.

Edit nodded. Susso leaned forwards slightly and peered in among the sparse pine trees. The neighbours' house, a white single-storey building painted blue around the windows, was visible through the trunks only a hundred metres away. She took a step sideways to keep her balance, but it was difficult and she had to put her hand down on the snow for support.

'Is that all he did? Stand there?' she shouted.

'Yes,' said Edit. 'Grinning.'

She rearranged her shawl and with her head bowed stepped into the track Susso had made. Her long waistcoat trailed behind her.

'Perhaps he was only making a face,' she said. 'It wasn't easy to see what he looked like. But I think he was laughing, because that's what Mattias said he was doing.'

'How old is Mattias?' asked Susso.

'Four,' said Edit, pulling the shawl and the collar of her blouse tighter around her. She looked cold, but it was probably only a shudder going through her because then she said, almost in a whisper:

'You see, I was standing in the kitchen and then I heard the boy. He was talking to someone. Out here. "Why are you laughing?" he said.' Edit had altered her voice to sound like her grandchild. 'I thought he was playing a game, but then he said it again: "Why are you laughing?" He sounded almost angry, I thought, as if he was getting impatient. I was curious, of course, because he doesn't have any friends. There are no other children in the village.'

She turned round to face the house, pointing.

'He was sitting there on the steps with his hands on his backpack, as if he was afraid someone would take it from him. Then he looked over here, and when I came out I saw him. The little man. Here. Where we are standing now,' said Edit.

Susso took out her snus tin and opened it without taking her eyes off Edit.

'He wasn't at all shy, and that was unexpected. You'd think a thing like that would be. That's what it's like – you want them to run away, given that they're so secretive people don't even know if they exist.'

Susso put a pouch of snus under her lip and nodded.

'But this one,' said Edit, sharply, 'he didn't run away and hide. Do you understand what I'm saying? He *didn't run away*. And it felt as if, I don't know, as if he wanted me for something.'

'Okay,' said Susso.

'But I certainly didn't want to find out what he wanted. I dragged the boy with me into the house and locked the door. Then we went into that room to watch him through the window.' She nodded towards the side of the house.

'And then guess what he did? You won't believe it. He came even closer. He was standing right below the window, looking at us. He was staring at us so intently I closed the curtain. I couldn't *bear* him looking at us like we were looking at him.'

'So you saw him close up?'

'Oh yes,' Edit said. 'I had a good look at him. He was wearing a jacket with a hood over his head. And his eyes . . . they were the worst thing about him. It was like looking at an animal's eyes. They were yellow, bright yellow, with pupils like slits.'

'Like a cat?'

'Yes,' said Edit. 'Just like a cat.'

Susso nodded and looked away to the trees.

'And it was obvious that he was thinking,' Edit continued. 'He was standing there planning something.'

After a few moments of silence she added:

'He had some kind of business here, you could tell that a mile off.'

She shook her head.

'We didn't know what to do so I phoned Carina – that's Mattias's mother – and when she pulled into the drive he ran off immediately. Straight over there, towards the Westmans'.' Edit pointed towards the neighbouring house. 'And since then I haven't seen him.'

'And Mattias's mother,' said Susso, 'did she see anything?'

'Carina? No, no.'

Edit leaned towards Susso.

'And she didn't *believe* us either. That was the worst part. She insisted we had made it up, all of it. Me and the boy. Even though I showed her the tracks he had left when he ran. Well, they're gone now. But I took pictures of them.'

Susso looked at her. This was something new.

'But you can't see anything,' Edit said, waving her hand. 'When you take pictures in the snow they don't turn out very well. It's all white. Anyway, when I wanted to show her the tracks she got angry. She put Mattias in the car and drove home. And they haven't been back since. He doesn't want to, Carina says. And Per-Erik, my son, won't say anything at all.'

'And the neighbours?' asked Susso. 'The Westmans, wasn't it? Have you spoken to them?'

'I have,' said Edit. She shivered. 'But I know what he's like. He just shrugged his shoulders. And that's just it,' she said. She fixed her gaze on Susso, who had turned to face the Westmans' house. 'If you don't know what he looked like, how strange his face was with those eyes, and how *little* he was – hardly a metre tall, I would say – then it's hard to be interested. Hard to take it seriously.'

Susso put her hand in her pocket and pulled out her mobile. It was almost half past two and soon it would be completely dark.

'You know what, Edit?' she said. 'I think this sounds very interesting, and that's why I'd like to set up a camera. If that's okay with you. It senses when anyone gets close to the house.'

Edit looked a little uncertain but did not protest, so Susso waded off and fetched her backpack from the car. The camera she dug out had a camouflage pattern. Two Velcro straps were wrapped round it.

The downpipe was the obvious choice. She positioned the

camera about a metre off the ground, with the lens aimed at a spot between the birches and the drive. She attached the top strap over the wall mounting that held the pipe in place so that the camera would not slide down. As she fixed the straps she explained to Edit how the sensor worked, how to check if the batteries had run out or the memory card had become full. Edit listened silently, leaning forwards in concentration, her eyebrows wrinkled sternly.

'Because he was here in the daytime,' said Susso, 'I'll set it to take pictures day and night. Remember that, so that you don't walk over there and we get masses of pictures of you.'

'Oh, right,' said Edit, taking a quick step backwards.

'But you can walk there now,' said Susso.

'Now?'

'Yes,' she said, rubbing her hat where her scalp had started to itch. 'So I know the camera is working as it should. Walk around the cars and come from that direction.'

Edit walked off and disappeared behind the Opel, and the second she came into the camera's field of vision the movement indicator began to flicker.

'Good!' shouted Susso. 'You've been detected!'

Out of his pockets he pulled a pair of work gloves that had dried into stiff knots. Snow met his face as he walked down the veranda steps. There was a yap from the dog enclosure and a low growling from one of the dogs, but no barking. He hit the chicken wire and the snow fell away, revealing the dogs. Two Swedish Elkhounds, a Finnish Lapphund cross, and the little Laika with her bushy arc of a tail. They all stood up and watched him.

'Were you up on the roof last night?' he said, and the dog put her head on one side.

The Volvo lay with its bonnet and windscreen on the ground, and the rear wheels were some way above Seved's head. He rested a hand on one tyre and rocked the car gently.

One of the wing mirrors was hanging loose, but luckily all the windows were undamaged. If any invisible damage had been done, they wouldn't know about it, of course. He had asked Ejvor whether the old-timers had picked up the car and thrown it or whether they had only overturned it, but she was unsure. Probably they had only tipped it over. It was doubtful the windows would have stayed intact otherwise.

He crouched down in front of the bonnet. There were no traces of oil as far as he could see, but water had leaked out, smelling strongly of antifreeze.

The front door of the house slammed shut and Ejvor came walking towards him with the hood of her down coat covering her head. The fur circled her small face like a fluffy crown.

'How the hell did you do it last time?' he asked.

'We just tipped it back,' she answered, making a pushing gesture with her hands. 'But then it was lying on its right side. And Lennart was with me.'

'I'll have to use the tractor.'

'Shouldn't you wait until Börje comes home?'

'It can't be left like this. What if I fasten a strap between the front and back wheels and hook the chain in the middle? Then I ought to be able to turn it upright with the tractor, don't you think?'

Ejvor stood silently and tried to work out what he meant.

'As long as the car doesn't drag along behind you like a plough.'

'I'll have to pull slowly.'

'I honestly think you should wait. It won't hurt the car.'

'What if something happens and we need to get away?'

He threw the question over his shoulder as he strode off to the barn. He knocked the bar across with his fist and opened up both doors. One door always swung shut, so he propped it in place with a pointed stake.

The chain and hook hung on a wall and rattled heavily when he laid them in the tractor's snow bucket, where patches of snow still lingered. He climbed up into the cab, took the headphones off the steering wheel and put them over his head. They were painfully cold on his ears but would soon warm them up. The engine spluttered a couple of times before it rumbled into life, spewing out exhaust fumes which rose to the roof of the barn.

After bringing out the tractor he jumped down. He pushed the strap's tapered end in behind the front axle, lifted the chain out of the snow bucket and placed the hook at the centre of the taut strap. He wound the other end of the chain around the arm of the bucket, then climbed up into the cab and put the tractor in reverse.

They ate Mekong soup that Edit had cooked from a packet. The taste eluded Susso, whose nose was streaming, but it was scalding hot and she liked that. It almost burned her palate. It was no more than thirteen or fourteen degrees in the house. She ate with her face over the bowl, strands of her hair hanging loose. Her skull felt worryingly heavy.

The old woman talked slowly but almost uninterruptedly. Carrying an experience like that had been unbearable, she explained. She had tried talking to her son but he did not know what to believe. Normally he always trusted her.

'But he's too scared,' said Edit. 'Afraid of conflict, as they say these days. He doesn't dare go against Carina, and she will absolutely not hear a word about . . . these things.'

Edit had phoned her sister, but had detected a sneering hostility. Talking about mythical beings and supernatural happenings was all right, it could even be amusing, but only as long as they were joking. When it was serious, the mood changed.

Edit sighed.

'So in the end I kept my mouth shut,' she said.

'So you haven't told anyone else?' she asked.

'Oh yes,' she replied. 'I phoned the *Kuriren,* of course.'

'You're joking?' said Susso, smiling.

Edit shook her head.

'They thought it was an amazing story and said they might send a reporter.'

'They said that?' said Susso, wiping her nose and still smiling. 'They said they would send someone?'

'Yes,' said Edit, and looked out of the window. It was completely black out there now. All that could be seen in the glass was the reflection of the candles and the white oval of Edit's face. 'But nobody came.'

And then she added:

'It's too far to come for something like this, I suppose.'

'Haven't they got a local reporter in Gällivare?'

Edit was not listening. She pushed her bowl aside and looked at her fingers before continuing.

'Hockey they can write about, and basketball, day after day. But the kind of thing Mattias and I experienced, something downright unbelievable? They won't touch it.'

They sat in silence for a moment.

'Was it a troll?' Edit asked.

Susso looked up and met Edit's clear eyes. They were asking her for something.

She sank down heavily, rested her elbows on the table and started picking at the cuticle of one thumb with the tip of the other.

'I presume you've asked the other neighbours?'

Edit nodded.

'I've gone to Randi and Björkholmen to ask, but it . . .'

Edit shook her head.

'What?'

'Same as with the Westmans. People just laugh at me.'

'Yes,' said Susso. 'That's what usually happens.'

Edit's bathroom was off the hall. The sludge-green wallpaper had begun to come loose and was bulging in places, making the large floral pattern come alive. When Susso carefully pushed the shower curtain to one side there was a soft scraping from the curtain rings. She stared at a row of plastic bottles of various colours neatly lined up on a little shelf.

The toilet was fitted with support rails. So she had not been on her own for very long. Surely no one would hang on to support rails for sentimental reasons?

Susso turned on the tap in the basin and opened the bathroom cabinet slowly so that the hinges would not creak. Inside there was dental floss, cosmetics, creams, nail clippers, toothpaste and a necklace with orange-coloured stones that could have been amber. But no pills. Not even a painkiller.

By the time Susso returned Edit had laid out coffee cups on the glass table in the sitting room. Susso took a cup and sat down on the beige leather sofa, which exhaled under her weight.

'How long have you been alone?'

Edit stood beside the coffee machine. The answer came immediately. It was as if she had been waiting for the question.

'Two years. At Christmas it will be two years.'

Susso told her she worked occasionally in homecare, so she knew how hard it was, being the one left behind. It was the worst thing.

'Everyone says so,' said Susso.

Edit disappeared out of sight, so she called after her:

'And how would they know!'

Edit came back into the room almost immediately with the coffee thermos in her hand. Susso smiled at her, but Edit did not seem to realise that Susso had been trying to be funny. With a pensive expression she poured coffee into the cups, which were decorated with small frosted sprigs of flowers.

'No,' she said. 'There's a lot that can't be proved.'

Susso agreed: there were philosophers who said that nothing at all could be proved, not even a thing like sitting at a table and drinking coffee, although that was taking things a bit too far, of course. If you carried on like that, you would end up crazy.

'Like me, for example,' said Edit, looking up and winking at her.

Susso had her cup to her lips but stopped. Had Edit heard her looking in the bathroom cabinet?

'You think I'm imagining things.'

'I don't think that at all.'

'Yes, you do. You think I've lost my marbles.'

'If anyone's lost their marbles, it's me,' said Susso, trying to force a conciliatory smile that somehow turned into a grimace. She sipped the strong coffee and then replaced her cup on the table.

'I've read it,' said Edit. 'On your website. About hoaxers and all the trouble they cause. The people who dug up that wraith burrow, or whatever you want to call it.'

Susso nodded.

'But I'm no hoaxer,' Edit said.

'No, of course not.'

They sat in silence for a while, listening to the fire.

'We'll have to wait and see if anything happens with the camera,' Susso said. 'You said that Mattias hasn't been here since it happened?'

'No. I don't know if Carina's stopping him or if he just doesn't dare. He was really frightened. But I'll phone and talk to Per-Erik.'

'Well, you needn't say anything about the camera. If that's their attitude, I mean.'

Edit snorted.

'Oh, no. That's our little secret.'

Seved had driven the tractor into the barn and switched off the engine, but he had no desire to climb down from the cab. He sat there, holding the headphones. The snow streamed down outside the door. The Volvo was a black mass in the pool of lamplight outside. It had dragged along after the tractor, just like Ejvor said it would, so he had decided to wait until Börje came home. If it turned out the car had been damaged, then he was likely to get the blame.

Why didn't they keep the cars in the barn, as a precaution? There was certainly room. But who knows what that might lead to. If the cars were missing, they might get anxious and agitated. They never liked being left alone, especially during the winter months. And what if they got into the barn and discovered the cars? That would confuse them, of course, and if the worst came to the worst they would also work out that the cars were being kept in the barn out of their reach. Then anything could happen.

He hung the chain on the wall and barred the doors again. Then he trudged back over the yard, stopping beside the car.

He tugged off the broken wing mirror and inspected it. He would probably be able to stick it back on with gaffer tape. Then he realised how stupid that was. It would just come loose again when they put the car upright.

As he stood there with the mirror in his hands, he stiffened.

He had heard something.

Bellowing.

He stood completely still for a moment or two before shaking his arm to reveal his watch. It was only three. Surely he wasn't hearing right. Thinking about the noise they had made the past few nights, and how badly he had been sleeping, it was not impossible that the noise was inside his head.

It came again.

First a muffled groaning.

Then a whimpering that gradually increased until it culminated in a melancholy, drawn-out howl.

Ejvor had also heard it. She was standing in the hall, putting on her jacket, her head bowed. She was fiddling with the zip, trying to fasten it at the bottom. Seved noticed that her red, roughened hands were shaking. In his hurry he had brought the mirror in with him, so he laid it on the hat rack.

'Are you sure you ought to go in?'

'It's not dangerous,' she said, pulling up the zipper. 'But if I get thrown up onto the barn I would appreciate it if you came and got me down.'

From one of the pegs on the hat rack she took down the head torch. She checked that it was working and fitted it so that the elastic strap lay under her knot of hair at the back.

'I'll think about it,' said Seved. He had walked into the kitchen and opened the larder door, scanning the shelves, where everything stood tightly packed. 'It might do you good to sit up there for a while.'

'Then you'll have to make your own food.'

'I thought I'd heat up some beef soup. Do you want beef soup?'

'Beef soup?' she said, taking the tin out of his hands and turning it round and round. 'The use-by date was last century.'

She slipped it into her pocket and said:

'But the trolls won't know that.'

It was time to set off for home. If Susso did not get the car home in time, there would be hell to pay from Cecilia, although that would probably happen anyway. She had not told her she would be taking the car all the way to Jokkmokk. She stood the cups and saucers in the sink, put in the plug and turned on the hot-water tap.

'Leave that,' Edit said, with a wave of her hand.

'As I already explained,' Susso said, as she put on her boots and hat, 'if it gets cold the batteries won't last very long, so you'll have to check that. Otherwise the memory card will be full in about three weeks. It all depends. Do you get many animals running about the place?'

Edit shook her head.

Susso walked outside and down the steps, looking for her car key. She turned round.

'I'll be in touch,' she said, and nodded at Edit, who was standing in the darkened hall with her hand on the door handle.

'Will you write that it was me who saw it? Will you put "Edit Mickelsson"?'

Susso took a deep intake of breath while she considered what Edit meant.

'Not if you don't want me to. Absolutely not.'

'No, I don't think I do.'

'I don't have to write anything at all. Not yet.'

'Perhaps that's best. For the time being.'

'Okay,' Susso replied, walking towards the car.

'Are you sure you have to go?' Edit exclaimed. 'In the dark, with the spray from the snow and everything? I've got an extra bed, if you want to stay the night.'

Susso smiled.

'Thanks, but I really have to get back. My sister,' she said, 'it's her car. She'll kill me if she doesn't get it back. And I've probably got to work tomorrow.'

Edit nodded.

And then before she closed the door, she said:

'Drive carefully.'

The light on a nearby mobile-phone mast glittered like a ruby-red star in the night, and way ahead another red dot blinked in and out of the haze. A car with its rear fog light on. Susso adjusted her speed to match, to have something to fix her eyes on. She held both hands on the cold plastic steering wheel. The fan heater roared at full pelt. The tarmac was scraped in dark, uneven streaks, so the snow plough could not be too far ahead of them.

In Porjus she had to stop for a pee. She had drunk far too much coffee at Edit's. Now her bladder was so full it was making her left leg vibrate. She reduced speed, threw a glance over her shoulder, swung off the road and parked by a viewing point overlooking the power station.

The facility lay far down below in the river valley, a burning fortress that filled the night sky with a dusky blue sheen. The pylons rose up like many-armed giants with straddled legs and handfuls of cables in their fists. The power cables rose in loops up the slope, from giant to giant, running over the tops of the birch trees and hanging over the road. Susso could hear they were making a noise.

They were speaking.

She wondered if it was caused by the snow or if in reality it was the sound of high voltage, of fast-travelling electrons. Did electricity make a sound? She had no idea. She pulled her hands up inside her jacket sleeves and walked closer to listen. They were emitting a humming noise, a secret song. She could not decide if the hissing came from snowflakes landing on the cables. All she heard was the song. Dark and strange.

It got to be four o'clock, then five and then five thirty, and still Ejvor had not returned. Seved thought it was odd. His hunger always meant a lot to her. She ran her life according to it, always producing food or asking questions about food. But perhaps she thought he had already made himself something to eat because he had been looking in the larder earlier. But he really could not be bothered. Beef soup would have been perfect. It only needed warming in a saucepan.

He sat by the window and looked at the pale facade of the building looming out of the darkness on the far side of the yard. It was still snowing but now strong winds were pulling the flakes along with them, lit up by the powerful lamp on the barn.

On the rare occasions she went in there during the evening she used to put a kerosene lamp on the draining board and the beam from her head torch would flash over the walls. But now the windowpanes were completely dark and shiny as steel.

He must have stood there waiting for fifteen minutes, but the ray of her head torch did not appear, and that could only mean she had gone downstairs. Probably because Lennart had forbidden it.

He looked at the clock again. Nearly six. Now he simply had to get himself something to eat. He opened the fridge and found a ring of Falu sausage. A tube of mustard. Margarine. He got out a slice of bread, spread it with the margarine, cut a few slices of sausage and lay them on top. He decorated the sausage with mustard, coarse-grained and strong, and ate while standing at the window, his hand cupped beneath his chin to catch the crumbs.

Shouldn't Börje and Signe have been back by now? He was still chewing his last mouthful as he went to the telephone hanging on the wall. Both the flat receiver and the wall mounting were made of the same ivory-coloured plastic, which had turned a shade of yellow. The spiral flex had coiled itself into a hard tangle.

He licked mustard from his thumb before tapping in the number.

'We're on our way,' Börje said. 'We're just passing the flooring factory.'

'Ejvor went into Hybblet and she's been there for almost three hours.'

'Then she's probably doing some cleaning. She said she was going to do that.'

'No, she went in because they called. She's already done the cleaning.'

Börje mumbled something that Seved did not catch. It was probably to Signe.

'We'll be home soon. Don't do anything until I get there.'

'I'll go in and have a look.'

'All right, do that. But stay in the hallway.'

Cecilia was sitting in a corner of the sofa wearing jogging pants and watching television when Susso stepped through the door, cold and out of breath. She dropped the car key onto the small, round glass table in the hall, making a demonstratively loud clatter. Ever since she left Vaikijaur she had been longing for a tissue, so she went straight to the bathroom and blew her nose. At the precise moment she flushed the paper away she remembered no one was allowed to make a noise because Ella woke up at the slightest sound.

'Don't flush!' demanded a voice from the sitting room.

All she could do was shut the bathroom door quietly and pull an apologetic face, which her sister did not even notice. With the tips of her boots on the metal strip between the hall floor and the parquet flooring of the sitting room she stood leaning against the door frame, looking at the TV screen.

'I've left the car in the square.'

Her sister nodded without taking her eyes from the screen. It was obvious she was pissed off. Susso tried to think of something to say to soften her up, but could think of nothing.

Finally she said: 'Have you spoken to Mum?'

Cecilia picked at the hem of her trousers and sighed.

'Not today.'

With a tug she removed a piece of thread, which she rolled

between her thumb and forefinger. On the table stood a thick purple candle on a pottery dish filled with shells.

'I don't think she's well.'

'Not her as well?' Susso said. She breathed in through her nose, making a sniffling sound. Cecilia looked at her with interest and asked:

'Can you work in the shop on Saturday?'

Susso knew they were negotiating the loan of the car and the cost of the fuel, which she had not even mentioned yet. There was no way out.

'I think so,' she said, wiping a cold knuckle under her nose. 'If I don't get any worse, I mean.'

'Because Ella's going to some dressing-up thing. A friend from pre-school.'

Susso nodded.

'I'm sure it'll be okay,' she said, getting out her mobile. She did this quite unnecessarily, looking at the digits of the clock without registering the time. She turned and walked towards the door but was halted by Cecilia's question:

'What have you been doing?'

She took a deep breath, wanting to avoid this part.

After a few seconds she said:

'I went to visit an old lady.'

'An old lady?'

'She saw something.'

'Where?'

It was pointless lying. She would see the mileage counter anyway.

'In Vaikijaur.'

There was a momentary silence.

And then it came:

'And where's that?'

Now she was really going to get it in the neck because she had driven the car more than five hundred kilometres. Her sister was enjoying dragging it out.

'A little village just north of Jokkmokk.'

Cecilia slowly tucked her feet beneath her as she reached for the silver-coloured plastic snus tin on the coffee table. She looked at her little sister with narrow, glittering brown eyes. A square of oily skin shone on her forehead where her fringe had parted.

'How did it go then?'

'She seemed pretty sound,' Susso said, shrugging her shoulders. 'So I set up a camera. The Reconyx.'

Cecilia inserted a snus pouch.

'Tell Mum', she said slowly, 'that you'll work instead of me.'

Not a day went by without Susso looking in on her mother. It seemed natural because they lived in the same block of flats on Mommagatan 1, Susso on the second floor and Gudrun on the third. It was a shabby concrete three-storey building with a dirty-pink facade, situated opposite the big hotel with its dark-brown brick permanently covered with expanding frost patches.

When she opened the door the dog started barking and thrashing its bushy tail. Susso crouched down and was forced to grab hold of a coat hanging in the hall to stop herself from being knocked over by the eager dog. He was part terrier but also part Spitz, as was evident from his curled tail. In the spirit of irony he was called Hound of the Baskervilles, but was also known as Basker. Her mother claimed he was registered with the kennel club.

'Hasn't he had a walk today?' she called into the flat.

'I'm not well!'

'So I heard.'

Susso removed her jacket and hung it from the hall cupboard handle. Through the doorway she saw half of her mother sitting at the kitchen table reading the paper. Her sleeve was pulled up, revealing her watch with its thin strap of blue leather. The radio was on, the volume turned to a pointlessly low level. There was a smell of burnt coffee.

When Susso sat down at the table Gudrun looked up and smiled quickly, wrinkles radiating out from the corners of her eyes. There were beads of mascara on the tips of her eyelashes. Had she been working in the shop anyway? Either that or her boyfriend Roland had looked in.

Susso pulled off her hat, put it on the table and kept her hand inside it, playing with the wool.

'Do you want coffee?'

'Coffee? What, now?'

Gudrun folded the newspaper and looked at her.

'Wine then?'

Susso shrugged: why not? She took out a stick of lip salve and rubbed it over her lips. They were always dry when she was out in the cold. There was something wrong with her, some gene that made her unsuited to the subarctic climate. Gudrun stood up, took two glasses out of the cupboard and walked over to the worktop, where the wine bottles lay in a cast-iron rack next to the microwave. She was wearing a loose-fitting apricot-coloured viscose top, the fabric so thin her bra was visible.

The glasses arrived on the table and Gudrun sat down, one foot beneath her, the way she always did when she drank wine: it was her relaxed mode. There was a short clucking sound from the bottle, then streams of red poured into the glasses.

Susso tucked a greasy strand of hair behind her ear.

'The woman I was with today might have seen something, I think,' she said slowly. 'The one in Vaikijaur. Edit, she's called.'

Gudrun pulled at her top but said nothing.

'It came sneaking into her garden. A little old man, or that's what it looked like, about a metre tall. She said he had cat's eyes.'

'Cat's eyes?'

'You know. Horizontal pupils.'

'That sounds strange . . .'

'Yes, I know.'

'But you believe her then? Has she got any evidence?'

'Not evidence exactly, but she saw him in full daylight, at a distance of about two metres, maybe less. Through the window. That makes it an absolutely unique observation.'

Gudrun placed the tips of her thumbs and index fingers on the foot of the wine glass and turned it a half circle.

'Did you set up the camera?'

Susso nodded.

'So in a few weeks' time I've got to borrow your car so I can drive up and collect it. I don't want to ask Cecilia again, she gets so shitty about it. She *lives* to lend me her car and then make me pay her back somehow.'

Gudrun nodded.

They sat without speaking for a moment, and then Susso said:

'I was thinking about something when I stopped in Porjus. There are cables there, running above the road, coming from the power station. And they kind of sing. Why do you think they do that? Does electricity sing?'

'I wouldn't have thought so.'

'But think if it is because of all the electricity streaming through them, and the trolls felt it. I've heard they disappeared when electricity came to the countryside. They must have felt the current really strongly, everywhere, in every single wire. Do you think that could have been why?'

'Susso . . .'

'But don't you think that sounds logical?'

Gudrun pushed up her sleeves and looked at the clock.

'Are you working tomorrow?'

After he had replaced the receiver on the wall he remained standing in the unlit kitchen, hesitating. He had detected an undisguised tension in Börje's voice and it made him uncertain. He regretted saying he would go in and look. Now he more or less had to.

He pulled on his boots and went out, but turned back immediately to get his torch, which was attached to the fridge door by a magnet. There was no lighting in Hybblet. There had been too much playing about with the switches.

The snow was biting cold against his neck and he stopped to zip his jacket all the way up to the top. As he walked across the yard he recognised a feeling of resistance.

The beam from his torch swept over the netting of the dog compound and met eyes suspended in a row. The dogs were uneasy, not surprisingly. The previous night had made them afraid.

Why had they never told him before what had happened in the dog pen? Why had no one told him they were capable of such meaningless cruelty? Börje and Ejvor had always assured him they were entirely safe. But if they could set on the dogs, where did they draw the line? Was there a line?

It is like some bloody frenzy.

That was all Börje would say when Seved asked him what had happened. He realised it was serious all right – more serious than Börje and Ejvor let on. Lennart had turned up no less than three times during the last month, and on one occasion he had been accompanied by a couple of people Seved had never seen before. A bearded man who had walked with a limp around the outside of the building and an older woman in a wheelchair. He had only seen her back. There was also a girl, pushing the wheelchair. Seved had not dared to ask who they were.

Now he had reached the veranda, and he stopped to listen before pulling down the door handle. It was so silent he could hear the snowflakes floating in and landing on the black sacks.

Because he knew the door was warped and difficult to open, he tugged it hard.

The stench hit him, a warm, sickening blast from the dark interior. It was a smell of rotten meat, rancid dry fodder and old piss, blended with fumes from a strong alkaline cleaning solution. And excrement. What it had smelled like when Ejvor had gone in to clean up he did not want to imagine. By then no one had cleaned in there for almost three weeks. All they had done was carry in plastic bags and boxes of food.

With his left hand covering his nose and mouth he stepped over the threshold and carefully kicked the snow off the soles of his boots. Not too hard – he did not want it to sound as if he was knocking.

He shone the torch on the circular pattern of the cork matting and then over the faded floral wallpaper on the narrow wall that separated the two doors on the opposite side of the hall. There was a rustling of small clawed feet in one of the rooms. He stood listening, feeling anxious, and after a while was forced to let go of his nose and draw in air.

Christ, what a stink! He twisted his face in disgust and fought as hard as he could against the impulse to run out.

Perhaps he ought to let them know he was here after all? It went against his instinct, but the big ones did not like people creeping up on them. They were exactly like bears in that respect. It could get dangerous.

'Ejvor?' he said.

He waited a few seconds and then he said:

'Mum?'

There was no way he would shout. Even sudden noises could irritate them, and it would almost certainly upset the little ones.

He could not see her, so she must have gone downstairs, as he thought. Because she couldn't be upstairs, surely? He shone his torch up the staircase but quickly lowered it. He did not know which of them was in the house, and considering Ejvor was hardly likely to be on the upper floor it was unnecessary to disturb them.

He looked into the kitchen. They had already made a mess. A real mess.

On the floor lay polystyrene trays with remnants of minced meat long turned grey. There were half-eaten packages of black pudding and liver pâté and bacon, and an upturned paper carrier bag from the supermarket with its contents of apples and potatoes strewn across the floor. It looked as if they had amused themselves by trampling on it.

Around the buckets lined up under the draining board the cork matting was black with pellets of dry fodder. Someone had dug down deeply to see if there was anything else at the bottom.

Normally they didn't crap in the kitchen, but judging from the smell they must have done, and it was when he was searching for their droppings with the torchlight that he caught sight of her, only a few metres away.

She was sitting with her back propped against the wall and her legs straight out in front of her, her hands resting limply on the floor. The head torch was resting on her chest like a large pendant.

It never occurred to him to approach Ejvor, so he must have immediately registered that something was wrong, but he aimed the torch at her for several seconds before realising that the back of her head with the shiny knot of hair was where her face should be, and that she was staring straight at the wallpaper without seeing it.

The long hours of daylight that fortify us and the unyielding darkness that wraps itself thickly around the shimmering green swirls of the northern lights – it is primarily these extraordinary and mutually opposed forces that led our family, the Myréns, to investigate and eventually reveal the existence of trolls.

Dad was drawn to the dramatic play between light and darkness, and to the landscape itself, of course. And he drew us with him.

This is what I remember him saying, or rather singing:

'Sweden, Sweden, country of wildlife, winter country of fiery northern lights.'

I used to wonder what kind of image foreigners have of our circumpolar land. A windswept and frost-ravaged expanse? A barren and for the most part wretched region, sparsely populated, if not to say uninhabited? A stag standing proudly on a mountain, with jutting chest, a nimbus of hoar frost around his raised antlers, the northern lights radiating behind him? Or is it a howling wolf, or the muffled sound of troll drums? I know. Perhaps I know better than anyone how that image has been formed, and that is because I come into contact with the hordes of tourists. The airport buses deposit their cargo literally outside my shop door, and the mine tours start and finish here. Naturally I'm grateful for that: if the shop had not been quite so central and located next to the tourist information office, lending it an unmerited official status, I would have frozen to death in seconds.

In winter the northern lights are our foremost attraction, and naturally enough the capriciousness with which they choose to reveal themselves increases their appeal. Many who come here like to think of the northern lights as some sort of compensation for the stolen daylight, that they appear every night in the same way that the moonlight is switched on. They stand with their faces turned skywards, waiting patiently. Then the next day they come into my shop and complain: 'No aurora last night.'

But it isn't the deep, solemn winter that brings the tourists here, it's the midnight sun. The light that never fades. People come from all over the world to see it. The majority are Germans, of course, then the French and the Spanish. They think it's amazing, seeing the sun hanging on the horizon. Odd, in fact. As if there must be something wrong.

That's our high season, when the shop is most crowded, the backpacks colliding between the shelves. And that is the time I think about Dad the most. He stands with me behind the counter, which is strange because he certainly never did that in real life.

The shop is named after him: Gunnar Myrén Ltd. Here, among all the other things, are his photos, reduced to postcard size or enlarged as posters. And books of photographs that are so large they have to be laid flat to fit on the shelves. Folios, they are called.

Like Dad I make a living from the landscape. My business is the exotic shimmering image of Lapland which Dad, in a not inconsiderable way, has helped to shape. The shop window says *Photographs Books Cards Handicrafts*, underlined with the billowing line of the familiar silhouette of the Lapland Gate, in far northern Sweden.

We stock what were previously called Lapland handicrafts

but are now known as *duodji*. There are knives with handles and sheaths made of reindeer horn. Cups, boxes and figurines carved from mottled masur birch, and Sami ceremonial drums.

We also stock a lot of random knick-knacks, because you have to: key rings and bottle openers; small round badges you can pin onto your lapel which say *Kiruna*, but also *Sverige* or *Sweden*; and sweatshirts with prints of wolf heads, the northern lights, reindeer herds and magic inscriptions. We have fridge magnets, and even Dala horses: it would never occur to a Swede to buy a horse from Dalarna while visiting Kiruna, but people from Spain are not so fussy and we get a lot of Spanish people here. So they sell well.

We also have trolls, naturally. The artist Rolf Lidberg, from Sundsvall, has made picture books about kindly, large-nosed trolls who live on the banks of the Indals River and fish for salmon, and we stock his books. These trolls are also pictured on napkins and paper cups and plates.

But the real troll – the family's troll, if you like – is not something we have tried to make a profit from. We keep that to ourselves.

At least, we did for many years.

It was my daughter Susso who changed everything.

Dad was a pilot. He flew a single-engine amphibious Piper. In fact, he owned three aircraft through the years, all Pipers, so in my mind they are one and the same plane. In this fragile but heroically reliable mode of transport he floated above the most northerly regions of Sweden. He was a genuine pioneer. No one had flown there before him. Not like that, not to look around and capture those fabulous views on paper.

Often he photographed Tjuonavagge, the valley commonly

known as the Lapland Gate. If you have ever seen a photograph of the Lapland Gate, there is a good chance it was Dad who took it, and if it is an aerial shot, then I can almost guarantee it was him. This particular motif did not interest him especially, but it was popular, and Dad was a businessman through and through, if perhaps a hot-headed and impatient one.

He would rather photograph the striking lowland fell in Rapadalen, the one he called the Lonely Mountain, though its real name is Nammatj. In the Sami language that means 'nameless'. He also loved the Skierfe: the 'sheer drop'.

There are dramatically sharp features on the face of the ancient landscape.

In the beginning he travelled on skis. He trained with the Ski Battalion in Boden, and it was during his military service that he became familiar with the most northerly parts of the country. He came into the world further south in Örnsköldsvik, which made him a man of Ångermanland, and I like to believe that I have Ångermanland in my heart as well, because I have never liked it up here. In a way I hate the life here: the coarse mentality that dominates the iron ore mining fields, the macho culture, the stubbornness and the corrosive, everlasting gossip. The darkness and the cold which leave deep and permanent frost damage in their wake, both in buildings and people. The reindeer and their pastures, as sacred as cemeteries.

But I got stuck here, somehow. Just like Dad. Although for him it was different: he was mesmerised by the mountains. During the war he was posted to Riksgränsen, the northern border, and liked the place so much that he settled there. 'A fells convert,' he used to say.

Riksgränsen was a dreadfully isolated place when Dad first

went there. It's almost impossible to imagine how isolated it was. So living there was more or less impossible. And I think that was what attracted him because few were as stubborn as he was. He bought a ski cabin by Lake Vassijaure and above the front door, which opened inwards, he nailed a sign with the words: MYRÉN'S PHOTO STUDIO.

He stayed there for as long as a person can be in one place. When he died he had been living in Riksgränsen for over fifty years.

He was a physically strong man, but fragile in spite of that. It changed from one day to the next. He was something of a hypochondriac too, if I'm honest. He often grimaced, bared his teeth and sighed, relating in detail how his body had let him down, and he complained despairingly that nothing worked the way it should: the plane, the cameras, his knees. There was always something letting him down.

The fragile side of him would carry him to unsuspected heights, however. That's how we'll have to look at it. Following a knee injury, when Dad felt as if the fell world was drifting out of his reach, he acquired an aircraft and then learned to fly. In that order. It was a large and risky investment, but it succeeded. No one had photographed the fells from above before.

With the plane he could reach in a few hours places that it had taken him days to get to before, or else had been completely inaccessible. It was revolutionary. The world saw the Swedish fells from above for the first time, and it was entirely thanks to Dad.

Reindeer appeared as small dots on the blindingly white mountainsides. Distant, silent hordes, such as only the hawks had seen before. The valleys were filled with shining, black, meandering water courses, veiled in driving clouds of rain. Remnants of snow appeared as lines on the hillsides, like white scratch marks. The bogs changed colour, as if a red-brown wind was blowing over them.

Dad demonstrated that he was a fully-fledged pilot by landing on the top of Kebnekaise – or, to be more accurate, immediately below the summit, because of course no plane can land on the actual mountain top – and he was the first person in history to do it.

He took a picture of himself up there, to capture the moment.

It was 1 May 1967.

Dad has his hands raised to the heavens and is leaping for joy. Landing on Sweden's highest mountain meant he could land anywhere. He was not too old for the world of the fells.

I look at that photograph often. Very often.

It is a moment of happiness.

If only it could have stopped there, I think.

The aircraft's wing casts a long shadow, and the trail Dad has trampled in the permanent snow cover is littered with small shards. The mountain tops in the background are disappearing in a milky-white haze that is growing larger, hurtling forwards.

I call it the troll mist.

Here it comes.

But it would take twenty years before it reached its destination.

There is an aerial photo from Rapadalen dated 18 April 1987. A bear is lumbering among the birches, but there is nothing remarkable about that: it has just woken up and is looking for something to fill its belly. It is moving away from the low-flying plane, probably driven on by the sound of the engine as it grows louder.

On the bear's hunched back is a lighter patch, and if you focus your gaze or, even better, look through a magnifying glass, you can make out a naked body with spindly arms and legs.

It looks like a monkey, but of course it most definitely is not a monkey.

It is not an animal.

And it is not a human being.

It is something else.

Something in between.

Dad sat for ages at the desk, staring at the bear's inexplicable rider. As he was flying through the valley he thought he had seen something strange on the bear, but decided it was just the sun illuminating the bear's fur. It was not until he was in the darkroom that he managed to see what the camera had captured. It gave him his first heart attack.

If only his eyes had seen it, well, that would have been different. Then he could have dismissed it as an apparition. But it was impossible to believe that his camera, his reliable Hasselblad, had been fooled. It was the model they had sent to the moon, the most reliable camera on the planet.

He banged the handle of the magnifying glass against the desk's green imitation-leather underlay. Then he put his eye against the lens and glided over the boggy ground, trying to get around the bear to see from the other side.

I could see him through the crack in the door. Sitting there, wanting to get inside the picture.

Could it be a Nordic monkey, unknown to science? A shy and lethargic creature, a kind of weasel, living off new spruce shoots and extremely averse to being on the ground or even, in fact, fearing the ground. A dark mass in the fork of a spruce, moving between the trees so carefully it is almost motionless.

But the naturalists Dad approached dismissed the idea of such an animal. Quite simply, it could not possibly exist.

And suddenly, there it was.

The word.

The thing clinging to the bear was a troll.

It was only a word, after all.

A name for something extraordinary and elusive.

A troll is quite simply something that will not allow itself to be categorised.

A hybrid that has not been given a scientific description or a habitat.

No one could explain what Dad had photographed, and that frightened him. He had developed heart trouble and could no longer fly alone. To save the business my stepmother Gunilla studied for a pilot's licence, as did my husband Arne.

But the truth was that he did not want to fly any more.

He did not dare.

The plane remained in the hangar.

From time to time he went off on the snowmobile and photographed the light that floated on the surface of Vassijaure. Slowly he made his way around the area, staring down at the points of his skis. He kept the lens in a cone-shaped leather case hanging across his shoulder, and the Hasselblad protruded like a growth under his winter overall.

And then he was gone.

We were taking a walk alongside the railway line, me, Dad and

Arne, on a beautiful day in October with a high blue sky. Dad grew tired and slowed down. When we asked if we should turn back, he told us to go on ahead and he would follow at his own pace.

I will never know what it was, a premonition perhaps, but after we had walked a short distance I turned round to see how he was getting on. He had grabbed hold of a small birch tree and I saw the leaves shaking as he tried, but failed, to keep himself upright.

I ran to him and watched him sink to the ground.

'Don't be afraid, Gudrun,' he said to me. 'Don't be afraid. I'm not afraid.'

And then he died. With a smile on his lips.

It was a heart attack. His second.

We travelled up to Vassitjåkka by helicopter to cast his ashes to the wind, because that was his wish. There was me and Arne, Gunilla and Susso – Cecilia couldn't come because she was living abroad at the time. The pilot flew us there for free. He said it was an honour, and he looked as if he meant it.

It certainly is a little strange up there at the top. The mountain is steep and completely untouched, and there, right in the middle, is a small hut, or at least that's what it looks like. Susso went into the hut and sat down. She was annoyed about something, I don't remember what, and it is only looking back that I realise it was because she was feeling sad and for some reason had the idea she mustn't show it. Because no one else cried, not even me. It was probably because Gunilla was there.

Afterwards I regretted taking her up there. It was as if the ash was flung back on itself in the strong wind raging up the mountainside and blew into her. As if Dad was carrying on his quest through her eyes. I know that's sentimental and irrational, but that is how I see it.

We stayed at Riksgränsen for almost ten years. Then Arne cheated on me with Susso's boyfriend's mother. I discovered them myself, in Dad's old workroom, of all places. They had not undressed or anything but were standing close together, and when the door opened they sprang apart and acted as if nothing had happened.

But I knew what I had seen and when I confronted Arne he confirmed it with his silence. When I carried on asking he shouted at me to stop.

It was a real mess, I can tell you. It was one thing that our marriage came to an end – it hadn't been particularly good for many years – but it also meant the end for Susso and her boyfriend Torbjörn. They were thrown together in a kind of sibling relationship and Torbjörn especially couldn't handle it. He told Susso he thought the whole thing was sick, and I comforted her by saying that if that was the case, the feelings weren't right anyway. But it was a pity they had parents who behaved like that, who didn't think!

The worst thing was not being able to move straight away. There was so much to sort out. Arne part owned the company and I was forced to buy him out. I did that by giving up my share of the properties, and in the autumn of 2003 I moved down to Kiruna. By that time Siv had already moved up and taken my place. It was like a slap in the face. Fifteen years younger than me and fifteen centimetres taller. She is a good-looking woman – slender limbs and raven-black hair – and I can't help seeing her in Torbjörn.

*

Susso was thirteen when Dad died and she didn't show any particular interest in the troll initially, at least not as far as I can recall. It was a strange but natural part of her upbringing, but we seldom mentioned it, especially in the years immediately after Dad passed away. We thought it was about time to bury the troll – Gunilla even suggested that we destroy the photograph. If anyone was to blame for Dad's death, it was the troll.

But then one day Susso told me she thought it was odd there was nothing about trolls on the internet. She thought other people would have seen something similar and written about it. She understood why reports of things like that didn't appear in the newspapers, but wasn't it weird that you could find no mention of it online?

That was in the mid-nineties, when I knew nothing about the internet. I knew it was something that existed on computers but that was as far as my knowledge went.

Susso started searching, and in actual fact she did it like Dad.

Because the search engine she used was called Altavista.

And that means 'view from above'.

She didn't find any trolls but she did come into contact pretty quickly with other people who were looking for the same things as herself, more or less. They were cryptozoologists. She introduced the word to me, wanting me to accept it. I didn't. To be honest, I was irritated by her lively interest in that troll. It had only brought unhappiness. I thought it was childish of her not to understand that. But she hadn't known Dad before he'd seen it. Before he became the person he became.

It was Cecilia who came up with the idea of setting up a website for the troll. It was Easter, and Susso had come up from Kiruna.

We were sitting on the terrace, all three of us, and Cecilia's daughter Ella was sleeping in her pushchair. The sun was floating on the lake and we were drinking coffee and eating biscuits we had baked using Dad's recipe. The wind rustled playfully among the willows down the slope. The mountain tops were sharp against the sky. There was a constant dripping from the roof, and from time to time huge sheets of snow came sliding down the roof tiles. I enjoyed every minute of it. Until Susso started talking about the troll, that is.

She wanted to know what we *really* thought about it.

I didn't say I didn't believe it, but that's the not the same thing as believing. It's something more evasive and perhaps cowardly, and she latched onto that. You could say she had my back against the wall.

'But do you think he forged the picture?'

The look I gave her made her understand that obviously I didn't think that.

'So what do you think then?'

'I don't know, Susso.'

'You don't know what you believe?'

'No. Actually I don't. Sometimes it's like that.'

Cecilia had been sitting quietly but now she moved, making the recliner creak.

'If there's one,' she said, 'there's got to be more.'

'More trolls?'

She shrugged under the fleece blanket she had wrapped around herself.

'Granddad can't be the only one to have seen something. That means there are more people out there thinking about it. Really thinking.'

'So why haven't they written about it on the internet then?'

'Well, you haven't.'

The answer silenced Susso.

'You can search, Susso. And you also can make people search for *you*.'

Susso was sitting in a ray of sunshine. She screwed up one eye and looked at Cecilia with the other.

'A website, Susso. That's what you ought to have.'

Once Susso had made up her mind things happened quickly. She has always been like that. She probably got it from Dad. When something interests her she puts all her energy into it, and her energy is considerable. It took no more than a couple of weeks for her to learn the programming language, buy a domain name and create a website.

I was worried at first, I have to admit. How would it affect our business if it became common knowledge that Dad had believed in trolls? It could only be positive, according to Cecilia, but I didn't like the idea of everyone *knowing.* I thought that a website could attract a lot of critical attention, which would be bad for business.

As it was, nothing much happened. The website came up and you could read about Dad's photo and trolls and wraiths and everything Susso had unearthed through the year, but the business was not affected in any way, as far as I could see.

Not many people visited it. Susso could see that on a web counter.

There was a bloke from Gunnarsbyn who sent an email about a wraith that had saved his life in the forest, and then there were some people in Östersund who said they had 'excavated' an authentic wraith burrow in their garden. Susso actually went there but she was convinced they were hoaxers, so she didn't write anything about it.

Nothing much happened after that.

She went out and set up wildlife cameras a couple of times, but that didn't result in anything.

Not until Edit Mickelsson from Vaikijaur got in touch.

The icy wind whipped in grainy blasts along Adolf Hedingsvägen. It tugged at the tassel of Susso's hat and made her eyes water. The moon was dissolving like an ice floe in a black ocean and her footsteps were heavy as she trudged along Gruvvägen. She really should have stayed at home because the walk had exhausted her. She was not completely better and there was a risk she would pass it on to the old folk. Turn up like an angel of death. But she could not afford to be ill, and anyway she had brought ginger biscuits for Lars Nilsson.

She took off her hat in the lift, straightened her hair and pulled a strip of tinsel out of her jacket. She wound it a couple of times around her head and after ringing the doorbell she opened the door, singing the traditional Lucia Day song:

'Outside it's dark and cold . . .'

Lars Nilsson was sitting in an armchair watching the Channel Four morning news. He was dressed in a tobacco-brown leather waistcoat and a green and black checked shirt. The light from the TV fell on his lined face like a mask. When Susso strode into the room he picked up the remote and lowered the volume, greeting her with a smile which spread into the grid of wrinkles surrounding his eyes.

'Good morning, Lars!'

She broke open the lid and held out the box.

'Ginger biscuits.'

The old man took a star-shaped biscuit from the tin, and half of it disappeared immediately between his teeth.

'So you're out spreading festive cheer . . .'

'Why haven't you lit the candles?' she asked, walking over to the window where the electric Advent candleholder stood, with a yellowing geranium on one side and an amaryllis on the other. It had seven carved arms and an impressive base of unvarnished wood. Around each candle was a small ring of fake lingonberry leaves. Susso twisted the top of the bulb furthest to the right. The reflection in the window made two candleholders light up the dark room.

'Have you eaten breakfast?' she asked, pinching off a geranium leaf.

After thinking for a moment Lars held up the ginger biscuit. Only one corner of the star remained.

'What would you like?' Susso asked, walking into the kitchen and opening the fridge. When there was no reply she called:

'Shall I fry a couple of eggs?'

While she stood by the stove under an extractor fan roaring away at storm force, the old man sat at the kitchen table with the palms of his hands resting flat on the *Norrländskan* newspaper, waiting. When the silence had gone on for too long Susso had to bring it to an end.

'Well, Lars?' she said, knocking the spatula against the frying pan.

'Why not?' came the reply.

Susso put salt and pepper on the eggs, slid the two glistening eyes onto a plate and, after moving the newspaper out of the way, placed them in front of him on the table.

After the coffee had been brewed and poured into the cups she read the newspaper out loud to Lars. Slumped at the table, the old man studied his fingers. They were well worn, gnarled and the colour of bronze, with cracks around the nails. He had owned reindeer once and also worked as a reindeer herder for many years.

Susso soon tired of her voice, which was nasal from her blocked nose, and put down the paper. What about doing the crossword? Lars nodded and Susso turned the newspaper so that they could both see the puzzle. They sat for a while, thinking, Susso wiping her nose repeatedly on sheets of kitchen roll. Eventually she sat up straight. This was not a good idea. She could pass on her cold to him if they sat like this, almost cheek to cheek. They would have to do the sudoku instead because numbers were not as hard to read upside down, or so she thought, and they could sit opposite each other. Lars had the paper the right way up, but to compensate it was closer to Susso. It was a compromise.

From time to time the old man's hand came inching over the paper and his index finger scraped against a square where he thought a number might fit, but he never said which number he was thinking of, so it wasn't much help. It confused her even more.

After a while she said:

'Have you ever been to Vaikijaur, Lars?'

She had to repeat her question, and he slowly shook his head and whispered something she couldn't hear. Perhaps it wasn't even in Swedish.

'I was there yesterday,' she said.

'Yesterday?' he said. 'No . . .'

'I was there,' she said, raising her voice. 'Yesterday. I met someone who had seen a little old man in her garden. Really little, I mean. About one metre tall. She thought he might be a gnome.'

Lars nodded.

'I set up a wildlife camera. So with a bit of luck I'll get a picture of him and then I can show you what a real gnome looks like. If he comes back, that is.'

'Oh, he will.'

'Do you think so?'

She reached out for the coffee pot and filled the cups.

Horizontal lines filled the old man's forehead.

'You'll get to the bottom of it,' he said, adding: 'Ossus.'

Susso raised her eyebrows, met his gaze and saw the twinkle in his eyes.

Then she looked down at her jumper and the swell of her left breast. She gave a lopsided smile. The flesh under her chin fell in folds as she undid the small safety pin on the yellow woollen jumper and turned her name badge the right way round.

'So you can read from that angle after all,' she said. 'Well then, we don't have to carry on with this boring sudoku.'

She leafed through the newspaper, folded it and flattened down the page containing the crossword.

'Let's get going!'

Seved stood on the veranda with his hands in the pockets of his down jacket, looking in the direction of Hybblet. It looked the same as usual: unlit windows with closed curtains, the long palisade of fir trees behind and the bulging drift of snow on the porch roof that formed the same shape every year. That was both strange but not strange.

The fact that Ejvor was sitting inside there, staring at the wall, was impossible for him to grasp, even though the sight of her lifeless body had been etched so deeply into his memory that he would never forget it. She ought to be in the kitchen now, or standing in the bathroom, pulling washing out of the machine and complaining about how badly it rinsed the clothes. Or leaning over the kitchen table with a small cup of coffee, reading the paper. Humming a Christmas song. All those songs she had inside her! Who had taught her? He didn't know because he knew nothing about her. He realised that now. And it was too late. She would fade away and be nothing more than an imprint inside him. An imprint alongside the one he already had, one that he had never mentioned to anyone.

He had almost made it across the yard when his legs refused to carry him any further. Later, when Signe and Börje had returned, the headlights of the Isuzu had picked him out slumped in the snow. Signe had hurried to help him up, but he had not wanted her to touch him and had wrenched himself free.

Afterwards Börje had come up to him, his ski hat pulled down over his ears and his mouth grim. He had left the engine running because he knew he might have to drive off immediately. When he had managed to get enough out of Seved to grasp what had happened he stood for a while, glowering at Hybblet, before cutting across the yard and walking up the steps to the veranda. He did not venture any further.

He leaned forwards and, after peering in through the doorway, he set off back to the car, opened a door and took out a box, which he carried in both hands to the house. A few seconds later he came out, shutting the door after him, quietly but securely.

'She can stay there,' he said.

'Aren't you going to bar the door?'

'No, that'll make it worse. We'll sleep in the car tonight.'

She can stay there.

Seved knew why. Of course he did. He knew it was a safety measure and nothing else. Börje was no coward. His desire to get Ejvor out of the house was at least as strong as Seved's.

But he did not want to take the risk. The risk of being inside there now.

The only thing they could do was keep out of the way.

They had driven down the drive and parked on the other side of the barrier. Wrapped in quilts over their jackets they had shivered through the night, Börje in the front with his large hooked nose pointing up at the roof, and Seved and Signe in the back.

He had heard Börje crying on the other side of the mesh panel, muted and almost silently. Seved had pressed his face hard against the cold plastic of the truck and had held a clenched fist to his ear. He had never heard Börje cry before and he didn't want to hear it. Not this close. Not now.

They hadn't been able to sleep much. As it began to get light he had no memory of being anything other than awake, but he must have slept because there had been dreams. He had seen things, but most of all it was the sound that lingered. The noise. As if someone had been bellowing continuously inside his head.

By now it was one o'clock, and Börje was in the leather armchair in the sitting room, his eyes closed. His head, with its combed-back greying hair curling at the nape, was lolling slightly to one side and his lips had fallen apart. He was wearing a short-sleeved shirt, black with silver-grey stripes. It was unbuttoned at the throat and a tuft of long, wiry chest hair poked out. Around his wrist he wore a leather strap with plaited pewter and a reindeer-antler button. He was clasping his left wrist and his sharp elbows stuck out on either side of the armrests.

Seved stood for a moment, watching him. He did not know whether to let him sleep or not. Leave him in peace. No doubt he was deeply distressed. But he felt they ought to be doing something because soon it would be dark again. One of the hares was lying asleep on the olive-green velour sofa, and Seved shoved it roughly to the floor before he sat down. The animal, afraid, scuttled away across the wooden floor, and the sound made Börje open his eyes.

His forehead was shiny, with sweat at the hairline.

'What's the time?' he mumbled, rubbing his face with the palm of his hand.

'She can't be left sitting there any longer,' said Seved.

Börje's nostrils flared as he filled his lungs with air, which he immediately exhaled in a snort. He righted himself in the chair.

It was incomprehensible that he had chosen to sleep sitting up after spending all night in a car, although the intention had not been to sleep. He grabbed a half-litre plastic bottle from the floor. It had once been filled with Diet Coke but now it contained something else.

'Börje,' said Seved, 'she can't be left there.'

Börje unscrewed the cap and held it as he drank. After he had swallowed and cleared his throat he said:

'Go in and get her then.'

Seved folded his arms.

'It's light now,' he said. 'There's no danger.'

Börje snorted. Or it could have been a laugh.

'If only it was that easy,' he said, digging out his mobile from the pocket of jeans that were too tight on him. He pressed the keypad a few times with his thumb and then sat with his eyes fixed on the dusty television screen. It was almost as if he had fallen sleep again, because his eyelids were closed.

'What do you mean?'

Without opening his eyes Börje said slowly:

'We don't know why they did it. Hopefully it was an accident, a game that went too far, and they put her there because they didn't know what else to do with her.'

Then he sat up and threw the mobile onto the smoke-coloured glass tabletop.

'But it could also mean they want to keep her.'

'Keep . . .'

Börje nodded.

'And that would make it dangerous to move her.'

Seved had to think for a while before he understood what Börje meant.

Keep her. A corpse to eat as required.

That made him feel intensely nauseous and he tried to push the idea to the back of his mind.

'What shall we do then?' he said, sounding defeated.

'Nothing,' answered Börje. 'Lennart will be here in an hour or so. Before three, he said. And until then we won't do a single damn thing. Have you got that?'

Seved nodded and lowered his eyes.

'What about the little shapeshifters then? Won't that help?'

Börje shrugged.

'A little, maybe. But it's not a long-term solution.'

'I don't understand it. Why would they do such a thing? To her?'

'It's what happens,' said Börje. 'When they don't get their own way. When we don't give them what they need.'

And he looked at Seved with sleepy, red-rimmed eyes.

'It's all our fault, this is.'

It had been dark for a long time when the dogs started barking. Seved stepped out onto the veranda and soon he could see the headlights down on the road, nosing their way through the darkness. He hadn't thought he could be filled with anything other than apprehension at the sight of Lennart's car, but now he was. If it wasn't gratitude he felt, then it was not far from it. He pulled the door shut behind him and called out:

'He's coming!'

Börje sat in the kitchen eating spaghetti, a sticky, pale-yellow skein that he was jabbing with a fork. He hadn't even put any sauce on it and he was drinking strong beer directly from the can.

They heard the car pull up and the six-cylinder engine fall silent. After a couple of minutes had passed and no heavy footsteps had been heard on the veranda, Seved walked over to the window. The car, a large Mercedes with a snout of additional lights, was parked outside Hybblet. The rear section of the champagne-coloured roof shimmered in the glow from the barn's lamp. He had gone straight in. Totally unafraid. But then there was no time to lose.

'Did you say where she was sitting?'

Börje didn't answer. Without looking up from his plate he said:

'Tell Signe to come down.'

Seved went into the hall to shout, but Signe was already on her way down the stairs. She had taken a shower and her body exuded the sweet fragrance of aloe vera.

He had made a clumsy attempt to talk to her during the day but had not got very far. He had only heard the sound of his own voice, the tremulous uncertainty of it, the empty words he had managed to stutter. Afterwards he wondered if she blamed him, if she thought he ought to have stopped Ejvor from going into Hybblet. That was probably what he was fishing for: confirmation that it was not his fault. It might be something of a consolation to hear those words. But she had said nothing. Now she was looking at Börje with a blank expression. The groove in her dry lower lip looked like a cut. She had been crying. Her eyes were swollen.

'We'll be talking down here for a while,' said Börje, 'so stay up there. Do you hear?'

She went back up without saying anything, thumping her feet on the stairs as she went.

Seved rinsed out the percolator and filled it with water, and because he couldn't find the measure he scooped up the coffee with a tablespoon. He pressed the switch with his thumb. There was some spaghetti left in the yellow plastic strainer standing in the sink on top of a pile of unwashed plates and cups. He had eaten nothing himself all day. The very thought of food made him feel nauseous. The memory of the smell of rotting meat kept threatening to well up inside him, and it made him gag.

The tall, heavy man stood in the door frame with his head bowed, glaring at them from behind his tinted glasses. His snow-white hair was combed in a sweaty side parting. His military-green thermal jacket was unbuttoned and the pocket flaps were creased. His left hand, which was wrapped inside a grubby light-blue sleeping bag case, was pressed to his chest.

Not until Lennart had stepped into the kitchen did Seved realise he had someone with him: a stooped man who hung back in the hallway. The top of his head was completely bald but his brown wavy hair streaked with grey fell down at the sides to join a beard that had turned white at the tip.

Seved recognised him. Lennart had brought him once before, along with the woman in the wheelchair. But he had no idea who he was. Seved could not help staring back because the bastard was wearing Ejvor's jacket.

Lennart pulled out a chair, but before he sat down he thrust his hand into his jacket pocket and groped around for something. When he found what he was looking for he slung them on the table in front of Börje's plate. Two dead mice.

'How many did you get?' the big man said, sitting down.

Börje put his fork on the plate and then pushed it to one side, away from the mice. He rested his elbows on the table.

'Eight, I think.'

'Eight? I said fifteen. At least fifteen is what I said.'

'They couldn't collect any more. Didn't have the time, they said.'

Seved studied the shapeshifted animals. There was a wood mouse with close-set eyes like peppercorns, and a shrew that looked as if it was squeezing its eyes shut in despair.

'I never thought they'd kill them,' he said.

Lennart looked at the mice for a while before answering.

'They haven't,' he said, laying his covered hand over the wood mouse. Using the fingers of his right hand he pinched the tiny head and bent it back. The white fur at the throat parted to reveal a shiny, fleshy slit.

'You see? They're killing each other. And I imagine these two poor little buggers are not the only ones. It's like a battlefield in there.'

The coarse fingers kept hold of the mouse, stroking its shiny coat, gently prodding the eyes. The thumb made its way into its mouth and felt the teeth.

'You weren't very old.'

His voice was tender, gentle.

'Ejvor,' Seved said softly. 'Have you brought her out?'

'No,' grunted Lennart in his normal gravelly voice. 'And unless you want to join her I advise you to leave her where she is. You don't set foot in Hybblet, understand? Someone has tidied up in there – was it her?'

Seved nodded.

'Well, you can damn well forget about that,' said Lennart. 'Stay indoors as much as possible and under no circumstances go out at night. Keep all the lights on in here. Start up the car from time to time, even if you're not going anywhere. Keep everything the same as normal.'

'And if they call out?' said Seved.

'Let them! Turn up the television or use earplugs or do what the hell you want. They won't be coming in here.'

Börje had been sitting silently, his thoughts elsewhere. But now he said:

'And how long can you guarantee that?'

There was a pause before Lennart answered.

'It will take a while', he said eventually, 'before they go that far.'

Seved pressed his thumbs against the rim of the coffee cup. He was aware it was getting close now. That they were getting close to explaining why Ejvor died. He would find out now.

'So she has to stay inside there?' asked Börje.

'For the time being!' The man with the long beard had shouted from the hall. But he stayed out there. He did not even look inside the kitchen.

'Until the child comes,' he added, in a singsong voice.

Seved felt a stab. So that was why. Then it was his fault. But did they mean she would have to sit in there *until then*? Even if he slept with Signe it could take months before she conceived, and then another nine months on top of that. How would they be able to put food in the kitchen? She had probably started to smell already. Börje couldn't agree to this, surely?

Oddly enough, Börje said nothing. He just looked down at his hands, at the bracelet with its button of reindeer antler. He was worn out. It looked as if he was struggling to keep his eyes open.

Lennart got to his feet. Slowly he dropped first one mouse and then the other into his jacket pocket.

'Tomorrow I'm driving up to Torsten and his aunt's,' he said, pinching his nostrils together. 'We'll see what we can come up with. But if you move her, then you've only got yourselves to blame. Just so you know.'

The water that flowed through the heating system in Susso's flat kept it at a constant if only mildly warm temperature, although the radiator in the bathroom was usually freezing cold, and that was yet another reason why she put off having a shower. With a pair of thick socks on her feet she went into the kitchen and put on the coffee machine. When the coffee was ready she sat down in front of the computer and wondered how to formulate her words.

It was not exactly straightforward.

It would be best to wait until she saw the photographs from the wildlife camera. At least then she could account for the measures she had taken, if nothing else, and compare the results with what Edit had told her. That would have to be enough.

She had poured too much milk into her coffee, so she returned to the kitchen and put the cup in the microwave, which was a robust appliance, almost as old as she was. It resembled an old-fashioned television.

She took out her cup, sat down again at the computer, opened a new file and wrote:

> Edit Mickelsson, living in Vaikijaur in the municipality of Jokkmokk, states that on Wednesday 16 November at approximately three in the afternoon she observed an unknown and abnormally short male person outside her house . . .

She then erased Edit's name and took a mouthful of coffee, which was now far too hot. She drummed her thumb on the edge of the keyboard and glanced at the clock. It was almost ten forty. She went into the bathroom, brushed her teeth and put in her contact lenses, relieved at not having to write anything.

It had taken Seved just over an hour to drive to Arvidsjaur and now he sat in the car, waiting for two o'clock.

Using his index finger he pushed back the cuff of his jacket to look at the scratched face of his watch. It was now one fifty. There was a car park to the rear of the pizzeria but there was no sign of the motorhome or the Merc. He breathed in deeply and then exhaled white air through his nose. The temperature in the car had dropped fast. The seal on one of the Isuzu's doors had fallen off, so it was always perishing inside. The clothes he had put on were not warm enough and he had not bothered with a hat or gloves.

He climbed out of the car, crossed the street and walked into the restaurant. Furthest in, where the chilled drinks cabinet hummed, an overweight man in a cap and knitted jumper sat staring into his coffee cup, but otherwise the tables were empty.

Seved sat down in a corner close to the exit. Lennart would only have to step through the door to catch sight of him.

There was a reflective sheet of glass over the tablecloth and on it stood salt and pepper mills and a bundle of toothpicks in a glass jar. He took one of the toothpicks to give his fingers something to do. When he had broken it into small pieces he took another and immediately began shredding it in the same way.

He didn't know what Lennart wanted to talk to him about but

he had his suspicions. He was going to get a bollocking. A proper bollocking. Because if anyone was responsible for Ejvor's death it was him, and now he was going to get it.

And what did he have to say in his defence?

That he couldn't? That in his eyes Signe was a child? A sister?

Two years had passed since Signe had first been given her instructions, as Ejvor had put it. In a low voice and sort of in passing she had told him about it. Confused and embarrassed, he had quickly walked away.

What did *that* have to do with him?

The information had actually disgusted him.

Then he had understood.

Small hints. You and Signe. When we're away and you and Signe . . .

They wanted them to have a child together. It had not been hard for him to work out that it was for the sake of the old-timers – he could remember how they had forced him to play in Hybblet when he was a little boy. But he had always thought that it was just for their amusement, so he had not attached much importance to Ejvor's instructions, and you could hardly say she or Börje had nagged him about it.

How could he have known it was so important?

That things would turn dangerous if there was no child for them to look at?

If anyone was to blame, then it was Ejvor and Börje, because they must have always known what could happen. This is all our fault, Börje had said. But perhaps he was referring only to himself and Ejvor, and not Seved and Signe?

He had just started breaking a third toothpick into pieces when he caught sight of Lennart outside the window. Stooping and with his arms hanging heavily at his sides he came puffing through the door. He took a look around the restaurant and then turned his dark glasses in Seved's direction. His lips were parted, revealing yellow teeth crowded together in his protruding lower jaw. He asked Seved if he was hungry.

Despite the fact that Seved had not eaten all day he shook his head – he didn't know why, it was a reflex action and he regretted it immediately.

Lennart shuffled over to the till and ordered some food. Seved heard him clear his throat and speak in a low voice. When he returned to the table he had two bottles of lager with him. A bottle opener rattled against the table. Seved picked it up and opened both bottles.

He had never before reflected on why Lennart was unable to do certain things. Simple things. Ejvor had said that the skin on his left hand had rotted away with some rare and incurable skin disease. The sores wept continuously and without explanation. He wore the bag so his hand would not make a mess or become infected. And to stop people staring, presumably.

He sat himself down, resting his trapper hat on the table. He had a rugged, deeply lined face with drooping cheeks. His hair shone white and looked soft. He downed a mouthful of beer and looked out through the window. Two marker poles were sticking out of the ploughed-up ridge of snow on the opposite side of the street. One of them was leaning contemplatively. It was like a barrier that was in the process of being lowered. Someone had probably driven into it. Why had no one put it upright?

'Börje said it was calm last night.'

'Yes. Well, at least they didn't come out.'

Lennart was silent for a moment before he said:

'It's going to get worse and worse.'

'But why? What's the reason?'

'I'm sure you know.'

The gaze that could just about be made out behind the tinted glasses did not shift from his face.

'Yes. I think it's a child they're after.'

A whiff of sweat hit him as Lennart shifted slightly in his seat.

'Ten, twenty years can pass – you never really know. Up in Årrenjarka there's no danger yet, even though Torsten's kids are pretty big by now. But where you live, well, it's already gone too far.'

'I don't know. Me and Signe . . .'

'There's no time left now for that kind of thing.'

That came as a relief. He even nodded. In that case he was prepared to do anything to put things right.

'There's only one thing we can do,' Lennart said.

What did he mean? Seved looked up but couldn't raise his eyes higher than the front pockets on Lennart's shirt, with their small white plastic buttons.

The waiter arrived with two steaming pizzas that he set down on the table. They had been cut into sharp triangles containing pieces of pork, banana slices, peanuts and pools of buttery-yellow Béarnaise sauce. Pearls of fat bubbled up through the red-flecked mass of cheese. Had Lennart known he had been lying about not being hungry, or was he going to shovel down two pizzas all on his own?

'Eat up,' said the large man.

Seved grabbed hold of his knife and fork, bent over his pizza and cut off a piece, which he ate with his mouth open. It burned him but he didn't care.

Lennart was in no hurry. He picked up a strip of pizza, which he folded in half, and when it had stopped dripping he crammed it into his gaping mouth.

'We've got to take a child,' he said as he chewed.

Seved nodded, even though he did not understand.

'And we want you to do it.'

By now Seved's expression was completely blank, and Lennart watched him for a moment before leaning forwards and explaining in a low voice:

'It's nothing special. A kind of transplanting, that's all. Children of that age forget so quickly. Just look at Signe. She's doing okay.'

'But we can't just take a child . . .'

Lennart leaned back in his chair, wiping the corners of his mouth.

'I'm sure there's a way.'

'But the police. They'll come looking.'

'Yes, we'll have to be prepared for that.'

'It's kidnapping,' said Seved quietly. 'I . . . I could end up in prison.'

That's when the bag struck. It slammed down on Seved's half-clenched hands with such force that it made the cutlery on the plates rattle. One hand escaped but the other was caught beneath the light-blue lump, which slowly and relentlessly pressed downwards and was so close to Seved's bowed, contorted face that he could see clearly the weave of the stained nylon fabric.

It felt as if his fingers were being crushed like twigs. Lennart waited, and when he was certain there was no feeling left in Seved's trapped hand he said:

'And what do you think will happen if we don't find a kid soon? Have you thought of that? Perhaps you'd like to ask Ejvor about it? I'm sure she's got an idea.'

Seved panted. He'll let go soon, he thought. He has to let go soon.

'But I might as well tell you what will happen,' Lennart continued, staring directly into Seved's face. 'One fine day they'll come and visit you. And then you'll wish you were in prison, believe me. They'll open up your stomach and pull out your intestines, metre by metre. To see how long they are.'

'It hurts.'

'Yes, it'll hurt a lot.'

'My hand. Please . . .'

'Do you want to know how long they are?'

Seved's neck was so tense and his jaw muscles so tightly clenched that small vibrations were running through his head.

'Let go,' he said. 'You've got to let go.'

'Answer my question.'

'Which question?'

'Do you want to know how long your intestines are?'

Seved shook his head.

'No,' he said. 'No, I don't.'

Then finally Lennart released his grip. At least, he allowed Seved to pull his hand back slightly. But the weight did not disappear, or the pain.

'You'll be paid, of course,' Lennart grunted, immediately bringing out his wallet and opening it. He grabbed a bundle of unfolded thousand-kronor notes, which he slapped onto the table beside the plate.

'Here's fifty thousand,' he said. 'You'll get a hundred more if all goes to plan.'

Seved stared at the money. There was something unreal about it and he felt a resistance building in the pit of his stomach, but it didn't get any further. It sat like a stopper in his chest.

He had never had any money of his own and naturally Lennart knew that, so that is where he could apply the pressure. And he did, cunningly. Slowly he pulled the money away, emphasising how hard it was to snatch a child. That there was an art to doing it properly. The old-timers were not interested in crying children. Crying children made them sad, and that could actually make things worse.

'Children's tears are corrosive,' said Lennart.

'Right,' said Seved with a mouth that had turned dry. 'Okay.'

'Taking a child with violence is no problem. An animal can do that. But to take a child so it doesn't realise – that's a completely different thing. You've got to be fast and wary, but not too fast and not too wary. It's a bit like plucking squirrels from a tree. Do you know how to do that?'

Seved shook his head.

'The squirrel has to be sitting on a suitable branch,' said Lennart. 'The branch must be thin enough for you to shake. A small tree is fine. When you shake the branch the squirrel clings on tight. That's how it protects itself when the wind blows. An innate defence, so it can't stop itself. And while you're shaking – not too hard or the squirrel will lose its grip, and not too gently or it will run away – you reach out and pluck it like a pine cone.'

The comparison left Seved none the wiser, and Lennart saw that.

'You attract the kid to you with a shapeshifter,' he said. 'Children that age can't resist them. Make sure it's wearing clothes, that's a good trick, and that it hasn't shifted into an animal. A little hat is enough. The child will never have seen anything like it before, at least not in real life. They become hypnotised, and then all you have to do is open the car door. Sooner or later the child will want to go home. That's unavoidable. And that's when you have to shake the branch, so to speak. It's best to get the shifter to do something amusing. But you know what they're like. They can never be trusted, so you have to be imaginative. Entertain the child constantly. Tell them something interesting. Sing, maybe. Persuade them with a present.'

Seved nodded.

'Okay,' he said.

Lennart picked up his tin of snus and flipped open the lid.

'Immediately north of Jokkmokk,' he said, inserting a crumpled cushion of snus under his lip, 'there's a village called Vaikijaur . . . are you listening?'

Seved nodded obediently, but in actual fact he could hardly think of anything apart from the pain in his hand.

'Vaikijaur,' he repeated.

'Right,' Lennart said, snapping the lid shut and rubbing his fingertips together, making crumbs of tobacco rain down. 'There's a young lad living there, three or four years old. Exactly the right age. According to Torsten he's often out playing on his own. They've been keeping an eye on him for a long time. But I've advised them against it because it's risky snatching a child who lives so close. That's why it's better if he can come to your place.'

'When?' said Seved. 'When does it have to happen?'

'As soon as possible. I don't know exactly where he lives, so you'll have to travel up to Torsten and talk to him.'

They left the restaurant and walked round the back because Lennart had something for Seved to take with him. By this time it was dark. He walked behind the stocky man, staring at his back.

After Lennart had opened the car door he bent over the back seat and lifted out a grey bundle. It was something wrapped in a woollen blanket. Seved took hold of it and heard a creaking metallic sound. He realised it was a cage.

'There are three of them,' Lennart said. Crooking his finger he fished out the pad of snus from his mouth. After spitting he said:

'Shapeshifters. That turn into lemmings. Make damn sure you take good care of them. The one with the white mark above its eye is very old and Elna says it can talk.'

'Talk?'

Lennart shrugged his shoulders and spat again.

'Let them out in Hybblet straight away and make sure the door to the hide is open so they can get down there. They always do some good.'

He walked round and opened the door on the driver's side. Then he ran his eyes over the car roof, which was covered in a layer of uneven glittery ice.

'If they get to you on the way home, just put the radio on,' he said. 'They hate music. And watch out they don't change back to lemmings again. We haven't got time for that.'

'But these little things usually run back after a few hours.'

'Not necessarily, especially if they find themselves in an unfamiliar place. And it always takes time, whatever the circumstances. The old one can easily take a couple of days to get back home. And we're short of time.'

After saying this he sank down behind the wheel, but it took a few moments until he shifted position and reached out for the door handle with his right hand and slammed the door shut.

Seved placed the cage on the passenger seat. Through a gap in the blanket he could see the bars arching over a plastic tray and straw sticking out. No sound was coming from the cage. Presumably the shapeshifters were curled up asleep, hopefully sleeping deeply enough not to wake up during the journey home. Having shapeshifters in the car was risky, most of all the ones who were not familiar with him.

To get the car key out of his trouser pocket he had to lift up his backside, and when he thrust his hand into his pocket it hurt like hell. He gripped his hand and rubbed the palm with his thumb, forming a fist and waggling his fingers. Was something broken?

He had known Lennart was strong, you could tell that a mile off. But not that he was *so* incredibly strong. He hadn't even squeezed his fingers, only held them down. And with his left hand too, which you would assume was weaker than his right.

Snatch a child.

Seved knew very well he could never snatch a child. But then he felt the weight of the bag-covered hand on top of his and he was no longer quite so sure.

There is only one thing we can do.

They were words Seved had to bear alone.

If he had understood how important it was . . .

He started the engine, threw a glance over his shoulder, backed up and drove out onto Storgatan. He followed it until he reached the roundabout that connected to route 45.

An articulated truck with a bar of blinding headlights rumbled past, and to avoid the cloud of snow from its wheels Seved waited until he could no longer make out the truck's rear lights before pulling out. He grabbed the top of the long gear lever and put it into second, accelerating to change straight up to fourth, but before he did so he leaned over the cage and fastened the seat belt around it.

In the evening Susso and Gudrun drove to the supermarket, a steel hangar surrounded by mountain ranges of ploughed snow in a deserted car park. They usually did their shopping either very early or very late; the store wasn't as crowded then. Rather empty shelves than packed with people, Gudrun used to say.

Afterwards Gudrun gave Susso a lift to her job at the care home on Thulegatan, next to the hospital. Nothing much was expected of her at Thulegatan, nor was she paid to do more. After emptying the dishwasher, she boiled water for tea. She stood looking blankly at the saucepan and the steam that floated ghost-like on the surface of the water. Small bubbles rose up from the bottom, rushing after each other in long strings. The packets of tea were kept in the cupboard above the cooker hood, so she stood on tiptoe, reached in and grabbed hold of a green box. Herb Harmony, it read. That sounded pleasant. Soft and mild.

'*Pehmeä ja mieto*,' she said, pulling away the little square of paper attached to the bag. With a spoon she pressed the bag into the steaming water and said: '*Mieto, mieto*.'

Talking to yourself at night, that was all part of it. It made it easier. The silence pressed against her eardrums, but there was no point in switching on the radio, for example. You had to talk, to say something. Anything at all. Hear your own voice echo inside your head. It was not madness but a way to banish the madness.

As usual she found herself sitting in front of the computer, because there was not much else to do after the scheduled duties had been attended to. She slouched on the wheeled office chair, the sleeves of her roomy fleece jacket rolled up. Her hair was tied back in two small pigtails sticking out from a crooked parting at the nape of her neck.

There were several cryptozoological sites she regularly visited. The best was Still on the Track, run by a man named Jonathan Downes. Downes's newsletter had links to CFZ, the Centre for Fortean Zoology. It was about as close to an official cryptozoological forum as you could get. Its mission was spelled out on the home page: 'At the beginning of the 21st century monsters still roam the remote, and sometimes not so remote, corners of our planet. It is our job to search for them.'

Monsters. How could she possibly read that word without sneering? What she was looking for were hardly monsters, but still it was here among the monster researchers that she found her sympathisers. Among the wackos! They spent considerable amounts of money on expeditions searching for ethnoknown cryptids – animals spotted by local people that somehow never revealed themselves to scientists for documentation.

But at the end of the day it was just a matter of semantics.

'Monster' did not mean 'beast', it meant 'warning', from the Latin root '*monere*'. It could also be interpreted as 'reminder'. The word 'monument' had the same origins.

But what was it a reminder of?

That everyone could be a monster?

The chair creaked as Susso leaned back in her seat. There was nothing new. The monitor showed an amarok: a wolf- or bear-like monster in Greenland that liked to eat the Inuit's children but could never catch them. Pretty much the same as the stallo.

In Sami folklore the stallo were a kind of troll. They were huge, terrible creatures depicted by the *nåjden,* or shaman, on his drum. Troublesome and stupid. Fond of human flesh.

She had written about them on her website, mainly because these creatures oscillated between myth and scientific knowledge in a way that interested her. In fact, many archaeologists were convinced there was some kind of underlying truth to the myths of the stallo. Ancient settlements and trapping pits that could not be linked to the nomadic Sami culture had been excavated in various places in northern Scandinavia.

The question was: what had happened to these mysterious creatures?

The road to Ammarnäs was unlit. There was only the glimmer of light from an occasional house, lamps deeply embedded in the darkness. But the curves of the road were imprinted in Seved's brain and he knew the places where snowdrifts could block the way.

During his school years the road had left its mark on him. The days began and ended with the road then, days when he set off in darkness and returned home in darkness. There had been daylight as well, but when he thought of that time it was only the molten, insatiable darkness he remembered. The night outside the windowpanes, the rough upholstery of the seats illuminated by the lights in the ceiling of the bus, the handrails reflected in the vibrating glass. His own taciturn face and growing hunger. He and the driver, alone, kilometre after kilometre. The long walk from the main road towards the glow of the lights on the veranda that seemed to be moving ever further away. And then his greed at the kitchen table, his only comfort.

The lemmingshifters had not made a sound and he had almost forgotten about them. He had been thinking of the money in his jacket pocket since he left Arvidsjaur. Fifty thousand would not go far. Not even a hundred and fifty went far.

But still. To have money that was all his own.

He knew Lennart was wealthy. He had seen the fat, untidy

wads of notes that Börje and Ejvor accepted from him, and once when he had been shopping at the Co-op he had asked the girl at the till how much was left on the pre-loaded card. There was over a hundred thousand, and he could see from the girl's face that it was a lot, that people did not normally have sums of that size on their cards.

He pressed his hand to his jacket and felt the notes. They were there, like a compact slab against his chest. He had still not decided whether to tell Börje he had been given the money.

Did Börje know what Lennart had wanted to talk to him about?

In all probability, he did. But did he care? At the moment he didn't seem to care about anything. That was not so strange. Letting Ejvor remain where she was must have been unbearable for him. Not being able to do anything except wait.

Signe had said that Börje had peered through the window several times, standing there with his hands on the windowsill. It was understandable that he wanted to see her, and perhaps even necessary, but why put yourself through it over and over again? Why torture yourself?

Seved could not understand why they had gone for Ejvor in particular. At first he thought it must have happened by mistake, that they just hadn't realised how strong they were. He had experienced that for himself once when he had been inside Hybblet, cleaning up. They had come upstairs, which wasn't something they normally did. Usually they would just shuffle about, sometimes barging into him, but on this occasion they decided they wanted to hug him. Seved had probably tensed his muscles too much because suddenly it turned into a battle of strength. He had passed out. First there was an explosion like fireworks going off, and then everything had gone black. When he came round they were running up and down the staircase, making it creak and groan, and Ejvor had said that was probably an expression of their remorse, to the extent they had those sorts of feelings. Seved was left with purple streaks across his chest, and Börje said he had probably cracked a couple of ribs but not to worry, they would heal on their own, and they did.

Don't fret, Ejvor had said, they wouldn't harm a hair on your head.

Soon he reached the curve where it had happened. It was many years ago now and he had been in the eighth or ninth grade. One Saturday he had gone to a party in a large house in Sorsele. It stood on the edge of the lake and was brightly lit up in the night. Doors and windows were open. There was shouting, a racket, and no parents to put a stop to it. The girl had just moved to the area. It was September and the school term had not long started.

He drove there on his moped. One lad from his class had brought a plastic bottle containing something cloudy. A witch's brew. It tasted revolting but it did the trick. He wanted more. He had searched the bathroom and found a bottle of perfume, and in front of a small audience, watching him with eyes blurry from alcohol, he downed the lot. They thought he was insane, but in a cool way.

Later he got his hands on a girl he did not know. She had a Norwegian name and he could not for the life of him remember it afterwards. She was the one who had hit on him. All he had to do was turn his cap round and take what was offered. They snogged on a sofa. He probed hard with his fingers but didn't get anywhere, although he had been close. He slipped out his dick and wanted her to hold it, but she pulled her hand away rapidly, as if she had touched a snake.

Someone had seen it and they did not like what they saw. Either that or they did not like him. As he was driving home afterwards in the grey dawn light, a car swung in front of him, its wheels screeching. A Volvo 740 with alloy wheels and music thumping from its loudspeakers. He had no time to stop his moped, so he ran into the car. That in itself was a good enough reason for a beating.

Two of them climbed out. Red cheeks, loud voices, caps. Thick neck chains outside their jumpers. They shoved his shoulders, but he was too drunk to fend them off. All he could do was try to avoid them. Get away. Home was not far away, only a few kilometres. And he remembered saying that. 'I'm almost home,' he had said, grabbing the handlebars, trying to roll the moped out of the way.

As if being close to home had anything to do with it.

As if that would make them leave him alone.

But in a way it did.

The next day, the newspaper said they had flipped the car over, made it do somersaults.

Three teenage boys killed on the 363.

The school had held a minute's silence. Seved did not attend because he got the idea someone had seen what had actually happened, that there were *witnesses,* and so he had phoned in sick. But he heard about it later. How the principal had spoken solemnly to the assembled students about the dangers of driving while drunk.

'Now you see how wrong things can go,' he had said.

Oh yes, he had seen all right. He had kneeled at the roadside and seen it all: the lads who had got out of the car to attack him had all of a sudden been grabbed, turned upside down and had their heads slammed bloodily against the surface of the road. Their bodies had flown in deep among the fir trees, to be met by snapping branches.

The car had been lifted up and dangled in the air. He saw the amusement of the old-timers as the car spun like a tombola drum between them. The piercing cries and shouts for help from inside the car seemed to fire them up, fill them with a crazy energy and make the car revolve faster and faster. The pumping music was distorted as the car turned and it did not fall silent until the vehicle lay crushed on its roof five metres into the forest.

Afterwards they had wanted to carry him home, and he did not dare refuse. They wanted to take turns carrying him too. One held him and one held the moped. Then they swapped. And swapped again.

He had never said a word to anyone about what happened that night. But he thought Börje knew because the following morning he had stared at Seved and said something about him being lucky. Lucky he was not the one who had killed himself driving.

The road up to the house ran behind a mountain. Unless you knew the drive was there it was almost impossible to see. Several times he had driven past it himself and had to turn back. The mountain was asymmetrical: the southern slope that faced the river had slipped. The precipice that remained was a hanging rock face, and when the meltwater froze, long yellow icicles formed up there in its jaws. From the road below they looked like fangs. When Seved was young and looked up at the mountain he always thought of it as a gaping mouth that could bite.

He stopped at the barrier and hurried out to open it. He

grabbed hold of the padlock with most of his hand tucked inside his jacket sleeve and inserted the little key. It trembled between his fingers, which were red in the light from the Isuzu's headlamps. When he got back in the car again he blew on his hands. They were stinging.

'Nearly there,' he said, and it wasn't until he heard the reassuring tone of his voice that he realised the shifters had got to him. They had gone inside his head to tell him they were cold.

With her hat pulled down over her forehead, Susso walked home through the darkness. The temperature had dropped even lower overnight: ice blocked her nostrils as she cut across Kyrkparken.

Curiously, she felt a muffled buzzing in her jacket pocket. Who could be phoning this early in the day? She pulled off one mitten and it took a while before she was able to get her mobile out. 0971 shone from the display. Jokkmokk, she registered, before realising it could be none other than Edit Mickelsson who was ringing.

'Sorry,' she said. 'I've woken you up, haven't I?'

'No, you haven't,' Susso said. 'I've been working a night shift.'

The cold was pinching her fingers. She cradled the phone against her cheek, keeping it there as she put her mitten back on.

'He . . . he's been here again. The man I saw.'

Susso came to a halt and caught her breath.

'You've *seen* him?'

'I woke up,' she said, and then her voice disappeared for a second or two before she cleared her throat and continued: 'I was woken by a knocking on the window, the kitchen window. And when I got up to see what was going on, there he was, outside. He was standing there, looking in. Just like last time. Except this time it was dark. I could hardly see him at first.'

'The camera,' said Susso, starting to walk quickly. 'Have you checked it?'

'No,' answered Edit. 'I don't really know how to. And I'm a bit scared to go outside, to tell you the truth.'

'But you're absolutely sure?'

'As sure as I can be.'

'Where did he go?'

'I went and got Edvin's rifle. And when he saw it, he dropped down. Perhaps that was a stupid thing to do. Because I'd really like to know what he wants.'

'Yes. Me too.'

Susso knew it would be nothing short of suicidal to drive as far as Jokkmokk after working a night shift, but she convinced herself she had no choice. With any luck they had captured the person on camera.

She could not gather her thoughts, she was far too tired for that. All she could do was walk as fast as possible. She let herself quietly into Gudrun's hall and snatched the car keys. Then she went down to her own flat to get ready. In the bathroom she let out a yell and, in a desperate attempt to relieve the pain, smacked the palm of her hand hard against the tiles, obscenities pouring from her mouth: she had put in a contact lens using fingers that had been in contact with the powdered tobacco in her snus tin. The stinging in her eye and the fury at bringing it on herself in such an idiotic way – she didn't know which came first – had the effect of waking her up. Her cheeks grew hot. She extracted the lens, crumpled it up and washed out her eye, groaning into the handbasin. Then she raked about in the cabinet until she found her glasses.

From her wardrobe she pulled out the military-green backpack that she had borrowed from Torbjörn. After putting on her boots and jacket she thundered down the stairs to the dark, cold garage where the car was standing, a grey Passat. She threw the backpack onto the rear seat of her mother's car, moved the driver's seat forwards and reversed out. A couple of times in the past she had scraped the left wing mirror on a concrete post, so she drove especially slowly up and out through the garage exit.

There was another car parked outside Edit Mickelsson's house when Susso pulled up and a wave of reluctance washed through Susso's stomach when she saw it. Her first instinct was to do a U-turn. Make a curved track in the snow and drive home again. But she knew that she could never do that, so instead she pushed the snus pouch as far up inside her mouth as she could with the tip of her tongue and parked at an angle behind Edit's car.

Behind the cafe-style curtains she glimpsed a sudden movement. There was a ringing in her head, but now she had woken up, found her second wind. She decided to leave the backpack where it was on the back seat. Why she had brought it with her she had no idea. If Edit was not alone in there, it was probably advisable to go in empty-handed and a little bewildered.

They were sitting at the kitchen table, Edit and a thin man in a padded vest and cap. The peak hid his face; only his chin and pinched mouth were visible. In the indentation below his lower lip he had a little goatee tuft sprinkled with grey. The man could be none other than Edit's son, Per-Erik.

Edit looked over her shoulder and her lips formed a swift smile. Was she looking rather ashamed? Susso had not said she was coming, not definitely. She realised that now. She had said she might come, and now suddenly it seemed as if she was intruding.

She wondered what to say, but the situation resolved itself when she caught sight of the wildlife camera on the worktop. There was no mistaking the fact that it was broken: only shards of the diodes remained. The plastic cover had been cracked open and the electronics were visible through the gap.

'What's happened here?' she said, walking over to the worktop.

Both Edit and her son watched her. The man had laid one hand over the other and was stroking his chapped knuckles. It looked as if he was contemplating something. Just as Susso thought he was going to open his mouth he turned away and peered out through the window instead, but there was nothing to see there.

The camera could never be repaired. It was not only broken – someone had *destroyed* it. Susso levered the plastic halves open as far as they would go, unwilling but curious to know what the contents looked like.

'It broke,' he said finally. 'When I got it down.'

There was a momentary delay before the fury rose up inside Susso, but she controlled herself. She poked her index finger into her mouth and hooked out the snus pouch, which she threw away in the rubbish bin under the sink. After she had slammed the cupboard door shut she folded her arms and studied Per-Erik's face in profile. She had detected a small grin, but he was now concealing it under a false expression of innocence.

'Typical,' she said.

'Anyway, you have to have permission,' he added.

Susso shook her head. All she could do was smile.

'There are laws,' he said, gripping the peak of his cap and nodding in his mother's direction. As he righted his cap the dark wisps of hair at his temples shifted.

'We'll pay you for the camera, of course,' said Edit.

'Like hell we will!'

Per-Erik leaned across the table and stared into his mother's eyes.

'Anyone putting up a camera does so at their own risk. That's what the law says.'

As he said 'the law' he tapped his snus tin on the tabletop.

'Is that what the law says?' Susso asked. She grinned at him. Was he being serious?

Per-Erik shrugged, clicked open the tin and probed with his fingers.

'Well, that's just the way it is,' he said.

Susso bowed her head, examining the rug on the floor. He was goading her. Not without success, she was forced to admit. But she kept quiet because it was risky to continue.

There was no more to say. They had reached deadlock, and for a long time it was silent in the kitchen. Per-Erik had opened the snus tin and taken out a pouch without taking his eyes off his mother, who was looking down at the tablecloth. He pressed the snus into his mouth, rubbed his large, rough hands together and shifted his heavy boots underneath the table. Then he stood up and muttered something Susso could not hear. He thrust out his head and stomped to the door. A small reindeer-horn knife dangled from his belt.

Then there was rumbling outside the house. Per-Erik's engine increased to a roar before he backed the car out of the driveway, causing snow to fly up from the tyres.

Susso sank down on one of the kitchen chairs. She pushed a finger under one lens of her glasses and rubbed her eyelid, releasing a long sigh. The memory card looked a bit bent, and that looked ominous, but probably the worst thing was that the camera had been trampled in the snow. She had no idea how sensitive the circuit boards were to damp.

Edit stood by the coffee machine holding an unbleached coffee filter. She had folded it and was busy pinching the fold as she watched Susso. The old woman looked genuinely sorry.

'Have you got a camera that can read this?' asked Susso, lifting up the tiny plastic card.

'Camera? No, not one like that. Not a digital one.'

'And you haven't got a reader, for your computer?'

Edit looked around, trying to remember where the computer could be.

'You've got to have a special memory card reader,' Susso said. 'You know, one of those little external gadgets.'

Using her fingertips she indicated the size of a matchbox on the tabletop.

'Have you?' said Edit. 'No, I haven't got one of those. Sorry.'

She scooped coffee out of a metal tin.

'So the pictures can be there even though the camera's ruined?' she asked.

'You never know.'

Edit shook her head.

'He went mad when I told him about the camera.'

'What did he say about what you saw?'

'That I had imagined it, of course.' Edit gestured towards the window. 'That I had seen myself in the window, my own reflection. But why don't you see for yourself? His tracks are out there.'

Tracks.

Susso leaned over the handrail and saw tracks. They were unmistakable.

Someone had stepped off the cleared path and taken a few steps in the snow up to the kitchen window, and even placed their hands on the windowsill, for there were indentations in the snow there.

Nothing much could be learned from the shape of the hand-prints because the snow was deep and loose and had slipped into the holes, but there was no doubt that whoever had made them had been there recently and was a relatively small person.

A child, Susso thought. Could a child have been here, in the middle of the night? But why? She got out her mobile and took some pictures, with and without the flash. They showed more or less nothing apart from shadowy impressions in the whiteness, but despite that she had to document the tracks in some way.

She had seen tracks before, of course, at least on photographs. Imprints made by peculiarly shaped paws. Naked feet with exceptionally long crooked toes. Funny little reindeer-hide shoes. But footprints were an elusive communication and to her they were of little or no value as proof. People through the ages had faked them to frighten or just confuse those around them. The Abominable Snowman in the Himalayas might not have materialised but it had been recreated time and again by a large footprint made in the snow, and it was obvious why Big Foot in the States had been given that name.

She walked down the steps and over to the corner of the house where the camera had been. The snow was trampled and the prints she and Edit had left were still there. They led straight towards the edge of the forest. She bent forwards to get a closer look. It had not snowed much since and it was hard to tell whether they had been made recently. The footsteps left by the mysterious visitor continued in among the trees, and she followed them all the way to the neighbouring plot of land. There they veered off and disappeared up towards the road, exactly as she had expected.

'Did you show him that?' asked Susso, as she walked in through the door, stamping the snow from her boots.

Edit nodded.

'And what did he say?'

'That Matti had made them.'

'And you're sure about it?'

'What?'

'That it wasn't Mattias who had left the tracks when he was last here.'

Edit folded her arms and leaned against the worktop.

'Well, of course I am,' she said. 'You were here yourself last Sunday. There were no tracks outside the house then, were there?'

'I never thought of that.'

'No, but I did. And there were no tracks. I'm absolutely positive about that.'

She pointed to the window.

'He was standing out there early this morning. Looking at me. It wasn't very nice, I can tell you. To think that he came back and even dared to get closer this time. And he's not as shy as he was. He'll be ringing the doorbell next. I don't know what I'll do then.'

There was a naked honesty in Edit's harassed voice, and Susso couldn't alleviate it with her own mumbling doubt. She wished she were not so tired, that her thoughts were not so muddled.

She picked up the warm cup with both hands and propped her elbows on the table, bent forwards and began slurping her coffee, which was strong and good.

'I am *so* tired,' she said.

'Perhaps you'd like to sleep for a while?'

Susso smiled at the suggestion, the kindly tone.

'No, I've got to get going.'

Edit stretched slightly, as if her neck ached.

'You shouldn't drive when you're so tired.'

'I know, but it's Mum's car and I have more or less stolen it. And I want to get home and look at the photos, to see if there's anything there.'

There was a soft clink as Edit stirred her cup.

'You had a different car when you were here last time,' she said. 'A red one.'

Susso nodded.

'That was my sister's.'

'Haven't you got a car of your own?'

'Yes, but it's not working and I haven't got any winter tyres. It feels like it's not worth repairing. It'll be too expensive, all of it.'

'What make is it?'

'A Volvo.'

'I've got some wheels you can have,' said Edit. 'If they'll fit.'

'Have you?'

'After Edvin passed away I sold the car to some lads, but they were just going to wreck it. It was perfectly obvious what their plans were. It was a shame, I thought, because there wasn't much wrong with it. Even the seat warmers were still working. Anyhow, I kept the studded tyres.'

'How many wheel nuts are there?'

'Four, I think.'

Without discussing it further they went out to the storage shed. Edit had to tug at the door because the snow was piled against it, and it flew open with a bang. The wheels were piled one on top of the other beside a workbench. A blurry pattern of rust had spread over the metal wheel hubs and small glistening stones were wedged in the tyre treads.

Susso examined the tyres.

There were four wheel nuts. She thought they would probably fit.

'They're not exactly new,' said Edit, standing in the doorway with her hands in her cardigan pockets. 'But I'm sure they'll do for one more winter.'

'One?' answered Susso. 'Two, at least.'

She pressed one of the studs with her thumb. Most of them protruded from the tyres by a couple of millimetres.

'But I can't just take them.'

'Oh, it'll be all right,' Edit said, holding open the shed door. 'I'll tell Per-Erik I gave them to you to compensate for the camera. That'll shut him up.'

Although Edit was short and slight it took her less time to carry the wheels from the shed than it took Susso to wedge them into the baggage compartment of the Passat. The night shift had caught up with her and she stood motionless, staring at the worn exhaust pipe, the number plate bearded with snow, the line of icicles hanging from the front bull bars, and at one of the backpack's grey-green straps poking out from underneath the car door.

Edit lifted in the last tyre herself and slammed the back door shut with such a loud noise that it made Susso lift her head and look around in confusion.

'You are going to get some sleep,' said Edit, nudging her towards the house. Susso tried to protest but gave up.

*

In the room where Edit had led her there was a bureau and beside it a bed with a brown crocheted bedspread. The bed had metal springs which creaked under Susso's weight as she sat down. Worn out, she collapsed onto her side and pulled up her feet.

She lay there, too tired to remove her jacket and hat, or even her boots with the snow-covered soles. There was a small embroidered cushion which she dragged under her cheek, but it knocked her glasses sideways, forcing her to take them off. She held them in her half-open hand because she was too tired to reach out and put them on the bedside table. Her eyelids closed, and the darkness was immediately pierced by a flickering pattern of dots and circles of different sizes. It was as if she was looking directly into the secret inner workings of her brain. She felt the waft of air as Edit dropped a blanket over her.

'Thanks,' she slurred into the hard little cushion, which smelled as if it had been stuffed with dust.

But by that time Edit had already pulled the door shut.

It seemed the lemming shapeshifters had been useful after all. Seved had not heard a sound all night – no banging and not a single shout – and when he went outside in the morning he saw no sign of anyone having been out of doors. It had snowed a little but there were no fresh footprints surrounding Hybblet. There were only his own tracks from the previous evening, when he had placed the cage in the hallway. He had done it swiftly, wary of the smell of the rotting corpse.

It had not struck him then that the Volvo was no longer lying on its roof. Börje must have righted it while he had been in Arvidsjaur. He walked over and looked inside, then opened the door and sat down. After sliding back the seat he knelt on it and started tidying the interior of the car, throwing into the back everything that belonged there. There was so much rubbish he ought to get rid of while he was at it, but he had no sack to put it in and could not be bothered going to get one, so he left it as it was. He picked up coins, a packet of chewing gum, cassette tapes, snus tins, a pen, a phone charger. Much of this had been lying under the seats, hidden and mainly inaccessible. That was perhaps the only advantage of having the car turned upside down.

Börje sat at the kitchen table eating crispbread. He slid a slice out of the packet, squirted a swirl of cod roe spread onto it from the tube and took a bite. Seved told him about the lemmings he had let out in Hybblet and how that might explain the silence during the night, but Börje said it could just as easily be a coincidence.

It would rise up in them and then subside, but it would not go away.

He rested the hand holding the crispbread on the table.

'What else did Lennart say? I can't believe he wanted to meet you just to give you the shifters.'

Seved had expected this question and had already decided how he would answer it.

'He wants me to do it.'

'Do what?'

'You know what I mean.'

Börje sat in silence for a few moments before he said:

'Will you be able to?'

'He gave me money.'

Börje worked another slice out of the packet without taking his eyes off Seved, eyes that narrowed and showed interest.

'How much?'

'Fifty thousand. And I'll get another hundred, he said. If everything goes according to plan.'

'According to plan?'

'Yes, if the child doesn't cry or scream or make a fuss, because that makes them sad and things will get even worse.'

Börje nodded.

'I'm sure that won't be a problem.'

'No?'

'As long as we're kind they keep calm. Children are polite creatures. Their politeness paralyses them.'

Seved was unsure if he should ask because they had never

discussed these things before, but after what had happened it seemed as if a wall between them had come down, and without thinking he blurted out:

'But have you ever done it? Taken a child, I mean?'

Börje said nothing. After putting down the tube, screwing the top back on and licking his thumb he said:

'How do you think she got here?' he said, nodding towards the ceiling. 'Do you think the stork brought her?'

'But isn't she adopted? I mean, really adopted? That's what Ejvor said. That you had adopted her.'

'We did, in a way. But there's no paperwork.'

'So you just took her?'

'I don't want you to say anything to her about this. It's getting close now.'

Seved nodded.

'It was Erasmus who told me to do it,' said Börje. 'Erasmus Partapuoli, that arsehole who was here yesterday. It was a crisis. Just like it is now. Erasmus had snatched a child in Finland, but we needed more. And they had to be girls – well, you know why. And dark-haired, because he'd worked out there was less of an outcry if you took a kid with black hair, and that's true. There's less coverage in the newspapers because it's not nearly as dramatic as when a Swedish kid disappears. People don't identify with it in the same way. They don't care because they don't feel it could have been their child. It's only some immigrant kid. And anyway it's much easier to hide children who aren't Swedish. No one recognises them. They all look alike.

'It was the summer of '97, and I travelled way down south because there weren't that many foreign kids up here, at least not then, and it's always better it happens far away, whatever the circumstances. I was in Småland, and by pure chance I passed a farm where a group of sodding immigrants was standing, gawping at me. They looked pretty strange, I can tell you, out there in the middle of the forest, and as I drove up they got frightened and some of them even ran off to hide, and I wondered what the hell was going on. And they had kids, masses of them, swarming around like chickens. I assumed they were refugees, hiding on this farm, and I thought I'd go back at night because surely they couldn't keep tabs on all those kids. But then as I drove away I caught sight of her. She had taken herself off maybe three hundred metres from the farm, and was playing with something in the grass. I told her that her parents were looking for her. She couldn't speak a word of Swedish, but I indicated she should get in the car. And then I told her I'd drive her back to the farm.'

He sniffed.

'But that didn't happen.'

After a pause he laughed and went on:

'Remember that ferret that was always in here before? Bloody hell, he was a laugh. It's like he had a sense of humour.'

After saying this he sat quietly for a second or two, looking at the table.

'I wonder what happened to it . . .'

'You mean the brown one? With the long mark on its throat?'

Börje nodded.

'I haven't seen it for several years,' said Seved.

'Well, whatever. I had it with me,' said Börje, nodding. 'And she liked it so much, she sat stroking it all the way up here. And everything went so smoothly that I drove back down again. She was mentioned in the papers, but not much, you know. That's the way it is. Most people think it's a family matter, that some relatives have come from their homeland and taken the kid for some unknown reason. So people don't care and neither do the police because there's not much they can do if the kid's been taken out of the country. People looked for her. There were search parties, but after a couple of days they gave up. Well, the papers did, anyway.

'So I drove around down there and came across another girl. She was dragging a black rubbish sack, collecting empty cans, and I thought she was a gypsy with her long black hair. Bloody perfect. So it was the same thing with her. All I had to do was let the ferret run out and get her. It was in Sävsjö, that's what the place was called. I drove with her all the way up to Kattuvuoma. To Erasmus. Skabram was living up there at that time. But he said he didn't want her and suggested I strangle the girl and throw her body somewhere on the roadside. Well, not just strangle her. It had to look as if there was a paedophile on the loose.'

Börje took a huge crunch.

'So I took her with me to Grete, and she's settled down really well there. I bet she's better off there than with her filthy gypsy parents down in Sävsjö.'

He thought for a while before he went on:

'Some people shouldn't have children, Seved. They can't cope. A refugee family with ten kids. I mean, shit, if they have so many kids they can't even look after them, then something's wrong. And the whole pack was allowed to stay, I heard, for humanitarian reasons, after they had lost the girl. So everyone ought to be happy all round.'

He licked a blob of cod roe from his knuckle.

'I did Signe a favour. That's how I see it.'

'Erasmus was wearing Ejvor's jacket.'

'Yes, I noticed that.'

'And is that supposed to be okay?'

Börje shrugged his shoulders.

'It's his jacket, in a way.'

'What do you mean, "his"?'

'It's his money we're living off.'

'But isn't Lennart . . .'

'Most of it comes from Erasmus. And from the Finns. And Grete, of course.'

Börje had stood up. He opened the fridge and put in the tube of spread and the packet of crispbread as well.

'There's nothing wrong with Erasmus, not really,' he said. 'He's a bit of an unsavoury character but he's only doing what's necessary. Just like Lennart. That's all there is to it. Erasmus loves his wolves and he'll do anything for them. Anything. And for us too. You'd better remember that.'

'I think he could have left the jacket alone.'

'Oh, get over it,' Börje said, sitting down. 'It's only a jacket. Tell me what else Lennart said. About that child. Is it a girl?'

'No, a boy. He lives in Vaiki . . . Vaikijaur. It's some village outside Jokkmokk. On the road to Torsten Holmbom. He's the one who told us he was there.'

Börje nodded.

'I know where that is.'

'So I've got to drive there and talk to Torsten.'

'I can come with you, if you like.'

Seved nodded.

'Yes, okay. Seeing as I don't know where it is.'

'That's settled then.'

'But what about Signe? Are we just going to leave her here?'

'I'm sure it'll be all right. As long as she stays indoors there's no danger.'

Susso's sleep was more like a hibernation, with intermittent explosions of insistent and vivid dreams filled with cries and unintelligible words. The room was cold but she was wearing her outdoor clothes, and that was probably what woke her eventually.

Not moving, she lay staring at the thin strip of light under the door, trying to recall where she was. When she moved her sleeve she heard the rasping sound of the jacket's stiff fabric, and then she remembered.

With an effort she sat up in bed and took out her mobile, pressing a key with her head bowed. Her hat was perched on top of her head like a cone. There was a crackle of static electricity as she pulled it off.

It was pitch black outside the window. 16:14, the display said. What time had she fallen asleep? Eleven, maybe twelve. It did not feel as if she had slept deeply, but even so she must have done because when she woke up her glasses were still in her hand. Normally she only slept in that immobilised state when she was drunk.

There had been a slamming of car doors, lowered voices, whispers. A small figure had stood motionless in the doorway, watching her for a long, long time, and afterwards a larger shape had blocked out the light and closed the door. A mobile had rung, an Ericsson. That little six-tone melody, over and over again.

She sat still on the bed for a while, listening, unable to move. From outside nothing could be heard except the rumble of the fridge. It was almost uncomfortably quiet.

After smoothing out the creases in the bedspread and placing the cushion symmetrically on the bed, she walked into the kitchen, where Edit was sitting reading with her head in her hands. She was wearing a bulky yellow knitted cardigan. The squeak of the door made her look up.

'Well, look who's here,' she said.

A long yawn escaped Susso's smiling mouth. She sank down on a chair and looked distractedly at the newspaper, which was spread out across the table.

After a while she wrinkled her brow and said:

'Were there people here?'

Edit looked up at her, surprised, and then lowered her eyes. She licked her thumb, flicked through the paper to the TV listings page and flattened it out with her hand.

'Per-Erik and Mattias looked in.'

Susso nodded, staring at the floor.

'So he's allowed to come and visit again then. Mattias.'

'What?'

'You said he wasn't allowed to come and see you after what happened. But now he can?'

Edit nodded.

Susso scratched her face and realised the cross-stitch on the cushion had left an imprint on her skin. She pointed at the door.

'Was he standing there *looking* at me?'

An embarrassed smile appeared on Edit's lips.

'Yes,' she said. 'He was curious, naturally, when he heard there was a girl asleep in there. In Granddad's old room. Something like that doesn't happen every day, so he immediately wanted to have a look.'

'Just wondering,' Susso said, shaking her head. 'Because I had such weird dreams. You can't sleep properly when you're that tired. It's something different.'

She fidgeted on the chair, thrust her hands between her thighs and yawned widely, exposing her teeth.

'Something not like sleep at all,' she said. 'Now my head feels like it's stuffed with cotton wool.'

After staring at the floor for a moment she said:

'But aren't you happy he can come and visit you again?'

'I suppose so,' Edit replied.

She sighed.

'It's just that I didn't know what to say about what we had seen. He must be wondering too. There's only the two of us involved – and you too, of course,' she added, nodding at Susso.

'Well, how did he seem?'

'He sat here with his glass of juice in front of him and didn't say a word. I asked him what he had been up to lately, and he told me about something he had seen on television. I couldn't say anything because of Per-Erik, so I'll have to wait until next time I see him.'

Edit had placed the camera and the straps in a plastic bag printed with *ICA Rajden,* and she held it out to Susso as they stood on the veranda steps.

The sky had cleared and there were stars. Far away on the other side of the water, along the road leading to Jokkmokk, there was a solitary light. A house. Or a lamp post at a slip road. Occasionally it flashed and then disappeared for a moment: no doubt there were trees in the way, swaying in the wind.

Susso opened the bag and looked inside. She didn't know what to say. They had hardly spoken about Edit's experience.

'I'll be in touch,' Susso said. 'As soon as I've checked the photos.'

Edit nodded.

'And if you see him again, give me a ring.'

There was a news programme on the television. Some social services bosses from a council further south were being chased with a blowtorch, but Seved had no idea why. Something about not doing their job properly. He was slumped in the armchair with his chin on his chest. He was cold but could not be bothered to shuffle over to the sofa and get a blanket. Börje had already gone to bed, and Signe was on the upstairs landing. From time to time she tuned to the same programme he was watching, but most of the time she sat there channel hopping.

That weary look in her eyes – he did not want to see it. That was the reason he thought he would put off going upstairs until she had gone to bed. It had to be soon. Or had she slept during the day? She often did. Then she sat in front of the TV all night, huddled under blankets.

Signe.

He knew that was not her real name, and he thought she knew that too, but they never talked about it. They never talked much about anything. They did not even look at each other in the kitchen, and he thought he hated her.

What was it he felt if not hate?

He had no real reason to hate her, but she made him feel uncomfortable, and perhaps that was enough. To get him through the days.

No one had told him she would be coming or who she was. She had suddenly been sitting there one day at the kitchen table, glaring at him, her black fingernails clasping a sandwich that Ejvor had made for her. A foreigner! He didn't understand a thing and afterwards he had asked Ejvor who she was. She would be living with them for a short time. That was all she said, and he had gathered from her voice that she wanted no more questions.

Unless it was unavoidable, they never even mentioned her name. Has *she* eaten? Is *she* up yet? Has *she* cleaned out Hybblet?

For a while.

That was over six years ago.

But she wasn't a child now.

When Susso entered the kitchen Gudrun was standing with her back to her, slicing a cucumber. She had rolled up the sleeves of her blouse and her bracelet was jangling as she sliced. Small chunky silver charms dangled from it.

'Where's your camera?' Susso asked, putting the plastic bag on the table.

Gudrun pointed with the wet blade of the knife towards the brown-stained cupboard visible through the open bedroom door, and after Susso had gone in she yelled:

'On the top!'

Susso stood on tiptoe and saw the black nylon shoulder strap with its white lettering. Holding the camera with both hands she walked back into the kitchen and dug the memory card out of her pocket. Strands of hair had come loose from her ponytail and were hanging down in two curls. They met at her nose as she bent her head over the camera.

'What have you got there?' asked Gudrun.

She had put down the knife and was taking bites from a slice of cucumber. She was so curious she was almost smiling.

'Wait until you see *this*,' said Susso, pressing the button to illuminate the display. An alert popped up on the screen saying there were no pictures on the memory card.

'Oh shit,' she said, rubbing her face.

She told Gudrun about the tracks outside Edit Mickelsson's window, and what had happened to the wildlife camera when that arse Per-Erik had removed it from the wall of the house. Gudrun did not appear worried about the fact that he had sabotaged it. All her attention was focused on the camera.

'Then we'll have to ask Cecilia. She's clever at this sort of thing.'

Susso and Gudrun sat close together, looking at the screen as Cecilia clicked her way to the folders. The computer took its time. Cecilia said it was lost in thought, and when computers were lost in thought it was time to take them out and shoot them.

'You see,' said Gudrun. 'What did I tell you?'

'It wasn't because the card was damaged that you couldn't see the pictures. It was because you moved the card from one camera to another,' explained Cecilia. 'Cameras don't always talk to each other.'

She double-clicked on one of the files, tapping her index finger impatiently on the mouse as the reader got going. Slender birches in a grey mist appeared.

'It's the warmth,' said Susso. 'As the sun rises. Either that or the branches are blowing in the wind.'

The next photo was practically identical, and the next, and even the one after that. After a while Cecilia grew tired of the birches.

'How many photos are there?' asked Susso.

'Just over a hundred.'

'Go on to the last ones then,' said Susso.

The final photo documented the brutal removal of the camera and was just a blur. They backed up a dozen images and found more birches, pale skeletons standing out against a background black as night.

Then Gudrun jabbed her index finger hard against the screen.

'There!' she said. 'See?'

Deep in the murky shade hung a small but penetrating dot of light. Susso bent forwards to get a better view, while Gudrun wrenched the mouse out of Cecilia's fingers and clicked on the next picture.

Now there were two dots, suspended beside each other in the darkness.

'There's something there,' Susso said.

Gudrun's hand trembled as she moved the arrow to the next file, so Cecilia took over the mouse again. Susso had pulled her sleeves down over her hands and was sitting leaning towards the screen, looking closely.

On the next photo both dots were enclosed in an oval of faint light that could only be a face. No one said a word. They just stared at the screen while Cecilia clicked with the mouse.

'Someone's coming,' said Gudrun, twisting her bracelet round and round her wrist.

Yes, someone was coming. Its eyes were shining white from beneath the hood of its jacket. It was an old man, a very small old man: the snow came up to his chest. His arms were open wide and he was wearing gloves.

The camera had taken a picture every ten seconds and the tiny figure was visible on a total of eleven, if you included the first ones showing only his eyes: seven as he walked towards the camera and two as he walked, or rather ran, off.

He could be seen most clearly in the seventh photograph. He was standing to the side of the shot, and his face glowed white in the cascade of infrared light.

He was not deformed exactly, but he had an unusual appearance, to say the least. His eyes were set far apart and deep in their sockets, and his nose was lumpy and large. Sparse white bristles protruded from his wrinkled cheeks and his chin.

Susso phoned Edit immediately, standing in the kitchen, staring at the laptop. Gudrun and Cecilia could not take their eyes off the screen.

For a long time Edit was silent at the other end of the line. Then she wanted to know what they planned to do next. Susso didn't know how to answer that. She was completely thrown and filled with conflicting emotions. She could barely keep still.

Her mother and her sister were involved in a lively discussion, and because she wanted to have her say she ended the phone call with a promise to ring the next day.

Cecilia agreed that the little man in the photographs looked strange – not even human, in fact – but she refused to believe it could be a troll. Or a gnome, for that matter.

'It could be a kid,' she said. 'Dressed up. Ella and I have been looking at masks online and they're so bloody realistic.'

'A kid?' Susso said, pointing at the screen. 'At nineteen minutes past five in the morning?'

'Well, it's a dwarf then,' said Cecilia, wide-eyed. 'He might actually look like that. It can be hormonal, you know.'

She angled the screen to get a better look at the picture.

'If I looked like that, I would only go out at night as well.'

'If that's the case, then wasn't it a dwarf Granddad saw too?' Susso exclaimed.

Cecilia took a deep breath and rolled her eyes. She took her mobile out of her pocket and looked at it.

'I've got to go home,' she said abruptly.

But Susso had no intention of letting her get away that easily.

'So you don't think it's remarkable that he turns up here, in this very village, just a hundred kilometres or so from the place where Granddad took his photo?'

'I hadn't thought of that,' Gudrun said, in surprise.

Cecilia stared at her phone, shaking her head.

'You are completely bloody unbelievable . . .'

'No, *you're* the one who's unbelievable,' muttered Susso.

Finally Cecilia looked up, her cheeks glowing red as she smiled.

'Susso,' she said, 'what do you want me to do?'

'You could at least be a bit interested.'

'But I'm telling you, I've got to get home to Ella!'

When Susso returned to her own flat upstairs she paced the floor in an attempt to calm herself down. She sent a text to Torbjörn. She didn't want to tell him about the photo over the phone, so they arranged to meet on the Friday at Safari.

That was where they used to go when they were together. It had been their favourite thing to do, sitting upstairs leafing through the papers, drinking coffee and playing games on their mobiles. Then he had moved to Luleå. He had been offered a place on some course at Luleå University of Technology. He had not said a word to her about applying, and she knew he had done it to get away from her and the family trouble at Riksgränsen. When she had confronted him he had asked if she wanted to go with him, but without really meaning it – he hadn't even tried to persuade her. Bloody Torbjörn.

Seved knew he would never be able to snatch a child. It would be easiest if he got Börje to do it for him.

Börje, who had done it before.

Although he had not snatched Seved.

There was a memory, and that was of being picked up, but he had no memory of crying or shouting, and that was strange because it would have been reasonable to expect that. Perhaps it had all been too much for him. He remembered hunger, or perhaps it was nausea. He was carried for an eternity. He vomited and saw his vomit run like porridge down a hairy back, a rough bark of grey skin covered with long hair hanging like tassels.

It was an image that never faded. That could never fade.

A hand, heavy as a log, had held him, and the nails sprouting from the tops of its fingers were claws that occasionally dug about in his mouth, forcing in bilberries and lingonberries, and bitter fungi that he was unable to swallow. It was only in the darkness that he had dared to look at the enormous wrinkled face turned towards him, with its small, single amber eye edged with slime. A fly crawled into the gluey mucus but still the eye did not blink. It was always watching.

He wasn't sure now if that had been Karats or Skabram. It definitely wasn't Luttak because his pelt was almost entirely grey, or so Börje had said, and the one who had carried him was dark.

It could also have been the fourth hairy old-timer.

Urtas.

The one who had disappeared without trace.

Ejvor had told Seved that he had been carried off by mistake and that he had to live with them until they could find his mother. He remembered that so well. She was gentle and friendly as she explained that it was hard to find his mother because no one had contacted the police to say they had lost a boy. And the huge creature had carried him all the way up to Norrland, so he was far away from home.

They would just have to wait.

And he waited.

Then came the moment that was far worse than the moment when the huge creature lifted him up.

Ejvor had been standing with her back to him, doing something at the sink. He had been quite big, seven or eight at least, and he had asked her something about his mother. He could not recall what it was.

She had turned round and looked at him severely, and said that he had to stop going on about a mother because now there was no other mother. She was his mother.

He had always lived with them.

'You've got such a vivid imagination.'

An aroma of coffee and cardamom met Susso as she walked into the cafe, and there was a din coming from the open kitchen door. A huge blackboard hung on the wall. She stood looking at it for a while, counting her money in her head. There was not a lot left in her account. She would prefer not to know how little. She was hungry but would have to settle for a drink. She ordered a Christmas latte. It had the flavour of spicy gingerbread and was laced with mulled wine. Holding it in her hand, she tramped up the old staircase.

He was sprawled on the red velvet sofa, tapping the keys of his mobile. His shiny black curls were sticking out from the edge of his white beanie hat. On the table was a can of Coke and beside it his tin of snus, with two crumpled pouches on the lid. She remained standing with her glass of coffee until he got up and gave her a hug. It was a stiff hug with one arm. A sour smell of snus came from his mouth.

Susso put her glass on the table and undid her jacket.

'Talk about slippery out there,' said Torbjörn, sitting up straight. Typically he had already started grinning at the story he was about to tell.

'I was coming home from work between shifts and it was okay until I got to the Statoil junction. Then I got into this massive great skid. And then that little hill, you know where I mean? I hardly made it up there. Sliding about all over the place. Then I kind of swerved all the way to the hunting school, where I made the final skid, landed on the wrong side of the road and of course there was this car coming and it didn't get out of the way and I couldn't move, so it was a right pile-up. Well, sort of.'

'Sort of?' said Susso, and took a gulp of coffee.

'She got a small dent and my car was totally okay,' he said, with a lopsided grin.

As he tapped out texts on his mobile Torbjörn told Susso a few more stories, but soon he noticed that Susso was hardly listening. He put his phone down on the table and looked at her. He had grey eyes and between his eyebrows was a scar, a small pothole.

'What's the matter?' he asked.

Susso reached out for his snus tin, shook off the used pouches and opened the lid.

'Something's happened,' she said quietly.

It was not even half past five in the morning when Seved was woken up by the loud flush of the toilet. Almost immediately there were two heavy thumps on his door, so he got up, nauseous with exhaustion.

Börje had been right. Barking dogs, grunts and tormented bellowing had kept them awake for most of the night. The car chassis had squealed and he had heard a window being smashed.

Freezing cold, Seved got dressed and went down to the kitchen, zipping up his fleece jacket. He saw through the window that the rear lights of the Volvo were on and Börje was standing out there, scraping the windows. The Isuzu was lying on its side, its roof a white wall.

Börje and Seved sat more or less in silence for the entire journey, and it was a long one: three hundred kilometres to Jokkmokk, and then maybe ten more on the road that curved alongside the river. The atmosphere in the car was strange. They had never spoken before about anything other than practicalities, and although neither of them wanted to admit it, something had changed between them since Börje had told Seved about Signe. Seved had been coming to his own conclusions during the night, and Börje knew that, of course. But he probably thought it was just as well, that it was about time. Either that or he had reached a point where he no longer cared. He didn't bring it up, and Seved did not ask. Deep inside, he wanted to know nothing about it.

So nothing was said.

The humped peaks of the mountains that had been huddled gently on the horizon were now increasing in height, and Seved realised they were getting closer. A peculiarly thick fog had drifted up from the lake, which was half covered in ice, and it lay ghost-like across the road that wound down the steep fir-clad slopes of the mountains. When they turned off the main road the pallid mist followed them a short way into the trees.

The forest road was narrow, and after a couple of hundred metres it was blocked by a barrier. Seved ran out and opened it. Torsten knew they were coming and so he had left it unlocked.

The tyres crunched on the crusty snow as they steered through the forest, with tall starved spruces on each side. It was a deep, wild forest, ancient and full of dead wood.

Soon they saw the farm: a collection of white-hatted blocks against a dark fringe of fir trees whose tops had all been blow-dried in the same direction. A few silvery-grey wooden sheds were keeping their distance from the other buildings. A thin band of smoke was rising from the house's chimney.

Börje pointed to the barn, and Seved leaned forwards to see.

The frost had edged its way far up the unpainted timber. It looked as if someone had started applying white paint to the logs but had stopped halfway up. There was a window with four panes on the side wall, and that was also white, blinded by the cold. Where the panes met it resembled a faded cross.

Up on the roof's ridge something was standing.

A small figure in a green anorak with the hood up.

Puzzled, Seved wondered if a child had climbed onto the roof.

But naturally it was no child.

It was only that Seved wasn't used to seeing the shapeshifters wearing clothes.

'How many are there exactly?' he asked, without taking his eyes from the little figure on the roof.

'Lots,' answered Börje, and changed down a gear before the final uphill stretch.

Then he added:

'And they live in the house. Well, not Luttak, of course. But the others.'

'They have the shapeshifters indoors?'

'Only the small ones.'

'That one doesn't look very small,' said Seved, nodding at the roof, where the creature had now moved back along the snow-covered tiles on the ridge so it could watch the approaching car.

'Yes, well, that one's a different matter,' Börje said, darting a look at the barn as he turned the wheel, letting his hands cross. 'He comes and goes as he likes.'

Seved looked away and faced rigidly ahead, taking care not to stare.

They parked between an old van and a large yellow tractor with frost-covered, studded ice chains draped around the wheels. Inside a compound the dogs were leaping around each other. Their barking and howling was deafening, and to make himself heard Seved was forced to shout as they got out of the car.

'How long will it take, do you think? Shall I connect the engine warmer?'

A tall and slightly crooked man in oil-splattered overalls came walking stiffly towards them from the barn. Seved realised it was Torsten, whom he had heard about all his life but had never met.

He had thin grey hair and unshaven cheeks, and the skin under his eyes was darkened by wrinkles. Without greeting them he asked tersely if they had locked the barrier after them, and Börje nodded.

He was alone. The others had gone to the village, he said, opening the door that led to the kitchen. The doors were unpainted and had old-fashioned locks and doorknobs. There was no electric cooker, only a wood-burning stove with a pearl-white microwave standing on it, and a coffee machine perched on top of that. The old floorboards were grey and covered with narrow rag rugs. Across the ceiling ran a fabric-covered flex, hanging in deep loops and leading to a lamp that hung low and had a thin shade made of what looked like hand-blown glass. On the wall above the wooden sofa was a wall hanging with the embroidered text: PEACE THROUGH THE BOND OF UNITY.

Torsten put on the coffee and then sat down at the kitchen table, where there was a Jokkmokk telephone directory. He licked his thumb and flicked through the pages to the maps at the back, and when he found the one he wanted he scrupulously smoothed it out with the palm of his hand. Then he picked up a ballpoint pen and circled a house.

'It's here,' he said.

Börje and Seved both looked, and when Torsten was sure they had seen the right house he tore the page out of the directory and slid it across the table.

'Of course, most little kids go to nursery these days,' he said. 'But this one doesn't. He plays outside on his own and he doesn't seem scared. We've seen him many times on the other side of the road, the side where the lake is, building grottos in piles of snow or whatever it is he gets up to. And for a long time we've thought it wouldn't be too difficult to snatch him, if we needed to. And it looks like you need to.'

He stood up to fetch the coffee jug and filled the cups.

'I heard about your sister,' he said.

Börje sat in silence for a moment, lost in his thoughts.

'It can't be easy,' Torsten continued.

'Of course, you do wonder.'

'What?'

'Well, if she really was that stupid.'

Torsten looked at him carefully and licked his upper lip with the tip of his tongue.

'You mean, you're thinking she found a way out of it?'

Börje shrugged his shoulders apathetically.

'It was hard for her,' he explained. 'I know that. She didn't want another child in the house. Having to go through all that again, comforting it, making it understand. She didn't want to have to do it.'

He took a drink of his coffee and then said:

'And now she doesn't have to.'

Seved could hear Torsten and Börje talking, but he could not take in what they were saying. His thoughts had drifted far away and he heard their voices only as a distant murmur. His field of vision shrank: it zoomed in on the embroidery on the linen tablecloth, the splashes of red paint on the sleeve of Torsten's overall, the steaming china cups, the telephone directory and the broken clip of the ballpoint pen. The plates on the painted wall shelf too, and the blackened glass chimney of the paraffin lamp.

Sister.

Were Ejvor and Börje *siblings*?

He had always thought they were married.

Well, that explained why they had no children. That explained why he had ended up with them. And Signe. It explained everything!

Trying to work out what Börje meant when he suggested Ejvor had found a way out of it was beyond him, but it occupied his thoughts, and that was why it took a while before he realised that Torsten was talking to him.

'The lemmingshifters,' the old man repeated. 'Did that work out?'

'It was calm the first night,' Seved answered, confused. 'But last night they were out again, carrying on, so I don't really know.'

'Then maybe you need more?'

Torsten stood up, rubbing his index finger in a shadowy groove above his upper lip. He looked at them enquiringly.

'I'm sure we can manage with what we've got,' said Börje.

Clearly it was not meant to be a question because Torsten had already opened the door to the hall. He walked up the staircase, and they could hear the floor creak as he walked backwards and forwards upstairs. Seved shot a look at Börje, who was sitting with one elbow resting on the back of the chair and staring unseeingly at the floor. There was no point asking him about Ejvor; it would only make him withdraw into himself.

He thought about Ejvor's behaviour before she went into Hybblet that afternoon. She did not seem to be depressed. She had actually joked with him. But perhaps that kind of thing never shows on the outside.

Seved drank the last of his coffee, ran his eyes over the tongue and groove on the kitchen walls and then out through the window, where he caught sight of the little man who had been standing on the roof. Now he was sitting in the raised bucket attachment of the tractor, leaning back casually and looking towards the kitchen window. His clear yellow eyes were surrounded by creases and shadows that gave them a troubled look. His face was leathery brown and wrinkled, and the thin white beard pointed in all directions.

And he was reaching out. Seved felt that immediately. It was like a fleeting caress inside his forehead. Swiftly he leaned back so that the old man could no longer see him – usually it was enough to get out of their line of vision – but to be on the safe side he pushed the chair back from the table half a metre.

'Him,' he said. 'The one that was on the roof. He's up to something.'

Börje peered through the window.

'Yes, he's a nosy little bugger, that one.'

He had no time to say more before the stairs creaked and Torsten walked into the kitchen holding a wooden box. It was a little chest, made from painted planks. The lid had a brass lock. He put the box down on the table and looked at them.

'I could only get hold of four but that's better than nothing. And they're small and entertaining. The old-timers like that. You have to take these with you, you understand. I've got a wood mouse and a few other things. A couple of shrews.'

He opened the lid of the chest and poked around in the hay. After a while he pulled out his hand. A grey-brown tuft of hair stuck up out of his fist. Torsten pressed his thumb against the little creature's chin and unwillingly it lifted its head. Its eyes were screwed up tightly and the mouth with its pin-like teeth was gaping open. It seemed as if it was trying to open its mouth as wide as it could to show how big it was.

'See?' said Torsten, grinning. 'See how he's laughing?'

'A week or so ago', said Susso in a low voice, 'I got an email from a woman in Vaikijaur who had seen a little man outside her house. He just stood there, looking at her. Vaikijaur is *relatively* close, so I drove up there. And she seemed pretty credible, so I set up a camera – you know, the one I got from Tommy, Cecilia's bloke.'

Torbjörn changed position on the sofa without taking his eyes off her.

'Then the other night, or morning it was, she phoned to tell me she had seen him again. He had been looking into her kitchen.'

From the front pocket of her parka Susso brought out a print-out of the photo. It was the seventh picture, the one where the wrinkled little face could be clearly seen. Torbjörn took a gulp from his can, and after putting it down again he wiped his mouth and leaned forwards, looking at the figure. His nostrils tensed and flared, but he said nothing. After studying the picture he leaned back in the sofa. It looked as if he was trying to stop himself from laughing. His eyes were glittering dark slits. One arm was stretched along the back of the sofa and he was drumming his fingers on the frame of shiny polished wood.

'What are you going to do with it?'

'I've posted it on the website.'

'Will it lead to anything then?'

'Probably not. I suppose I ought to promote it somehow. Do

you know any journalist who would want to write about it?'

She meant the last sentence mainly as a joke.

'No, but you ought to go to Jokkmokk and ask around. A person looking like that – well, someone ought to know who he is, don't you think? If he lives in that area.'

Susso stood up and walked to the window. A wind had started blowing and it made the globes of the street lamps move slightly. The snow that had settled on the pale-green facade of the house opposite looked as if it had attached itself like lichen.

'What if it's just a dwarf?' she said. 'That would be embarrassing.'

'Then you'll have to ask what the hell is he doing running around in that old woman's garden in the middle of the night,' Torbjörn replied. 'He's not supposed to be doing that.'

She nodded.

'I know one or two people in Jokkmokk. I could ask them if they know of a dwarf living in the area. People normally know about that kind of thing. There's a dwarf up in Haparanda, and you can ask anyone you like about him. Everyone knows who he is.'

The snowsuit stood out like a red dot against the piles of snow.

Börje and Seved said nothing to each other but they both knew.

This had to be the boy.

He was walking along the other side of the road. Towards them.

Börje slowed down to give himself time to think, and then he stopped. The wipers swept across the windscreen. He sucked his teeth and looked reflectively in the rear-view mirror.

'We could run him over,' Börje said. 'And then get him in the car to take him to hospital. If anyone sees us, that's what we could say. That we only wanted to help him.'

Seved stared: was he serious?

'Well, he is walking on the wrong side of the road,' said Börje.

'Yes, if you're coming from that direction,' said Seved, pointing. 'You can't run him over from this direction.'

'I'll just have to turn round and do it then!'

Seved rubbed his forehead hard and looked in the wing mirror, in the star-shaped hole left by the ice crystals. Could Börje really consider doing such a thing?

The boy was not far away now. Soon he would reach the cones of light radiating from the car, picking out the streaming snowflakes.

'So what shall we do then?' Börje said loudly.

Seved pretended to think and eventually he said, with lips that had turned dry:

'We wait. Until we have another car.'

'Nothing shows,' said Börje. 'The car's completely covered in snow.'

'But Torsten told us we weren't to do it with this car. Someone could have seen us when we drove up to his place. Then they'll come here looking. It's too risky.'

Börje shook his head.

'We'll do it now,' he said, and pressed the button so that the window began to go down slowly with a scraping sound. 'Give me one of those.'

Börje leaned out of the open window. He was holding his hands cupped against his chest.

'Happy Christmas!' he called.

The boy carried on walking for a few steps before he stopped and looked at the car.

Then he started walking again. Faster.

'Where are you off to?'

There was no answer.

'We want you to help us with something,' Börje said, turning to Seved, indicating he wanted him to play along. 'Your mum just phoned and told us.'

Seved leaned forwards and nodded.

'We've got something for you,' he said. 'A Christmas present.'

The words aroused the boy's interest and he stopped walking. After looking both ways he crossed the road. A few metres away from the car he stopped. He was wearing a hat with a spider-web pattern and his cheeks were red. It was cold, as low as minus fifteen, and clouds of snowflakes were being buffeted around in sudden gusts of wind.

'Where are you going?' said Börje, sounding tense. 'Are you going home?'

He had already asked that, and it was obvious that the boy had become scared but without exactly knowing why; a feeling told him something was not quite right. He screwed up his eyes against the wind. Snow fastened in his eyelashes and the thumb of his mitten came up to rub it away.

'Your mum said you don't have to go home,' said Börje. 'She said you could help us with something, if you like. But we've got to make sure you're the right boy. What's your name?'

'Mattias.'

Börje nodded.

'Mattias. That's right. Then it's you we're looking for. That's lucky.'

Börje turned to face Seved.

'Shall we show him then?'

Seved nodded.

Börje lifted up his cupped hands slowly and secretively until they appeared in the open window, like a puppet show. He gradually opened his fingers, and from between them poked a tiny delicate snout, although to be exact it was not a snout. It was a nose. A smile spread across the boy's face and he quickly approached the car door, pressing himself against it to get a better view. But then Börje pulled his hands away.

'No,' he said. 'They're very nervous.'

'What is it?' asked the boy. 'Is it a gerbil?'

Börje took his hand away as if he was sliding back a screen and revealed the agile little shapeshifter shivering in the cold air streaming into the car. Its grey furry tail lay coiled in the hollow of Börje's palm.

'You can have one of these, if you like,' Börje said in a friendly voice, gently pressing his finger on the little creature's back, where its shoulder blades protruded. 'Not this one, but one just like it. In our pet shop in Jokkmokk we've got masses of them, and we need to give a few away because we haven't got room for them all. But we can't give them away to just anybody because they've got to be looked after properly. So if you like, you can have one to take care of. Would you like that?'

Mattias nodded.

'Jump in the car then.'

The boy was allowed to hold it. With his hands pressed tightly together he made a little balcony against his chest, and there the mouse shapeshifter lay on its back, watching the boy's face. It looked as if it was sunning itself in the wonder radiating from the child's eyes.

'What's its name?' he asked, as they swung south onto the motorway.

Seved could not see him: he was clutching his forehead with his right hand and staring out through the window. He must not start crying, but he felt very close to it. It was rising up inside him.

'It hasn't got a name,' said Börje, over his shoulder. 'But you can give it a name, if you like.'

'Can I have it?'

'No,' said Börje. 'Like I said, not this one. But you can give it a name. It makes them happy if they have a name. And we have so many it's impossible for us to find names for them all.'

The boy was silent.

'Have you got a good suggestion?' he went on.

'Perhaps Jim.'

'Jim?'

The boy nodded.

'Jim,' said Börje, as if testing the sound of it. 'That's not a bad name, is it? Did you hear what a good name he thought up? Jim.'

Seved nodded.

'It's nice,' he said softly. By this time he had twisted his face towards the glass so that the tears welling up in his eyes would not show. They would be streaming down his cheeks any second.

Time.

It was only a matter of time.

Everything passes with time.

He had been told that himself, and he knew it was true in a way. Time blotted things out. They lost their hold. Although of course there was no telling what would fade and what would remain. But it would get better. He would get used to it, even if he was sad to begin with. It vanished with time. A shell formed.

They had to drive through Jokkmokk, and they knew that was not entirely risk free. Partly because the boy would realise they had no plans to stop at a pet shop, and partly because they would have to drive relatively slowly through the built-up area, and then someone who knew the boy might catch sight of him. On the other hand, it was fairly dark.

They were not particularly worried that he would start screaming and struggling. It would take a lot for the boy to do that. But there must not be silence. Seved tried to think of something to say but his mind was a complete blank. It would be a disaster if the boy heard the crying in his voice.

They turned into the road that ran past the police station. Lights were shining in the windows of the ground floor. Seved tried to see if Börje was nervous, but it was hard to tell.

'Jim,' repeated the older man loudly, and craned his neck to get a glimpse of the boy in the rear-view mirror. 'That's a really good name. How clever of you to come up with such a good name, Mattias.' He put the indicator on and the Volvo began to tick. 'If you like, you can name a few more, because I can never think of names that suit them. They have to be names they like, of course. And you can't ask them because they can't talk. But they can nod. They understand!'

'Do they?'

'Of course. Ask him if he would like to be called Jim.'

The boy sat and thought for a moment.

'Do you want to?' he said quietly.

He looked for a long time at the mouseshifter, which was lying very still and looking at him with eyes like dark dots. The little object did not understand a thing, it seemed.

'Well?' asked Börje. 'What does he say? Would he like to be called Jim?'

'I think so.'

The streets of Jokkmokk were lined with frozen birches, cars covered in white and high mounds of snow left behind by the ploughs. In the windows, Advent stars and candlesticks were shining. They passed an ICA supermarket and a pizzeria. Some way along a side road a car was parked with its headlights on full beam.

'Well, Mattias,' Börje said, 'perhaps you'd like other toys too? What toys would you like to have? Do you like Lego?'

Mattias nodded.

'You can build a house with your Lego for Jim to live in, can't you? You could build a block of flats, and then Jim's friends can live on the other floors, and you can build a castle . . .'

It was clear from Börje's voice that he was running out of things to say, and Seved tried desperately to think of something. He swallowed, repeatedly. He was unsure of his own voice. It might let him down.

'They like to wear clothes,' he said, turning round in his seat to study the boy, who was trying to pat the little mouseshifter with his finger. 'Like the mice in *Cinderella*. Have you seen *Cinderella*?'

Börje turned his head with a look that stung Seved's cheek. That was exactly the kind of talk that had to be avoided. Nothing about home, nothing outside the car.

They approached a junction, and Börje slowed down because a car in front was pulling out. At the same time a woman came along with a kick sledge. Her glasses had misted up under her fur-edged hood and she passed by on Seved's side. He looked at her and she looked at him. Stared, in fact.

As they began to move again he met Börje's eyes.

And now he was no longer unaffected.

Seved looked at his watch. Over half an hour had passed.

'Shall we phone Lennart?' he said quietly.

Börje nodded, extracted his mobile from his trouser pocket and gave it to Seved.

'Better still,' he said, 'send a text.'

Seved had never owned a mobile phone. He didn't know how to send a text; he didn't even know how to unlock the phone.

Börje had to instruct him, step by step.

When Seved had found the right place and worked out how the keys functioned he wrote:

'WE HAVE THE BOY.'

Then he held up the phone so that Börje could check.

'Now what?'

'You've got to send it as well. Press YES.'

Shortly afterwards the phone rang.

'LENNART BRÖSTH,' it said in black letters against the grey display. Seved handed the mobile to Börje. He answered Lennart's questions in monosyllables, and when the conversation ended he threw the phone into Seved's lap.

'Have you cleaned up the cellar?'

Seved shook his head.

'Then you'll have to call Signe,' said Börje. 'Lennart was in Glommersträsk, on his way to Skellefteå. But he's going to turn round straight away, so it looks like he'll be there before us. Tell her to clean up the worst of it. And make the bed.'

'I think I want to go home now.'

When Seved heard the boy's high voice from the back seat he felt a knot form in his stomach, and for a few seconds he could not even draw breath.

'Home?' Börje said at length. 'Didn't you want your very own little troll mouse?'

'Yes, but I have to go home.'

'We'll drive you home as soon as we have collected the mouse,' Börje said over his shoulder. 'That'll be all right, won't it?'

Mattias had stiffened.

Seved unclicked his safety belt, put one boot on his seat and squeezed himself between the front seats and into the back, almost falling on top of the boy, who was holding his cupped hands in front of him. They were empty. The mouseshifter had slipped away. Now it could be anywhere in the car, and it would not be easy to get hold of it again.

Mattias stared out through the window. A tear had left a shiny stripe down his cheek. His hat had ridden up his head and one ear was visible. It was a little red nine shape, surrounded by tufts of brown hair.

'You mustn't be sad,' Seved said, using the back of his hand to wipe his own cheekbones, and then his moustache to get rid of the mucus that had collected there in a sticky fringe.

'It'll be all right, you'll see. It'll be all right.'

When they pulled up outside the house someone was moving about in the spotlight. It was Signe. She was on her way into the house and glanced at the car before disappearing through the door. Lennart's Merc was parked in front of the dog enclosure, and they pulled up alongside it.

'Come on,' Börje said, opening the door for Mattias.

The boy did not move at first, so they had to help him out.

He walked between them, holding the mouseshifter in his cupped hands. Seved had heard a scratching in the moulded pattern of the floor mat and managed to catch hold of the little creature again. That was lucky. From what he could see the boy was once again mesmerised. The small eyes had fixed themselves on his.

Strangely, there was music in the kitchen, lively Christmas music. The notes from the CD player came from a disc that Seved had never heard before, and he realised Lennart must have brought it with him. On the plastic case lying on the windowsill there was a red price sticker.

The big man sat at the kitchen table, looking towards the door. The lump of his left hand was hidden under the tabletop and he had taken off his jacket. Seved realised he had never seen him without a jacket before, not even in the summer.

The table was laid. Two plastic bottles of cola were standing in the centre. There were ginger biscuits arranged on a red napkin on a plate, and on another plate were clementines. And bags of sweets in a big pile: chewy cars and jelly dummies and chocolate rice puffs. Lennart must have emptied the confectionery shelf at Q-Star.

Signe stood with her back against the draining board, her arms folded. At her feet sat a hare, staring vacantly ahead. Its ears were pressed back. Shapeshifters in the kitchen, thought Seved. What about that, Ejvor?

Lennart was distractedly rolling a chocolate egg wrapped in foil on the table, and when Mattias appeared in the doorway he immediately began playing with it.

'Can you help me with this, little fellow?' he said.

Oddly enough, the boy showed no shyness. He strode into the kitchen, let the mouseshifter leap down onto the table, and took the egg from the old man's rough hand. He unwrapped the foil as Lennart watched him with his eyes half closed.

'You'll have to open it too.'

Mattias purposefully broke apart the two chocolate halves and removed the plastic egg inside. It was yellow.

'Was that all?'

The boy nodded.

'Is it an egg yolk?'

Mattias shook his head.

'What is it then?'

'A toy.'

'A toy?'

Mattias shook the container, and it rattled.

'So there's something inside?'

The boy nodded.

'Is it a chicken?'

He shrugged his shoulders.

'Open that one too. Then we can see what we've got.'

The brown halves that Mattias laid on the table instantly attracted the little mouseshifter's attention, but it seemed as if it was afraid to touch or even approach the chocolate. The boy struggled with the plastic egg but his small fingers kept sliding off.

'I can't do it.'

Lennart took the yellow container and pressed it together until one side came apart from the other with a popping sound. Then he shook out the contents onto the table. There were colourful pieces of plastic and a slip of paper, coiled from being rolled up. When Seved bent under the table to pick up one of the plastic halves that had fallen down he saw the hare looking at him. It had lowered its neck exactly as if it had been a cat about to run up and play with something that had landed on the floor. It was an old hare and its whiskers were thick and unpleasantly long.

'What is it?' asked Lennart.

The boy sorted through the pieces, picked them up and examined them.

'A dinosaur, I think.'

'Do you want it?' Lennart asked.

Mattias shrugged.

'What about some sweets then?' the man grunted, resting his hand on the pile of sweet bags. They rustled as he moved his hand among them.

'There are all sorts here,' he said. 'Dummies and things.'

'I'd like some cola,' said the boy, scratching his head under his hat.

Signe unscrewed the cap of one of the bottles and it started to spray, so she hurried to the sink as the brown liquid overflowed.

'They've been in the car,' Lennart explained.

After wiping the bottle she poured out a glass, which she placed in front of Mattias. He took hold of it in both hands and drank.

When he had finished he put the glass down in front of him and asked:

'Can I go home now?'

'You want to go home?' Lennart asked.

The boy nodded.

'Why so soon?'

'Can I?'

'Listen,' said Lennart, 'I've just spoken to your mum, and she said it would be good if you could stay here overnight. Then you can go home tomorrow. They have lots to do, seeing as it's nearly Christmas.'

'I want to phone her and talk to her.'

'And they were very tired,' Lennart continued. 'They were very tired and were going to go to bed early. They didn't want us to phone and wake them. But we can phone tomorrow.'

The boy did not move. He was fighting back the tears.

'Tomorrow we'll phone your mum,' said Lennart. 'And when you have drunk your cola I think you should go to bed, so that you will be wide awake tomorrow and can play with your friend. You're going to have your very own room to stay in, you and your friend. That'll be nice, won't it, little fellow?'

Torbjörn sat up, reached out his slim arm and pulled the pizza box onto the floor. Then he went into the kitchen. There was a clatter as he searched in the drawer for cutlery. Everything was in a mess, and he searched for some time before coming back and sitting cross-legged against the sofa. First he cut the pizza into slices, and then into smaller pieces which he put into his mouth with a fork.

He stabbed a piece of pizza and said with his mouth full:

'You've got to follow it up somehow.'

'My sister reckons it's someone dressed up.'

'Cecilia?'

Susso nodded and shoved the grease-stained carton onto the floor, then lay on her back and stretched out her legs.

'It's like . . .' she said, and then fell silent because she had to think. 'It's like I want Cecilia to be right – that it isn't real, that it is only someone in disguise. Or else it's a completely normal dwarf – you know what I mean, a really short person who is interested in Edit Mickelsson's house for some reason. I can't bear the thought of it being anything other than a human being. Even I can't bear that. Do you understand?'

Torbjörn had eaten less than a fifth of his pizza and it seemed enough for him because out came the snus tin. Holding it in his hand he stood up, ambled over to the computer and switched it on. The seat of his trousers hung low, exposing the lettering on the wide waistband of his underpants. A string of fine dark hair clambered up his lower vertebrae. Susso knew how silky it felt under her fingers.

'It could be a mask,' he said, leaning towards the screen. 'But then again, you can see how tiny he is. Less than a metre tall, I would guess. How old are you when you're a metre tall? Three? And the photo is taken at five thirty in the morning. Not many three-year-olds out at that time.'

After a while he said, without turning round:

'Do you trust her? The old woman?'

'I'm a hundred per cent sure she's not a hoaxer, if that's what you mean.'

He spun the chair round.

'In that case there are two alternatives. It's either a dwarf who looks like this, or a dwarf who is wearing a mask. And for some unknown reason he's sneaking around up there in Vaikijaur.'

'Three,' said Susso, looking up at the ceiling. 'There are three alternatives.'

'Yes?' he said. 'And what's the third?'

'That it's a real troll.'

It was silent for a long time.

Eventually he said quietly:

'Okay. Three alternatives.'

Then he stood up and asked if he should switch off the computer, but Susso told him to leave it on, so he returned to where he had been sitting in front of the television.

'Come here,' she said, holding out her hand.

He was holding a snus pouch between his fingers and looked at her with his mouth open. Then he turned to face the television again.

'No,' he said, inserting the snus.

'I only want you to see something.'

'What?'

She rolled onto her stomach, folded the pillow into a pad and placed it under her chin.

'My bruise,' she grinned.

He snorted.

'I don't want to see your fucking bruise.'

'It's not a fucking bruise. It's my bruise. My *lovely* bruise.'

'Susso,' he said, 'cut it out. I know your tricks.'

'Come on,' she said, beckoning with her finger.

He shook his head.

'C'mon here, boy. Good boy.'

'Cut it out, for God's sake!'

They didn't fall out exactly but there was irritation and silence between them, and the television droned on, unremitting and soporific. Susso nodded off, and when she woke Torbjörn had gone. But the sheet under the pillow was soaking wet. When she patted it she could feel that not all the snow had melted. He always did that: brought in lumps of snow and put them in the bed. It amused him enormously. She swore at him, but still she was happy that he had played the trick on her. It meant he couldn't be too annoyed.

She did not know what to make of him. He seemed embarrassed, only partially present. But she did not want to ask him if he had met anyone else. If he was forced to say it, there was a risk he would hear his own words. And that could sway him. Make him clam up.

It had been fairly okay between them, but he had left anyway.

Although it was probably like Gudrun said: if his feelings were stronger, he would not have minded. That scared her. Because she did not mind. She thought the situation was pretty difficult, naturally, but not insurmountable.

About six months after he had moved to Luleå he had turned up at Ferrum, out of nowhere, wearing a new shirt and with his hair spiky and a beer in his hand. She had screamed at him and had enjoyed seeing his face flatten in a grimace. She could not remember what he had said in his defence. Probably nothing. Later that evening he had got involved in a fight, rolling around on the ground outside, standing there afterwards with his jumper caked with snow, pestering the doormen who resolutely pushed him away. And he had lost the cloakroom ticket for his jacket and had to spend the night at her place. The cold was ferocious and naturally he had no taxi money – he had shown her his wallet. In bed he had indifferently stroked her hip with limp fingers, but had then given up and fallen asleep with the snus still in his mouth. After that they had not been in touch until he came back home and started working for Wassara.

After she had pulled off the sheet and thrown it in the laundry basket she picked up the pizza boxes and pushed them into the bin. They stuck out at the top and the cupboard door would not close.

She sat with her back against the cold stone wall and watched television, holding the remote. She clicked on teletext. There was a film on at nine, but it was not even six thirty, so she walked to the bookshelf and stared at her DVDs for a long time. There were about twenty. She ran through some of the scenes in her head but nothing really appealed.

Her mobile began to buzz on the coffee table. Susso stretched forwards and saw that it was Edit. For a moment she hesitated, trying to decide whether to answer or not. Eventually she picked up the phone.

She could hear immediately that something was wrong. Edit apologised for calling like this on a Saturday, and when Susso assured her it was not a problem she said in voice almost like a whisper:

'Mattias is missing.'

The boy was dressed in his outdoor clothes and holding the mouseshifter he had named Jim close to his chest. The little creature sat stock still, with its rounded cheek against the boy's snowsuit. It looked as if it was listening to the boy's heartbeat. Below the worried creases on its forehead the eyes showed like black peppercorns.

Signe asked the boy if he wanted his hat, and when there was no answer she pushed it down on his head and then straightened it so that he could see properly.

'It's cold in there,' she said in a low voice.

Lennart had opened the door to Hybblet and was standing on the porch steps waiting for them. He had opened a couple of windows as well, to get rid of the worst of the smell.

They walked across the yard, Signe first, then the boy and lastly Seved. Börje was not with them. He had gone to lie down again. He had told Seved that Lennart had taken care of Ejvor's body, and when Seved had asked what he had done with it, he had mumbled that it did not matter. Did this mean he did not know or that he did not want to say? Seved was unsure. Börje had looked so grey and fragile he had not wanted to question him any further.

The door to the kitchen was closed and Seved was careful not to breathe in through his nose. The stench in Hybblet had always been hideous but he did not want to know if there was a different kind of smell. Like something new had been added to it.

The room known as the jumping room was empty apart from a green-painted metal bed frame standing in the middle of the floor. A dirty yellow foam mattress was lying on it.

'Here,' Lennart said, pointing to the bed. 'This is where you can jump if you want to. That's what this bed is for.'

Through the open window where net curtains were flapping a parched light fell onto the floor tiles dotted with mouse droppings.

The boy looked at the bed.

He did not understand a thing.

He pressed the little object hard to his chest and ran his eyes over the walls.

Seved remembered standing there himself.

How Ejvor had forced him to jump.

How she had held onto his hands and jumped with him.

How he had hated it.

'You have a go,' he said.

'Yes,' said Lennart. 'You have a go, little fellow.'

Susso told me to put on teletext, and when I didn't do as she said immediately, because I thought she only wanted to see what was on the other channels, she told me again, this time almost shouting. At first I thought she was annoyed because my boyfriend Roland was over and we weren't properly dressed, which made *me* annoyed because I thought we had the right to be completely naked if we chose. Her habit of walking straight into the flat often got on my nerves.

I grabbed the remote and changed to teletext:

FOUR-YEAR-OLD BOY ABDUCTED IN JOKKMOKK

At first I didn't understand at all: which four-year-old boy? My thoughts were still grinding slowly, or unwillingly, after the hour we had spent in the sauna earlier, so Susso had to explain that the missing boy was Edit's grandchild.

'The one who was with her when she saw!' she said.

'It's two minutes to,' said Roland. 'Switch the news on.'

Dazed, I changed to a different channel. My left hand picked nervously at the collar of my silk dressing gown. It was not so much the news as Susso's peculiar behaviour that worried me. I had never known her to be so solemn.

The television wouldn't obey the remote, so I stood up to get as close to it as possible.

Flying above the snow-topped fir trees was a police helicopter, chasing its powerful light over the ice of Lake Vaikijaur. And there was a voice saying:

'Four-year-old Mattias was visiting his grandmother on Friday. At five o'clock his mother realised that he had not come home and alerted the police.'

A squinting police officer from the Luleå police force was standing in front of a furry grey microphone from Nordnytt TV.

'The charge,' he said, and then he paused. 'Is kidnapping.'

'Oh God,' I said, and sat down on the coffee table, carefully so it would not tip. 'Oh my God.'

'A witness saw Mattias in an unknown car, a brown Volvo 240, in central Jokkmokk at four fifteen on Friday afternoon. The police are appealing to the public.

'If anyone has seen anything in the vicinity or has any other information, please contact us,' the police officer said. 'However small, it could help.'

Susso stood immobile, concentrating, her arms folded. She had lowered her forehead as if to confront the news head on. The item was over, and I searched the channels looking for other news bulletins.

'But what does she say?' I asked, pumping the arrow-shaped button with my thumb. 'What does Edit say?'

Susso went into the kitchen. She returned with a wine bottle in one hand and a glass in the other. She poured the wine and drank deeply.

Roland had crossed his arms and was leaning back in the sofa.

A feeling of uneasiness came over me. My stomach was in knots.

'His parents,' I went on. 'What do his parents say?'

Susso shook her head, not in answer but more to indicate that she hadn't the energy to answer. She sat in the armchair, holding the wine glass in both hands. Her eyes were directed at the wooden floor. The bottle stood on the glass-topped table, shining a deep red.

'What if he's the one who's taken the boy?'

'Who?' I asked. '*The troll?*'

Susso nodded.

'What troll?' Roland asked, sitting with his hands on his knee-caps, his eyes wandering between me and Susso.

I kept quiet for a moment, fiddling with the small clip of my watch strap, which rubbed against the veins where the skin is so thin.

'It's like this: Susso has taken a picture of a troll,' I said finally, slowly placing the remote on the table. 'Or maybe a gnome. At least, we think that's what it could be. And it was there at that little boy's granny's house.'

I told him the whole story and how the picture had been taken with a wildlife camera outside Edit's house.

A deep exhalation of breath came from the sofa. Roland was staring grimly out of the window. He's not going to put up with us, I thought. He's not letting on what he really thinks. He's going to give up now. It's making him cocky. Any minute now he'll snort and maybe come out with a sarcastic remark. Oh God, what if he does? Susso will be furious. We had spoken about the troll several times before, me and Roland, so it couldn't just be avoided, but even though he had never mocked me I got round it by pretending I didn't believe it. From habit, because I was afraid of scaring him off.

'Can I have a look?' he said.

Roland sat wordlessly looking at the laptop on the kitchen table. He had pushed his glasses down the bridge of his nose. After a while he grabbed the screen and angled it a fraction as he leaned closer.

'So this is supposed to be a troll . . .'

'We don't know,' I said. 'But it certainly could be, couldn't it?'

He gave a laugh.

'Could be? Well, yes, perhaps.'

He craned his neck and shouted in the direction of the sitting room:

'Have you shown this picture to the police?'

'I haven't,' Susso answered. 'But I think Edit has. At least, that's what she said she'd do. Tell them it's on the website.'

Roland nodded.

I went back to Susso. She was lounging in the armchair, her hand against her chest, tapping on her mobile. In the gap between her trousers and her jumper there was a roll of fat with her navel in the centre. It was snowing and I stood looking out. Mainly because I didn't know what to say.

'Did you ever meet him?' I said eventually.

She didn't answer, so I turned round.

'Susso. Did you meet the boy?'

She shook her head, texting with both thumbs.

'What about his mum and dad?' I said. 'Do they live together?'

'Yes,' she said. 'I've already told you.'

'Because it's usually a parent who steals a child. If it's a custody issue or something. Or another relative.'

'Yes, but in this case it isn't.'

She had stopped texting and was staring at me.

'Someone has taken him. Don't you get it?'

'He'll come back, you'll see,' I said. 'Children aren't kidnapped just like that.'

The squeaking from the metal springs hurt Seved's ears but it was more than the noise that made him want to get out of Hybblet. Not only did he know what was going on inside the boy, he felt it. And he felt it with an intensity that took him by surprise.

He saw him standing there in his red snowsuit but he could not believe it was real. That they had actually taken him. It had all happened in a flash. Before Börje wound down the window and called the boy over, the thought of kidnapping him had been nothing more than a thought – it had not even been a plan. He never believed it would happen. That it really would happen.

The boy looked down at the little thing he was holding tightly to his chest. He had comfort from that, at least. Or perhaps it was the boy who was comforting the little shapeshifter. Seved knew how they could nestle their way in. Unobtrusive and eager. So it was not easy to say who was comforting who.

Signe had brought a thermos with her and he heard her unscrewing the stopper. When she gave him a cup he squatted down with his back against the wall. Normally it was about ten degrees in the house, but now, with the window open, it was colder. A white mist hung in front of Signe's mouth and it changed shape every time she breathed out, so Seved could clearly see how nervous she was.

What were her memories of this room?

He had no idea because they had never talked about it, but

he assumed that she disliked being in here as much as he did. Perhaps it was worse for her because it had only been five or six years since she was that child jumping on the bed.

Heavy footsteps could be heard on the cellar stairs and both Seved and Signe stood up, afraid. They stared at the door, which was opening.

It was Lennart.

He came in and joined them, standing for a long time looking at the boy, who had stopped jumping and was now sitting, prodding the little mouseshifter. The boy was letting it run free on the mattress and then crawl back into his hands to be picked up again.

'I've just spoken to your mother,' said Lennart. 'She says you're to stay here another night.'

Instantly the boy looked up. He didn't want to.

'Your mum said so,' Lennart grunted.

'Phone her,' said the boy. 'She'll come and get me.'

Lennart strode to the bed and sat down, making it creak.

'I didn't want to have to tell you this, but your mum is angry with you, little fellow. I don't know why.'

Lennart rubbed his cheek with the hand that was inside the bag.

'Do you know why?'

The boy shook his head.

'Don't lie.'

'Perhaps because I went to Granny's house?'

'Exactly,' said Lennart, nodding. 'That's what she said. She is angry because you went to your granny's. Even though you weren't allowed to. So she thinks you ought to stay here for a while.'

'But I want to phone her. I want to say sorry.'

'You can't. There's no telephone here.'

'But you've just talked to her.'

'That was over at the neighbour's house,' Lennart said, standing up. 'And I can only use their phone once a day.'

'But why can't I go home?'

'You can go home. Just not today.'

I had been sitting so long at the laptop that I had given myself a stiff neck reading everything the newspapers had written about Mattias's disappearance. Pictures from Vaikijaur were rolled out on the evening news: helicopters circling, a deserted Kvikkjokk Road. But no progress had been made by the police in their search. Susso had been down in her own flat all day but came back up in the evening. She sank to the floor with her back resting against the fridge.

'Have you heard any more?' I asked.

Susso shook her head and picked up the dog.

'They were talking to the police on the radio an hour or so ago,' she said. 'They're not looking for him any longer. Out of doors, that is. So now they're looking . . . in different ways, I suppose. I don't know.'

I took a mouthful of wine and sat there with the glass in my hand.

'And the police have phoned me,' Susso said.

'They've phoned *you*?'

'It's the photo,' she said, rubbing the back of her head against the fridge door. 'They want to talk about it. I don't know any more than that. I'll drive down to Jokkmokk tomorrow.'

'But what do they want to ask about it? And why do you have to go there? Surely they can come here? There has to be someone you can talk to here, at the police station.'

'Well, how do I know?' Susso snapped.

Susso losing her patience like that made me shut my mouth. It was clumsy of me to go on about it. Naturally, this was tough for her.

'They've set up some kind of base there,' she continued. 'Or whatever they call it. And I said I could go, it was no problem.'

She put the dog down on the floor and brushed off her trousers.

'Do they think you're involved in some way?'

'Of course they don't.'

'How do you know?'

'All they want to do is ask a few questions. I expect they want to find out what kind of person I am, spending my time photographing trolls. That's not surprising.'

'No,' I said, sighing. 'I suppose not.'

'Are you making a grotto?'

Seved peered at the boy from below, at the sliver of his withdrawn little face that could be seen between his jacket collar and fur hat.

He had climbed up onto the heap of ploughed snow that was piled up in the middle of the yard, and was standing there wearing the winter clothes that had been stored in a cardboard box ever since Seved was a boy: the black padded trousers with braces; the blue down jacket with a red and white border across the shoulders, the one Börje insisted was a snowmobile jacket. Even the hat had belonged to Seved. It was made of chocolate-brown leather lined with fur, which was tinged yellow on the ear flaps and the folded-back section above the forehead. But the boots were modern. They had Velcro fastenings at the front, and reflective strips. They were the boy's own boots.

Seved walked up the veranda steps and fetched a snow shovel. The greying wooden handle was furry with frost.

'Here,' he said, climbing up the heap of snow and hacking at it with the steel blade.

The boy took a step back, watching him with a wary but not uninterested look. His cheeks were red raw. He stuck out his tongue to lick at the clear mucus running from his nose.

'You've got to have a plan for building it,' Seved said eagerly, digging away at the snow. 'So it doesn't go wrong. Otherwise it will collapse. If you're in the cave when it collapses, you'll get trapped.' He straightened up to rest his back for a few seconds. 'That's why you have to think about it before you start. The walls have to be straight. That's very important. And you have to dig like this. Scrape away the snow to make it nice and even.'

The boy knelt on one knee, looking at the growing hole.

'And you can have windows in it,' said Seved. 'Do you want it to have windows?'

The boy nodded.

'Then we'll make some. But first we've got to dig it out properly.'

By now Seved had stepped down into the grotto opening, and from there he explained:

'You make the windows by getting water to freeze in a cake tin or a bucket. And you can put things in the water too, to make decorations in the windowpanes. I'll show you how to do it. You can put leaves in it, for example, although they'll be hard to find at this time of year. But I'm sure we'll find something else.'

To Seved's great astonishment the boy suddenly leaned forwards and grabbed hold of his arm with both mittens. The grip was surprisingly strong and Seved didn't understand what had got into him. Was it some kind of clumsy hug? But then he saw the frightened look under the furry edge of the hat and he understood why.

One of them had come out onto the porch.

It was Karats.

He stood there with his shaggy, flattened head to one side so that it would not hit the roof. His eyes were dark slits on either side of the coarse nose and his cheeks were moving as he chewed something. One of the hares was sitting at his feet like a little dog.

Seved crawled up out of the grotto and put his hand on the boy's back, pulling him close as he looked towards the immobile giant on the porch.

'It's all right,' he said. 'He won't do anything. You don't have to be afraid.'

But the boy was petrified. He refused to let go of Seved, so Seved helped him down from the pile of snow and carried him inside.

The police station in Jokkmokk was a yellow wooden two-storey building.

Susso had never been inside a police station before, never had anything to do with them, so she didn't know what to expect. The ramp leading up to the entrance had been conscientiously cleared of snow and scattered with brown swirls of sand. She opened the door and went into a reception area, where two women were busying themselves behind a glass screen. It seemed as if they were searching for something. They were looking down and did not even notice her.

Susso took off her hat and pushed her hair to one side.

'Hello,' she said. 'I'm here to meet a Lars-Göran Hannler, or I think that's what he's called.'

One of the women, who was heavily overweight and had a bleached fringe, told her to sit down and wait.

'He won't keep you long.'

Susso sat herself down on the waiting room's small sofa, which was tucked behind a fig tree taller than she was. She crammed her hat into her jacket pocket and found her stick of lip balm, which she pulled out and rubbed over her lips. They had cracked in the cold.

She wondered whether the receptionists were police officers. They did not look like police officers – at least, not the fat one. Though you could never tell.

*

Ever since Edit had phoned and told her that Mattias had disappeared, Susso had blamed herself, and nothing could persuade her otherwise. The guilt felt like a bitter grey lump inside her. However hard she tried she could not supress the thought that she had triggered all these events by driving to Vaikijaur and setting up the camera.

The photos taken by the wildlife camera had scared her. Those white eyes were aimed at her. 'It's like I've been fishing and caught something I don't want on the end of my hook,' she had said to her mother. And so it was.

Lars-Göran Hannler was wearing a light-brown corduroy jacket and dark-blue jeans which he drew up at the waist before stretching out his hand to greet her. His palm felt rough and warm. He had a suntanned face, pale probing eyes and light-grey hair in a flat side parting. On the skin beneath his shirt collar shone a slender gold chain.

'I'm glad you could come,' he said.

They walked up a staircase with framed photographs on the walls. Susso rested her hand on the bannister and studied the policeman's back. A distended pocket containing a wallet came into view occasionally in the jacket's back vent.

In silence they walked down a short corridor and rounded a corner. She glanced at the name plates placed at eye level on the doors. *Kvickström* it said on one of them, and she recalled the same name written on one of the mailboxes in Vaikijaur. Somewhere a phone was ringing. There was absolutely nothing to show that the police did their investigative work from here – or perhaps she had completely misunderstood everything and that kind of work was carried out in Luleå instead.

'This is where I live,' the police officer said as they arrived at his office.

He waved towards the chair, indicating where Susso was to sit. After sitting down she pressed her palms together and pushed them between her thighs.

Lars-Göran Hannler exchanged a few words with someone further down the corridor. 'That'll be great,' he said, before pushing the door closed and sinking down on the chair behind the desk. Susso looked at the computer. The screensaver consisted of the emblem of the Swedish police force, which was slowly rebounding from one side of the screen to another. It looked desperately unimaginative.

'As I mentioned on the phone,' Lars-Göran said, rolling the chair back a few centimetres, 'we want to know how you went about taking the photo in Edit Mickelsson's garden.'

'And as I mentioned on the phone,' she said, repeating his own words, 'it was a wildlife camera. I didn't take the picture.' She mimed taking a photograph.

The police officer regarded her for a long time. He had folded his plump arms across his chest.

'So all you did was set up the camera on Edit Mickelsson's house?'

Susso nodded.

'And you have no idea who that is in the picture?'

She shook her head.

'Obviously, if I knew I would have told you.'

The officer nodded.

'Did you ever meet Mattias?'

'No. Or rather, yes. He stood watching me once while I was

asleep. In Edit's house. But, no, I have never met him or spoken to him or anything.'

The police officer inhaled through his nostrils and cleared his throat. He placed one elbow on the back of his chair and locked his fingers together over a stomach that stretched his shirt and revealed skin in the gaps between the buttons.

'Because there is no room here for any kind of hoax, as I'm sure you understand.'

'Hoax?'

'Some internet scam . . .'

'It isn't,' she said, leaning towards him. 'It's nothing like that. It's genuine. On the level, or however you want to say it.'

All at once she felt exhausted. What did he actually want to know? She stared at the grey mottled vinyl flooring and tried to collect her thoughts.

'It's like it's unreal but . . . I don't know what to say.'

There was a long pause before the policeman spoke again. It was as if he wanted to let her sit there, squirming. Let the silence take effect. With any luck it might result in her revealing something new and useful.

'I've looked up your website, you know. Read what's on it.'

'It's only . . . a project. That's all,' she said feebly.

'And we are familiar with your maternal grandfather, Gunnar Myrén. But I have never seen this bear before. Or the troll, or whatever it might be. That's new to me.'

'We . . .' she began, but was interrupted when the door opened behind her. Instinctively she turned her head, but by that time the door had closed. She looked quizzically at the officer. His gaze was clear and unchanged.

'He was afraid,' she said hesitantly. 'Afraid of not being believed.

Because people didn't believe him. And then there's Mum. She's afraid of making herself look stupid.'

She smiled as she said this, but the police officer did not return her smile.

'And you're not?' he said.

Susso shrugged her shoulders.

'I don't care. Not as much.'

He nodded his head.

'And this is the first time you have captured something on a photograph?'

'Yes,' she replied, nodding emphatically. 'I have photos other people have taken, but they're not very good. If you have visited the website, you will have seen them already.'

He received this information with a nod, but she could not decide whether he nodded because he had seen the pictures, or whether he simply wanted to move on.

'But it's the first time I've . . . captured anything on a photo myself. I've set up the camera before but never got anything. So this is the first time.'

He watched her for a few seconds, waiting in case she had anything more to add. There was nothing. When she shut her lips and raised her eyebrows to indicate that she had finished he stood up.

'Wait a minute,' he muttered, and walked out of the room.

He returned with two other men trailing behind him. Both were in their sixties. One was short and bald, with a flattened nose, and she thought he looked like an old boxer. He was wearing a light-blue police shirt with a dark-blue tie, and a ballpoint pen was attached to the edge of his breast pocket. His name was Kjell-Åke Andersson and he told Susso that he was leading the investigation.

He spoke slowly, emphasising every syllable, and she could tell he came from Tornedalen. He pulled up a chair and sat down diagonally opposite her. His eyes were red and bloodshot, but he kept them fixed on her.

A trail of aftershave followed the second man into the room. He had a leather jacket and a white, well-trimmed moustache. Before he took his place by the window, scanning the car park and the street, he introduced himself briefly as Wikström from the county CID. The black jacket shone like the protective shell on a beetle's back, and Susso thought there was something odd about him. The jacket and the overpowering smell of aftershave did not correspond to his age.

She now had three pairs of eyes directed at her, and she did not like it. Only intermittently did she succeed in looking unconcerned. She worked her tin of snus out of her pocket but she could not bring herself to open it, and sat pressing the lid, making it creak. She was fully aware that she gave the impression of being nervous but there was nothing she could do about it.

'It is extremely rare for a child to be abducted in this way,' said Kjell-Åke ponderously. 'That's why it's hard for us to know how to go about looking for him. But we do know that every hour is vitally important now, at the beginning.'

When he had said this he fell silent, and judging from his enquiring look it was clear that Susso had to confirm that she understood. She nodded.

'For that reason,' he continued, 'it can be disastrous if the investigation is focused in the wrong direction. Even at this stage, after a few days.'

With small nods of her head Susso indicated that she understood this too.

'So before we go any further we want to be sure that this picture, the one you took with your camera, is not a hoax, or whatever you want to call it. That it's not someone dressed up, that it doesn't have anything to do with this website of yours in any way.'

She kept quiet, waiting for the rest, which was about to come.

'That is the most likely explanation we have,' he said, inhaling deeply, 'considering the person's actual appearance.'

He breathed out and gave her a meaningful look. His eyebrows were like cotton wool on a forehead crowded with lines.

'It's not a wind-up,' Susso said. 'Not as far as I know, anyway.'

'You know,' said the man by the window, craning his neck as if he had caught sight of something that interested him outside, 'we could draw a line under all this today. But if at a later stage of our investigation it emerges that you have lied, or withheld information, you could be prosecuted. For impeding police investigations. It's a crime that can result in a prison sentence. You need to be aware of that.'

'Furthermore,' interjected Kjell-Åke, crossing his arms and wrinkling his tie, 'it could have significant consequences for the boy. Today he might be alive, but in a couple of days he might not be.'

When Susso looked up she saw the detective in charge of investigations had tilted his head to one side.

'Now you wouldn't want that on your conscience, would you?' he said kindly. 'So it's best you tell us straight away whether it's an internet hoax or something.'

'I can only tell you what I've done,' Susso said, 'and all I did was set up a camera at Edit's house.'

Wikström had picked up his mobile, and an unhappy look

spread over Kjell-Åke's face. It was as if he pitied her for not fully understanding the implication of what he had said.

She shrugged her shoulders.

'I don't know what else I can say,' she said. 'Perhaps it was a stupid thing to do. But all I did was set up the camera. I don't know any more about the man in the photo than you do. Believe me, on my life.'

'Right,' said Wikström, snapping his mobile shut.

'Yes, let's give them that,' said Kjell-Åke, pushing his fists into his thighs and straightening his back as if it was aching.

'Give them that?' she said. 'What does that mean?'

'Give it to the media.'

Susso's head started to spin.

'But what if he hasn't done anything?' she said. 'What if it's just a coincidence that he was at Edit's house. If he hasn't done anything . . .'

'Then of course we will want to *know* that,' said Kjell-Åke.

From a small packet he shook out a piece of chewing gum and slid it between his lips. Susso smelled the waft of mint that emerged from his mouth.

'So we can exclude him from the investigation.'

Susso's face took a direct hit from the cold as she came out of the police station. Darkness had settled over the white rooftops. It felt as if she had been sitting in Hannler's office for hours. An elderly woman on a kick sledge loaded with shopping glided past on silent runners.

The car's windscreen had iced over, so she had to use the scraper. Her fingers were stinging with the cold because her gloves were on the seat inside the car, pressed together in prayer.

Slowly she drove along the main road, uncertain which direction to take. She ought to eat but she wasn't hungry. She didn't feel sick but something was wrong. There were not many people out and few cars, the occasional pair of headlights driving past. Between the buildings hung strings of lights like bead necklaces against the frozen sky. She picked up her mobile and held it to her ear for a moment before ringing her mother.

'TV?' said Gudrun.

'Yes.'

'When?'

'Don't know. As soon as possible, I guess. I don't know when it's on.'

'But will they say anything? About Dad, I mean? And the website?'

'I find that hard to believe. That can't be relevant, surely.'

'And the newspaper too. Isn't that what you said?'

'Yes.'

'Oh Lord . . .'

Gudrun went silent for a moment, but then she said:

'What does Edit say?'

Susso held the phone tight between her ear and her shoulder so that she could change gear without letting go of the steering wheel.

'I'm going to drive there now,' she said. 'So she doesn't know anything yet.'

It felt hard tapping in the number: Susso had not spoken to Edit since she had phoned to say Mattias had disappeared. She had told Susso that he had come to see her even though he was not supposed to. When Mattias had knocked on the door she had phoned Per-Erik's mobile and told him that the boy was with her. She had given him some juice and then he had left for home. But he never reached home.

She rang Edit, who was at Carina and Per-Erik's house. They said she was welcome to drop by if she wanted to. Even though she was scared at the thought of seeing Mattias's parents, she said she would come. She could not pass Vaikijaur without looking in.

The Mickelsson family lived in an ochre-painted house on the north side of the road, a few hundred metres from Edit's house. A rope of lights circled a flagpole, making the pole itself invisible. All that could be seen was a glowing strand spiralling up into the twilight.

Leaning against the garage wall was a metal snow shovel, and the driveway was scraped clean. When Susso had parked the car and slammed the door shut she thought she heard someone scream far away. She held her breath and stood completely still so that the soles of her shoes would not make the snow underfoot creak. A heat pump hummed behind the house, but otherwise there was not a sound in the white landscape. She looked along the road, mainly to see for herself where it must have happened. Somewhere behind those walls of ploughed snow.

Per-Erik was not at home when Susso arrived, and she was grateful for that. She had not forgotten his behaviour. Or his hostile expression.

Carina Mickelsson was sitting in a corner sofa next to Edit, who had a shawl wrapped around her shoulders. Susso had imagined that Carina's face would be red and swollen from crying, but she looked composed. Her hair was almost black and she had scraped it back in an untidy ponytail at the nape of her neck. She looked as if she was concentrating intently on something – holding back the tears, perhaps. She was wearing a burgundy hooded sweatshirt with the cuffs pulled over her hands. Her arms were folded. She immediately began questioning Susso about the photo. Susso answered as best she could. She did not take off her outer clothes, not wanting to barge in on their grief.

When she explained that the photo might be shown on television Edit broke out of her immobilised state and reached for her mug on the glass-topped table.

'It might just be a coincidence that he was here a few days before . . . before it happened,' said Susso. 'But I don't think they have anything else to go on. Not at present.'

'It's no coincidence,' Carina said. 'Of course it's him.'

Susso was quiet. She nodded guardedly and looked around the room. The television was on with the sound turned down.

'I'm so glad you set up that camera,' said Carina, looking at Susso. She had stern grey eyes and thin pencilled eyebrows. 'Otherwise he would be lost without trace,' she went on. 'Disappeared into thin air. Now at least they've got something to go on. And that's thanks to you.'

'I've been feeling it must be my fault,' said Susso softly, dropping onto the armrest of the sofa, which creaked under her weight.

Carina was not listening. She was talking continuously.

'I simply cannot work out why that revolting little object has taken him,' Carina said. It sounded as if she was about to start crying, but she held the tears back. 'I don't understand *why*. Why Mattias?'

The wretchedness in Carina's eyes receded suddenly, as if something had occurred to her.

'Perhaps he hasn't got any children of his own,' she said, 'and he wants Matti to be his child. There are people who do that, aren't there? People who haven't got any children of their own. Who take children. People who are kind. Who don't mean to harm them.'

She talked hurriedly, looking from Edit to Susso.

Edit was looking down, her eyelids swollen, but Susso nodded in agreement. She tried giving an encouraging smile.

Squashed behind the television was the Christmas tree, shining brightly. There were a few jagged cut-out paper decorations hanging on it, strewn with too many gold sequins. There was a framed photograph of Mattias standing on the wall unit, the same picture that had been in the newspaper.

The brown hair parted in the middle, flopping down each side; the big eyes with small folds underneath. There was a trace of gleaming mucus running from his little nose. They could have wiped his nose before taking the picture, Susso thought. He had an identity tag around his neck, a shining silver rectangle which lay outside his Spiderman sweatshirt. She was about to ask if Mattias was wearing the tag when he disappeared, but said nothing because she thought it might come out wrong.

IS THIS THE MAN WHO TOOK MATTIAS?

Seved recognised the little man immediately.

He was the one who had been standing on the roof of Torsten's barn and had stared at him from the digger bucket. The one Börje had called a nosy little bugger.

'What's this . . .?'

'Don't you recognise him?' asked Börje. 'It's Jirvin. We saw him.'

'But why is his picture here? What's he done?'

He skimmed through the article. It described how the police suspected the person in the photograph of being connected with the kidnapping of four-year-old Mattias Mickelsson. Anyone with information about the identity of the man was requested to contact the police without delay.

'But where does that picture come from? Who's taken it? Why?'

Börje shrugged.

'It was probably taken outside the boy's house.'

'But what was he doing there?'

'They don't know.'

'And what does Torsten say? Have you asked him?'

'Asked?'

Börje sneered and raised his voice as he repeated:

'Asked? Do you think you can get any kind of information out of that man?'

'Yes, but this is serious,' said Seved. 'What if someone has seen him up at Torsten's? Or in the area? It's not completely out of the question, all the years he's lived there.'

Börje nodded.

'You're telling me it's serious. Damned serious.'

He dropped into a chair and after a short silence said:

'Lennart wants us to move him.'

Seved looked up from the newspaper.

'Mattias?'

'No, the little old man. We've got to drive up there and fetch him. He'll have to live here for a while until all this fuss about the boy has died down.'

'But why? There's no chance . . .'

'He doesn't know people are looking for him,' Börje said in a low voice. 'Someone might catch sight of him up there. If we're really unlucky, the police will get wind of it. Torsten doesn't want a visit from the cops.'

He cleared his throat before continuing:

'We'll have to try and get hold of as many of those little shape-shifters as we can today because Torsten wants them back. He goes on about it non-stop, so I thought the boy could help out. It'll be quicker that way. And it's good if he stays in there. Let him keep that little one if he wants to, but all the others have got to go back. You can drive up with them. I don't feel up to it. You'll have to go.'

Seved nodded.

'I haven't repaired the window on the Isuzu yet, so you'll have to take Lennart's car. He's coming here this evening.'

Torbjörn stood holding the coffee-filled glasses, glaring at the sofa. Three girls had taken the place where he and Susso always sat. Between them glowed the display of a mobile phone. Their hair fell into the fur-trimmed hoods of their jackets in glossy coils. They seemed to pick up on Torbjörn's expression, though, because all of a sudden they gathered together their belongings and stood up.

When they had left Torbjörn put the glasses down on the table, removed his jacket, threw it onto the sofa and unwound his military-green knitted scarf.

Susso checked her pockets for her mobile before hanging her jacket on the back of a chair and pulling the phone out. She sat down and brought the hot coffee to her lips.

As Torbjörn settled into the sofa, moving to the corner where he always sat, where the dip in the seat cushion was shaped to fit his bony backside precisely, he knocked against the unsteady table with his knee, spilling some coffee.

'Do you know who Mattias Alkberg is?' he asked, lifting up the glass that was dripping brown milky froth. 'You know, the singer in the Bear Quartet?'

Susso nodded and then shrugged.

'Well, I know his name, but I don't know who he is,' she said.

'I got to know him when I lived in Luleå and we keep in touch.

I spoke to him yesterday and he said he knows a guy in Jokkmokk called Magnus. Magnus Ekelund. And he told Mattias that his mum knows who that dwarf is – or at least where he lives. That everyone down there knows.'

'Seriously?'

Torbjörn nodded.

'They reckon there's some place down there that's completely bloody mental. Some sect or whatever.'

'And the Vaikijaur man lives there?'

'That's what they're saying,' he replied, drinking his coffee.

'Well then, surely someone's phoned the police and told them?'

Torbjörn shook his head.

'That's the thing. It doesn't look as if anyone has. Mattias said that when things like this happen – you know, something nasty like this – people in general always assume that someone else has already done what they should be doing themselves. And I think he's right. But he didn't know for sure.'

'What else did he say? How far from Vaikijaur is it?'

'I don't know,' said Torbjörn. 'But we could drive down there, if you want, and talk to Magnus's mum, because she's the one who knows. I need to go to Gällivare anyway, so we can do it at the same time.'

Susso stared blankly ahead for a few moments before nodding.

'Have you heard any more?' Torbjörn asked. 'From the police?'

She shrugged.

'I don't know any more than anyone else.'

'I mean, because it's your photo.'

She leaned forwards, stirring with the long spoon.

'I haven't spoken to them since I was there for questioning. Or whatever you want to call it.'

She sighed before continuing:

'I'm torn, really. If he is mixed up in it, then it's good I got a picture of him, no question. But if he *isn't* involved, then the picture has only made things harder for the police. They might be spending time looking for him when they should be looking elsewhere.'

'Of course he's involved,' Torbjörn said. 'He has to be.'

Susso shrugged.

'It's just such a massive responsibility. It feels like it all depends on me.'

'It's not like that,' said Torbjörn. 'They were the ones who wanted to have the photo, weren't they?'

'Yes, I know, but . . . everything got so serious all of a sudden.'

'Do you regret going down there? Putting up the camera?'

'Yes,' she said, nodding. 'At times I do.'

'Then don't think like that. Think instead that if it wasn't for you and your photo, then the police would have sod all to go on.'

They stayed until the place closed, and afterwards stood in their creaking boots under a street light outside the cafe. Light streamed down from a couple of globe-shaped lamps suspended from iron hooks at the top of the post. Wreaths of fragile icicles had formed around the metal fittings.

The swishing sound of ski trousers came down the hill. A man and a woman strode past, their arms swinging. The woman was wearing a zigzag-patterned ski hat, and the man a fleece headband. Through the cloud that billowed from her mouth Susso watched as the couple disappeared beyond the town hall. She was freezing cold and moved reluctantly. In the icy air her face had set to a mask. Her cheeks felt stretched tight.

'It's so cold,' she said, rocking up and down on her heels.

Torbjörn sniffed and nodded.

They began to walk. Neither of them wanted to be the one to lead, or perhaps neither of them wanted to decide how fast they should walk. Slowly they moved towards Meschplan and the shops that surrounded it. As they crossed the square Susso threw a melancholy look at her own dark shop window. It was as if the grouse and the dolls and the moose and the bears behind the glass were watching her pass. She always felt like that.

'What do you want to do?' asked Torbjörn, as they reached Susso's front entrance and stood there in the darkness. 'Shall we go tomorrow?'

'To Jokkmokk?'

He had tucked his chin into his scarf, and he nodded.

'Okay,' she said. 'What time will you be here?'

'Can we take your car?'

'Sure. If you pay for the petrol.'

He tugged at the padlock a couple of times before returning to the car and slumping down behind the wheel. He gazed at the dashboard, stupefied. Why the hell had they not told him the barrier would be locked? It had to be at least two kilometres up to the farmhouse from the barrier, and the surface was icy. Worse than that, it was cold out. He couldn't very well slither all the way up carrying the box of shapeshifters and then drag the little man back behind him – what would that look like?

Then it struck him that this was Lennart's car. The key might be inside. He leaned across, opened the glove compartment and pulled out ice scrapers, papers and the instruction manual. He stretched out across the seats, put his hand into the passenger-door compartment and found a key ring. Ten keys threaded onto a length of twisted steel wire. Of course. Lennart would never get out himself and unlock the barrier. That is what he had Jola for.

He was lucky. There was only one key that matched the manufacturer's name engraved on the padlock.

He had to kneel for a long time on the icy crust of the road, blowing on the frozen steel, before he dared to grab hold of the key and turn it all the way.

As he pulled the key from the lock he noticed it had buckled. That was bad. He pulled on his gloves and moved the creaking barrier aside. He decided to leave the barrier open because he did not want to risk not being able to get out – *that* would be really worrying. Was it possible to turn the Merc on this road now that the ploughed ridges of snow had made it narrower? It was doubtful. He visualised himself reversing from the house with that disgusting little man sitting on the rear seat. He did not even want to think what that would be like.

He drove a few metres before flooring the brake pedal – it was as if his foot had thought for him. He flung open the door and leapt out, swung the barrier back across the road and replaced the padlock without locking it.

The sound of hoarse, agitated barking broke through the noise of the engine, and soon he could make out the light from the porch lamp, disappearing and reappearing between the fir trees. As he swung into the yard he glanced up at the ridge of the barn roof, but of course the little old man was not up there.

They were sitting at the kitchen table, the three of them: Torsten, Patrik and Bodil. But there was no sign of the wife, Elna. Torsten had pushed the metal frames of his glasses down the bridge of his nose. He was the only one to look at Seved.

'Did you lock the barrier?' he asked. Seved nodded. He would soon be leaving. They would never know.

'Do you want coffee? Bodil, put the coffee on.'

He did not seem at all angry, so it was likely he knew nothing about the car. Maybe he had not seen the paper? Seved stood motionless for a while, not knowing whether to hang up his jacket or not: he wanted to get away as quickly as possible.

Bodil had moved silently towards the corner of the kitchen, where the coffee machine was plugged into an extension lead. Her dark-blonde plaits were fastened to her head in two loops which moved when she reached up to get the tin of coffee from the cupboard.

The floor tiles creaked behind Seved, who turned and moved aside to make room for Elna to get past.

'There's some in the thermos,' she said.

'We want fresh coffee,' Torsten said, sitting up straight and casting an enquiring glance at Elna, who sat down at the back of the kitchen on a sofa with tartan cushions.

He pulled out a chair and sat opposite Patrik, who was resting his elbows on the table and looking out of the window, where it was slowly getting light. He was wearing a black cap with something written on it in small lettering. On the windowsill was a green ceramic plant pot. Its uneven rim made it look handmade. There was nothing in it.

'Perhaps you're hungry. Are you hungry?' Torsten asked. Seved shook his head.

'No, I'm all right.'

'What about the little fellers?' Torsten asked. He reached out and chose a thin slice of crispbread from the basket on the table. 'You've got them with you?'

He spread a thick layer of butter on the slice and took a bite. Crumbs rained down on the tabletop, and he brushed them aside.

Seved nodded.

'Well, five or six, at least. Lennart was going to bring the rest.'

'Where are they then? Did you leave them in the hall?'

'They're on the back seat of the car.'

The old man stared at Seved, his eyes round and blue.

'Have you left them in the *car*? It's thirty below out there! They'll freeze.'

'Well, shall I bring them in here? Is that okay?'

'No!' shouted Elna from the sofa. 'You'll have to put them in the garage. It's been so quiet and peaceful in here. And the floors are clean for once.'

Torsten's shoulders dropped. He stroked the table with his little finger, moving the crumbs, gathering them in a pile.

'Bring the box in,' he said.

Seved stood in the hall. The cold air was wrapped like a membrane around the box and it was worryingly quiet inside. He tried shaking the box a little as he moved his ear towards it. A very faint, high-pitched sound came from inside.

'Shall I leave it here then?' he called.

'You can bring it in,' Torsten answered, putting down his coffee cup with a clink. 'I want to see which ones you've brought with you.'

Seved walked into the kitchen and after Torsten had pushed the bread basket and the linen tablecloth aside, he placed the box on the table.

'There, there,' said the old man. His voice had an odd tremble as he opened the small metal tabs that kept the lid in place. 'Here we are. Calm down. You're home now. Back home again.' He opened the lid and looked down into the box.

They hissed and chirped like hungry baby birds in a nest.

'It's only the shrews,' he said. His fist rummaged about in the straw. 'And two wood mice,' he added.

'It's so hard getting hold of them all,' said Seved, pushing his hands into his jeans pockets. 'They didn't all want to be together.'

'You have to have more boxes,' said Patrik. 'It works better that way.'

'And this one is dead,' said Torsten, holding up a tiny shrew by its tail. 'Seved, this isn't the right way to do it!'

'Watch out,' said Patrik and Bodil simultaneously, and Bodil pointed to the tail, which was so damaged in places it was barely in one piece.

Elna had hurriedly opened the cupboard under the sink. She took out the green metal dustpan and brush, which she conveniently held out, but Torsten shook his head.

The shrew lay in his broad calloused hand and he prodded it with his index finger, rolling the little body over to examine it. Its eyes glittered, its mouth was wide open in surprise, and on its dark-brown, slender back there was a shiny stripe, as if the fur was damp.

'We were in a hurry, that's all,' Seved said. 'We might have put it in there even though it didn't want to. It just happened.'

'"Just happened",' said Torsten, looking at the shrew with heavy, half-closed eyes. 'It's dead. It could be twice as old as you, Seved, and now it's *dead*. What have you got to say to that?'

There was sorrow in his voice.

'I don't know what to say. It's a pity.'

'"A pity",' repeated Torsten. 'Didn't I say that if you borrowed the creatures, you had to take care not to throw them in together on long journeys? I was very clear on that point.'

'I know,' said Seved. 'We didn't think. Sorry.'

Sorry? He heard how stupid that sounded and immediately regretted saying it. To erase the feeble word that hovered over the kitchen table he said:

'I'm sure Lennart can compensate you.'

'What do you mean?' asked Torsten, glowering at him. He banged his elbows hard on the table as he leaned forwards.

'With money?'

'Yes. I suppose so.'

'I don't want any money,' muttered the old man, shaking his head from side to side as if to demonstrate he wanted nothing to do with the idea. 'What he can do instead is bring us more little creatures. If he's got any to spare. You can tell him that from me!'

Seved nodded, knowing that was one message he would not be passing on; at the same time, he knew that Torsten was only being sarcastic.

'And now you're going to take Jirvin from us as well?'

Torsten had closed the lid of the box, but his hands were still resting on it.

'Only for a while,' Seved said. 'Until everything's calmed down.'

'Until it's calmed down,' muttered Torsten. 'We'll just have to wait and see how that turns out then, won't we?'

They had decided to meet Magnus Ekelund at a pizzeria called Opera in central Jokkmokk. A dump, according to Torbjörn, who had been there once and knew how to find it. They left the car in a car park across the street and walked quickly through the snowfall and into the warmth.

Magnus sat in a far corner with his back to a plastic Christmas tree, reading an evening paper. There was a pizza in front of him and his hand was wrapped around a half-empty glass of beer. He was younger than Susso had expected: not yet twenty, she guessed. And short, no taller than she was. That was obvious even though he remained seated. Lap blood, she thought. Strands of hair hung down over his square face, and on the lapels of his grey military jacket with its outsized insignia was a cluster of badges: KISS, she read on one. RAMONES. Wrapped around the fingers of his left hand were white plasters, which she thought strange. Was that because he played guitar? He seemed to have finished with the pizza. The two pineapple rings and the slivers of ham looked colourless, as if they had been under water.

'Pizza for breakfast?' said Torbjörn, pulling out a chair.

'Too right, man,' said Magnus, grinning widely. 'So fucking rock and roll, that's me.'

He had a surprisingly deep voice.

'I know what you're thinking,' he said, grinning again. 'But allow me to say I haven't got a hangover, I'm just wiped out. Stayed up far too late. Don't even know if I went to bed.'

Susso walked over to the counter and the globe-like coffee jugs. There were fifty-öre coins welded to the hotplate and she wondered what the coffee would taste like. Cat piss, probably. The man by the till waved his hand: she could help herself.

She put the cups on a tray and carried them to the table.

'I didn't know if you wanted milk,' she said. Magnus shook his head.

'Black,' he said. 'Black, like my heart.' He gave a hoarse little laugh. It was as if he was incapable of being serious for any length of time, and Susso wondered whether what he had said about the Vaikijaur man and the sect was some kind of joke. What if Torbjörn had misunderstood everything?

'Magnus,' she said, 'tell me again. Do you know anything about the Vaikijaur man, who he is or where he lives?'

'Not me,' he said, shaking his head. 'Mum. She says he lives out Kvikkjokk way. With the Laestadians.'

'Whereabouts?'

He shrugged.

'If you want to know exactly, you'll have to ask my mum,' he said. 'She's shopping in ICA but she'll be here soon.'

Jirvin had come out of the barn and was standing there in his mildew-green jacket, as small as a child. Elna slid the bar into place behind him and then hurried back across the yard. Before she went into the house she said softly to Seved:

'It's not a good idea to talk to him.'

Talk to him? What the hell would he talk to *him* about? The very idea brought on a shudder that quickly spread through his body. Driving him all the way down to Jillesnåle would be absolute torture.

The little old man approached the car slowly, stopping often. It looked as if he was considering turning back to the barn. His yellow, deep-set eyes could barely be seen below the rim of his hood, which was drawn in tight. He was wearing snowjoggers on his feet. They were a bad fit.

The dogs were barking frantically and continuously. Seved was sure it was because of him and the little old man. But the dogs at home did not usually bark like that. Börje must have better control over them. It was hardly because their dogs were more used to the shapeshifters. He had no idea how many of them were in Hybblet, but he was sure there were more here at Torsten's. If you counted them, that is. Except they would not let themselves be counted. He and Signe had tried once but had given up.

He held the door open for the little man, who climbed up onto the seat without looking at him. He curled up in the furthest corner, twisted his head and looked towards the dog enclosure. I expect he is sad, thought Seved, and slammed the door shut. Who knew how long he had been here? How old was the farm? Two hundred years, certainly – agricultural buildings this far west of the cultivation boundary were usually pretty ancient. The old house did not even have exterior cladding and the barn's guttering was made of wood.

He knew the shapeshifters disliked being moved. They attach themselves to places, Börje said, not to people. Maybe he had been there for *generations*? Seen Torsten grow up, and perhaps Torsten's father. And grandfather.

Of course it was painful for him.

To the extent he could feel emotional pain, that is. Ejvor had frequently told him he should not allow himself to be fooled. They have faces, but that is all. Any other human attribute you think you can see comes from your own imagination.

Suddenly Patrik came running out onto the veranda and leaned over the railing.

'It's the police!' he shouted.

Instantly Torsten was there with his binoculars. 'You didn't lock the barrier behind you!'

Seved felt his stomach sink into a gaping hole. His mouth quickly filled with saliva and he swallowed, uncertain what to do next. Now he really had dropped them in it. He did not dare think of the consequences. He let go of the car door handle and cast an indecisive glance at the veranda, but Torsten was no longer there. Only Patrik stood there, with his hand held against the peak of his cap. He looked scared, like a child. Defeated and pale, with no trace of his arrogant, squinting gaze.

'Patrik!' There was a roar from the interior of the house, and the next instant Patrik had run inside. Then Torsten came out. He had pulled on a large fur hat and Bodil was behind him, swathed in a dense, grey woollen coat.

'Quiet!' Torsten yelled at the dogs, who obeyed instantly. It was like flipping a switch.

The police car rolled into the yard.

Behind the wheel was a man in uniform, and beside him a white-haired man in an unbuttoned down jacket bisected by the black strip of the seat belt. The car came to a halt and Seved could see that both men were talking. Then they drove up slowly, stopping as close to the Merc as they could possibly get.

'This is Anette,' said Magnus with a grin. 'My mum.'

Susso stood up and took Anette's hand. Her eyes shone blue behind her glasses and her blonde hair was cut to ear-lobe level and combed in a side parting. She had on a low-cut top in a flimsy dark-grey fabric. On the front a black tree spread its branches across her chest, where a silver pendant in the form of a snake was hanging. The chain ran right through the snake's head.

Anette had not contacted the police, but she was absolutely sure they knew. There might not have been many who had seen the dwarf with their own eyes, but after his photograph had been in the newspaper people had started to talk. And they all seemed to know where he belonged: a few miles west, in the direction of Sarek, on a farm.

'Are they Laestadians?' Susso asked. Anette nodded.

'The silent kind,' she said. 'If you know what I mean.'

'Where do they live?' Susso asked.

Anette unfolded the map she had brought with her. Leaning over the vast area she ran her finger along the lakes which fed the river, and carried on up in a northwesterly direction.

'Here,' she said. 'It's up here, along this road. But as I say, I'm fairly sure the police already know he lives up here.'

'Årrenjarka,' Susso read.

'Årre-njarka,' Anette said. '"*Njarka*" means promontory in the

Sami language. I'm not sure I know what "*Årre*" means.'

'It's maybe twenty kilometres from Vaikijaur,' said Susso, looking at Torbjörn.

'Well, you might as well go there and have a look,' said Magnus. 'Do a bit of spying.'

'I wouldn't do that,' Anette said, giving her son a reprimanding look. He rolled his eyes.

'They could easily shoot at you,' she went on. 'I remember that from when I was a child. There was someone from school who had been chased off their land, and they had fired a rifle at him. It might only be gossip, but I wouldn't go snooping around up there. Leave that to the police.'

Ivan Wikström was the name of the plain-clothes police officer. He was a detective chief inspector with the local CID. His colleague's name was Police Constable Tony Kunosson.

Seved tried to smile but his face was not complying, as if it had set rigid from the fear that had flooded his body like an icy fluid. The only thing he managed to force out was a parody of a smile that was hard to remove afterwards. He wanted to wipe it off with his hand.

'And you are?' said Wikström.

'I . . . I don't live here,' mumbled Seved. 'I'm only visiting.'

'But you have a name?' the chief inspector said, leaning closer. Seved nodded.

'Jola,' he said.

Jola? He had no idea why he had said that. How stupid. He noticed straight away that the lie only heightened his nervousness. What was he going to do if they asked about Jirvin? If he lied and then they caught sight of him sitting in the car, that would be it. What the hell should he do?

His eyes flitted about, seeking support from Torsten, whose face had twisted into a hard expression, the downturned corners of his mouth framing his jutting chin. To prevent the detective chief inspector's gaze coming anywhere near the old man in the back seat, Seved glided one step sideways to hide him from view.

'Are you Holmbom?' Wikström asked, turning to Torsten, who nodded. His eyes had narrowed to thin lines under the fluffy rim of his fur hat.

'Can we be of assistance in any way?'

The chief inspector put his hand inside his jacket and pulled out a folded sheet of paper.

'How many people live here?' he asked. He turned round, running his eyes over the barn, the garage, the dog enclosure, the house and the outhouses among the pines.

'Me and my wife, and our two children.'

'No one else?'

Torsten shook his head.

Wikström unfolded the piece of paper, which he showed first to Torsten and then to Bodil, who craned her neck in curiosity.

'See him?' he said. 'Do you know who it is?'

Seved could not see what was on the paper, but he knew only too well. Once again the saliva welled up in his mouth and he made an effort not to swallow in case the uniformed constable standing next to him heard. He looked down at the snow, blinked and raised his eyes slightly, only to see the policeman's heavily weighted belt: radio, a small torch, handcuffs and the butt of a revolver, black and shiny inside its holster.

'Don't recognise him,' Torsten said convincingly.

'Isn't that him?' asked Bodil in an unassuming voice. She tucked in the lock of hair that had fallen from her hood. 'The one in the paper?'

'So you read the papers, do you?' said Wikström.

Bodil looked quickly at her father, whose expression did not change.

'Yes,' she said quietly. 'I do. Sometimes.'

'And why wouldn't we read the papers?' said Torsten loudly.

Wikström shrugged his shoulders and folded the sheet of paper.

'I was only thinking of the isolation. Your self-imposed isolation. That you avoid keeping up with the news.'

'We don't,' Torsten replied. 'We keep up as well as we can.'

After saying this he gave a yellow smile.

'And I see you have curtains,' said Wikström, nodding towards the window.

'Are you harassing us?' said Bodil, glaring at him. The fierceness of her question and her hostility made her eyes glitter, and Wikström raised his eyebrows. The words came like pistol shots from her mouth:

'We haven't seen him. We don't know who he is. So you can leave now.'

'Aren't you curious about why we're looking for him?' he asked.

Torsten was quiet for a long time, thinking.

'We know why,' he said eventually. 'We've read about it in the newspaper. He's taken some lad.'

'You didn't recognise him, you said.'

'That's not what I said. I said I didn't know who it was.'

'No,' answered Wikström, smiling. 'You said: "Don't recognise him."'

'But that's what I meant!'

Wikström nodded. He took in a deep breath and puffed out his mouth. Then he turned suddenly, released the air and held up the photograph for Seved to see.

'Do you know who this is then, Jola?'

Seved knew that he should go closer in order to give a plausible answer, but he dared not move from the car window that he was obscuring with his body, so he bent forwards slightly and squinted, and then he shook his head.

'I've also seen him in the paper. And I don't know who he is either.'

Clearly he leaned too far forwards because a second later he heard the police constable's voice behind him.

'Ivan . . .'

Tony Kunosson was leaning forwards with his hand on his belt, looking through the rear window, and when he made eye contact with DCI Wikström he nodded towards the car. This took place directly in front of Seved, and there was nothing he could do except step aside. He wanted to run but realised that would be pathetic.

With his head to one side and a deep line etched between his eyebrows, Ivan Wikström walked towards the car, and when he saw who was sitting inside he stroked his moustache with his thumb, reflectively. He showed no sign of surprise.

He thought for a while before grabbing hold of the handle and slowly opening the car door. The little man was sitting stock still inside, staring straight ahead. Seved looked at Torsten, but he seemed to be lost in thought. He was standing with a blank look on his face.

With one hand on the car roof Wikström leaned inside the car and almost shouted:

'Hello. Can I have a chat with you?'

There was no answer, obviously. Jirvin gave no indication whatsoever that the policeman was even talking to him.

'Hello?'

When the little man continued to ignore him, Wikström climbed into the car and sat down on the back seat, but in a flash the little man reached out, took hold of the handle on his side and after a moment's fumbling got the door open and slipped out.

He headed towards the barn, but Tony Kunosson had already rounded the car and blocked his path, so the old man hurried off to the garage instead. He slithered about in his cumbersome boots. The policeman ran so fast his equipment rattled, but by the time he reached the garage the old man had opened the door, shut it and locked it behind him. Kunosson tugged at the handle and battered on the door with his fist.

'Open up!' he shouted.

Wikström had been calmly watching the chase from inside the car, but now he stepped out.

'Give me the key to the garage,' he said, reaching out his hand to Torsten, who began searching his fur coat.

'I'm not sure exactly where it is . . .'

This was too much for the detective chief inspector. Without waiting a second longer he walked over to the patrol car, opened the boot, took out a crowbar and walked briskly off towards the garage.

There was a crash from the direction of the garage as Wikström started to break open the door. The noise was immediately picked up by the dogs and they started leaping around inside the wire netting. A small brown Spitz barked crazily as it backed away, as if afraid of its own barking, but the other dogs kept quiet. The largest, a shaggy grey Siberian with heavy paws and clear shining eyes, lay down with its tongue hanging out, seemingly watching the policeman with interest. Wikström worked steadily and methodically. From time to time he threw broken shards of wood aside.

Moments after he had broken open the door and entered the garage with the crowbar in his hands, something red slipped out into the yard. Seved glanced at Tony Kunosson as he caught sight of the fox running towards the barn, where it sat down outside the door, elegantly sweeping its bushy tail over its paws, concealing them. The policeman's eyebrows creased and thickened, but that was all.

There was a clatter from the garage. It sounded as if a metal can had fallen to the floor, but it took almost a minute for Wikström to reappear. He was still holding the crowbar.

'I can't find him!' he shouted loudly, and it was clear from his voice that he could not help finding it comical in some way. 'There was only a blasted fox in there!'

Kunosson jogged across the yard and took over the search while Wikström stood thinking, the crowbar resting on his shoulder. He was keen to get round to the far side of the garage but the snow was almost up to the guttering, which made things difficult for him. He tested the snowdrift by stepping upon it but regretted it almost immediately and took a few paces back instead, to see what it looked like on the roof. Then he walked to the other side, but the snow was just as deep there.

Torsten was holding his gloves under his arm as he got out his snus tin and rapped it with his knuckles. He twisted off the lid, inserted a pouch under his lip, then snapped the lid back on and glanced sideways at Seved. He had pulled his hat so far down that his eyes were shaded, but Seved could see the trace of a grin among the wrinkles.

Seved felt momentarily relieved. Torsten had experienced this before. But then he remembered that the policemen had actually *seen* the little man in his car, and a knot formed in his stomach again. There was no way out.

Wikström came walking towards him, but then he stopped and pointed over his shoulder with the crowbar.

'Is the fox tame?' he asked.

'Yes,' replied Torsten. 'You could say that.'

'You know it can infect the dogs if it's got scabies?'

'That's kind of why we keep it in there. In the garage.'

It was clear from Wikström's expression that he knew this was a lie, and a contemptuous lie at that, but he kept quiet and carried on walking to the patrol car. He replaced the crowbar in the boot and slammed it shut.

On his way back he took out his mobile, and when Torsten saw the phone in his hand he turned away quickly to face the house. Then he approached the police officer, holding up the palms of his hand in a gesture to suggest there was no hurry.

'No need for you to phone until we have discussed this properly,' he said. 'To make sure we understand each other.'

'I'm waiting,' Wikström said, lowering the hand holding the mobile.

'It was unfortunate', said Torsten, 'that he was photographed, and he had no business being near that old lady. But he's not quite right in the head and we wanted to protect him. That's why we . . . we were less than truthful when you asked us about him. Because we didn't want him to get into any trouble. But I can guarantee he had nothing to do with the disappearance of that lad. It's all an unfortunate coincidence.'

By this time Torsten had come so close to the officer that his palms were almost touching him, and the policeman took a small step backwards.

Wikström nodded at Torsten's explanation. It looked as if he actually believed it.

'But where is he now?' he asked. Torsten stroked the stubble on his chin.

'Oh, he has his hiding places, that one, so I don't actually know.'

'He ran into the garage and he's not there now. I want you to tell me where he went.'

'He's little, you know. And a genius at hiding.'

There was the sound of rapid footsteps in the snow and Kunosson came running up. In his hand he was holding a bundle, which he held out to Wikström. It consisted of the old man's anorak, hat and boots, and the constable said he had found them shoved in a box just inside the door.

Wikström studied the clothes carefully. He straightened his glasses and looked at his colleague and then back at the clothes, before lifting his eyes to the garage.

'Now would you please do us a favour and tell us where he went,' he said.

Torsten burst out laughing, and it was so unexpected and so loud that Tony Kunosson instantly took a step backwards and put his hand to his hip where the pistol was hanging.

But all Torsten could do was shake his head.

'Come with me,' he said, still laughing. 'I'll show you something.'

Elna had come out onto the veranda, holding the wooden box in her outstretched arms. The lower edge rested against her thigh to help her bear the weight. She had not put on any old-fashioned clothes, and Seved could not understand why. Did she want no part in Torsten's Laestadian performance? Did she think it was unnecessary?

Torsten took the box and carried it over to the policemen. He put it down gently in the snow at their feet.

'Now, gentlemen,' he said, 'let me show you what we have here.' And with that he opened the lid.

After Magnus and his mother had left, Susso and Torbjörn stayed a while longer at the table in the flashing glow of the Christmas-tree lights. The map was spread out, and Susso looked at it as she ate the remains of the pizza.

'They must have been there, don't you think?' she said.

'Yes, you'd think so,' replied Torbjörn. 'If it's as well known as Anette says.'

'But I don't understand why Edit and Mattias's parents haven't heard anything about it. They ought to be told, if anyone.'

'Have you spoken to them then?'

Susso shook her head and leaned back.

'Not for a while,' she sighed. 'But I think Edit would phone me straight away if they found out anything. Even before Mattias disappeared she was asking people if they knew who was running about on her land. And no one knew anything. Weird, isn't it?'

Torbjörn nodded into his coffee cup.

'Perhaps you should talk to her?'

'We could drop in on our way past,' said Susso quietly.

'Is it difficult?' he asked. 'Talking to her?'

She shrugged her shoulders, and Torbjörn went on:

'You know he's dead, don't you?'

She looked up.

'No one knows that for sure!'

'No kid goes missing for this long and comes back alive.'

'It's happened before.'

'Has it?'

'Steven Stayner,' she said. 'He was kidnapped in the States in the early seventies, and he came back after seven years. Fusako Sano was a Japanese girl who was trapped in a flat for ten years with a psycho. And what about Dutroux, that Belgian – two of those girls he kidnapped came out of it alive. And there are even more children who have come back.'

'But it's bloody unusual,' Torbjörn said.

'It's also bloody unusual for a child to be kidnapped by a person completely unknown to them.'

'Yes, you're right,' he said. 'Though you don't even know if this is a kidnapping. Maybe he's just been murdered and his body hidden. Maybe he's lying under the snow somewhere.'

'Maybe,' she said, getting up. 'And maybe not.'

Detective Chief Inspector Ivan Wikström put the small bundle of clothes on the bonnet of the patrol car and stood with his hands in his pockets, studying the elderly man who was kneeling in front of the opened wooden box, talking to it in whispers. Strange whispers. The constable had positioned himself behind Wikström, his thumbs once again hooked into his belt.

'What have you got there?' asked Wikström.

When there was no answer he leaned forwards.

'I said, what is it?'

Torsten did not appear to have heard him. His head had almost disappeared inside the box. There was a rustling as he moved his hand carefully through the straw. The fox also came up to have a look. Seved flinched as it padded past, just like a dog. He was about to shoo the animal away when he realised it no longer mattered. It would all be over soon.

They got to the constable first.

He suddenly took a step backwards, raising his fingertips to his forehead, which had become deeply lined. Then his left hand gripped his head as he sank to one knee. He looked stunned and scared. His cheeks had turned ashen.

'What's up with you?' Wikström asked.

After a couple of unsuccessful attempts to get to his feet,

Kunosson sat down, breathing heavily and loudly. He knocked off the cap of his uniform.

'I don't feel very well,' he said, looking at the lining of his cap. 'I think I'll just sleep for a while.'

Then he rested his gloved hand on the ground and stayed like that for a moment, panting, before sinking down onto his elbow and rolling into a foetal position.

'Wake me up before you go, Ivan,' he said, his lips slurring against the snow. 'I'm just not feeling so good, that's all.'

Wikström had been walking forwards to help his colleague, but he came to a halt, looking at him with complete indifference.

And there he stayed.

Eventually Torsten stood up and brushed the snow from his knees. He walked over and gave the detective chief inspector a shove in the back. Wikström took a small step forwards but did not even turn round.

Even Seved had been affected. He leaned against the car and swallowed repeatedly. It felt as if his head had been filled with ice-cold meltwater.

He could have cried. Not just because of the whisperings from the shapeshifters but from the tension as well, which was receding now that the policemen had been disabled.

Torsten watched him with interest. He had closed the box and handed it to Bodil, who had put it in the hall. Seved felt the old man's searching gaze.

'I'm not used to it,' he explained. 'That's all.'

Elna had walked over to Tony Kunosson to see if there were any signs of life. With her arms folded she prodded his body with her foot. It moved involuntarily. He was completely gone.

His eyes were open but he saw nothing. She bent down, undid the buckle of his belt and wrenched it off him with such force that he rolled over and remained lying on his back with his face to the sky, from where occasional snowflakes were fluttering down. They settled on his cheeks and even on his eyes, which did not even blink.

By this time Patrik had come out. The narrow barrel of a rifle was resting on his arm, and Seved realised that he had been standing inside all the time, hidden by the curtain, ready to shoot if anything went wrong.

Torsten walked over to Wikström and searched inside his jacket. Seved knew he was looking for a weapon. It was attached to his belt and he had to turn the detective over to get at the holster with its metal clip at the back. When he had worked the holster free from the belt he opened the door of the patrol car and dropped both Kunosson's belt and Wikström's weapon on the seat.

'Fetch the snowmobile,' Torsten said. 'And attach the sledge.'

Patrik strode off and disappeared into the barn, and shortly afterwards an engine roared to life inside.

'What are you going to do with them?' Seved asked, watching the snowmobile driving slowly towards them. Patrik was standing up behind the windscreen with both boots on one footplate. The rifle was in the sledge.

'Luttak is going to have a few words with them,' said Torsten, and holding his cupped hand under his chin he spat out his snus, hurled it away from him and added:

'After that they won't even know their own names.'

Enveloped in exhaust fumes from the snowmobile, they loaded Kunosson onto the sledge. It took a while because he was such a weight, over a hundred kilos at least. When he was finally in place he lay there like a slaughtered ox, staring vacantly. Seved tried not to look at his face.

Wikström was even more difficult.

When they pushed him towards the sledge he tried to resist. A whimpering sound came from his lips.

'Pack it in!' grunted Patrik, tugging at the detective's jacket.

Torsten rummaged in the back of the snowmobile and brought out a length of light-blue bailer twine. He tied it round the officer's arms and legs. When he had secured it he took a step away and placed his foot on Wikström's back. He fell forwards, his chest thudded against the ground and his glasses flew off.

Patrik and Seved lifted him onto the sledge as if he were a parcel.

'Now take that fox and get out of here,' Torsten said.

He picked up the glasses lying in the snow and rammed them in an inside pocket of the prone detective's jacket.

'And lock that barrier after you!'

Edit Mickelsson was sitting in the kitchen in front of her laptop with a sombre expression on her face. Her fringe was pinned back with a small clip. She looked up when Susso and Torbjörn walked in through the door, and when she saw Susso was not alone she shut the laptop and stood up.

'This is Torbjörn,' Susso said.

'Would you like some coffee?' the old woman asked.

'No thanks,' Susso answered, as she sat down at the kitchen table without taking off her jacket or her hat. 'We've just had some.'

Torbjörn sat down on the small chest of drawers in the hall, resting his elbows on his knees.

'Can I get you anything else?'

Susso smiled and said, 'No thanks,' and Edit sat down again.

'How are you?' asked Susso.

'Well, you know how it is. You sit here, waiting.'

'No news?'

She shook her head and then turned to face the window.

'They've started talking to people in the village again,' she said. 'Asking things they've already asked. So I suppose they've run out of ideas.'

'Do you know of a farm near Årrenjarka, where Laestadians live?' Susso asked, getting out the map. But there was no need to unfold it because Edit nodded.

'Oh yes,' she said.

'We've just heard that he might come from there,' Susso said.

'The person who was here?'

'Yes, and I thought you might have heard something about it too . . .'

'As far back as I can remember there has been talk about those poor people,' she said. 'Edvin said they were intimidating Lars and Gun, who run the Fells Holiday Village over there. They had plans to expand, a restaurant or whatever, but it came to nothing because the digger broke. And when they got it repaired it broke again. And again. Then there was the year the campsite was invaded by lemmings. They even wrote about it in the *Kuriren*. There were so many lemmings the visitors couldn't put their feet down on the ground. It was literally heaving with them. And they were vicious, those creatures. So soon the cabins were standing empty. Until they were filled with researchers and ecologists from every corner of the globe, that is. So the Mannbergs didn't lose out. But they still insisted it was the Laestadians who caused the invasion – treating the ground with some kind of manure that attracted the lemmings, whatever that might have been. The things you hear.'

She shook her head.

'So I can't say I'm surprised if people are saying they're the ones who have taken Mattias,' she continued. 'They get the blame for all the trouble that goes on around here – unless it's the Poles or the Estonians, of course.'

'No one is saying they're the ones who have taken him. Only that the dwarf lives there.'

'The Vaikijaur man,' Edit said slowly.

It was clear she hated the name so much she could hardly bring herself to say it. Susso was aware that all the negative attention had resulted in ugly, indelible graffiti being painted on the village sign, and she guessed there were neighbours who blamed Edit for the damage. Quite possibly she blamed herself as well, far more harshly than anyone else. It was the same for Susso: she could not see how she could have acted any differently. If she had not set up the camera, the police would have nothing at all to go on, but that did not make her feel better. Susso had no idea what to say, so she sat looking at her hand, which was still resting on the folded map.

'Shall we get going?' Torbjörn said after a moment of silence.

Susso nodded.

'We're on our way to Årrenjarka,' she said, getting to her feet. 'To do a bit of snooping.'

Getting the foxshifter into the car was easy. Like an obedient dog it leapt onto the back seat when he opened the door, followed by its bushy tail. It sat in exactly the same place as when it had been in its other form.

Seved reversed to get past the police car, and just as he was putting the car into first gear and was about to drive off there was a thump on the roof. It was Elna. Seved reached across the seat, grasped the handle and opened the door, a puzzled look on his face.

'The clothes,' she said, scraping a tangled lock of hair from her face. 'He's got to have his clothes.'

She indicated the patrol car with a nod of her head, and the bundle lying on its bonnet.

Seved waited while she ran to fetch them, and after she had handed him the clothes he placed them on the seat beside him. There were wood shavings on the anorak and stains on the nylon fabric of the boots, probably piss. It smelled like that anyway. He nodded his head at Elna, who returned the nod, and then he drove slowly off down the slope. Creaking gently, the car trundled along the narrow forest road. Seved could see the fox's eyes in the rear-view mirror. Yellow and ringed with black they were watching him intently. There was no doubt Jirvin was concealed in there, in those narrow pupils. It was exactly the same look.

Seved knew he was very old. He had been living in this country when people were eating marsh turtles, so Torsten had said. That was an exaggeration, of course, but how old could he be? Five hundred years? A thousand?

When Seved had passed through the barrier and locked it behind him, he saw in the mirror that the fox was lying down. He felt a sense of relief and glanced over his shoulder to see what it was doing. Its head was resting on its front paws on the seat. Its eyes were glittering slits. Perhaps that was what it was going to do. Sleep.

After swinging onto the main road he turned round again, and this time he saw that the pelt had already started to disappear from around the eyes. And there was a patch on the forehead where grey leathery skin was shining through, and the nose had paled and begun to change shape.

He did not want to see this.

He picked up the old man's anorak. Without letting go of the wheel or taking his eyes off the road, he tried to cover the fox but failed, so he began to pull over to the side of the road.

Three hours to get to Jillesnåle. Would that be enough time to shift shape? It was doubtful. Larger varieties usually took a long while. Karats had taken over a week last time, ominous and growling. They had not been allowed to go into Hybblet then.

It was extraordinary that he was shifting shape in a strange car in close proximity to a human he had never met before. Had Torsten told him where he was going and how long it would take to get there, or did he just know?

In the distance, at the furthest point of the white road, he saw a car driving towards him. It was shrouded in a halo of snow flung up by its wheels. When he realised it was not a police car he put on the handbrake. Then he turned round and spread the jacket over the bony old animal, which had begun shuddering, and he could feel the peculiar heat of the shapeshifting process radiating towards the palms of his hands. It was like warming yourself at a stove.

As the car passed, Seved looked the other way, towards the ploughed wall of snow. The risk of being recognised was practically non-existent, but in these parts he felt like a criminal, and he had an idea it showed.

'You going up to Riksgränsen for Christmas?' Susso stared at the road, and waited for an answer.

'Yes, I thought I might,' he said.

She turned and looked at his profile.

'Seriously?'

Torbjörn snorted and moved the pouch of snus under his lip. Which meant: 'I don't think so.'

'Well, I thought I'd go up anyway,' she said.

Torbjörn nodded, and after a moment he said:

'Say hello to my mum from me.'

They sat in silence for a few kilometres, watching the peaks grow larger. The slopes were jagged with fir trees. Torbjörn leaned forwards and squinted.

'It's near here somewhere,' he said.

A short distance further on there was a break in the wall of ploughed snow on the right-hand side. Susso depressed the clutch and switched her foot to the brake pedal.

'Are you sure?'

'There's nowhere else it can be.'

The Volvo lurched as it made its way through the snow lying in thick ridges on the small road. In front they could see tyre tracks, the edges marked out in sharp shadows, and although she was not sure if they had been made by a vehicle with greater ground clearance than her own, she took it as a sign that there was no risk in going on. After about fifty metres the road was blocked by a barrier. There was a circular steel notice hanging from it, and even though the text was hidden by snow, the message was unmistakable: they would not be welcome here.

Susso stopped the car.

'Well,' she said, taking a quick look in the rear-view mirror. 'What do we do now then?'

'We'll just have to walk, I guess,' Torbjörn said, folding up the map.

Susso sighed and thumped the steering wheel.

'But we can't leave the car here,' she said. 'I'll have to reverse first.'

She rested her right arm on the back of the seat and looked over her shoulder, then quickly unclipped her seat belt.

'You're going to have to do that anyway,' Torbjörn said, nodding towards the road ahead.

A police car was coming towards them. Blue letters on the bonnet and on the roof the shining blue plastic of the lights. The car was moving slowly, and when it was about twenty metres from the barrier it came to a halt and stood there with its lights on in the half-darkness: cold, blinding xenon headlamps. Inside were two men, looking as if they had no plans to get out.

'What are they waiting for?' Susso said. 'Do they want us to open it for them, or what?'

'Or maybe they want us to reverse out of the way,' replied Torbjörn.

'What shall I do then?'

'Reverse.'

Susso gripped the gear lever, put the car into reverse, turned her head and began to drive backwards. It was dark in the ravine that opened up between the fir trees, so they made slow progress.

'Are you going to talk to them?' Torbjörn asked.

'Not sure,' Susso answered quickly. 'Do you think I should?'

When she reached the main road she asked Torbjörn to check if any cars were coming, and he strained his neck to see. When he gave the all-clear she reversed out, turned the car round and parked parallel to the wall of snow at the roadside. They waited with the engine idling. Neither of them said anything.

A harsh light flashed over the trees, and immediately afterwards the police car appeared. Susso opened the door, stepped out and stood facing the oncoming Volvo. She hardly needed to wave: naturally they would understand that she wanted something.

But they did not.

To her utter amazement they drove straight past.

The driver was wearing a police cap and was sitting stiffly behind the wheel. He did not even glance to the side. Susso ran after them for a few paces, waving her arms, and she noticed that the man in the passenger seat was one of the police officers she had spoken to in Jokkmokk. The one with the leather jacket. Wikström!

He looked directly at her but seemed not to recognise her.

The police car drove off in the direction of Jokkmokk, its engine whining as it shot off at top speed, leaving behind it a whirlwind of snow and exhaust. Susso waved both her arms above her head, but it was no use.

She flung open the car door.

'Shit! Why didn't they stop?' She was practically shouting.

Torbjörn did not answer. He merely shook his head, and when she had climbed in and started the engine he mumbled:

'Perhaps they were in a hurry.'

'But I've spoken to one of them,' Susso said, getting out her mobile while turning the car around. 'In Jokkmokk. He was there when they questioned me. And I *know* he saw me.'

'Maybe he didn't recognise you.'

'What do you mean, not recognise me? What the hell does that matter? They should have stopped anyway, if someone's waving them down. What kind of fucking police are they? What if something had happened?'

'Well, at least we know they've been here,' Torbjörn said.

'Morons,' said Susso under her breath, looking from the road to the keys on her mobile.

'Who are you ringing?'

'I want to know! If he was there.'

She tapped in the number for Kjell-Åke Andersson but got through to voicemail. The instant she began to say her name it struck her that it might not be appropriate for her to be spying on the Laestadians, and so she coughed and said only that she wanted to know how the investigation was going. When she had finished she held the mobile in her hand as it rested on the wheel.

For the last ten kilometres or so Jirvin had been talking to himself in the back seat – at least, he moved his lips and a whispered word came out from time to time. They were unintelligible sounds, but Seved could hear they were words. He did not like it and he drove far too fast. He just wanted to get there. He had not yet started to be affected but he had no idea what he would do if he began to sense the old man taking him over inside. It could very well end in an accident.

'We're nearly there,' he said, and because talking made him feel calmer he carried on: 'We live near a little village called Jillesnåle. That's where you are going to be. For a while.'

No sound came from the back seat. It could have just been a green jacket lying there. With a tail, thought Seved, after taking a look over his shoulder. The feet were visible too. They looked like a child's feet that had grown old. Like the feet of a mummified child. Black nails. Or rather, claws.

It took a while for the door to open and, when it did, it opened slowly. Börje was standing on the veranda, watching as the little man climbed down from the seat. The dogs barked, but that was probably because the shapeshifter was wearing clothes and had his hood up. It made them think something suspicious was going on. The little man held his boots in one hand and pressed the other to his chest while his yellow eyes looked at the dog enclosure.

'Is he going to be in Hybblet, or where?' asked Seved, slamming the car door behind him.

'The barn,' Börje said.

Seved walked across the yard and opened the barn door. The little man was right behind him and he picked up speed when he saw the darkness inside the barn. The dogs did not like it when he ran, but Börje roared at them and they instantly fell silent. But it was impossible for them to be still. Whining and with their tails erect they paced up and down inside the fence.

No sooner had the little man stepped inside the barn than he let something go, something that quickly glided up to the greying roof beams and was gone. A bird, Seved thought, astonished, and he took a step to one side to see where it had gone. Something tiny flew past him and then darted back, and he realised it was a bat. Seved looked at the little man, who was also standing with his head turned up towards the roof. It almost looked as if he was smiling.

'I heard you had a close shave,' said Börje, throwing his snus into the rubbish bin under the sink. Seved stood beside him drinking milk from a carton. He nodded without moving it from his lips.

'What will happen with those policemen now?' he asked, after he had swallowed.

'They'll have a little chat with Luttak,' Börje said.

'Yes, but what will happen to them? Will they forget everything, or what?'

'If he could just make them forget, then he would,' said Börje, who was standing looking out of the window with his hands in his pockets. 'But he can't. When he scrapes the details of the event out of them, other things come too. And the memory of it will sit inside them like an old nightmare. They will never be themselves again, believe me. In many cases it ends in suicide.'

'Because no one believes them?'

Börje shook his head.

'It's more like a burn. They'll feel the pain but have no memory of the fire. They won't know what they've experienced, but it will hurt and they will suffer a personality change, as the newspapers say. Start to drink. Slap the wife about. And then it ends with a gun in the mouth. Either that or they kill themselves driving.'

'The key to the padlock was bent,' Seved said in a low voice. 'So I didn't lock the barrier after me. That's why they could drive all the way up to Torsten's and take us by surprise like that.'

Börje nodded.

'Things happen.'

'But if I hadn't done it, those policemen wouldn't have been hurt.'

'If they'd wanted to take a closer look at Torsten's farm, a broken barrier wouldn't have stopped them. So don't you worry about it. It turned out all right.'

Seved nodded.

'I feel bad anyway.'

'We've got other things to think about,' said Börje, and walked out of the kitchen.

They had pulled in at the Statoil filling station in Gällivare. Susso bought a yoghurt drink and a cheese and ham baguette, and carried her purchases in a rustling paper bag to the car. She ate everything and crumpled up the wrapping. When she had thrown the rubbish away in the bin beside the petrol pump and brushed away the crumbs from her jumper, she hurried back to the car, where her mobile was lying on the seat with the display lit up.

She answered and heard Kjell-Åke Andersson's voice at the other end.

'I just wanted to know how everything was going,' she said. 'With the Vaikijaur man, I mean. Because I heard he might be living in that area, around Kvikkjokk, with some Laestadians. Do you know anything about that?'

'Yes, we know about that.'

'So you've been there then?'

'Susso,' he said, 'naturally we are grateful for your photograph and your interest in the search for Mattias, but I'm sure you understand that I can't answer that question.'

'But I only want to know if you've found him.'

'When, or should I say if, we find him, you will be informed.'

Seved took a dish from the washing-up rack, put it on the table and then fetched a carton of yoghurt and a tube of cheese spread from the fridge. The boy lifted the carton with both hands and poured some into the dish. He took his time, making sure not to spill any. From the basket of woven birch bark he took a slice of crispbread and crumbled it over the yoghurt.

Seved felt a pang when he saw how the boy broke the bread, because it gave him an insight into the life he must have had, a life they had taken from him. That *he* had taken from him. Who had taught him to crumble crispbread into his yoghurt? Seved tried to push the thought aside but it was not easy. It worked its way in and spread, forcing to the surface a lingering anxiety. Much of the boy's chest was visible in the opening of his shirt: it was like a bib of pale skin, lined with the shadows of his ribs. He had been with them for several days now and had not been eating well. He mainly wanted to drink. He liked apricot smoothies and yoghurt and clementines. Seved had asked him what he liked to eat. The boy never replied.

The boy bent over his bowl, pressing his elbows tightly to his body. It was as if he was trying to take up as little room as possible. He had a slight cold and was breathing through his mouth. Below his nose lines of mucus had dried to a crust.

'It's Christmas Eve today,' Seved said. 'Lennart will have presents with him when he comes back, you wait and see. What would you like for Christmas?'

There was no answer.

Lennart turned up around four o'clock with four plastic bags full of Christmas presents. The boy sat alone on the sofa, and his shoulders were so narrow he practically disappeared into the crack between the olive-green velour cushions with their large buttons.

'We've got to have some Christmas music as well,' Lennart said, and went to fetch the CD player. He fumbled with the buttons but nothing happened, so Seved had to hurry and put in the plug before the big man got angry with it.

Once the CD started spinning and the music streamed out of the loudspeakers, Lennart sang along. He was unsure of the words. All he knew was '*hejsan hoppsan*' and '*fallerallera*'.

As he sang and hummed he emptied the plastic bags onto the wooden floor, grabbing hold of the bottom of each bag and turning it upside down. Out tumbled rattling Lego boxes, athletic-looking plastic figures with cheerful grins, cars with big tractor wheels, board games, jigsaw puzzles, soft toys, a shining silver pistol, a sword and dinosaurs with stiff gaping jaws. There was a drawing pad and a box of tricks with a magician on the front in a high top hat and a cape.

Wide-eyed, the boy slid from the sofa and kneeled among the toys. Jim the mouseshifter was sitting in his uncombed hair.

'Bet you've never seen this many toys before,' said Lennart, grimacing as he clenched and unclenched his fingers inside their protective bag.

No, the boy most certainly had not.

'We didn't know what you wanted, so we took everything.'

The boy lifted up a robot and turned its arms.

'There are games too,' Lennart said. 'The kind you play on the TV.'

Börje was sitting in the armchair with a can of beer in his hand. He was drunk and he had said nothing for almost an hour. It was as if he had forgotten how to talk, and if anyone spoke to him, he only raised his eyebrows, startled. His eyelids had drooped so that only the lower half of his eyes was visible, but every time it looked as if he was about to shut his eyes completely all he did was slurp another mouthful from the can.

The snow was falling gently and sparkled in the light from the lamp on the barn wall. On the windowpane two white patches appeared in front of the noses of the gigantic figures standing outside, draped in tarpaulin, watching the child playing.

Sigrid Muotka tentatively felt a bag of walnut kernels. She squeezed the cellophane and inspected the contents. The walnuts looked like brains. Her knitted beret was an intense splash of colour and a round reflective tag dangled from a twisted cord emerging from the pocket of her poplin coat. Susso stood behind her holding the wire basket. It was already quite full and she was holding it with both hands.

'Do you want the nuts?'

As if in answer to Susso's question, Sigrid let go of the bag and walked on, her rubber-soled shoes shuffling on the shop floor. She looked timidly along the shelves but could not see what she wanted, and perhaps she did not even know herself. Susso wanted to help her and frequently offered suggestions, but the old lady either shook her head or appeared not to hear.

There was a muffled buzz from Susso's jacket. She put down the basket, dug her hand into her pocket and pulled out her mobile, along with a crumpled tissue. Unknown number. Normally she would be curious to find out who was phoning but lately she had not wanted to know. Because what if it was the police and they had discovered something? She did not answer and the caller left a voicemail message.

They made their way to the till and Susso began to empty the basket onto the conveyor belt – milk, tins of mackerel, a sliced loaf, knobbly potatoes, a packet of coffee and four rolls of kitchen paper.

Leaving the store, the two women pulled on their gloves, turned up their collars and lowered their chins, and went out to face the biting cold. It was almost three o'clock and the sky was grey. Sigrid Muotka lived on Föreningsgatan. There was not far to go but the final stretch was steadily uphill and Susso felt as if the cold was gouging out her eyes. She was pulling the sledge with the bags stacked one on top of the other, grimacing and glancing at little Sigrid, who was struggling along with the kitchen rolls in her arms, her eyes fixed on the snowy ground.

'Not far now!'

When they reached the block of flats the old woman walked straight in through the entrance doors, while Susso unloaded the sledge and took it to the carpet-beating frame, which doubled as sledge storage. There was not much room and to find a place Susso had to step in snow that was yellow and corroded by dog piss.

Then her phone rang again.

Unknown number.

She realised it could be important, so this time she answered.

It was a woman's voice. She said her name too quickly for Susso to make it out, but she did hear the next sentence:

'. . . and I'm phoning from *Expressen*. I'd really like to talk to you a bit about this website you've got . . .'

TROLL HUNTER'S PHOTO ONLY POLICE LEAD

The Vaikijaur man is not a man. At least, not if you believe cryptozoologist Sussie Myrén, who has captured him on film.

'It could be a genuine troll,' she says.

Sussie Myrén's wildlife camera took the picture, which is the only lead the police have in their search for four-year-old Mattias Mickelsson, who was abducted by two unidentified men on 17 December in Jokkmokk. But she had not set up the camera to take pictures of animals.

She wanted to document something completely different. Trolls.

In the family

Ever since she was a child Sussie Myrén, who works as a care assistant in Kiruna, has dreamed of seeing a supernatural being with her own eyes. She inherited this unusual interest from her maternal grandfather, a fells photographer. Towards the end of the eighties he took an aerial photo of a bear with an unidentifiable creature on its back.

'No one has ever been able to explain the image in the picture. I have puzzled about it all my life. You could say I absorbed it with my mother's milk. If anyone has an explanation they are welcome to contact me,' she says.

Her own website

In the interest of gathering information about authentic dwarfs and trolls she has created a website, and it was through the website that

Mattias Mickelsson's grandmother came into contact with her.

'She saw a figure in her garden that she thought was some kind of goblin or gnome because he was so small and he looked so strange,' says Sussie Myrén, who for the sake of simplicity uses the term 'troll' for all supernatural beings in the Nordic region that have a human form and anthropomorphic characteristics.

'Abominable Snowmen and Big Foot are not trolls, of course, but if similar beings were observed here I would call them trolls. So it is quite simply a question of geography,' she says.

Unknown species

Sussie Myrén thinks in cryptozoological terms. She believes the beings we call trolls could, in fact, be animal species that have avoided scientific explanation.

'I am fairly certain that Abominable Snowmen and Yeti exist or have existed. And Sweden has huge areas of forest. Remember, these creatures are more wary than lynx and considerably more intelligent.'

But why have troll skeletons never been found?

'That's a good question. The answer is probably that these beings are extremely rare and can be similar to other animals, even humans. Have you ever seen a skinned bear, for example? It is uncannily like a human corpse.'

Mobile cameras

She believes that the explosive increase in the number of cameras in our society, such as those in mobile phones, will result in a flood of photographic evidence.

Now she hopes her picture will be able to assist the police.

'It could be a troll, but not necessarily. The most important thing is for anyone with information about the person in the photograph to contact the police.'

*

My jaw dropped when I read that, and I had trouble catching my breath. That's what Roland told me anyway, when he came in with the newspaper and handed it to me with an inscrutable grin below his moustache. He had no idea why it made me so upset.

'"Absorbed it with my mother's milk,"' I said. 'What will people think!'

'But that's true, isn't it?' he said.

I read our name in the paper with horror.

Myrén, Myrén, Myrén!

And they had spelled Susso's name wrong. Luckily Dad's name wasn't mentioned – it would hardly be good for business if the actual name of the company was linked to something as awful as child abduction. Although Cecilia said the connection didn't matter and that the publicity could only have a beneficial effect on business, if that's what I was worried about. But I was still thankful the reporter had not dug any deeper.

The police got nowhere with their investigation. Apart from the fact that they knew Mattias had been taken by two men in a brown Volvo estate, the photograph was their only lead, but such an elusive and doubtful lead that they had no idea how to follow it up, or even if there was any point in doing so. And because the boy had been missing for so long they were more or less certain he would never be found alive. You could read that between the lines. There were thirty investigators working on the case full-time. Every dark-coloured Volvo estate registered in the province was being checked out, and it would be hard to find a more common make of car in Norrbotten, so they had their work cut out. It's a never-ending job, so Roland said, and judging by the look of Kjell-Åke Andersson, the detective in charge, he thought the same. He was on TV: a short grey-haired bloke who spoke slowly and looked pretty pathetic standing in the wind outside that steel building in Luleå where the County Police have their headquarters, and which is so horribly ugly that people with an interest in architecture come from far and wide to visit the place, just to look at the awfulness of it.

'It's a total mystery to us,' he explained.

When he was asked if they had any leads he shook his head. 'Nothing new, anyway.'

And the man in the photograph? The Vaikijaur man?

'We're not excluding anything from our enquiries. That means we are interested in any tips we receive. And we are entreating the general public to continue passing on tips, so if anyone has any information please phone 114 14 . . .'

Occasionally I asked Susso how she was getting on, and although I noticed she was a bit down – to be honest, she just wasn't herself – I never had the strength to break through that shell of indifference she had built around herself. When she said she was fine, I contented myself with that answer, which was of course cowardly of me because inside I knew it was a lie.

The same day she had been in the national newspaper she was phoned by the local papers *Norrländskan* and *Kuriren*. She had answered their questions politely and even agreed to be photographed. I suggested they take the picture outside our shop, and that's what they did. We had to make something positive out of all the fuss.

Susso thought the more that was written about Mattias, the better. The more often his picture appeared in the press, the greater the chance of him being recognised by someone who had happened to see him. But the local press was only interested in

Susso, the girl who believed in trolls and whose grandfather was famous in the county.

Susso was embarrassed about the way she was portrayed in the papers, and naturally people talked. The attention was too much, we all felt that. It made all of us feel bad. Business in the shop suffered too, and I could see no logic in that. And as for Roland, he just walked around with that grin on his face.

'There are gremlins in the works,' he said.

Lennart sat with the open newspaper in front of him, staring at the greatly enlarged photograph of Jirvin's aged face. There was also a picture of Mattias, and one of a cryptozoologist named Sussie Myrén from Kiruna. Naturally Seved and Börje knew the article was disturbing, and they were waiting to hear what Lennart had to say about it. He sniffed and shifted his weight from one buttock to the other, making the old chair creak. The bag lay on one side of the paper and his bronzed right hand on the other. The creases on the knuckles of his fingers were deep crevices.

'The other day,' he said at last, 'when the police made their unannounced visit to Torsten, this person was here, nosing about. Patrik noticed a car on the other side of the barrier. A green Volvo 240, registered to Susso Maria Myrén.'

Lennart prodded his index finger on the cryptozoologist's face.

'But how did she know he was there?' Seved asked. 'And how did she find the house?'

'She found it', said Lennart slowly, 'because our friend here has been running around the village for some unknown reason. He has been to the boy's grandmother's house on at least two occasions. And he can't just have been there by chance. We have no idea at the moment why he did it, but it's important you keep an eye on him.'

'What, you mean he was trying to warn her? Is that what you're saying?' said Börje.

A growl formed in the base of Lennart's throat.

'I'm saying you've got to keep an eye on him! No one knows what goes on in his head.'

'There's not much we can do,' Börje said. 'Not if he starts causing trouble. Such an old . . .'

'He won't dare cause any trouble,' said Lennart. 'Not down here. Not with you. Because otherwise Karats would make a fox-fur collar out of him. And he knows it. That's another reason we moved him. With Karats and Skabram close by he won't be getting up to any mischief. But you've still got to keep an eye on him, understand? Make sure he doesn't slip away.'

Börje nodded, and Seved noticed a layer of perspiration had formed on his forehead. He had never seen him look so tense before.

'Jola and I have had a closer look at that website Susso Myrén has set up,' Lennart continued, his fingers scratching inside the bag. 'And I can tell you this much: it needs to be got rid of.'

When he had said this he looked at Börje challengingly.

'But what does it say, this website?' Börje asked.

Without taking his eyes off him, Lennart said:

'It's got to go.'

Börje pursed his lips and swallowed hard.

'Do you understand what I'm saying?'

'I'm a bit out of touch . . .'

'Jola can help you,' muttered Lennart, folding the paper. 'You travel up to Kiruna next week. We're taking a trip to Östersund, but after that you'd better see to it. Right away.'

One evening at the beginning of the new year I was sitting in the shop, holed up in the darkness like a little owl. I had closed long ago but it was savagely cold outside and I was putting off going out in it, just sitting there in my jacket and staring into space. I was vaguely thinking about whether I should improve the Christmas decorations or simply take them down, even though there were several days left until the thirteenth of January, St Knut's Day.

There was a sudden sharp rap on the shop window, and there outside stood Susso. She was wearing her Inca hat and the large, light-blue down coat that reaches to her knees, and she was holding her mobile in her gloved hand. She had used it to rap on the glass.

'I'm just leaving!' I called through the window, waving my gloves as proof, but she pointed to the door, so I had to go and open up for her.

She held up the phone and said in an eager voice that she had just been speaking to a man who knew who the Vaikijaur man was.

The man who had phoned was called Mats. He didn't know the exact identity of the Vaikijaur man but apparently he had lived in his loft for over a year at the beginning of the eighties. He was not a hundred per cent sure, but he was so similar that he had contacted the police. They had not been particularly interested, however. On the other hand, he couldn't offer them much information: he didn't know what the man was called, not even his first name or where he came from – in fact, he knew practically nothing about him at all.

I pursed my lips and pulled on my gloves, studying the leather that shone over my knuckles when I curled my fingers.

'Anyway, he's going to send a photo,' Susso said.

'A photo?'

She lifted up her mobile and the display lit up, but the picture had not arrived yet. She pulled off her hat, ran her fingers through her hair and sat down on the chair at the end of the counter. You could tell she was excited because she kept repeating herself.

'He said he had met him at the end of the seventies and that he had lived in their storehouse. For almost a year.'

'In their storehouse?' I said. 'What kind of storehouse?'

'I don't know, but he also said he had saved their son's life and that he seemed extremely interested in the boy. And he was four years old, just like Mattias.'

'But what do the police say?' I said.

'They kind of didn't care. I'll phone Andersson because it seems weird they don't want to take a closer look at it at least. Seeing as they don't have any other tip-offs.'

'Perhaps tip-offs are all they have,' I said.

'Leads, then. If they don't have any leads.'

The mobile gave a signal, and Susso held it up as I walked round to look. I can't deny I was curious. With her stubby thumb she tapped a few keys to access the image.

It took a few moments for the picture to materialise, but when it did we were hugely disappointed. The only thing you could see was a little person in green clothes standing on a slope in a forest.

It was impossible to tell whether or not it was the same person the press had christened the Vaikijaur man.

I took the phone out of Susso's hands, pushed my glasses up onto my forehead and looked closely at the display.

'It looks like a juniper bush covered in moss.'

'He's got him on film too. Thirty-five millimetre.'

'I see,' I said, handing back the phone. 'Can't he send that then?'

Susso shook her head.

'It's on a reel. He hasn't digitised it.'

She took a deep breath and turned to face the shop window, where long shadows reached out from the souvenirs that had been caught in the headlights of a car outside in the parking lot.

'I ought to go there and take a look at it,' she said. 'But I'll have to take your car to Dalarna.'

'Dalarna!'

'He lives outside Avesta.'

'Do you know what I think, Susso?' I said, rooting around in my bag for my lip balm. 'I think you should leave it alone. He could easily be some kind of lunatic. I think the police ignore tips like this for a very good reason.'

'But I want to help him. I can't just sit here doing nothing.'

'Help him? Who?'

'Mattias!'

I couldn't help sighing.

'You've helped enough already. If it hadn't been for your picture, the police would have had nothing to go on. You don't have to do more.'

'What if he's got nothing to do with the case? Then it is my fault that they wasted masses of time looking for him. And Granddad's fault.' She pointed to the wall, at a framed photograph of mountain flora showing colourful clumps of berries.

'All right, all right,' I said, trying to calm her down. 'But I still think you ought to let the police take care of this. They know what they're doing, don't you agree?'

She shook her head.

'If it's a troll, they'll never find him.'

'But, Susso . . .'

'Trolls don't exist in any kind of register. They don't have fingerprints. They can't be found by using criminal sodding profiling. I've spent the best part of my life searching for them and even I don't have the faintest idea where they keep themselves hidden or what they look like.'

After sighing again I reached for the tin of ginger biscuits, found a heart-shaped one and bit off the pointed end.

'I think you should phone the police and talk to them. Ask them how it's progressing and what they think about this latest tip about the old man in the loft. In Avesta.'

'It drives me mad,' she said. 'They're so slow following it up.'

'Let's go home now,' I said. 'We can pick up some Thai food on the way. And then we can watch a DVD. That'll take your mind off it for a while.'

That was my way of trying to look after her. In all honesty I was probably afraid to give her too much encouragement. I was worried about what all this publicity in the press would lead to in the long run. What if she was never able to get a job because of it? Who wants to employ someone who spends all their time looking for trolls?

Susso was under a lot of pressure, and instead of supporting her I gave in.

When she talked about trolls I quickly tried to talk about something else, some everyday topic. In my defence I can say I didn't do it consciously. It was just that I couldn't deal with it, that's all. My reserves were too low. Drained. It takes a considerable amount of energy to maintain the pretence of self-pity.

But naturally we are stronger than we think.

And if it hasn't been obvious before, it certainly becomes apparent when you find yourself in a crisis.

In mortal danger.

Lars Nilsson had cut out the *Norrländskan* interview with Susso and stuck it on the fridge door with a magnet, and when they sat down to eat lunch she said:

'So, Lars, you've been reading about this crazy person who believes in trolls?'

He looked up at her, considered the question with a puzzled expression and then shook his head as he lifted the fork to his mouth. They were eating enchiladas with a sweet and sour sauce.

'I'm referring to myself, Lars,' she said, pointing her knife at her chest. And then she pointed it at the fridge door, and he understood.

'Have they found the boy?' he asked.

Susso shook her head. 'No, and it doesn't look as if they're going to, either. Not alive, at any rate.'

Lars Nilsson chewed for a long time, and after he had swallowed he said:

'I remember when I was little. How two children disappeared, a brother and sister. We heard stallo had taken them and eaten them.'

Susso took a drink from her glass and waited for the old man to continue.

'But that wasn't what happened,' he said. 'Many years later someone saw the girl in a market. She wasn't a girl any longer but a fully grown, fine young woman. It was a relative who had seen her, the lost children's uncle, and he was certain it was her because she was so like her mother. The man's own sister, that is. But she didn't recognise him, and when he went to embrace her she ran off into the crowd and was gone. And that's when people said stallo had taken her, not to eat her but just to have her, as their own child.'

'Yes,' said Susso, 'that's what we're hoping. The boy's mother, who I've met, talks about that. She says the person who has taken Mattias doesn't want to harm him. But that's probably how you have to think, to be able to bear it.'

'They're tasty, these enchiladas,' said Lars.

'Do you think so? I think they taste terrible. Or rather, taste of nothing. Makes you wonder what's in them.'

The sound of a television was coming from the upstairs landing. When Seved came into the hall and heard it he stamped up the stairs without taking off his boots. Profanities simmered in his mouth. Didn't she understand anything!

She was sitting cuddled up to the boy, who was curled under a blanket with only his face visible. They had been eating clementines, and the peel lay in a pile on the coffee table. They both stared at him wide-eyed as he strode across the floor and forced his way behind the old TV. With a powerful tug he wrenched the aerial cable out of the socket. A fizzing sound filled the room before he pulled out the plug as well. Then all he could hear was his heavy breathing.

Signe sat up. 'It was only a children's programme.'

Seved did not answer. There was no point in arguing about such things when the boy was in the room. Because of that he had no release for the fury that had welled up inside him and driven him up the stairs. His hands shook as he rolled up the cable.

'You can look at a film instead,' he muttered. 'There are plenty of films you can watch.'

Seved did not want to hear anything about what had happened in Kiruna. That was the real reason he had forbidden Signe to put on the television. But he could not tell her that because naturally she knew nothing about the things Börje did. He had to deal with this on his own, and that made it so much worse.

The risk of the boy seeing his own face on the TV news was practically non-existent by now. The police had interviewed several hundred people but had got nowhere, and therefore there was nothing to report. Moreover, almost every news programme was full of pictures from south-east Asia, where an earthquake had triggered a tsunami that had rolled in from the sea and taken the lives of a shockingly large number of people. On the paradise beaches of Thailand corpses lay like bundles of rotting seaweed in the sand. Many of the victims were Swedish. They were mangled and swollen and unidentified. As many as ten thousand Swedes could have drowned.

Lennart had grunted with satisfaction when he saw it. It certainly could not have come at a better time, he thought. The wave had swept away the Vaikijaur man as well.

'If it's true he's been living with those Laestadians in Årrenjarka,' said Susso, as she and Torbjörn sat at their usual table in Safari, 'then we ought to have heard something by now.'

'It was probably just talk,' Torbjörn replied. 'Like Edit said.'

'Yes, it seems like it.'

Susso, who had been quick to grab the sofa, undid the laces of her boots and pulled up her feet so she could rub them.

'And that guy in Avesta?' Torbjörn asked. 'The one who phoned?'

'He seems a bit confused,' Susso answered, shaking her head. 'I wanted to see the film, but then he started going on about how it wasn't digitised and he didn't know how to transfer it to his computer, and so on. And that's what usually happens when people are lying. The simplest things become difficult. I mean, how hard can it be? The quality doesn't matter. I just want to see if it really is him.'

'My dad could never manage a thing like that,' said Torbjörn.

'No?'

'Not a chance.'

They walked home in the darkness. Torbjörn lived up in Matto, in a bedsit on Per Högströmsgatan, and Susso went with him part of the way so that she could buy food for breakfast at the ICA store. Torbjörn said there would be a few seconds of sun the next day and his accelerator thumb was itching. Susso thought that sounded like an invitation, so she suggested they go out for a run on a snowmobile. He shook his head and said both of them were broken.

They walked into the shop, and Torbjörn began talking about *Lost*.

'You've got to see it.'

'I can't stand Channel 4. All those crappy ads.'

'You can always download it,' he said.

'My internet is so slow. It'll take forever.'

'You can borrow it from me. I've got all the episodes.'

They watched *Lost* on the laptop Torbjörn had propped on a chair at the end of the bed. Susso tried to follow the story, but there were no subtitles so she found it hard to understand everything. She was also tired. Torbjörn lay next to her, explaining what was happening. A character called John Locke was hunting a wild pig and came across a monster you never saw, and then it ended.

'But what was it then?' Susso asked.

'Hmm,' said Torbjörn. 'That's the question.'

'Tell me!'

'I don't know. We're never told.'

'I bet you it was a dinosaur. If so, I'm not watching it any more.'

'Have you got something against dinosaurs?' Torbjörn said, unexpectedly reaching out his long arm and pinching her shoulder hard.

'Ow!'

'That's what happens when you talk shit about dinosaurs.'

Susso giggled and hit back, calling him a variety of names. The harsh words seemed to bring them closer. Before it had always been bickering, coarse jokes and wrestling that ended with one of them pinching the other on the inside of the thigh and making them howl in pain. Between this and the other there had been no physical contact at all. It was as if neither of them knew how to go about it.

Torbjörn asked if she wanted to watch another episode, but she slid off the bed, stretched and said she probably ought to be getting off home. He did not try to stop her.

While she put on her boots and tied the wet laces, he stood leaning against the hall mirror, one foot angled in front of the other, his hands plunged into his pockets, watching her.

'Don't forget your things,' he said, nodding at the plastic bag she had put beside the door.

She stepped out of the front door and buried her head deep inside the collar of her coat, covering her mouth. It was snowing. Sharp grains blew in all directions at once, stinging her skin. Probably the worst kind of snowfall. Blinking was no help. The only thing she could do was look down at the ridged layer of snow, yellow under the street lamps lining Hjalmar Lundbohmsvägen.

When she reached Hermelingatan a Volvo trundled past with large clouds pouring from the exhaust at the back. Otherwise it was completely dead. It was past eleven. There was no sight or sound of roaring snow ploughs either, despite the fact that the snow had started to fall heavily. When they had left Safari the sky had been as dark as an empty blackboard.

The shadow of her hurrying form alternately lengthened and disappeared, only to reappear again suddenly. She cut across the street and carried on in the direction of the playground in the park. She usually went this way, mainly to avoid the wind, but this time there was something pulling her in that direction.

The glow from the lamp posts beside the narrow path swelled into circular patches in the darkness. The snow was easing off. It was as if she had entered a different zone where everything was untouched. The bushes were soft mounds under their white covering and the branches of the trees in the park were thickened by the snow.

Then she heard a sound, a dull squealing inside her skull. Or rather she felt it. She thought it was a car with faulty brakes, someone slowing down at a red light.

She heard the squealing again, and this time it pierced her brain so distinctly and painfully that she had to stop. Leaning forwards slightly she moved the bag to her left hand and lifted her glove to her ear. This time she had not experienced the sound as external: it was like a cry inside her head. Was there something wrong with her?

As she stood there, wondering if the sound was going to recur, she heard footsteps. She whirled round and saw a man walking towards her. He was big and wearing a dark waist-length jacket and a hat pulled down to his eyebrows. He walked with determined, loping strides and was less than ten metres away.

A strong urge to run welled up inside her but she controlled it, and instead walked on as fast as she could.

She dared not look back, wanting only to get out of the park as quickly as possible, and found herself jogging. She had reached the middle of the park and could already see the light from Adolf Hedinsvägen beyond a small hill. The plastic supermarket carrier swung to and fro in one hand, while with the other hand she managed to pull out her mobile, which had been bumping about inside her coat pocket. It was difficult to focus on the screen. But who could she call? The police would hardly have time to get there if the man attacked her. She dropped the phone back in her pocket and felt around for her key ring, thinking she could use the largest key like a small knife. Then she decided to use the bag instead. Two litres of milk weighed two kilos. That would leave an impression.

With relief she saw that someone was standing over by the crossing.

A person wearing a lingonberry-red jacket – Roland.

He met her with an amused look and did not seem especially surprised to see her, even though it was so late. He was bareheaded and snowflakes were scattered in his hair. The cord coming from the handle of a retractable dog lead looped behind a snowdrift.

'Look, Basker,' he said. 'Look who's coming here.'

Susso turned round, but the man was no longer there. She gasped for air and felt it sting inside her chest. The dog came running up to her, wondering why she was not greeting him. Its snowy paws climbed up her jeans.

'What's up?' Roland asked, pulling the lead gently.

The dog walked alongside them for a few steps but immediately wanted to go back.

'Nothing,' she said, panting. 'I just . . . I just got a terrible headache. And then . . . I don't know. It was . . . I don't know . . .' She shook her head and crouched down to pat the dog, which was standing on its hind legs, boxing with its paws. Roland's thumb clicked to shorten the lead. His pointy eyebrows had shot up.

*

Gudrun was sitting in front of the television watching a blaring action film. When she heard what had happened, that Susso thought she had been followed by someone in the park, her lips tightened to form a wide, serious fissure in her face. She fumbled with the remote and turned off the sound.

'But are you sure . . .?'

Susso sat with the cold shopping bag on her lap and was silent.

'No,' she said, after a moment. 'It was just so . . . horrible.'

Gudrun walked into the kitchen and looked down at the street, as if she was expecting the man Susso had told her about to be standing in the light of the street lamp, waiting.

Roland was still in the hall. He had not removed his jacket but had unclipped the dog and placed the lead on the chest of drawers.

'I'm going out for a while,' he said. 'To have a look around.'

'Are you mad!' Gudrun exclaimed, quickly turning round.

'I'm only going to look,' he said, shutting the front door behind him.

'We have to phone the police.'

'Drop it.'

'What if it had been a rapist! And now he'll attack someone else instead because you've slipped out of his grasp.'

Susso snorted.

'Slipped out of his grasp?' she said, bending over with an amused smile as she put the bag on the floor. She pushed away the dog, who was interested in the contents.

'What if you read about it tomorrow? How would you feel then, if you hadn't reported it?'

Susso could only shake her head. Gudrun sank back down in the sofa and folded her arms.

'You have a duty to phone the police.'

'But what can they do, Mum? He didn't actually do anything.' Susso pulled off her hat and leaned back in the armchair.

She rubbed her forehead.

'Have you ever had migraine?'

'Migraine?'

Susso nodded.

'No, I don't think so. Why, have you got a headache?'

'I'm not sure. It's . . .'

The dog leapt up and trotted out to the hall, and immediately afterwards Roland came walking into the sitting room. His face was shiny and his glasses had steamed up, so he had pushed them down his nose.

'Did you see anyone?' Gudrun asked.

He shook his head and sat down on the edge of the sofa.

'I walked all around the park and up the road a bit, but there was nothing.'

'It's just me . . .' Susso said, burying her head in her hands. 'I expect I'm imagining things. It's all this Mattias business, and the photo, and everything they wrote in the papers. It's hard, that's all. And now I think I've got a migraine as well.'

'Migraine?'

'Yes. Do you know what that feels like?'

'Well, it's probably like a really bad headache.'

'There was a kind of screaming inside my head.'

'You need a holiday,' Roland said. 'I can hear that all right.'

'I could borrow your snowmobile,' Susso said.

'You need to get further away than that if it's going to do you any good.'

'It's better than nothing. Can I? We thought of taking a ride.'

'What do you mean, we? Gudrun asked.

'Me and Torbjörn.'

There was a sharp intake of breath from Gudrun.

'Are you two getting back together?'

Susso had no intention of answering that question. She turned to Roland.

'May I?'

He sat thinking about it for a long time – either that or he was taking his time answering just for the pleasure of it. He pulled a tissue from his jacket pocket and examined it, before pressing it to his nose and moustache. He sniffed and said she could take the old Lynx. If she was careful with it.

'Torbjörn will be doing the driving, I expect, and he was practically born on a snowmobile.'

Roland pushed the tissue back into his pocket.

'Hasn't he got one of his own then?'

She realised the trap too late.

'Yes, two. But they're out of action.'

'That sounds very reassuring,' Gudrun murmured.

'That's always the way with snowmobiles,' said Roland. He grunted. 'You spend as much time fixing them as driving them. But take the old Lynx. I've got it up at the cabin. We were also thinking of going for a ride tomorrow, so we can meet up there. It's in Holmajärvi, on the Kiruna side.'

First there was barking. Then beams of light.

The camper van came driving up between the spruce trees. It was beige with a horizontal brown border halfway up and gathered grey curtains hanging in the windows. The wheels looked disproportionately small and the hexagonal hub caps were dark with rust. A shiny steel ladder climbed up the rear of the vehicle all the way to the roof, where there was a skylight.

Seved sat at the kitchen table and watched Lennart step out and make his way towards the house. He had an unusual gait. For every step he took it looked as if he would fall forwards, as if he was about to lose his balance, but he regained it each time at the last minute. He was holding the bag-covered hand against his stomach.

He appeared not to notice Seved but walked, panting, directly to the sink, where he turned on the tap, bent his head down and took a long, noisy drink. Then he turned round, wiping his jaws.

'I'm so damned thirsty.'

He took a glass from a cupboard and filled it with water, swallowing it down in one gulp. Then he opened the fridge and lifted out a bottle of cola, which he slammed on the table, only now looking at Seved. While he drank glass after glass he asked where Jirvin was.

'He's in the barn,' Seved said.

Lennart coughed up some phlegm, which he swallowed down with the cola, never taking his eyes off Seved.

'He is?'

'Yes. I think so, at least. I haven't seen him.'

Too late Seved realised he had just made a confession. Lennart had told them to keep an eye on Jirvin, and he could honestly say he had failed to do that.

In fact, he'd been avoiding him. He had taken food out once a day – cooked macaroni with smoked reindeer heart and slices of cured pork, because Torsten had said he liked that – but he had left the bucket inside the door and not so much as glanced into the gloomy interior. The fact that the bucket had been empty every time he collected it was no proof. No doubt there were eyes peering through the gap in the curtains upstairs in Hybblet, watching him walk up and down with the bucket, and it wasn't hard to work out what it contained.

But Lennart did not lecture him.

He merely looked down at the glass.

'And the boy? How is he getting on?'

'He doesn't say much.'

'But he plays?'

'He plays. Mostly the video game. He likes that.'

'He has to get out as well. It's important he goes outside.'

Seved nodded.

'It was absolutely necessary,' said Lennart. 'What we did. It was the only thing we could do. And he'll be fine here, with you.'

After he had said this he put his hand inside his jacket, coughed and brought out his wallet.

'So, payment.'

Seved accepted the notes. He sat holding them for a moment before rolling them up and stuffing them into his pocket.

'That feels good, doesn't it? Having some money?'

He nodded.

'Fetch the boy now,' Lennart said. 'I've got to have a word with him.'

Seved walked down to the cellar, and when he returned with the boy Lennart was sitting on a chair holding the hare in his arms, slowly stroking its fur.

'I was at the county court today,' he said, not looking up from the hare. 'Do you know what the county court is?'

The boy shook his head.

'Well, they're the ones who decide. About children and things. And they said Börje can look after you. That means you are going to live here from now on. Börje is your daddy now. They've also changed your name. Your new name is Bengt.'

It was a while before the boy could get any words out.

'I don't want a new name,' he said. 'I want to go home.'

He was almost shouting. The hare's ears twitched.

'Your parents don't want you any more,' Lennart said calmly.

'Yes, they do!'

'I know it's hard to understand. It's not really that they don't want you . . . have you heard your parents talk about any problems lately?'

The boy did not know.

'But they have been arguing, haven't they?'

They had.

'And what have they been arguing about?'

'Money.'

'Exactly. Your parents can't afford to look after you. They know

Börje will take good care of you and bring you up well. And you can have all the toys you want.'

'I want to talk to them.'

'I know,' said Lennart, nodding. 'I know. I thought you could talk to them too, and say goodbye properly, but it's been so hard for them financially that they've had to move, and now they live in a flat somewhere in another town, and I don't know how to get hold of them. But don't worry, I'm sure they'll phone as soon as they've got themselves sorted out.'

The sky was layered. Dark blue highest up, then greenish-yellow, and below that a pink strip where the moon floated like a pale marble. The sun was still below the horizon, hesitating, but soon a sparkling shimmer would cover the fields of snow surrounding the flat white lakes to the south of the city.

When they had driven through Ön, the residential area that lay in the shadow of the ore mountain and had been abandoned since the seventies, there had been a lot of activity. It was a shanty town of snowmobile garages, and now, after midwinter, when there were a few moments of sunlight in the middle of the day, everyone wanted to be out. It must be something biological, thought Susso. Like insects swarming.

She was sitting very still with her hands clasped between her knees, her eyes fixed on the ridge of snow lining the road as it rushed past the car window. It had become very warm in the car and she should have taken off her jacket a long time ago, but now she didn't feel like moving a millimetre. She had not yet told Torbjörn how scared she had been the previous evening. After sleeping on it and going over those seconds of being followed, she felt like an idiot. She had overreacted and felt almost sorry for the man who had been walking behind her.

Torbjörn had peeled off the upper part of his snowmobile overall. The sleeves of his thermal vest underneath had a pattern of broken stripes and had seen better days. The blue synthetic fabric was knobbly and smelled of smoke and old sweat. He was wearing a plastic watch outside his sleeve on his left wrist. He had owned that watch for as long as she could remember, at least since secondary school. There was so much about him that was familiar. Unchanged. But even though he was the same old Torbjörn, she could not reach him, however hard she tried. He had always looked shy, but these days she could only occasionally catch his eye.

It was light by the time they reached Holmajärvi's northern shore, and they could see far out over the ice. Susso pointed at Gudrun, who was standing with a snow shovel in her hands outside a log cabin with snow piled up to the windowsills. A second later Roland came walking out of the cabin. He was looking very satisfied with himself, holding a packet of raisins in his fist and chewing.

The doors of the shed used as a garage were open and the snowmobiles had been brought out. One was a heavy Lynx with a wide track and a black aluminium chassis, tinted extra-high windscreen and wing mirrors. Behind the dual saddle was a back support with a grey, mottled reindeer skin hanging over it. The second snowmobile was also a Lynx, but an older model with taped handlebar grips.

Susso hoisted her backpack onto her shoulder, took out the helmets and shut the car door by pushing it with her foot. Torbjörn lifted a plastic container of petrol out of the boot and carried it at arm's length to keep his ski overall from getting dirty. He greeted Roland and Gudrun with a brief nod of his head and walked once round the snowmobiles, scrutinising them with eyes like slits. Roland leaned against the veranda railing, watching him. From below the sides of his cap his hair protruded like small upturned wings, and the tip of his nose was comically red. He said it was a ninety-seven and that he had extended the track for better performance.

Torbjörn leaned forwards.

'This can't be the original belt?'

'No, I've fitted a wider one. I didn't think it cleared the snow very well.'

Roland was surprisingly pleasant, explaining that the little kitty cat had a full tank and was ready to ride. He started his snowmobile, put on his helmet and glasses, then stood with his padded leather gloves on the handlebars.

'What have you got yourself?' he shouted above the rattle of the engine.

'A fifty-nine,' Torbjörn answered, fastening his overalls at the neck. 'And an old Polaris.'

'Polaris,' snorted Roland, as he turned the machine around slowly to allow Gudrun to climb on and sit down. 'They're like reindeer. They head for roads at the first sign of snow.'

Then he revved the engine, making Gudrun throw her arms around his waist, and let out a muffled shout from inside his helmet. Not until they had ridden out onto the ice did Roland sit down. In a flurry of fine snow they raced off across the lake towards the far side and the dark jagged silhouette of the pine forest against the sky.

Grains of snow flying in the raw air struck her ski glasses. They did not touch her, but even so it made her frown. If she turned her head, her helmet hit Torbjörn's shoulder, and occasionally there was the sound of plastic colliding with plastic, so she tried to sit still. She huddled down and looked at the trees, at the firs in their patchy overcoats of snow, crowded together. The lines of willowy birches with frost-covered branches. The hissing white clouds around the skis as they ran over the ridged trail.

They were not going fast. He's afraid of damaging the snowmobile tread on a rock or something, she thought. He had always been a careful person. Considerate. Wanting to do things properly.

There was a load of logs on the back, held together with a strap. They planned to find a place to sit for a while and make a fire.

They had been travelling for less than a kilometre when they caught sight of a wide trail leading steeply upwards among the trees. Torbjörn's helmet turned sideways, he pointed and Susso nodded.

Torbjörn stood holding a load of logs while Susso kicked the snow aside, revealing moss and low, shrubby bushes.

'That's enough,' he said, taking a step forwards to show that he wanted to put down the load he was carrying.

They had found a small plateau where the wind had made soft drifts of snow, revealing the ground in places. Spruce saplings and willow twigs peeked through. Stunted, knotty birches bowed down around them. Hanging from the lean branches were mourning veils of lichen, and the icy crust of the birch bark glistened in the rays of the sun, which was already on its way down.

Torbjörn poured the petrol, a yellow stream that splashed against the logs.

Then he threw on a lighted match. Squinting, he stood for a while watching the flames before going back with the petrol can and attaching it to the rear of the snowmobile. While he was there he kicked the footplates a few times to get rid of the clumps of ice that had collected there.

He took a thermos from the backpack. He twisted off the lid, which split into two mugs, one of steel and one of black plastic.

'Steel or plastic?' he said, but when there was no immediate reply he poured coffee into the steel mug and handed it to her.

She put her lips to the coffee but thought it was too hot, so she put the mug down in the snow.

Torbjörn sat leaning forwards and stared down at the reflective mirror of coffee in his mug, thinking. He had sucked in his lips until his mouth was a thin straight line, and she could see he was about to say something that was important to him. But instead he stretched his neck and wrinkled his eyebrows. Something behind Susso had attracted his attention.

'What is it?' she said, turning round. He had raised himself up, straining his head to see.

'What could that be? Is it a . . . bat?'

'What?' she said, smiling in disbelief.

At first she thought it was a small bird that had become caught up in the birch behind her, unable to get free. But then she saw its snout and the dog-like face. The domed folded ears. Its mouth was wide open and it seemed to be screaming at the top of its lungs in anguish. One of its wings was closed and the other unfolded, the thin skin a pale grey and criss-crossed with veins like cracks. The claws on its hind feet gripped the delicate frosty sprigs. It looked unnatural. As if it wanted to sit in the tree but was unable to.

Susso's eyebrows rose in astonished arcs. She had never been this close to a bat before. And in winter?

Slowly Torbjörn took a step through the smoke that was coiling sluggishly over the ground. He had taken out his mobile and was directing it at the bat.

'It must have woken up,' she said. 'From its hibernation or something . . .'

He nodded and crept closer, but clearly he overstepped some invisible boundary because abruptly the birch twitched and the bat flew off, a grey rag that fled into the shelter of the trees and was gone.

'I wonder if it will be all right?' he said, sitting down by the fire and putting his mobile back into the pocket on his trouser leg.

Susso was quietly watching the flames crackling upwards. Her face had become so hot it hurt and she straightened up and moved back a step. But the pain did not go away. She rubbed her forehead, which had filled with the same piercing noise that she had heard in the park. She was about to say something about her headache when there was a crack from the bottom of the slope.

Then she froze.

In among the trees stood a man, watching them. His eyes were staring through the gap between his hat and the woollen scarf he had wrapped around his face up to the bridge of his nose. An axe head glinted down by his knees.

A second later another man appeared diagonally behind the first. He was heavier and struggling to walk. Against his chest he held a moose-hunting rifle with a telescopic sight. The shoulder strap hung in an arc of shiny leather. He was wearing a thigh-length woollen jacket in black and grey check, and a cap that shaded his flabby, almost spherical face, with its pink cheeks and patches of stubble. He was peering at them with his deep-set eyes.

Both pockets on the legs of his baggy, faded combat trousers were open. It was impossible to tell his age. He could have been twenty or forty.

No one said a word. All that could be heard was the sound of the fire gently crackling. The fat man lifted the rifle, grinned, and glanced at the older man, who had taken a step forwards. The snow had fastened in chunks among the laces of his heavy boots. The axe he was carrying was one used for splitting logs. He raised it slightly, seeming to weigh it in his hand.

'Did you want something?' Torbjörn finally asked.

There was a whooshing sound, and the next moment the man with the masked face rushed forwards with the axe raised above his head. But Torbjörn was already on his feet. He rammed his shoulder into the man and with his left hand grabbed the arm holding the axe. Susso screamed as they collided.

Locked together they fell to the ground and rolled over and over, grunting and panting. Snow and sparks flew around them. Boots scraped and thudded.

'Drop the axe!' yelled Torbjörn. 'Drop the axe, for fuck's sake!'

The overweight man seemed uncertain about leaving the shelter of the trees. He had raised the butt of the rifle to his shoulder and stepped to one side, and was following the fight with his eyes. From time to time he raised his rifle but did nothing more than take aim before lowering it again.

The scarf had slipped from the face of the man lying on the ground and he bared his teeth in a wet grin. Susso realised it was the same man who had tailed her in the park. He had long grey hair and looked about sixty. It did not take long for Torbjörn to overpower him and end the fight. The axe landed a short way off and Torbjörn was trying to hold the man and press him into the snow to get him to keep still. It soon became too much for the older man. His chest was being crushed and his face was turning a deep blood-red. A couple of veins stood out on his forehead. Torbjörn had landed a few forceful punches across his mouth and blood-stained saliva was oozing from his lower lip. The only part of him that had not given up was his eyes.

They burned with rage.

'Shoot then!' he yelled at his companion.

When Torbjörn heard the rasping command he rolled onto his side, using the older man's body as cover. Immediately the man came to life. Perhaps he was cunning enough to have been lying there gathering his strength. The fight picked up again but it was not long before Torbjörn regained the upper hand. He pressed one of his elbows hard against the man's jaw. Powerless, the man turned his cheek to the ground and spat out red flecks, which were absorbed by the snow.

'Shoot,' he mumbled. 'Shoo-o-o-t!'

A faint click was heard from the little trigger on the rifle as the barrel was raised. The younger man's cheek fell in folds against the oily surface of the rifle butt as his eye peered through the crosshairs of the sight.

Susso realised she had to do something. The axe was too far away, so she reached for the thermos and sprinted a few steps until she was a couple of metres away from the man with the rifle. Then she threw the thermos with all her strength.

She missed. But the man was so surprised when the thermos flashed past his eyes that he stumbled backwards, and Susso reached him quickly. She hurled herself at him, grabbed hold of his rifle and tried to pull it away from him. The man was stockily built but had been caught unawares, so when Susso shoved her boot into his stomach and pressed as hard as she could she managed to snatch the gun away from him.

Hands flailing, the man fell backwards and crashed into a greying spruce, which clawed at his jacket, ripped off his cap and covered him in a sheet of snow. Almost immediately he was up on all fours, studying Susso, who was standing with a firm grip on the rifle a few metres above him. He got up and loped down the slope. After about ten metres he stopped and turned round. He was breathing so hard it looked painful.

'What are you going to do now?' he shouted, resting his hands on his knees, panting and dribbling saliva. 'You little slag!'

He spat out the words, sneering at her.

Susso raised the rifle but the man did not attempt to move. He stood where he was, his fair hair standing on end above his perspiring forehead, and glared at her with a disdainful expression.

Was he stupid? She had a good mind to fire off a shot between his legs just to see the fear hit him like a fist in the face. On the other hand, she wasn't convinced he would be afraid – at least, not so it would show. He's crazy, she thought. A fucking psycho.

'Susso . . .'

Torbjörn was standing behind her, tall and at an angle, as if he had hurt his leg. He was very pale and sucking in short gasps of air between his tense lips.

'Come on,' he said, pulling her jacket, trying to get her to leave, to get back to the snowmobile.

'But what about him?' she said, wrenching herself free and pointing the barrel at the man, who had picked up his cap and was brushing it off.

'Forget him. We're leaving.'

The older man was lying stretched out beside the fire. Although

Susso was unwilling to look at him, her eyes were drawn to the lifeless face. His eyelids were dark grey and blood had dried in the stubble on the slack chin. His leather gloves were fur-lined and enclosed wrists that were skinny.

'What have you done? Is he dead?'

Without answering Torbjörn put on his helmet, grabbed the handle of the starter cord and with a powerful pull started the engine. As he turned the snowmobile the headlight swept the trees around them. He stood up, letting the engine nose forwards, finding its own way. Exhaust fumes mingled with the smoke from the dying fire.

It took a while for Susso to realise it was time to jump on, because she was shaken and most of her concentration was fixed on the direction the man in the military-green trousers had taken.

Reluctantly, she stood the rifle against the snowmobile, picked up her helmet and pressed it onto her head, feeling the lining cold against her cheeks. Then she climbed up behind Torbjörn and rested the weapon on her knees.

'Leave it there!' he shouted.

'Not fucking likely!'

Before he accelerated away he leaned forwards slightly, and Susso, who had rested one hand on his shoulder, moved with him. They drove down in the same tracks they had made on their way there, and not until they had reached the trail and Torbjörn had accelerated as hard as he could, the wind blowing bitingly cold against Susso's throat, could she gather her thoughts and get them in some kind of order.

The police arrived at Holmajärvi only thirty minutes after Susso had phoned. It must be a county record, I said to them as they stepped out of the patrol car, but either they didn't hear or were pretending not to. No doubt they are used to dealing with people who are agitated and want them to get there instantly. Every minute seems like an eternity when something terrible has happened.

Torbjörn was sitting in the cabin knocking back coffee topped up with something stronger by Roland. He was leaning heavily on the solid pine table, pulling at the hairs on his lower arm, convinced he had killed the man he had been fighting with. I suggested he phone his parents, but Susso gave me such a sharp look that I backed away.

When the police returned a couple of hours later without having found even a trace of blood, and Torbjörn had convinced himself that they had been looking in the right place – on the laminated map the police inspector had unfolded Torbjörn had pointed out exactly to the millimetre where the attack had taken place – I saw the misery in his tense face dissolve in relief. He began firing questions at them instead, encouraged by the alcohol and the adrenalin that was probably still rushing through his body, but of course the police had nothing to say. All they had to go on was the statement he and Susso had given them. They were clearly puzzled and spoke quietly among themselves. The woman, her hair pulled back in a short ponytail, moved away to make a phone call, and then sat in the car and talked over the radio. I heard her mention the moose-hunting rifle.

'A class one weapon,' she said. 'A Remington.'

Susso explained that she had seen one of the men following her the previous evening, and that she thought it was all related to the kidnapping of Mattias Mickelsson, there was no other explanation, but the police were only mildly interested in that theory. They wanted a detailed, factual account of what had taken place, and nothing else. It was insulting and almost off-hand, the way they dismissed Susso when she tried to explain how it was all connected. I did my best to convince them she was telling the truth, but in the end I had to go outside and stand in the cold. I was hot from the warmth in the cabin and my suppressed rage, and as I stared at the patrol car, a V70 with a fringe of icicles at the front, only then did it occur to me that of course they knew who Susso was – they knew very well who was phoning when the call came through. That she was a Myrén.

It was morning, bitterly cold with a high, cloudless sky, and Seved was clearing snow when he heard the door of the camper van creak. The stocky man squeezed through the doorway with a grunt and upturned a plastic bottle. It gurgled quickly as it emptied, leaving a yellowish-brown hole in the snow. The big man flashed Seved a grim look and then disappeared inside the van. When he came out again he was wearing his sunglasses and a peaked hat. His cheeks were red and blotchy. No doubt it had been a cold night.

'You've got to get the boy outdoors,' he said. 'Make sure he plays out here for a bit.'

'Okay.'

'He can build a snowman or whatever the hell he likes, just as long as he's out of doors.'

He took out his mobile and looked at it as he lifted it up towards the pearl-grey sky. He was annoyed with the reception, that much was clear.

'You haven't heard from Börje?'

Seved shook his head.

He made sure the boy played outside for a few hours during the morning, and for a couple of hours in the afternoon as well. Signe had found a sledge somewhere and she pulled him round and round the yard with seemingly limitless energy, and the boy thought it was fun.

Even the foxshifter seemed to enjoy it. Seved caught a glimpse of him by chance in the darkness inside the barn door. He was standing there, staring out, and when Signe and the boy came into view he stepped out to watch them. And even though he wasn't smiling, because he could hardly do that, he gave the impression of feeling something other than the deep sorrow Seved always thought he could see in his expression.

Börje came home late that evening. He sat in the kitchen, coughing. There was a spreading purple bruise above his top lip and one of his eyes was swollen. Seved asked nothing because there was nothing he wanted to know. It was not until the following morning, when he heard Lennart's gruff tone, that he realised there had been a screw-up in Kiruna.

Susso sat in Torbjörn's kitchen reading the newspaper. Torbjörn was cooking. He was holding a fork that he jabbed into the saucepan from time to time.

The attack at Holmajärvi was reported in the paper, and as she read the article Susso regretted speaking to the reporter who had phoned. She must have been suffering from shock to a certain extent, but she also felt she had to tell them about it. The police had shown little interest when she told them why she thought that she, in particular, had been attacked, but the newspapers had listened. Except they made it look as if she was convinced it was Mattias's kidnappers who had tried to attack her, and when she saw it all in black and white, it did not look very logical.

'I want to get away,' she said. 'Last night I slept at Mum's – well, I didn't sleep exactly. I lay awake most of the night. I keep thinking of those men who turned up at Holmajärvi. I know they won't come but it *feels* like they will. I don't want to stay here. Not until the police have picked them up. So I can find out why. That's almost the worst thing, not knowing what I've *done*. It's got something to do with Mattias, I get that. But not why someone would want to kill me.'

'Going away for a while might not be such a bad idea,' said Torbjörn, nodding.

'Can't you come with me?'

'Well, it's a long way,' he muttered. 'What do you think, fifteen hundred kilometres, times two?'

'Eleven hundred.'

He lifted the saucepan from the stove, and as he tipped the macaroni into the colander his face disappeared in a cloud of steam.

'I don't know if I want to travel that far in your car,' he said.

Susso leaned her elbows on the table and picked at her thumbnail.

'Let's take Mum's car. She's said she'll pay for everything. Food, hotel – the lot. She wants me to leave town as well. She's afraid too.'

'She seemed angry in Holmajärvi,' he said.

'That's what happens when you're scared.'

He nodded.

'She wants to leave as soon as possible. Tomorrow, preferably.'

'Is she coming as well?' asked Torbjörn, looking surprised.

'Well, yes, of course.'

'But she, like, hates me.'

'No, she doesn't,' Susso said, folding the paper so that Torbjörn could set the saucepan down on it. 'Your mum, maybe. But not you.'

Seved and Signe were building with Duplo bricks at the kitchen table with the boy when Börje walked in through the door. He stood by the sink for a while, watching them. They had built a castle with battlements for the mouseshifter, which was sitting on the table, watching.

'Bengt,' said Börje, and when the boy did not react he leaned across the table, trying to catch his eye, but no eye looked back.

'Bengt,' he repeated, louder.

The boy raised his hand and scratched the side of his nose, and when he had hidden his hand under the table again he said quietly, almost in a whisper:

'I'm not called that.'

'Yes, you are. You are now.'

'I'm called Mattias,' he insisted.

'Not any more.'

The boy was silent.

'The quicker you understand your name is Bengt, the better it will be,' Börje said kindly. 'It will be easier that way. I promise.'

When the boy lifted his head, tears had welled up in his eyes and started to stream down his cheeks. He was holding a plastic brick but seemed unsure what to do with it.

'But that's not my name,' he said, his voice high-pitched from crying. 'I'm called Mattias. And I want to go home!'

Börje took a deep breath and tried to keep calm. But he did not succeed.

'No!' he roared, slamming his fist onto the table and making the boy jump. The mouseshifter fell to the floor, making an unhappy chattering noise. 'Your parents don't want you any more, don't you understand that? They're not able to look after you. They can't afford it! I'm looking after you. I'm your daddy now and you should be pleased about that. You should be grateful about that. Because where else would you have gone? You would have ended up in a foster home, and you wouldn't want that. They're nasty places.'

After he had said this he bent down and picked up the little creature.

'This is your home now. You've got to understand that! And your name is Bengt. It says so in the papers, the adoption papers.'

The boy lowered his head. It was shaking.

'Play with Jim now,' said Börje, dropping the little object onto the table. 'Otherwise he'll think you don't want him.'

Torbjörn must have been standing waiting in the entrance hall because he came out as soon as we pulled up outside his apartment building. He seemed a bit shy when he said hello to me. He looked away quickly. We had not met since that awful day in Holmajärvi and I suppose we were unsure of each other. To be honest, I'd always had a problem with him because his mother had turned my life upside down, but that was hardly his fault. Even so, I held it against him. It's easy to blame anyone who is even remotely involved.

Susso was curled up in the back under her jacket, with her feet up on the seat, so Torbjörn had to sit in the front. He rested his backpack on his knees as if he was going to be getting out any minute. I told him to put it in the back, and he did so immediately. My voice had sounded unintentionally abrupt and so I hurried to thank him for coming with us.

He nodded and looked out of the window.

'And thank you for saving Susso's life.'

'She saved mine,' he mumbled.

'Yes,' I said, 'but we're the ones who got you involved in all of this. Our family.'

He didn't answer.

South of Överkalix we pulled in at the Vippabacken motorway cafe to get something to eat. It was my decision: I hadn't been there for fifteen years at least. A wooden sculpture of a Laplander stood outside the door, welcoming in the customers, and I remembered him. We had both aged fifteen years since last time. Even the stuffed bear was still there. It was standing in the small shop and staring into the restaurant, its gaping lips as black as liquorice. I said hello to it.

While we waited for the food I walked around looking at all the stock. The restaurant resembled a disorganised living-history museum but everything was for sale – even the bear in the entrance. I thought I could probably learn a thing or two from the place.

There was a stuffed jay and a stuffed pine marten. A conductor's bag with empty coin dispensers, and a spinning wheel. Reindeer antlers at various stages, and moose antlers, shovel-shaped and pronged. Small landscape paintings with animals. A salmon spear. A bicycle with an old-fashioned saddle. Bread paddles, second-hand and new. Stickers with pictures of moose and the Swedish flag. Chests – the ones that were not empty were locked. Christmas-tree baubles, single or in bunches. Fishing line. A Finnish harp. A yoke with rusting hooks. A bear trap with a diameter the size of a hula hoop. Father and Mother Christmas dolls, with steel-rimmed spectacles. Old wooden pulleys. Nostalgic postcards and posters. Wooden ladles. Leather gloves and woollen gloves. Trolls with huge noses and tangled hair, with labels showing they came from souvenir wholesaler Allan Flink in Järpen, which is also where some of my stock comes from.

Sitting in a tiny painted chair right at the back was a doll, an old bronzed Sami man with a miserable expression. His traditional coat fitted badly and he had lost his left hand. All that was left were a few dangling threads.

Beside him logs had been piled up in crates and his best blue outfit was covered in woodchips, so you could understand why he was in a bad mood.

'Where's Susso? ' I asked Torbjörn, when I got back from looking around.

From the ceiling above our table hung an ancient gun, a vast chandelier with electric light bulbs, Sami boots with hooked toes, ordinary leather boots, bowls and copper pans.

'She's talking to the police,' he said, squirting ketchup over his food.

He was eating Falu sausage, fried egg and fried potatoes, the same as Susso had ordered. I was still waiting for my hamburger, so I stole a slice of potato from Susso's plate at the very moment she walked back between the tables.

'It was a stolen weapon,' she said, sitting down. 'It belongs to someone called Holmqvist, but he has nothing to do with the case, they're positive about that. His cabin in the fells was burgled four years ago and the theft was reported.'

She cut a piece of sausage and put it into her mouth.

'But the sight wasn't his,' she said, chewing. 'So that arsehole must have attached it.'

'But what about fingerprints and things?' I asked, reaching out for another piece of potato. She stabbed my knuckles with her fork.

'They're still waiting to hear about that,' she answered, waving the fork to indicate I could take the potato if I wanted it. 'My fingerprints will be all over it, that's for sure, but he was wearing gloves.'

'But he might have handled it without gloves earlier,' I said.

She nodded.

'We'll have to see,' she said. 'It would be such a relief if they found them soon.'

My food arrived. I unscrewed the top of a large container of seasoning and sprinkled it over the thin fries. I hadn't eaten since breakfast and I was starving.

'But what did they say?' asked Torbjörn. 'Do they think it's because you took that photo? Do they think that's the reason they attacked us? Because in that case it proves the dwarf is mixed up in the kidnapping. And that more people are involved.'

'I've thought about that,' Susso said. 'Let's say that's the case. That it's this Vaikijaur man who has taken Mattias, and that the photo I took means him and his partners will get caught. Assuming he has partners. But why attack me, in that case? What good would that do? The damage had already been done. It can hardly be a kind of revenge.'

'No,' said Torbjörn. 'That's true.'

'I can see only one explanation. They don't like what I'm doing.'

'You mean your website?' I asked.

'The very fact,' she said in a low voice, glancing quickly at the two men sitting at the next table, 'the very fact that there are people out there who hate my website so much they're prepared to murder me proves I'm right. It proves the Vaikijaur man *is* a troll.'

'Then perhaps you'd better take it down,' I said, with my mouth full.

Susso sprinkled salt on her potatoes as she shook her head.

'I'm not planning to sit here and wait until it all calms down. I'm going to get those bastards. They'll regret it. What do you think, Torbjörn?'

Torbjörn looked up and then nodded.

'I feel sorry for them,' he said. 'Seriously.'

*

I felt revived when I sat in the driver's seat again, and despite the worrying and fairly extreme decisions Susso had talked about in the restaurant, the atmosphere was noticeably improved after we had eaten something and drunk a cup of coffee. We were getting closer to the coast too, so it felt as if we were making headway south. The blanket of snow on the fir trees formed a long wall along the roadside, shimmering pale pink. As I drove, Torbjörn told me about his training. He had taken an electronics course at Luleå University of Technology, and it seemed well worth it because he had found work straight away.

I also asked him about his mother and whether she liked living up at Riksgränsen, but Susso yelped like a little dog from the back seat.

'Oh, give it a rest, can't you?' she said. 'Leave him alone!'

And so I did.

But he hadn't been offended. He smiled at me in secret when Susso wasn't looking.

I had booked rooms for us at the Höga Kusten Bridge hotel, and we ate dinner at the restaurant there. We sat in silence looking at the menu and then we all ordered the meat loaf with mashed potato and salted cucumber, the speciality of the house. I looked out of the panoramic window but it was pitch black outside. The bridge looked like two glowing arcs in the night.

I noticed that Susso and Torbjörn's eyes met from time to time. It wasn't over between them, you could tell that a mile off.

'We'll have to share a room,' I said, after the food had been served. 'I hope you don't mind.'

They said that was all right.

'I think it will make me feel more secure,' Susso said.

'What about you, Torbjörn?' I said. 'How do you feel about it, really? Will you be able to sleep?'

He shrugged his shoulders.

'I thought it would feel better once we got away from town. But I'm still feeling tense, like someone's going to leap on me. Even the waiter. It affects you deeply, so deeply you can't calm yourself down.'

'You'd better have some wine,' I said.

He nodded and emptied his glass.

It was not only the fact that Susso Myrén was still alive. The attack was all over the newspapers as well, which no doubt meant her website was receiving even more attention. So Börje and Jola had made the situation even worse by trying to shut her up. Seved was not allowed to know the content of the website – he was not even really sure what a website was – but he could understand what the fuss was about. She had come too close. Others might have suspected something in the past, but this was different.

She was investigating.

And Lennart wanted to put a stop to it, at any price.

Which is why he went ballistic with rage when she suddenly disappeared.

Jola, who had travelled up to Kiruna to finish what he and Börje had started, phoned Lennart to say she was nowhere to be found. He had parked outside her flat for over twenty-four hours but there was no sign of her. Her mobile was switched off and had been for a long time. The following day he had phoned her mother's shop pretending to be a journalist. He had spoken to Susso's sister, who told him Susso had gone away.

Where?

Somewhere in Dalarna, she thought.

That same evening Lennart had set off. And he was not travelling alone. Seved saw how heavily laden the camper van had been.

They slept late and then ate breakfast sitting at the same table as the night before, and this time the view was revealed. Beyond the fence the ground dropped steeply away. There was a cluster of snow-topped pines on the slope, keeping watch over the gigantic pylons and the cars like small splashes of sunlight travelling along the road far below. Susso was bent over the newspaper. She had slept badly. Thoughts had raced around in her head and both Gudrun and Torbjörn had snored, keeping pace with each other, or so it seemed. Susso had thrown money at them to try and get them to stop. When Gudrun woke up and found her bed covered in one-krona coins she had sat up and cried: 'I'm rich!'

She was joking all the time, trying as hard as she could to lighten the mood. Susso knew she was doing it for her sake, that it pained her to see Susso depressed and so afraid that she looked with suspicion at everybody they came in contact with.

On the opposite side of the bay there was a dark ridge of forest, with three wind turbines rising above it like huge white flowers.

'Look, they're not moving,' said Gudrun, pointing with her coffee cup. 'That means they've run out of diesel.'

Susso rubbed her eyes and smiled. She couldn't help herself.

Torbjörn was driving. Gudrun sat in the front and Susso in the back with her arms folded and her head resting on her jacket, which she had rolled up against the door. It was easier for her to sleep now. Torbjörn and Gudrun's chatter and the vibration from the car made her feel drowsy.

After a couple of hours they stopped at a filling station to stretch their legs, as Gudrun put it, but Susso stayed where she was, unfastened her seat belt and lay down on the seat. She was certain her mother would tell her to fasten it as soon as they were out on the road again, but she didn't. She let her sleep. And she slept deeply for a long time. When she woke up they were travelling through a forest with trees standing like black crystals beside the road. All that remained of the snow was an occasional isolated patch.

'Where are we?' she asked, sitting up.

'Gävle,' said Gudrun.

They were travelling on a B road and it was beginning to get dark. Torbjörn had to change constantly from full beam to dipped, and the road ahead shot into view and then disappeared, shot back into view and disappeared.

Torbjörn nodded his head in the direction of a dark opening in the forest.

'This is where Gudrun passed through,' he said.

'Is it?' Gudrun said, craning her neck to look out of the window. 'Was she this far north?'

'Why did they call the hurricane Gudrun?' asked Susso. 'Did it come on your name day then, Mum?'

'Don't you know when my name day is?'

'Seventh of January? Eighth?'

'The twenty-fourth of November. One month before Christmas!'

'But who cares?'

'I care.'

'When's my name day then?'

'You haven't got one.'

'No, and that's because I've got a Lapp name.'

'It was your dad's idea. You're called Maria as well. You can change to that if you're so keen on having a name day. It's the twenty-eighth of February.'

'So why *was* the hurricane called Gudrun?' asked Torbjörn.

'Firstly,' said Gudrun, 'she wasn't a hurricane, she was a cyclone at best. Or worst. Roland teased me about it, naturally, so I looked into it. The Norwegian Institute of Meteorology decided on the name. Storms are given names so you won't confuse cyclones and hurricanes that happen at the same time. They alternate between male and female. All in alphabetical order from ready-prepared lists.'

'When's your name day, Torbjörn?' asked Susso.

'Ninth of March. I know because it comes after Siv, and that's why Mum wanted me to be called Torbjörn. If I'd been a girl, I would have been called Edla.'

'Edla?' snorted Susso.

He nodded.

'What would I have been called, Mum, if I'd been a boy?'

'I don't know. I knew you were a girl.'

'Yes, but if!'

'Didn't you hear what I said? I knew you were a girl!'

Seved stood with the red bucket in his hand, looking into the barn. The gaps in the walls were compact streams of radiant light. There were large windows near the ceiling at both ends, but it was black and uncertain below the loft. The space was a mass of shadows that overlapped and became successively darker. From under a tarpaulin poked the shafts of an old sleigh. There were kick sledges in there as well, in a tangle of rust-brown runners and turned wooden handles: he counted five all together. The wood on most of them was old and grey but one was bright-yellow and even had reflectors. He knew it was Ejvor's.

Next to the kick sledges was a moped. Was that his old moped? It was so old it was impossible to see the make. Oh yes, *SACHS* it said at the base of the engine cover. He saw it as he crouched down to examine it. The tyres were as thin as bicycle tyres. With his fingertips he brushed away the dust and wood shavings from the glass cover of the speedometer. The dial went up to seventy but it was doubtful the moped could reach even half that speed. Unless it was souped-up. Of course. Had Börje done that? He actually had no idea. Börje had tried to get him interested in engines, kneeling on the ground and pointing to cylinders and carburettors with black oily fingers, explaining how they worked, but he had not taken it in. He had nodded but not really listened.

There was left-over macaroni in the bucket, stuck together

in a yellowish block at the bottom, clearly frozen solid. It was glittering.

The foxshifter was eating less these days. He was unsure whether to tell Börje about it. He did not want to worry him unnecessarily. A kind of darkness had settled over his face and he was often snappy, even with the boy. Probably it was easier for him that way. Under the anger he could hide all his other feelings.

There was a click far back in the gloom of the barn and he knew at once he was being watched. He felt the little man's eyes on him, even though he could not see them. But was he up in the loft or down below?

He had taken a step to one side to be able to see better when he heard someone call out. At first he thought it came from outside and he turned to the barn door. Was it Signe?

He heard it again and realised the cry was inside his head.

It was a woman calling and she was far, far away. Only a shard of her desperate cry reached him. It was as if her voice was drowning in the sighing of a thousand treetops.

Seved walked swiftly out of the barn without even closing the door behind him.

It was him. He had got to him. Reached out and got to him.

In the yard he met Börje, walking fast. When he caught sight of Seved he turned round immediately and called over his shoulder:

'There's a phone call for you.'

'For me?'

Seved walked into the hall and put down the bucket. The receiver was dangling near the floor, and he lifted it up and said hello.

Lennart's voice came through over the sound of traffic. He was practically shouting.

'You've got to get up to Kiruna.'

Seved wanted to protest but all he could say was:

'Right.'

'I've got to find out where she's going, that Myrén woman. What she's doing. Jola has tried but he's getting nowhere. So you've got to go up and talk to her sister.'

'But how am I going to . . .'

'Those lemmings I gave you in Arvidsjaur . . .'

'Yes?'

'Take them with you. Then she'll speak, you'll see.'

'But they're down in the hide, I think.'

'You can go down there now. There's no danger.'

Go down in the hide? He had never even put his hand on the cellar door before.

'But make sure you go carefully!'

'But how can I . . . what if they've hidden themselves and don't want to come . . .?'

'You'll have to tell her you work for a newspaper or something. Tell her you've got to get hold of her sister as soon as possible. And if she won't say anything, use the lemmings. It'll come out then all right. But it's important she doesn't get suspicious because then she'll warn her sister and we'll never get hold of her. So watch your step! And it's got to happen now. You've got to leave today, Seved.'

Börje was lying on the sofa in the sitting room, watching the boy with tired eyes. He was sitting on the floor holding a small car made of green metal. There were more cars scattered around his outstretched legs. Seved recognised them all. They had once been his. He had heard the boy run the cars over the wooden floor but had not thought Börje would be anywhere around. That surprised him. He was even holding a car, a red pickup.

'What are you doing?'

Börje lifted up the car.

'We're playing with the cars. It's one of those demolition derbies.'

'You having fun?' Seved asked the boy, who did not answer.

He stood silently for a while, thinking about what Lennart had said.

'Is it empty down in the hide?' he asked. 'Did he take both of them?'

Börje shook his head and knocked the car against the sofa cushion.

'Who did he take with him then?'

'Who do you think?'

The answer calmed Seved a little. He'd rather deal with Skabram than Karats.

'Lennart wants me to go up to Kiruna, and I'm to take Torsten's lemmingshifters with me. I've got to go down in the hide and fetch them.'

'Are you taking them up to Jola, or what?'

Seved shook his head.

'I've got to talk to the sister. Me and the . . . lemmings.'

Börje drew in a few deep breaths and Seved saw that he was furious but keeping it under control.

'It's not a game, you know,' he said, looking seriously at Seved. 'Those are nasty creatures, not to be messed with. Did he really say that you've got to talk to her? Isn't Jola going with you?'

'Not as far as I know.'

Börje stood up.

'I'll get them for you.'

'Are you sure?'

He pushed the toy pickup into Seved's palm.

'You drive carefully.'

The village where Mats Ingvar lived was about twenty kilometres south of Avesta. They drove along a gravel road through colourless agricultural land. There was no snow apart from patches in the roadside ditches.

Beside the narrow road lay thick branches, brought down and dragged from the forest by the weather. They drove past a farm where a tractor was parked beside a gritty snowdrift, and shortly afterwards caught sight of a leaning building. It looked as if it would topple over onto the road at any moment. A piece of bright yellow cloth was dangling from one of the eaves.

A man was standing in the driveway in front of a Hyundai with a dirty rear window. He was squinting and it was clear from his red cheeks that he had been out of doors for some time. His jacket was half unzipped and it filled out like a balloon with each gust of wind.

He pointed at a pile of sand further along the roadside, motioning for them to park there. On each side of the road were paddocks surrounded by electric fences. One of the paddocks stretched back up to the field and surrounded a huge barn built partly of stone, and behind it stood quite a large farmhouse.

Mats stood on the road waiting for them, with his hands in his pockets.

'This is Gudrun, my mother,' Susso said, indicating. 'And this is Torbjörn.'

They shook hands and exchanged a few words. Susso asked about the paddocks: did they have horses there? Yes, but they were not his. He only owned the paddocks.

'They're kept on my land,' he said. 'That way I don't have to mow the grass. And it gets fertilised at the same time. So it works out well.'

Gudrun folded her arms and turned her gaze towards the field. There was not much to see apart from frozen clay and one or two strips of snow. Torbjörn had taken out his mobile and began tapping the buttons.

Mats zipped up his jacket. He grimaced in the wind, which had turned much colder.

'Shall we look at the film straight away, or would you like to see where he lived first?'

'The film, I think,' Susso replied.

They walked towards the red farmhouse that lay directly beside the edge of the field. Torbjörn was left behind with his phone.

'Are you coming?' Susso asked.

He nodded but showed no sign of hurrying.

With their feet crunching on the gravel they walked beside a severely pruned lilac hedge up to the front of the house and stepped in through the door. Below the hall mirror was a large, white-painted chest, and Gudrun put her handbag down on it.

Mats lumbered ahead of them.

'What about some coffee?' he said.

'Yes, please,' Gudrun said, removing her jacket. 'I could certainly do with some.'

The house had been extended and the kitchen was in the

old part, where the ceiling was low. Torbjörn had to duck as he stepped over the high threshold. It was a little kitchen, clean and shining, with white tongue and groove panelling, stained with resin over the knots in the wood. A curtain with narrow stripes hung like a skirt in front of a humming dishwasher. On the windowsill stood a pile of bird books, with a pair of binoculars on top. At the rear of the house was a small lawn and two towering birches, and beyond them the fields, stretching into infinity in the twilight.

When the coffee machine started to bubble Mats opened a cupboard and took out a half packet of biscuits, which he placed in the bread basket on the table.

It was silent for a few moments and then Mats cleared his throat. 'Well, perhaps we should look at the film?'

The projector was set up on a solid pine table facing a tripod with a small screen, which Mats pulled down like a roller blind.

'Right, let's see,' he said, getting the projector started.

Susso and Gudrun sat down on chairs, but Torbjörn remained standing. He had brought a biscuit with him and ate it while he waited.

Soon the film spluttered into action.

'It's a bit further on from here,' said Mats. 'About two and a half minutes into the film.' They watched children running around on a lawn in a downpour of scratches and flickering on the old cine film.

'That's my son, Tomas,' Mats said, as a boy went by in a pedal car on a gravel road. 'Right,' he said. 'Keep an eye out now.'

The children were naked and skinny, splashing about in an inflatable paddling pool on the grass outside the storehouse. It was high summer. The birches were like green foam, the colours very bright. A girl got ready to jump and then landed on her bottom in the pool.

All of a sudden he appeared in the door furthest away in the leaning storehouse. He was in shadow at first but then stepped out almost into the light.

'There,' Mats said. 'Did you see?'

It was him. There was no doubt it was the Vaikijaur man. A green tracksuit hung like a sack on his crooked little body. Gloves. Beneath a knitted hat pulled down low over his face two yellow eyes were gleaming as he watched the children. He seemed not to notice the camera.

Gudrun had covered her mouth with one hand.

'His eyes!' she shrieked. 'Look at his eyes!'

When Susso went outside she looked at the leaning building in a completely different way. She felt a strong sense of unease, as if he was still in there. As a result she was careful not to go any closer.

The old man in the film was stunted and strange, but very *real*. A freak, she had thought when he had first shown himself in the doorway. Oh my God, a genuine freak! She had to go round the house and stand on the perimeter of the field to get good reception. Kjell-Åke Andersson answered almost at once. He asked her to calm down because he was not at all sure what film she was talking about. He knew nothing about someone called Mats in Avesta.

'Has he phoned us?'

It was impossible for her to stand still, so she walked up and down in the frozen grass.

'He phoned after he had seen the photo on TV,' she said. 'On that true-crime programme, *Efterlyst*. But nobody seemed to care. And now I've seen the film and it *is* him. It's the same person as the one in my photo. I'm one hundred per cent sure.'

The police officer said nothing.

'You have to see this film,' she pleaded.

'Yes,' he said. 'Perhaps we should do that.'

'I can film it and email it to you. That will be quicker.'

He gave her his email address and she hung up.

Mats was standing with his hands in his pockets, watching her.

'I've spoken to the police,' she said. 'They want to see the film.'

'Shall I send the reel, or what?'

'No,' Susso said. 'I'll film it. We've got a video camera with us. Then I'll email it to him.'

'I'm glad he listened to you,' he said.

'It's totally bloody unbelievable. To think they never showed any interest in any of this! I can't make out what's wrong with them.'

'Do you want to have a look?' asked Mats, pointing. 'At where he lived?'

The storehouse had three black creosoted doors, with an opening for a cat in one of them. Stakes entwined with wilted hop vines leaned against the wall, where there was also a wooden plough that had been given a new colour late in its life: turquoise shone against the red wall.

Mats walked briskly across the lawn and lifted the hasp on the door closest to the forest, where the old man had stood in the film. The hinge creaked as he pulled the plank door wide open.

Inside were potato-storage boxes full of various tools: rakes, spades, cultivators, fishing rods. On the floor were bags of old newspapers. A staircase made from rough-hewn planks led up to the loft: it was as steep as a ladder and crooked.

'It's up here,' Mats said, climbing up.

Susso motioned for Gudrun to go first. She leaned forwards, grasped one of the steps and began to climb up. Susso went next, followed by Torbjörn.

Mats had positioned himself by the window. The frame was rotten and some of the wooden wedges holding it in place had worked loose. There was not much left of the curtains. They were tatters hanging from a plastic rail. Someone had hung them up to make the barn look homely from the outside. Through the smeared window they could see the gravel road.

'That's Tomas,' said Mats, pointing at a graduation placard leaning against the wall. It was an enlarged photograph with the words 'Congratulations Tompa!' written underneath. The boy in the photo looked about six years old.

'What happened exactly?' asked Susso. 'You know, that incident with the car you told us about?'

Mats leaned his shoulder against the wall and moved the curtain aside with his index finger.

'We were out picking wild strawberries,' he said. 'The whole family. Up by the road over there. When it was time to go home Tomas didn't want to come with us. He liked wild strawberries. If I remember correctly, there was something I wanted to watch on TV, a football match or something, so I got impatient. When I tried to catch hold of him he ran away. And stupidly I ran after him.'

He stroked the top of his head.

'It was almost as if I was driving him towards the road by chasing after him. When I realised what was happening I stopped immediately, but he carried on. He probably didn't realise I had stopped running after him.'

Mats looked at Susso and then at Gudrun, who was standing a short distance away with her hands in her pockets.

'Do you see?' he said. 'He was right at the edge of the road and it was impossible for me to catch up with him. "Stop," I yelled, and Monika, my wife, she shouted as well, at the top of her voice. I can still hear us shouting, both of us. But it was too late. The car was already there. And it was going fast.'

He cleared his throat before going on.

'The very second we thought Tomas was going to be run over, a little figure dashed across the road and pulled him down into the ditch.'

Mats grabbed one hand with the other to show how it had happened.

'He literally appeared out of thin air! A little old man in overalls and a hat,' he said, smiling, lifting his hand to hip height. 'It was so unexpected. So amazing. That feeling of powerlessness. First this abyss that opens in front of you and then . . .'

Mats shook his head.

'We didn't even think to say thank you. We just lifted the boy up and hugged him and then . . . well, we staggered home, I suppose.'

There was a creak from the floorboards as Gudrun took a step closer. Her head was tilted and her expression had given way to one of compassion.

'It wasn't until later that evening,' Mats went on, 'after the shock had worn off, that we realised how incredibly lucky we had been, and what an unlikely rescuer he was. What kind of creature was he, actually? The following day he was wandering around here on the edge of the forest. It was Monika who saw him. We ran up to him to say thank you. We were overwhelmed, naturally, and happy to have the opportunity to thank him. It wasn't until then, as we stood there looking at him, no longer in shock, that it occurred to us what a remarkable person he was. And it wasn't just that he was a dwarf, or whatever you call it, and that he had such an unusual appearance. It was those eyes. And even though it was the middle of the summer he was wearing a thick winter hat and it looked . . . well, it didn't look normal. He was wearing gloves too, stiff with dirt and mud, and a fingernail was sticking out through one of the fingers. It was absolutely black, that nail. I remember it.

'We invited him for dinner. That was the least we could do. He ate greedily and was totally lacking in table manners. It was as if he had never seen food before. He kind of panted between each mouthful. The children couldn't take their eyes off him and wanted to know what he was called, which was a reasonable question under the circumstances. I asked him, but he didn't answer. It seemed like he was mute. We thought he was homeless and asked if he would like to stay with us for a while. He agreed to that, but only if he could stay in the storehouse. So I carried a mattress up here. It was right there,' he said, pointing. 'That was his sleeping place.'

'Didn't he leave anything behind?' asked Gudrun, looking around. 'A few of his possessions or anything?'

Mats shook his head. 'He didn't have anything, as far as I know.' He nodded at the flattened cardboard boxes on the floor. 'The only thing he left behind was that hole, in the flooring here. But don't ask me why he did that.'

'A hole?' repeated Susso.

'There's a hatch there,' said Mats, 'or an opening, rather. The actual lid is missing. That's probably where they brought up hay in the old days, or grain, I'm not sure. There are planks there so no one falls through, and some old cork flooring underneath. He made a big hole in it.

'Can I have a look?' asked Susso.

They knelt down and moved planks, boards of various sizes and a piece of window frame coated with cracked linseed oil. Underneath there was a folded sheet of cork flooring and in the middle was an oval hole with ragged edges. The opening looked down on the top of a dirty wardrobe on the floor below.

'I didn't discover it until after he left.'

Susso crouched down and looked.

'As I say, he had no belongings. We let him borrow a torch and Emma gave him a doll, but he left that behind. It sat in the window afterwards, and we thought that looked a bit sad. Like a reminder.'

Then he added, in a low voice:

'And he left the torch behind too, in fact.'

Torbjörn had walked warily over to the stairs and was looking at the contents of the plastic boxes stored there.

'What did he do about food?' he asked. 'Did he eat with you?'

Mats shook his head and said in a raised voice that could be heard the length of the loft:

'He really didn't like to go into the house. We left the food at the bottom of the stairs because that was how he wanted it. He brought the basket up here with him and then put it back on the bottom step when he had eaten the food. It was as simple as that. On Christmas Eve I put a little bottle of schnapps there, but he didn't touch it. Otherwise he ate everything, even the skin on the potatoes.'

'And how long did he live here?' Susso asked, brushing her knees after standing up. Mats looked up as he worked it out.

'From summer '79,' he said, 'until spring 1980. May. So it was almost a year. But we hardly saw him. Only a light shining in the window here in the evenings. It seemed he didn't just use the torch for light but also for entertainment. He would sit here flashing it on and off for hours. When the batteries finally ran out he gave it back and I put in new ones.'

Mats rubbed his mouth before carrying on.

'Time passed and we . . . well, we didn't have the heart to turn him out, to be honest. It didn't feel right when we thought about what he had done for us. So he was allowed to stay. But it had its drawbacks, as I'm sure you understand.'

Mats raised his brows and sighed.

'We couldn't invite people round, for example, at least not at night because they might have seen the light out here and started asking questions. We had no idea what we would say. It all sounded so odd.

'Then one day Tomas's babysitter asked us if we knew there was a little gnome living in our loft, an old man with cat's eyes who stood looking out of the window all day. She thought it sounded rather frightening and wondered if perhaps Tomas had been watching something unsuitable on television. We realised then that the situation had become unsustainable. So one evening I banged on the door and climbed up here. He was sitting on the mattress, looking at me. Staring, actually. I had never come up to where he lived before. I had quite a shock I can tell you, because it stank. It stank of piss. And he had carried in a load of sticks which he had laid on the floor, and he had even been in the room underneath here and brought things up. Toys. Plastic pots. Old ornaments. I told him it was time for him to move and I offered to drive him wherever he wanted to go. He said he wanted to go to Gränna, and that was the first and only word he ever spoke to me.'

'Gränna?' Gudrun said.

Mats nodded.

'He had a slight Finnish accent.'

He looked down at his shoes, battered deck shoes with dry leather laces that he had tied in loops so big they brushed the dusty floor.

'I thought it was a bit odd that he wanted to go there in particular. But he was very determined about it. I asked if he knew anyone there, and he nodded. We set off the following day. I tried talking to him, because it's quite a long drive to Gränna. Once it was obvious he could speak, I tried to get him to tell me a little about himself. But all he did was sit in the back and look out of the window. It was like driving a car with a dog. I heard him sitting there panting, and from time to time he moved, or sighed deeply and yawned. When we reached Gränna I let him out on the outskirts of the town. He knew exactly which way to go. I opened the door for him and he leapt out, ran down a path and disappeared onto a headland there, without saying goodbye or even turning round. He just ran. And after that I never saw him again.'

Mats shrugged his shoulders to indicate the end of his story.

'But where did you drop him off?' Susso asked. 'What was the address?'

'No special address, it was only a bus stop. And then he ran out to the headland. That's all I know.'

'A headland?'

'Yes. It was close to a lake.'

'But were there any houses there or was it open country?'

Mats shook his head.

'I don't know. It was so long ago. Almost twenty-five years.'

'You don't remember the name of the bus stop?' asked Torbjörn, who was holding onto a roof beam in the middle of the loft space.

Mats smiled.

'No. I didn't look. I just wanted to be rid of him.'

'Could you point out on a map where it was?' Gudrun asked.

'I think so. More or less.'

Susso pulled her laptop out of her bag. While it was starting up she looked for the cable for the video camera. She rummaged about in her pack, until she felt the plastic against her fingers.

'Right, you can run it now,' she said, and switched on the camera.

Mats started the projector. She watched the film through the video camera's small flip-out screen to avoid having to see the old man directly on the projector screen.

'It's hard to imagine that he's mixed up in this kidnapping,' said Mats. 'I can't understand it. After all, he saved Tomas and was always kind to the children – well, he was never directly unkind, anyway. I know he was a bit scary but I simply can't understand how he could be capable of such a thing.'

Susso transferred the film to her laptop and saved it on a memory stick, which she inserted into Mats's laptop and sent to the police inspector.

'Shall we look at a map?' Gudrun said. 'So you can show us where you let him out?'

Mats sat with his neck bowed, clicking the mouse.

'Now let's see,' he said slowly. 'Gränna. Örserum. The 113. Right. Bunnström . . . there's a beach there. Now then . . . Ekhagen. It has to be there. Can you see where it says Ekhagen?'

He hovered the cursor over a light-brown headland.

'That's where it was. By the road here.'

There were two properties on the headland, but no addresses or telephone numbers.

'You're going to have to phone National Land Registration,' said Mats. 'Or the council.'

'Or a neighbour,' Susso said. 'We could phone someone who lives close by, someone whose number we could get hold of.'

'There's no point,' Gudrun said.

'Why not?' Susso asked, straightening her glasses.

'If it's true he isn't human, or whatever you want to call it, and he knows someone who lives on the headland, do you think they are going to tell you where he is?'

Susso folded her arms.

'Yes, I do,' she said. 'If they hear what he might be mixed up in.'

Gudrun shook her head.

'We have to go there.'

'To Gränna?' said Torbjörn, looking at Gudrun.

'An unannounced visit is our only hope,' she said.

'But how far away is it?' Susso said.

Gudrun shrugged.

'Three hundred kilometres,' said Mats.

Gudrun's mouth was pursed and ringed with deep lines.

'We can't turn back now.'

Animals were not allowed in the hostel, Seved was pretty sure about that, so he left the cage in the car, hidden under a blanket. He would have to get it later, after reception closed. There was a girl sitting behind the glass, no older than twenty, if that. He mumbled the false name he had used to book the room and paid. The girl gave him a key with the room number engraved on a plastic tab. He took the lift up to a narrow corridor with green vinyl flooring and found his room at the far end on the right.

It was considerably bigger than he had expected. A bunk bed of white-painted steel stood on one side of the window and a single bed on the other. He felt relieved as he put his bag down on the table. The thought of having to sleep in the same room as the shapeshifting lemming had been worrying him ever since Lennart had ordered him to drive to Kiruna. For a while he had even considered booking two separate rooms, but this room was big enough for him to stash the cage far from the bed. On the table lay a pile of folders. Tourist brochures. He sat down and opened one of them. It showed a map of the town surrounded by advertisements. *Hotel Kebne: the hotel that raises your expectations.* Café Safari. The Nanking restaurant. He turned the map over. *Kiruna is special,* it said.

Gunnar Myrén Ltd. There was a picture of a light aircraft, which made him remember what the newspaper had said, that

Susso Myrén's grandfather had been an aerial photographer.

He had no plans to go and see the shop. Lennart had said there would probably be too many people there. He had written down the sister's address on a piece of paper, and also the address of her fiancé. If she was not at one address, he would be sure to find her at the other.

He ought to get going straight away. According to Lennart, this was an urgent matter. But he knew, as he sat in the silent, spartan room, that he was going to wait a while. He had to prepare himself mentally. Brace himself. That was what he told himself, anyway. In reality he wanted to put it off as long as he possibly could.

Until he no longer had any choice.

What the shapeshifter was going to do to the sister was unclear to him, nor did he know how much he would have to do to her himself. And what could he resort to if he failed to get anything out of her? He had seen what the little creatures in the box had done to the policemen in Årrenjarka, but he was not nearly as good at handling them as Torsten was. But of course Lennart knew that. He would not have allowed him to take the thing with him unless he had been confident of its influence over human beings.

Or was Lennart getting desperate? Was he allowing himself to be controlled by something other than the objective common sense he was always guided by? Was he afraid? Or had someone else told him to deal with Susso Myrén? That bloke Erasmus, perhaps?

And why was there such a rush? She would be home again all in good time. Börje made him believe that it was something else, that there was more at stake than simply shutting her up.

There was someone further south she must not come into contact with.

But who?

He looked at the clock. It was nearly eight. Reception closed at ten. That meant he could rest for a while. He needed that. The snow was piled up in a huge drift outside the window and the light from the street lamps was falling in strips through the slats of the Venetian blind. Without removing his jacket or his shoes, he lay down on the bed with his hands clasped over his chest and stared up at the ceiling. For the first time in ages he would be able to sleep without the worry of being woken up by the old-timers. He appreciated the murmur of voices coming through the hostel wall. Unfamiliar voices. Indistinct. Soon he was asleep.

Mats had recommended the Mas Grill when they asked him if there was a place nearby where they could get something to eat. When Susso and Torbjörn walked in and went to look at the illuminated menu board above the counter, the man working there glanced at them and then went back to watching television. Susso thought he was probably on his tea break. In front of his feet, under the table, was a pair of slippers. A second man quickly appeared, ready to take their order.

Susso pushed her hands into her pockets and realised that she was not really that hungry after all.

The door opened and Gudrun came in.

They all sat down at a table at the back of the restaurant. The tablecloth was flattened under a sheet of glass that reflected the wall lamps and the lighting above the petrol pumps outside. Susso studied the gaudy pattern of the tablecloth with its small birds sitting on snow-covered branches and star-shaped ginger biscuits hanging from red ribbons.

They sat in silence for a while. All Susso had was a can of soft drink.

'Have you told the police we're going to Gränna?' asked Gudrun.

'I put it in the email,' Susso said. 'When I sent the film.'

'Has he answered then?'

'I don't know about the email. But they've got your number.'

'Perhaps you ought to ring Edit as well?'

'Not yet. There's no point if we can't get hold of anyone who knows who the Vaikijaur man is. I don't want her to say anything to Mattias's parents, either, in case they start getting their hopes up.'

'It's lucky we've got Torbjörn with us,' Gudrun said. 'This isn't entirely risk free, you know.'

'What do you mean?' he said, finishing off his hamburger.

'He might have relatives down here, or accomplices, and here we are, snooping around. We already know what they're capable of.'

'They won't still be living there,' Torbjörn said.

'Why not?'

'It's not usual for a house to have the same owner for a quarter of a century,' he answered. 'It's more likely someone else lives there now.'

'It's not that unusual either,' Gudrun said, wagging her head. 'And even if it isn't the same owner now as it was in 1980, they're certain to know who lived there before and can give us the name. I'm sure that we'll find them sooner or later. And then, as I said, who knows what might happen.'

Susso sat with her hand around her drink can, looking at the television.

'Have you ever been to Gränna?'

Gudrun wiped her mouth with a napkin.

'Yes, I have,' she nodded. 'It's at such an angle it drives you mad.'

'What do you mean, angle?'

'It slopes,' Gudrun said, moving her hand in a diving gesture towards her plate. 'Everything is built on a steep slope. If you fall over at the top of the town, you won't stop until you've rolled all the way down into Lake Vättern.'

Did it get into his mind? Could it really radiate that far?

It seemed impossible, but that's what he was thinking as he sprinted down the corridor towards the lift. It felt as if the little creature had been inside him, as if it had tunnelled into his head from far, far away.

Why else would he have woken up?

It was almost one thirty and he must have slept heavily.

The car windows were white and opaque and the roof glittered. What the hell was he going to do if it had frozen to death? When he opened the door, which had stuck to the frame in the extreme cold, he was relieved to hear signs of life coming from the cage. After only a second or two, the shapeshifter had forced its vibrating fear into his consciousness.

'I know,' he said. 'I know.'

He took the blanket-covered cage in his arms, shut the car door with his foot and walked swiftly to the entrance. His head was pulsating. It felt as if it would split open.

The little shapeshifter must have calmed down a little because once they were in the lift the pressure in Seved's forehead eased. He closed his eyes and leaned his head against the wall.

They had taken the left exit at the roundabout south of Gränna and knew they were close now. Susso sat up and looked from side to side through the car windows. A lake appeared on the left-hand side of the road, widening out in a southerly direction towards an expanse of water beyond the sound. There were small islands out there, clusters of forest that had torn themselves away and were drifting to the far side.

'It must be here,' Gudrun said, easing her foot off the accelerator pedal. 'This must be Lake Bunn.'

Susso protected her eyes from the blinding reflection of the sun and leaned against the window, which was scaly with dried, dirty water. A carpet of pines covered the distant hills, following the ridges like a fur coat.

To think it was so hilly. She would never have thought that of Småland. Earlier, when the motorway had quite unexpectedly run alongside Lake Vättern, she had been astounded by the precipitous, lacerated rocks and the brilliance of the ice-covered lake dissolving into a remote mist. It had not even occurred to her that Lake Vättern would be here. A sea encompassed by land. A deep gash.

The sight of the mountains rising up on the opposite shore of Lake Bunn had a similar effect. It struck her that this part of the country was completely unknown to her. It had always existed on the map, but only there. She had never *been* here, not even in her thoughts.

'It's first right after the beach,' Susso said, squashing herself between the two front seats and pointing. But Gudrun did not need any directions. Torbjörn, who had been woken by the ticking of the indicator, hooked his fingers over the door handle and pushed himself upright.

'Are we there?' he asked.

In the flattened grass at the side of the road were double wheel tracks that turned off towards the lake and followed the shoreline. NO UN UTHORIS D VEHI LES, a notice said. The missing letters had worn away from the metal disc and the post leaned and was disfigured by rust. Torbjörn knocked on the window to draw their attention to the sign, and Gudrun muttered something. The Passat crept along. Susso was looking in the other direction at a yellow brick building standing beside the main road.

A couple of cycles were propped against the wall and a rag rug was hanging over the veranda railing.

'This can't be it, can it?'

'No,' Gudrun said, without looking. 'That's a different house. We've got to go out on the actual headland. Assuming that's possible.'

Down towards the lake, alder and birch saplings were growing in a tangled mass and the lake shone through the gaps in the foliage. Gudrun had leaned so far forwards her chin was almost touching the steering wheel.

The track was bordered on one side by a garden fence marked with round patches of lichen. The fencing criss-crossed at right angles and at every join was a small square of grey-green chipboard, partly eaten away by the damp. Beyond the fence, ground elder was growing in huge clumps, huddled together in the cold. Raspberry canes formed a stiff mesh in the background. Someone had tied a cat-shaped plastic reflector on the fence.

'There's no one here,' said Torbjörn. 'You can tell from the grass that no one has driven here for a long time.'

It came to an end in front of two tall wrought-iron gates with an ornate pattern of welded feathers. A plastic-coated chain with a hefty padlock linked the gates together. The posts were made of stone capped with black steel. There were two yellow plastic signs that read UNAUTHORISED ENTRY PROHIBITED and BEWARE OF THE DOG.

'If the dog is as old as the signs, then we don't have to worry,' said Gudrun, turning the wheel.

Next to the gates was an old storage shed. The red paint on the wooden panelling had worn away, exposing long strips of silvery-grey wood. It had two sets of double doors with hand-wrought iron hinges, held shut with steel bars. Gudrun drove up to the shed, reversed and parked with the rear of the Passat facing the gates.

'Well, here we are then.'

Susso had not expected it to look quite so sealed off. It made her think. The gate and the signs were signals that could not be misunderstood. They were not welcome. There was little chance they would get any answers here.

She stayed where she was in the car.

'What kind of people live here, anyway?' she said. 'More Laestadians?'

'Perfectly normal people,' Gudrun said, looking at the gates in the mirror.

'Normal?' Susso said.

Gudrun nodded.

'Signs like this are generally put up for good reason.'

There was a wind blowing up from the lake and a waft of sodden vegetation hit Susso. A smell of ditches. The clumps of reeds slumped behind the trees and were silent. The only sound came from the motorway in the distance. Susso had put a few printouts of the Vaikijaur man's face in a plastic folder, which she rolled up as she approached the gates.

Gudrun craned her neck and stood peering through the gates. She had turned up the collar of her jacket and pushed her hands into her pockets.

'Is it there, do you think?'

They could see a white-rendered stone house with a semi-circular extension at the edge of the forest a few hundred metres away. The facade was made darker by the shadows thrown onto it by the trees, making it look as if half the building was painted dark grey. All the windows of the extension had curtains that were shut. A house with closed eyes. Was this where he had run to?

Torbjörn slammed the car door and clicked open the lid of his snus tin.

After he had inserted a pouch of snus under his lip and shoved the tin back in his pocket he repeated his earlier remark, saying that there was no one here.

How could he know that? Susso stepped up to the fence connected to the gate posts. It was low enough for her to straddle the pointed slats and swing her legs over without difficulty. She then glared at her mother, who clumsily lifted one leg. Her long jacket got caught and Torbjörn came to help free her.

Susso walked purposefully towards the white house. She was holding the roll of photographs tightly. They were documents proving she had the right to be there, though she had no idea what she was actually going to say when they found someone. That made her nervous because this meeting must not go wrong. It was likely she would only have one chance.

Ringing on people's doors was something she did every day in her job, but approaching like this was something entirely different.

And then to start talking about trolls . . .

Naturally the word 'troll' was not one she could use.

She was here about a person, a very unusual little person, but a person nonetheless. Possibly one mixed up in child abduction. A person wanted by the police. And she had a picture of him.

On the two visible sides of the house were many doors, all of them made of glass. She aimed for the nearest one. The door had a column on each side supporting a little balcony with an iron railing, and Susso thought it looked like the main entrance. There were stone steps up to the house and the railings were made of wood. It looked rather makeshift. She ran up the steps and knocked on the door. Two knocks followed by four in quick succession. The pane of glass rattled.

When no one opened she peered in.

There was a small console topped with marble. There were paintings but she could not make out what they were because of the reflection in the glass. An umbrella was hanging from the coat rack, along with a wooden hanger and a small shoehorn in light-green plastic, all on different hooks. It looked abandoned.

Gudrun and Torbjörn stood close together under the birch trees, watching her as she returned to them with her arms folded. She shook her head and walked past them.

The second building was a little further off.

The trail they followed wound behind a dense grove of tall spruce trees. Torbjörn walked behind Susso, muttering that he was sure there was no one out here on the headland. If there was, they would have seen a car.

'They could have come by bus,' Susso said irritably.

She walked quickly, swiping at the yellow blades of grass with her rolled-up folder, looking down at the ground.

'People who live like this don't travel by bus,' he said.

He was right, of course, but even so she walked on. The trail to the Vaikijaur man ended here, in this place. They had to find someone to talk to; they had travelled over three-quarters of the country to get here. She was about to say that when she came to a halt. She had caught sight of a small wooden sign in the grass to the side of the trail. BJÖRKUDDEN, it said. Just beyond it were three large rocks piled on top of each other. On the top rock someone had painted an ugly laughing face. The nose was covered with warts. Large ear lobes were weighed down by rings. In the grinning mouth a front tooth was missing. The hair was a cushion of moss.

'Have a look at this,' she said. 'Could this just be a coincidence?'

'Well of course it is,' answered Torbjörn, looking up at the treetops to emphasise how little the stone troll interested him. 'It's like a garden gnome,' he went on. 'If we hadn't come here to ask about a troll, you would never have bothered about it.'

'Mum,' Susso said, 'do you think it's a coincidence?'

Gudrun stared at the stone troll. After a moment she shrugged her shoulders. 'It's only a troll,' she said.

They carried on along the path, which was criss-crossed with roots. The fir trees were crowded together and their lower branches were straggly. The ground underfoot was brown and covered in pine needles and old leaves.

Torbjörn asked if they thought it was illegal to defy no-entry notices.

'We're only going to ask,' Susso said, taking a long step over a fallen branch. 'Surely we're allowed to do that.'

The house that became visible through the trees had a red exterior with white corners, barge boards and window surrounds, and a steeply sloping roof. The roof tiles were patterned with grey-green lichen. There were so many mullioned panes of glass that the windows looked as if they were behind bars.

Susso walked closer and stood on her toes to look in but could only see curtains. They hung there, ghostly white, and a wooden seagull poked its long beak out from behind one of them as it gazed to the side. Brown fern fronds curled in the flower bed running parallel to the foundation's base of natural stone.

All they heard was the wind as it passed through the trees and bushes in a repeated combing movement. Stooping slightly, Susso moved forwards, preparing to make her excuses and bring out the photograph of the Vaikijaur man.

At the front-veranda steps she halted and glanced around the corner of the house. There a lawn sloped down towards a dilapidated fence made of wire netting, with old pasture land beyond and an outcropping of birches, juniper bushes and a few oaks. Sunlight radiated down between the branches, illuminating the frozen grass and turning the blades fuzzy in the light.

'Hello!' she called.

She paused for a second or two before walking up the concrete steps to the front door. She knocked and peered in through the faded cotton curtains, but there was nothing to see except an entrance hall with a worn and crumpled rag rug. There were more sea birds and some sparkling glass ornaments in the window.

Gudrun crept up beside her, keeping her hands in her pockets. It was obvious that no one was at home, and that had made her a little bolder.

'Nobody here,' Susso said, and walked down the steps.

On a green-painted plinth stood a sundial in the form of a sphere of welded iron circles. The arrow had an oily brass shimmer and the fletchings splayed out like the tail of a salmon.

Behind the house she saw a rocky hillock where a pair of large oaks soared up, capturing sunlight in their branches. From the dry fragments of leaves came a gentle rustling sound.

Susso continued circling the house without any clear idea of what she was looking for. She was just not ready to leave. A feeling rising from deep within her tethered her to this place. There had to be something here. It was magnetic. She was prepared to break into the house to look for answers, but she knew her mother would oppose that idea.

She came to the back door and saw that someone had fastened a picture to an upstairs window with long strips of freezer tape. Susso stood on tiptoe and backed away, but she couldn't make out what the drawing portrayed, only that it was painted in green. In pastels, perhaps.

A child, she thought.

In the above-ground foundations, immediately below a windowsill, was an aperture big enough to take a whole foot. It was extraordinary. In front of the opening lay a couple of boulders. She bent forwards and tried to see inside, crouching down to get a closer look.

Inside she could see a few oak leaves that had shrivelled into small grey cylinders and beyond that only impenetrable darkness. Was it something to do with ventilation? But why have such a big hole? Fairly large animals could get in, surely?

After getting up, supporting herself against the wall, she checked the palm of her hand for signs of the red paint. It was clean. She took a last look at the hole and walked back.

Torbjörn was inspecting the sundial and holding up his watch, and as Susso walked towards them he grinned at her.

'The time's right,' he said.

'It's probably a summer cottage,' Susso said, and she twisted the arrow, making it squeak. 'So we'll have to phone, I guess.'

'Or else we find out where they live,' said Gudrun, pulling her jacket collar closed to keep out the wind.

'And drive there?' Torbjörn said.

Gudrun nodded.

The shop was empty when Seved arrived. A woman was sitting behind the counter looking at a computer screen, and he knew it must be her. The sister. Cecilia Myrén.

He walked around outside a couple of times to summon up the courage to approach her. He had no idea what it would lead to, or whether he would be forced to break into her home later that night. Everything had to happen unobtrusively. With great care, Lennart had said.

From time to time Seved felt a twitching against his chest. It was the little lemmingshifter, changing position. It was in his inside pocket, directly over his heart. It could feel his heartbeats and presumably his nervousness. Did it have any thoughts about that?

Cecilia looked up the moment Seved entered the shop.

She was about forty-five. Her hair was shoulder length and tinted chestnut brown, and she had pushed her glasses up onto her head like a hairband. Her fingers were covered in silver rings and she wore bracelets on both wrists. She smiled as she greeted him.

Without introducing himself, Seved muttered that he was a journalist who wanted to write about Susso Myrén but could not get hold of her, so he wondered if she could help him track her down.

'Well, that might be difficult. She's in Gränna.'

'Gränna?'

She nodded.

'What . . . what's she doing there?'

'Buying peppermint rock. No, I don't know – it's got something to do with her website.'

Seved rubbed his hand gently against his chest. She seemed chatty enough. With a little luck he might not even need the little lemmingshifter's help. But he had better watch out and not go too fast. There was a risk she would back off.

'Are you the only person working here?'

'No, my mother works here, and Susso too, sometimes. And in summer during the busy season we take on extra staff. Mum is really retired but she can't just sit at home, that would drive her mad. So we all help out. I've got my pedicure business as well, of course. I do that part-time.'

She reached across the counter and picked up a business card from a transparent plastic holder. Cecilia's Pedicure Salon, it read. Seved nodded.

'Perhaps your feet need looking at?'

He had started to shake his head, but then he suddenly changed his mind.

'Why not?'

Susso had wandered off towards the pasture in protest. She was still not prepared to leave. There was something here, she was convinced of that. She *felt* it. There was a small gate in the fence but it served no purpose because the wire netting was sagging so low between the rotting fence posts that she could easily step over it.

She strolled around among the birch trees and the prickly juniper bushes, kicking the thick matted carpet of grass. Here and there the vegetation was hidden by a patch of snow that was slowly being eaten away.

She walked down towards the beach to get an overview of the lake, but a straggly wall of rushes blocked her way and the ground was boggy and coated with crackling shards of ice. She did not want to get wet feet.

Not far from the gate she had spotted a short jetty, so she turned back and walked quickly in that direction. She heard the tones of a ringing mobile coming from over by the house – her mother's ring tone, a rock song. Her gaze wandered over the tree-covered islands and the murky strips of forest rising up on the other side of the bay. Beyond that ridge was the motorway and Lake Vättern.

In silence, heads bowed, Gudrun and Torbjörn came walking towards her. Torbjörn had put on his woollen hat and his head looked like a small bud on top of his gangly body.

'There's been a journalist in the shop, asking about you,' Gudrun said. 'Cecilia said you were away.'

'But she didn't say where? She didn't say I'm here?'

'It won't matter. No one could figure out exactly where in Gränna you are.'

Susso reached her hand out for the phone.

Cecilia was taken aback by the anger in Susso's voice.

'If you're fifteen hundred kilometres . . .'

'Yes, but what if it wasn't a journalist! Shit, I was attacked! Someone wants to kill me! Don't you get that, Cecilia?'

'Oh, come on! It was a journalist. He seems really nice. He's even booked a pedicure session. You've got nothing to worry about.'

Susso ended the conversation with a furious tap of her thumb.

'Look, it's not a problem,' Torbjörn said.

Susso wanted to get away. She had already begun walking fast.

'You're getting paranoid now,' he said, hurrying after her. 'No one knows where you are.'

'They didn't have any trouble finding us when we were out on the snowmobile!'

'I know,' he said. 'But they had probably followed us. No one could have followed us down here. That's impossible. Calm down.'

Close to the house, tucked into a small copse of conifers, stood a shed with a sheet-metal roof. On one side was a hatch and above it, hidden away under the eaves, was a bird box. The doors had diagonal wooden handles. Susso recalled that the dwarf had lived with Mats's family in an old outhouse. If he had ever stayed here, it was likely he had lived in this shed.

'Wait a minute,' she called.

But before she could even open the door, she caught a flash of dark-blue fabric moving along the path in the gloom below the trees. It was a woman walking briskly towards them. She was wearing a knitted jumper with the sleeves rolled up. Her grey hair was tucked behind her ears and she was holding a mobile phone.

'Who are you?' she shouted.

Susso took a few steps back and began fumbling with the plastic folder.

'We're looking for someone,' she said, pulling out a sheet of paper which she tried to flatten out. 'Someone who has disappeared. Who we think might be here. Or who has been here, at least.'

Gudrun forced a smile. 'We only want to know if you've seen him. The police are looking for him too. We've driven fifteen hundred kilometres.'

'So perhaps you know something?' Susso added, waving the piece of paper in front of the woman.

'This photo has been on television,' Gudrun said. 'He could be involved in the kidnapping of the boy in Jokkmokk at Christmas. I'm sure you've heard about it.'

'You should go now,' the woman said.

As they walked sheepishly towards the car, Susso and Gudrun tried pleading with the woman, who was following on their heels like a sheepdog.

It had not been their intention to do anything illegal, they explained, and Susso told her that the person in the photograph had run onto the headland in the spring of 1980 and no one had seen him since. The only way to track him down was to come here and ask.

'But you can't just come marching in here when you feel like it,' the woman repeated. 'This is private land! There are signs!'

Their appeal went unheard and finally they gave up. It seemed as if the woman was not even listening to them. All Susso wanted to do now was get away. She walked as quickly as she could without running, and she could hear her mother panting behind her.

By the time they reached the gate Torbjörn was already in the car and had started the engine. White fumes were pouring from the vibrating exhaust pipe. They climbed over the fence and were about to get into the car when they were stopped.

'Wait a minute!' the woman called, stepping over the fence rails.

Judging from her voice she was prepared to talk now that they were on the other side of the fence. Susso said she had not been able to find the telephone number and that the directions, which were based on a journey taken twenty-five years ago, were all they had to go on.

'The trail leads here,' she said, nodding out towards the headland. 'Literally.'

The woman took the sheet of paper Susso held out to her. After turning it the right way up she snorted, grinning.

Gudrun leaned against the car to study the woman as she looked at the picture. Torbjörn switched off the ignition.

'Have you seen this photo before? It's the one that was on TV.'

'No,' she said. 'I must have missed it.'

And then she said: 'But it has to be a joke, doesn't it?'

The smile lingered at the corners of the woman's mouth.

'Well, no,' Susso said. 'It isn't.'

'It isn't?' She raised her eyebrows.

Gudrun shook her head.

'He does look a bit unusual, but . . .'

'In that case', said the woman, 'someone's pulling your leg.'

'This is what he looks like,' Susso said. 'The picture has been in the paper as well as on TV. The police are looking for him. We really do want to know if you've seen him before.'

'It's supposed to be a troll, isn't it?'

The word made Susso stiffen.

'Yes,' said Gudrun hesitantly, moving nearer. She straightened the scarf around her neck. 'Perhaps' – she was almost whispering – 'perhaps it does look like a troll. But it certainly isn't a joke, I can tell you that. A boy has been kidnapped. So it's no laughing matter.'

The woman turned sideways and waved the piece of paper in the direction of the headland.

'Do you mean you don't know who used to live here?' she said.

She waited for an answer but no one spoke.

'John Bauer,' she said. 'This is John Bauer's old house.'

'Now you're the one who's joking,' Gudrun said.

'No.'

Susso and Gudrun looked at each other, and then Susso insisted they had had no idea who had lived in the house. It came as a complete surprise. She turned to Torbjörn, who was staring through the gap in the half-open door with a look of disbelief.

'John Bauer?' he said. 'The man who painted the trolls?'

The woman explained that there was no limit to people's curiosity, which is why they had put up the gates and no-trespassing signs. In the summer, boats circled the water packed with tourists craning their necks to get a glimpse of the fairy-tale artist's idyllic home, and hopefully a troll as well. Hot-air balloons floated disrespectfully low over the headland and people leaned over the edge of the baskets, waving.

None of this was appreciated by Herr Dahllöf, the current owner of the house, who had inherited it from his father's two sisters. He had been more or less forced to invest in a gate because sometimes people who had seen the house from the lake or from the air came tramping all over the garden afterwards, wanting to have a look at whatever could not be seen from further away. Since the gates had been installed no one had come onto the land. Until now.

'We had no idea, truly,' said Gudrun. 'We were told that the person we are looking for, the Vaikijaur man, set off for this place in 1980. That's all we know. That's why we are here. Not because John Bauer lived here. It's . . . well, I don't know what to say.'

'It seems like someone is having you on,' the woman said, studying the photograph of the Vaikijaur man's face.

'Well, I don't understand a thing. Do you, Susso?'

Susso shook her head.

'The man who lives here, what was his name again?' she asked.

'No one lives here,' the woman replied. 'It's a summer house.'

'Well, the owner then?'

'Dahllöf. Fredrik Dahllöf, he's called. And he lives in Helsingborg.'

'Have you got his phone number?'

Subdued music met Seved as he opened the door. Pan pipes, he thought. Supposed to be relaxing. On a table in the small entrance hall a candle was floating in a dish of water and over the doorway to the treatment room hung a curtain of ruby-red beads. There inside stood Cecilia Myrén with her back to him. She told him to take off his jacket, but, of course, he could not do that so he told her he was cold.

'It's not that cold today.'

'I'm not used to it, that's all.'

'Oh, right. Where are you from?'

He did not reply and only stared at the floor.

She waited a moment for an answer and then gave up.

'But you'll have to take your shoes off, you know.'

'Yes,' he said, and began to untie his boot laces.

'It would be a bit difficult otherwise,' she laughed.

The chair reminded him of a dentist's chair. It was adjustable and the seat covers were shiny and flesh-red. He really had no desire to sit down but he could hardly get straight to the point of his visit. She watched him as he climbed up into the chair and she seemed amused. Her eyes had narrowed.

'Socks as well,' she said.

He pulled off his socks and sat with them in his hand, unsure what to do with them. Then he pushed them into his jacket pocket. She stood with her back to him, unscrewing the lid of a little bottle. She had wide hips and was wearing a black skirt with a knee-high pleat at the back.

'So, you're a journalist then?' she said, without turning round.

'Yes.'

'For a newspaper, or what?'

He said nothing. He had not been prepared to answer questions.

'Or are you a freelancer?'

'Yes. Freelance.'

'That's nice,' she said. 'Being your own boss. I've got this and it suits me perfectly, combined with the shop.'

'It's exciting, what she's doing. Your sister.'

At first he thought she had not heard him, but then she said softly:

'Scary too.'

She came up with a bowl full of water, set it on the floor and then began to roll up his trousers. He wondered if he smelled. He had never soaked his feet, let alone taken care of them. When his toenails grew too long he usually tore them off with his fingers.

'A few weeks ago a couple of men tried to kill her,' she said, lifting up his feet and putting them in the water. 'Here in Kiruna.'

'Kill her?' he said. 'Why?'

'There are so many sick people around,' she said, standing up.

'But what's she doing now, in Gränna?'

'As I say, she's a bit upset at the moment, so if you want to talk to her you'll have to wait until she gets home.'

'I only want to know what she's doing. And see if I can talk to her.'

'She doesn't want to, not at the moment.'

When was the lemmingshifter going to start working on her?

He had no idea what would happen if he started asking her too early, if he *demanded* an answer from her. That could make her clam up. But at the same time he did not want the visit to drag on too long.

'I might have seen a troll once,' he said.

'You have to sit with your feet in the water for fifteen minutes,' she said. 'To soften them.'

'A real troll, I mean.'

'Really? Where?'

'Do you think your sister would want to write about it?'

'Was it here in Norrbotten?'

He noticed his mouth had gone dry.

'You could ring and ask her if she wants to.'

There was no reply. She had turned her back to him again and was doing something with the jars. He was going too fast, everything seemed to indicate that. It made him uncertain, so he raised his hand to the top of his jacket zipper, and once he had started to pull it down he thought he might as well continue.

'Look,' he said. 'Look what I've got here.'

Cecilia swivelled her head, her eyebrows raised, and when she saw the curled-up little creature in Seved's palms she turned round and pressed her hand with all its silver rings to her chest.

'What?' she gasped. 'What's that . . . why have you got . . . what is it?'

'It's to make you tell me where she is.'

'What is it, why have you got that . . .'

'You must tell me,' he said. 'Do you understand? You have to tell me now. And then I'll go.'

He lifted his feet out of the warm water and put them down on the floor, one at a time. One of his trouser legs had rolled down and he left a trail of wet prints behind him as he slowly walked towards the woman, who backed away.

'Stop,' he said. 'Stand still. We only want to know. We have to know.'

But Cecilia was not listening. She continued walking backwards. Beside the wall in the entrance hall was a low unit with foot-care products on a glass shelf, and she tried to support herself against it. Jars and small bottles were knocked over by her groping hand and some fell to the floor.

A buzzing swelled in Seved's head and he did not notice that he had wet himself until the warmth spread down the inside of his left leg. It felt so uncomfortable that he had to move the creature to one hand to try and dry himself with the other.

'You've got to stay,' he said, rubbing the wet stripe on his trousers, but naturally that did not make it any better. 'There's no danger. Stay and you'll see.'

She did not stop. She stared at the thing in Seved's hand and all of a sudden one of her legs gave way, as if it had snapped. She spun her arms until her bracelets rattled, and the next moment she sank to the floor, her eyes squeezed tightly shut. It was as if all her body had given up but her eyes refused to accept it. From beneath her a pool spread quickly over the floor.

Presumably the little shapeshifter had come on too strong and damaged something inside her. Seved held the little creature in front of him and stroked its rough golden-brown hair with his thumb, from the back of its head and down over the cold skin of its neck, while he tried to think what to do next.

She had collapsed and he had not got a word out of her.

That was bad.

Anxiously he glanced over his shoulder, towards the street.

What if someone came in?

He took a step towards the door curtain but stopped and let the little creature down on the floor before he hurried into the hall and locked the front door. At least no one could come into the salon now.

There were no curtains he could close, so he would have to get her into the next room. After throwing a second swift glance at the salon window, he stood behind the collapsed woman and forced his hands under her limp arms, which were sweaty underneath. Laboriously he dragged her into the other room. Her thick hair gave off a heavy aroma of musk. It made him want to turn his face away. The lemmingshifter sat inert for a while in front of the pool of urine before scuttling after Seved on all fours. He heard the scraping sound as it ran up the steel legs of the massage table in the next room.

Seved moved a chair and propped Cecilia against the wall, with her head hanging to one side. Her eyes were still shut tight and she was breathing so fast through her nose that her nostrils flared.

It did not look good.

There was a paper-towel holder on the wall and Seved drew out a long piece which he crumpled up and used to wipe his trousers, mostly because he did not know what else to do. Should he wipe the pee from the floor as well? Was there time for that?

Not a word had he got out of her. Nothing.

'Can you hear me?' he said, rubbing the paper against his trouser leg, but she did not react. She just sat there against the wall, eyes closed, panting. The little creature had hopped down from the massage table and was beside Seved's naked foot, nudging his heel with its nose. Probably the salts in the bowl of water had made his skin smell exciting. He let it continue. He was actually afraid of it. He never imagined it could be so powerful.

Seved crouched down and was trying to open one of Cecilia's eyelids when a trilling noise made him turn his head.

A mobile phone.

At first he was afraid and he dared not move until the tones had stopped. Confused, he had the idea the phone was ringing because someone was coming. Of course, he understood that was not the case but he could not shake off the growing uneasiness that told him to get out as fast as possible.

The ringing had come from the treatment room and he stood behind the door frame for a while, hiding himself from anyone walking past outside. A handbag stood gaping open on top of a small chest of drawers. It could be inside. He hurried out and rummaged around in the bag but the phone was not there. Then he continued out into the hall.

He found it in her coat. A red mobile with an antenna. Lennart could use that in some way, he was sure. Maybe there were messages on it? As he shoved it into his pocket he discovered his rolled-up socks. He put them on, followed by his boots.

The little shapeshifter stood in the middle of the floor, watching vigilantly. The eyes in its wrinkled, distorted face were like a couple of chocolate buttons.

'Come on,' he said, picking up the lemmingshifter and letting it glide down inside his jacket. It scratched around in the lining of the sleeve before it found its way into the pocket.

He zipped up his jacket, put on his hat and went out. There was not a single person in sight. The cold soon homed in on his wet trousers and, with its icy grip on his leg, he hurried towards the hostel.

They found themselves on the outskirts of Mjölby. Swollen clouds hung low in the sky and sleet had started to fall. The slivers hitting the windscreen could hardly be called snow. Ahead of them the asphalt was black and water sprayed up from cars' tyres as they passed. Susso was holding Gudrun's mobile, moving her thumb indecisively over the worn, loose keys.

'I don't know what to say,' she muttered. 'Can't you ring instead?'

Gudrun was sitting in the back seat, her head leaning heavily against the window.

'I'm too tired, Susso.'

Her voice was weary, almost whining.

Susso waited a few moments longer. She could not understand why Mats Ingvar would want to mislead them. Clearly the Vaikijaur man had stayed with him and his family, but why send them to John Bauer's house? She could not equate Mats's sorrowful expression with someone who was conning them when a little boy's life was at stake. It did not add up.

There had to be another explanation. She had toyed with the idea that Bauer might have made the same observations as her grandfather and had some connection with authentic trolls. Perhaps the Vaikijaur man was acquainted with Bauer?

'Okay, I'll phone,' she said, pressing the keys.

She pressed the mobile to her ear and rested one foot on her knee. A yellowing pine needle had hooked itself onto one of the laces. She picked it off and rolled it between her fingers. The phone rang at least twenty times before she gave up. She was relieved that he had not answered. Her anger had not lessened but it was diluted with doubt. There was so much she did not understand at the moment. She borrowed Torbjörn's smartphone and typed 'Bauer' and 'Björkudden' into the search box.

After a short delay a list of links appeared on the screen. The first was to the John Bauer museum.

'Look!' she said triumphantly. 'I've found something.'

The screen filled slowly with text, and as sleet splashed against the car windows Susso began to read aloud from the phone as it glowed in the dark interior of the car:

> Upon their return from a trip to Italy, John and Esther Bauer found Villa Björkudden, beautifully situated on a small headland beside Lake Bunn, south of Gränna. They rented the house from the artist Pelle Malmborg and lived there between 1910 and 1911. But Esther was not happy living at the isolated property through the winter, so for a couple of years they lived at Björkudden during the summer months and rented a home in Stockholm for the winter. In 1914, John and Esther decided to buy the house at Björkudden, and the following year Esther gave birth to their son Bengt, who was given the nickname Putte. This was a harmonious time for the family, who appeared to have settled happily in the idyllic location.
>
> The house was surrounded by thick forest, essentially untouched. Here John Bauer found the silence and tranquillity necessary for his creativity. They planned several ambitious renovations and extensions to the property, but these were never realised. It became obvious that Esther was not smitten with Björkudden like John. She was lonely in

> the wild forest and longed to return to Stockholm. John's father paid for a plot of land in Djursholm, on the outskirts of Stockholm, where the couple built a new house. They were on their way to the newly built house on the steamer ferry *Per Brahe* when it capsized on Lake Vättern in November 1918 and the whole family died.

Susso clicked on the link '*Per Brahe* capsizes' and continued reading:

> The accident was widely discussed and contributed to John Bauer's fame. Perhaps it can be regarded as fitting, if tragic, that the artist who illustrated fairy tales met his death in the mysterious depths of Lake Vättern.

Susso dropped her hand to her knee. Torbjörn said nothing. He pulled at the edge of his hat and then replaced both his slender hands on the wheel.

'I didn't know he drowned,' he said. 'Did you?'

Susso shook her head.

'I don't get it,' Susso said. 'It can't just be coincidence, can it?'

'What?' said Torbjörn.

'That he wanted to be given a lift *there*, of all places.'

'No, of course it can't!' snapped Gudrun.

'So what was he doing there then – assuming Mats isn't making the whole thing up, which I find hard to believe,' Susso said. 'How would he have been able to do that? It's perfectly obvious it's the same person on the film and in my photo. There's no mistaking it.'

'Maybe he felt he belonged there?' Torbjörn said. 'It's like it was a leper colony, or however you want to describe it. A sanctuary . . .'

'Ring that man,' Gudrun said. 'The one who owns the house.'

'Ring him yourself,' Susso said. 'You're much more polite.'

Gudrun keyed in the number she had written on the back of a receipt.

'Is this Fredrik Dahllöf?' she said. 'My name is Gudrun Myrén and I'm phoning you because . . . well, because I'm looking for a missing person and I think this person could have visited you in the spring of 1980. At Björkudden, your holiday home in Gränna . . . I was given it by your neighbour . . . He looks quite unusual. He's short, very short in fact. So if you have met him, I'm sure you would remember . . . Hello? Yes. Like a child, except he isn't a child, he's . . . old. He looks a bit like a troll. Or a gnome perhaps . . .'

She sat in silence for a moment before folding the phone shut and saying:

'He hung up.'

'But what did he say?' Susso asked.

'He hung up. He didn't say anything.'

'But why didn't you say anything about Mattias?'

Gudrun took a deep breath, and after she had exhaled she said:

'I didn't have time. I just told you, he hung up!'

'You'll have to ring again.'

'Ring him yourself.'

'Mum!'

'You ought to phone,' retorted Gudrun. 'You know more about the boy than I do.'

'Give me the phone then.'

'Use Torbjörn's.'

Susso gave a laugh.

'Why are you being so silly?'

'I'm not. He hung up on me! If he gets another call from the same number, it's highly likely he won't answer.'

*

They pulled in at a petrol station. Gudrun and Torbjörn vanished into the shop but Susso stayed in the car. Outside the illuminated circle of the filling station it had become night. The beams from their headlights lengthened in the rainy darkness and turned into spiralling veils, and Susso could not tear her eyes away from them.

Later, as they swung back out onto the motorway, she said:

'He wasn't lying. I'm sure about that.'

'You can never be completely sure,' Gudrun said, chewing.

She had bought a hot dog and the whole car smelled of sweet mustard and grease.

'I can be sure of that, at least.'

'You ought to phone Tomas,' Torbjörn said. 'His son. To get it confirmed.'

'Yes,' said Gudrun. 'That's not a bad idea.'

'It is him on the film,' Susso said. 'Definitely.'

'Why don't you ring Dahllöf again?' Gudrun said, her mouth full of food.

'But he didn't know anything,' Susso said over her shoulder.

'I didn't say that.' Gudrun finished her mouthful. 'I only said he hung up.'

Susso held out her hand, and when Torbjörn saw it out of the corner of his eye he fished his phone out of his pocket and unlocked it.

'Give me the number then,' she said.

'Dahllöf.'

'Please don't hang up,' Susso said, 'because what I want to tell you is important. It concerns a child who has been kidnapped.'

'Look, what is this all about . . .?'

'You've probably read about it. Mattias Mickelsson, who disappeared at Christmas. In Jokkmokk. We're looking for someone who might be involved in that.'

'Who am I speaking to? Are you the police?'

'My name is Susso. You spoke to my mother a minute ago.'

'No, I did not. Goodbye!'

'Stupid bloody man,' Susso said, pressing the disconnect key hard with her thumb.

'You ought to phone the police and ask them to phone him,' Gudrun said, crumpling up the hot-dog wrapper. 'That'll make him talk.'

'It's a bit suspicious, I think,' Susso said. 'Hanging up like that and refusing to answer.'

'Maybe he's mixed up in it,' Torbjörn said.

'We might have to track him down,' Gudrun sighed. 'And make him understand.'

'Where does he live then?' Susso asked.

'Didn't she say Helsingborg?' answered Gudrun.

Torbjörn snorted.

'How far is that?' said Susso.

'It's in Skåne,' Gudrun replied.

'If we go there, we've practically driven down the entire country,' Torbjörn said. 'And judging from his response on the phone it's not going to be a very rewarding journey.'

'He'll understand how serious it is,' Susso said, 'if we come to him.'

'Unless he's protecting someone,' said Gudrun. 'It's like Torbjörn says – they might both be involved in the kidnapping.'

'You've got to phone the police,' Torbjörn said. 'And explain.'

'Explain what?' Susso said, unscrewing the lid of her snus tin.

'That the person they're looking for visited the headland where John Bauer lived? Twenty-five years ago?'

She inserted a pouch under her lip, pressed it into place with her tongue and went on:

'It's hardly a hot lead.'

Seved was sitting in his shirt and underpants, eating a meal he had bought at the fast-food kiosk. He had hung his trousers over the radiator below the window after rinsing them under some running water in the handbasin.

Cecilia Myrén's telephone was locked, so he could not get into it. He thought about phoning Lennart again. Perhaps Jola would know how to unlock it? If it proved to be impossible to get into the phone and find some useful information, he would be forced to make another attempt with the sister, and this time it would be considerably more difficult. His only chance would be to break into her place at night, and if her bloke was there, who knew how it would end? It was tempting to talk to Lennart instead and tell him there had been a cock-up, that he had tried but had not been able to get anything out of her. That she had collapsed. And that was the truth. But Lennart would not give up until he had pushed Susso Myrén's sister so hard she died.

Seved felt distinctly uncomfortable when he thought about what the little creature had done to her, and he wondered what would have happened if he had taken all three, as Lennart had told him to do. Could it be that he had made a mistake in taking only one? But he trusted Börje. It was Börje who had fetched the cage from Hybblet and told him one would be enough.

The lemmingshifter had found a place in the top bunk bed.

It was impossible to know what was going on up there. Every so often there were minute, indeterminate sounds, and Seved had seen yellow flakes fall to the floor. They were pieces of foam rubber that the thing was tearing from the mattress. Either it was a kind of vandalism or just something to pass the time.

The phone had rung four times – 'TOMMYBOY', it said on the screen – and every time the twittering signal cut through the silence the creature came out to have a look. It seemed very interested in the sound, standing there with its little wrinkled face half hidden behind the metal frame and staring expectantly.

From beneath his floppy hair Seved peered at the little object, but he had to be careful not to catch its eyes. They were a kindly brown but he had noticed a nasty piercing gleam in them, something hard and sharp that wanted to force its way inside him.

Evil beings, Börje had said.

Seved realised now what he meant.

It was nine by the time they stepped out of the car, stiff and tired. They had found their way to the Scandic Hotel at Järva Krog on the northern outskirts of Stockholm. As soon as they entered their room Gudrun collapsed on the bed, still wearing her clothes and shoes, her neck creasing into more than one double chin. She groaned, and Torbjörn, who was sitting in a small armchair with his legs splayed, grinned at her.

Susso sat down on the bed beside her mother and began to lever off one of her boots.

'What are we going to do then?' she said.

'Sleep!'

'Are we going to Helsingborg? We'll fly, surely. Won't we?'

'I've got to call Cecilia,' said Gudrun, yawning again.

Susso and Torbjörn went down to the restaurant. Lamps cast a cold light over the bar and its dark wooden counter, and there was low music coming from the loudspeakers, but there were no people about.

'Perhaps it's closed,' Susso said.

A man appeared wearing a white shirt and a waistcoat. His sideburns grew down to his beard and the top of his head was bald. He was carrying a plastic crate full of washed glasses.

'Are you open?'

The man nodded without looking at them.

They each bought a large glass of draught beer and sat down at a round table at the back of the restaurant. Through the window they could see the motorway and the cars rushing past in an unbroken stream.

'So, are you coming with us if we go to Helsingborg?'

Torbjörn took a mouthful of beer and set his glass down carefully.

'No, I think I'll wait here.'

'You understand now that I'm not mad.'

'I never said that.'

'No, but you've thought it.'

He shook his head as his eyes wandered around the room, indicating that he would prefer to avoid the subject, and that in itself meant they were halfway to an argument. Susso filled her mouth with beer. After she had swallowed, she said:

'But you can't deny he's not . . . human.'

'He does look flipping weird, I agree with you there. But that's not the same as saying he's not human.'

'But you saw', Susso said, leaning forwards with her elbows on the table and gesticulating, 'his eyes. They're not human.'

Torbjörn shrugged.

'It was an old film. Colours go a bit strange.'

'But you *saw* it!'

'He's deformed, that's all.'

'That's what I thought at first. But not any more.'

'You said yourself that could be the reason why people started believing in trolls in the past,' said Torbjörn. 'People saw some poor sod who had been driven out into the forest because of some defect and they thought it was a troll, because what else could it be?'

Susso smiled down at the froth on top of her beer, which had thinned to a ring around the edge of the glass. She had tried to have an objective conversation about trolls and folklore with Torbjörn before, but he always kept his mouth shut because he hated it when she got irritated. This time, however, he was not backing down, so she wanted to take it slowly.

'As I said,' she went on, 'I used to think the same way. Poor people, I thought. But when I add up everything I know and everything I've seen, I'm not so sure. The Vaikijaur man could actually be a real troll and connected in some way to the thing in Granddad's photo.'

'Yes, but that could have been something totally different,' Torbjörn said.

She looked at him for a long time, studying his face.

'You've never actually said what you really think about the photo.'

'I have.'

She shook her head.

'Do you think it's a fake?'

Now he was on dangerous ground, and it showed because he did not move a muscle. He sat still, holding his glass. Soft footsteps could be heard as the barman made his way over to them, a tea towel thrown over his shoulder, and asked if they wanted anything else.

They ordered two more beers. Torbjörn paid from the small bundle of notes he had in his jeans pocket. He asked the barman if he had any snus, but he said no.

'It could be a troll,' he continued. 'Or at least some strange animal no one has discovered yet. I can go along with that. But I don't think the Vaikijaur man is one of them.'

'And so he is . . .?'

'A freak of nature.'

'But what about John Bauer then?' Susso asked him. 'Why did he go to his old house, of all places?'

Torbjörn took a drink, and after replacing the glass on the table he shrugged his shoulders.

'Like I said, maybe he felt it was some kind of sanctuary. I get that. I'm sure he believes he's a troll himself, if that's how people have treated him all his life. That was the place he wanted to see. For reasons we can't understand. Maybe he thought he could find others like him in the area. What would you do if you were so like a troll you actually thought you were one? A changeling.'

'Drown myself. Swallow poison and then drown myself through a hole in the ice.'

'Well,' said Torbjörn, leaning forwards, 'perhaps that's what he did. He might have decided to do away with himself somewhere close to Bauer's house. Or in Lake Vättern. To follow him down into the depths, so to speak.'

There was a gleam of amusement in Torbjörn's eyes, but she ignored it.

'Clearly that is not what he did,' she said, a fixed expression on her face. 'Because he was in Jokkmokk just before Christmas. I have photographic evidence of that.'

They went up to their room. The fitted carpet muffled their footsteps and Susso heard from Torbjörn's breathing that he was trying to come up with something to say to placate her, or even cheer her up, but he was uncertain what her reaction would be. So he kept silent.

She took out the keycard, pressed it into the slot and opened the door. Then she walked straight to the bed and ripped off her jumper, but it fastened in her hair slide, so she had to pull that out at the same time.

Gudrun was asleep, curled in a heap under the duvet, her face to the wall lined with wardrobes. Her glasses lay on the bedside table. There was a faint shimmer from the little glittery butterfly on the frames. Beside them was her mobile. It was flashing green.

The springs of the extra bed gave a groan as Torbjörn lay down on his back. He put his hands behind his head and stared up at the ceiling, which pulsed with the light from passing cars. Susso stepped out of her jeans and looked at him, because she knew he was about to say something.

'Shit, it's so . . .' he began.

'What?'

'Sensitive. These things.'

She could only sigh.

'I ought to be able to say what I think,' he said softly.

'But you never do. You only hint at things. It's the same old story. All you do is grin and make jokes.'

She imitated his grin for an instant before looking at him angrily. He had turned onto his side and propped himself up on his elbow.

'It's just that I don't think this has anything to do with your troll. It's probably some paedophile who has taken Mattias.'

'Why do you have to keep on joking about it then? Saying he could have drowned himself and all that. Why can't you be serious?'

'It was . . . it was only a theory,' he said, slurring his words.

She waited for him to go on, but there was silence.

'A theory?' she asked.

He did not answer, and she knew he had fallen asleep.

When Susso came down to the dining room the following morning Gudrun and Torbjörn were already there eating breakfast, bent over their newspapers. Torbjörn was wearing his white beanie, and when he caught sight of her his mouth widened into a thin smile which was gone in an instant.

The room was full of chatter from the people at the tables, and the sun was shining through the large windows. She filled a mug with coffee and sat for a while looking at Torbjörn and Gudrun's plates before going over to the breakfast buffet. After queuing behind a fat man with a greasy plastic comb sticking out of the back pocket of his baggy jeans she piled scrambled egg onto her plate. It had grey layers and left behind a pool of water. She helped herself to shiny chipolatas and crumpled bacon slices, white bread with ready-sliced cheese and rings of red and yellow pepper. She poured herself a glass of orange juice and started drinking as she walked to the table. She had a slight hangover, strangely enough, that manifested itself only in a raging thirst.

Torbjörn was sitting with his spoon in his hand, staring at the newspaper. He was eating a bowl of yoghurt with muesli and raisins. She couldn't work him out: eating so healthily when there was so much tasty food. He lowered his head as he spooned in the cereal, and there was a crunching sound as he ate.

'Shall we fly there, or what?' she said, cutting into her sausage.

Gudrun cleared her throat.

'You haven't heard anything from the police?'

Susso took a bite of her sandwich.

'Me?' she said. 'They'll phone your mobile in that case, because that's what I told them to do.'

'No,' Gudrun said. 'We won't be flying.'

'We won't?'

A piece of pepper dangled from Susso's mouth and she pushed it between her lips before going on:

'Why did we come to Stockholm then? It's in completely the wrong direction.'

'You never know,' Gudrun said, licking her fingertips before turning the page of her paper. 'Might give us time to collect our thoughts.'

'We could just as easily have done that in Gränna,' Susso retorted, looking at her mother in bewilderment. 'It's significantly closer to Helsingborg from there. Now we've driven two hundred kilometres in the wrong direction!'

She suspected that Gudrun had slowly begun to plan their return journey. That made her angry. As if she was in charge of everything! It might be her car and her money, but this was so important that she had no right to make all the decisions about what they were going to do. Soon she would be saying something about the shop, that Cecilia had phoned to complain. Or that Roland was having trouble with the dog, or that he had to go somewhere and did not want to leave the dog alone.

'So we're *driving* to Helsingborg from here?' Susso asked.

She wanted confirmation. Possibly she could get her mother where she wanted her by waiting and leading her gently along, and pretending that she did not know she thought it was time to go home, but by now she had lost patience.

Gudrun sat cradling her coffee cup. It was white and some coffee had dribbled down the side, like a brown tear.

'Are we?'

Gudrun looked up and gave Susso an irritated look before returning to her newspaper.

'No,' she said, distractedly. 'We aren't.'

'Well, what are we going to do then? Are we going home?'

'No, I don't think we will.'

'So?'

'I thought we might drive into town.'

'To do what? A bit of shopping?'

'We're going to visit someone.'

'Who?'

'Someone called Barbro. Barbro Jerring.'

'Really? And who's that?'

'Barbro Jerring,' Gudrun said in a low voice, 'the widow of Sven Jerring.'

That made Torbjörn look up.

'And he is?' said Susso, taking a mouthful of coffee.

'Honestly, Susso,' Gudrun said. 'Don't you know who Sven Jerring is?'

Susso shook her head.

Then Gudrun turned to Torbjörn.

'Torbjörn, surely you know who Sven Jerring was?'

'He got some kind of prize,' he began doubtfully. 'Didn't he?'

Gudrun was amazed and she gaped at them.

'He's only one of the most famous people in Sweden!'

'Obviously not,' Susso said, 'because otherwise we would have heard of him.'

'Before that! When I was young. Uncle Sven! Have you never heard anyone talk about Uncle Sven and his *Children's Letterbox* programme?'

Susso shook her head and Torbjörn kept quiet.

'That's absolutely shocking,' Gudrun said. 'Cecilia was on *Children's Letterbox.* Not on the actual programme, of course, but she was invited to Stockholm. Susso, you must have heard about the invitation?'

'I know there was something about a radio programme, but that's all.'

Gudrun stared at them, astonished.

'Fancy not knowing who Sven Jerring is . . .'

The phone had started ringing as soon as I had put the tray on the table and taken a bite of my bread roll. It was a mobile number I did not recognise. I swallowed the mouthful before answering. At the other end was a woman speaking very fast in a southern Swedish accent.

'You phoned yesterday and spoke to my father.'

I considered the situation for a moment. I was about to be on the receiving end of a slap on the wrist and I wondered whether it would be simpler to deny that it was me who had phoned. But then I felt a sudden surge of irritation that someone wanted to tick me off for making a phone call about a kidnapped child – and at the fact that my own daughter had been attacked and her life had actually been in real danger.

'Yes, that's right,' I said.

'Dad doesn't want to talk to you, but I think you ought to know that you are not the first person to ask about that boy Magnus.'

'Don't you mean Mattias?'

'No, Magnus. Magnus Brodin.'

I tried to explain to her that there must have been some kind of misunderstanding, but she interrupted me.

'In 1979,' she said, 'Sven Jerring came to see us at Björkudden and he talked about that boy, the one who disappeared.'

I said nothing. Had I heard correctly?

'Children's Letterbox,' the woman said. 'Uncle Sven!'

'Yes, I know who it is. But the boy we are looking for went missing this Christmas just gone. Mattias, he's called. Which boy are you talking about?'

'Oh, I see. I thought you were asking about Magnus Brodin . . .'

'Magnus Brodin,' I said. 'I recognise that name. He was kidnapped, wasn't he? In the seventies?'

'Seventy-eight. The summer of '78.'

'And you're saying Sven Jerring came to your house on Björkudden and asked about him? What did he ask?'

'He said he had come because of Magnus. He had an idea that the boy had been abducted by trolls. Dad didn't know what to believe. He thought it was all a joke because the house had belonged to John Bauer and that perhaps it was going to be part of a radio programme, but he's realised since that it was no joke.'

'But did he say anything about a very small man? Did Sven Jerring say anything about a dwarf?'

'A dwarf? I was only little then, I don't really remember . . .'

It was starting to sound vague. I cleared my throat.

'You've probably read in the papers that the police are looking for a person known as the Vaikijaur man,' I said. 'We drove to Björkudden because we had heard that he had been there. In 1980.'

'The little old man who was in the papers?'

'Exactly. The Vaikijaur man.'

'And he was supposed to have been living at Björkudden in 1980? Well, I can tell you he wasn't, most definitely.'

'I don't know about living there as such. We only know he visited the place. That he had some kind of business there.'

'It sounds strange. No, I don't believe that's right.'

'And you're completely sure about that?'

'Yes, of course. What is all this, for God's sake?'

'What did your parents say to Sven Jerring?'

'Nothing! They hardly believed him! And I don't think his wife did either.'

'So she was with him?'

'Yes.'

'Is she still alive?'

'How would I know?'

I sat for a while wondering what to do next, before calling directory enquiries and asking for Barbro Jerring.

'I believe she's living in Stockholm,' I said. 'If she's still alive.'

She was. Or at least, she had a phone number.

I looked around. The dining room had started to fill, with people gathering around the breakfast buffet, so I got up and went over to a small group of sofas where I could sit hidden behind a pillar and a palm.

There were seven or eight rings and then a rustling noise.

'Jerring.'

'Hello,' I said. 'Is that Barbro Jerring speaking?'

'Yes.'

'May I ask if you were married to Sven Jerring?'

'Yes, I was.'

'Then I have the right number. My name is Gudrun Myrén and it so happens that I've just been speaking to Fredrik Dahllöf's daughter. I don't know her name, but anyway she said you and Sven visited Björkudden in 1979 in relation to Magnus Brodin and the fact that Sven thought he had been taken by trolls. Is that correct?'

'Are you a journalist?'

'No, we're trying to track down the so-called Vaikijaur man. The police suspect he is involved in the kidnapping of Mattias Mickelsson. Have you heard about that?'

'I've read about it in the newspaper, yes.'

'We're lending a hand, you might say. It was my daughter who took the photograph of this person. The Vaikijaur man, that is. So we're trying to find out who he is. And it seems as if there could be a connection between the disappearance of Magnus and Mattias. You see, the Vaikijaur man visited Björkudden in 1980.'

'He was at Björkudden?'

'Yes. We know he was there, but not why.'

'What has Dahllöf told you?'

'He doesn't know this person at all. Or so he says. But we definitely know he was there, so we think perhaps Dahllöf is keeping something from us.'

'No, I don't think he's doing that.'

'You don't?'

'No.'

'What do you think then?'

There followed a moment's silence, and just as I was about to say 'Hello?' Barbro added:

'I think I have an idea who he was looking for.'

The dark-red mobile swivelled and buzzed on the table.

'MUM,' it said in the oblong window.

And below: 'Answer?'

Seved picked up the phone and held it uncertainly for a moment before pressing the key.

'Hello! Can you hear me?'

It was a woman's voice. It was loud.

Seved waited quietly, not even daring to breathe in case it would be heard.

'Hello? Cecilia?'

He cleared his throat.

'I can hardly hear you. Listen, we're in Stockholm.'

Seved kept silent. Stockholm. He had been expecting an address in Gränna. This was better, but Lennart would not be happy with the news. There was a risk the woman would hang up, so he made a humming sound.

'Do you know where we're going? You'll never guess!'

'No,' he whispered.

'We're going to Sven Jerring's home. To see his widow, Barbro Jerring.'

Seved hung on. Was she going to say anything else?

'I'll have to tell you about it later. Hello? Can you hear me?'

*

Oh yes. He had heard all right.

He dug about in his bag and brought out the phone Börje had given him, followed by the slip of paper with Lennart's number on it.

'Yes?'

'It's me. Seved.'

'Yes?'

'I know where they're going now. Where they're heading.'

'Right.'

'To someone called Barbro Jerring, I think.'

'You think?'

'Yes, that's what she said.'

'Barbro Jerring? Jerring? As in Sven Jerring?'

'Yes. It's his widow, that's where they're going. She lives in Stockholm.'

'So what was all that crap about them going to Gränna then?'

'Don't know.'

It was clear from Lennart's voice that he was unsure whether to be satisfied or annoyed.

'Can . . . can I drive home now?'

'No, you stay where you are! Until I've got hold of them.'

When the conversation ended he sat staring at the mess on the table in front of him. He had left a few stumps of hard, overcooked fries and some onion and the remains of the dressing in the sticky hamburger wrapper, but now it was all gone, every last scrap, and the polystyrene container that had held his burger had been shredded into pieces the size of rice grains.

The feeling of disgust that welled up inside him was so strong he gagged.

To think it had been sitting there, eating in the darkness, while he had been sleeping.

He looked around the room because he had no idea where the little shapeshifter could be. Not in the cage. That was shut.

It was probably on the bed. He looked up at the top bunk, then walked over and gently lifted the duvet that was folded next to the pillow, but it was not there. He looked under the duvet on the lower bunk as well and then kneeled down and looked underneath the bunk bed, but saw only his empty can of cola, which the lemmingshifter had presumably knocked from the table.

Where the hell had it gone?

Could it have escaped somehow?

His eyes scanned the room to check for any openings, and there, right above the door, was a round hole that had probably once had a cover. Could it have climbed all the way up there? The wall was covered with shiny textured wallpaper, so that seemed unlikely. But perhaps there were other gaps? A few millimetres would be enough for it to force its way out.

The thought that the creature had taken itself off filled him with an overpowering sense of relief. Now there would be absolutely no reason for him to stay in Kiruna. He could set off for home immediately. It was not his fault the little being had decided to run away. It probably did exactly as it chose. Lennart had to know that.

Seved put on his jeans, sank into the chair and quickly pulled on his socks. He was in a hurry now. It might have just slipped outside for a while to have a look around. If he hurried, he would be away before it came back.

He picked up his shirt and pushed his arms into the sleeves, glancing at his watch as his left wrist appeared through the cuff.

It had just turned ten. Quickly he fastened the buttons. Then he put on his down jacket, pushed both mobiles into a pocket and zipped it closed. He tied his boots, hurried over to the bed and began rolling up the sleeping bag. He knew he would not be able to get it into its case unless he rolled it up properly, getting out all of the air, so he dragged it to the floor and knelt down beside it.

Then he felt something inside.

A small lump.

He straightened up immediately, staring at it.

The creature had crept into the sleeping bag and had slept by his feet. All night it had been curled up there, enjoying the warmth from his body. He stood up and noticed a small movement making a crease in the dark-green synthetic fabric. It had woken up and was on its way out.

Now, he thought. I've got to do it now.

And he lifted his foot and stamped as hard as he could.

Tessin Park was ringed by tall chestnut trees with spreading black branches. A woman was pushing a pram on the gravel path bisecting the park, but otherwise there was no one in sight, which Susso thought was odd. To think it could be so deserted in the middle of Stockholm, in the middle of the day, and in such a large and lovely park.

They followed the pavement along De Geersgatan, nobody saying a word. Gudrun's hand gripped the metal ring linking her handbag to its plaited shoulder strap. Her other arm swung up and down as she walked ahead, fast. She had taken a pair of brown leather shoes from her suitcase and their heels were clicking and scraping against the gritted paving stones. The smudges of blusher on her cheeks looked like bruises.

Susso had stuffed her hands deep into her pockets and one of them found an old receipt that she crumpled between her fingers as her eyes ran over the facades of the apartment blocks. They were light yellow with balconies of corrugated steel, and were mottled with the shadows of the trees in the park.

During breakfast Gudrun had told them about Magnus Brodin, the boy who had disappeared in the summer of 1978 in Dalarna. For some reason, Sven Jerring had been convinced that the boy had been taken by trolls.

Gudrun had the door code on her mobile. She pressed the

buttons with her index finger, and when the lock buzzed she opened the heavy door.

'Come on,' she said, waving the hand that was still clutching her phone.

The walls of the stairwell were painted with horses and naked people. There was no board listing the names of the residents, so they had to go from floor to floor looking for the right apartment. The curved bannister was made of copper that slid shining and cold under Susso's palm as she jogged up the stairs. When, breathless, she reached the top floor and started reading the name plates on the doors, she heard Torbjörn's voice from below. He was trying to whisper but it sounded like a loud hissing:

'Susso! It's here.'

It was a solid panelled door of gleaming wood, with the name JERRING in ornate lettering on an oval brass plate above the letterbox.

The doorbell was attached to the frame on a level with the handle and its button was as small and black as a liquorice cough drop. Gudrun pressed it and straightened the apricot-coloured scarf tied around her neck. Susso could see she was nervous.

No one opened, so she rang again, longer this time. When she removed her thumb the sound remained in their ears because it was noticeably silent in the stairwell.

'Isn't she supposed to be at home?' Susso asked.

'Yes,' Gudrun answered, taking out her mobile. 'I thought so.'

She scrolled to Barbro's telephone number, and soon a muffled ring was heard from inside the apartment. She let it ring about ten times before flipping her phone shut.

Susso sighed.

'And of course she has no mobile?'

Gudrun opened her bag and took out her lip salve. After rubbing it over her lips she replaced the stick in her bag and zipped it shut.

'We'll just have to wait,' she said, unperturbed.

They sat down on the stairs, Susso and Gudrun on the bottom step, the soles of their shoes resting on the floor of shiny marble slabs with their scattering of fossils, and behind them in the darkness Torbjörn, his eyes narrowed and alert.

In the car on the way into the city Gudrun had told them all about Sven Jerring and his radio programme *Children's Letterbox*, how it had broken the record for the world's longest series with the same presenter. There was probably no one of her generation who had not at some point fantasised about walking into Sven Jerring's studio to sing or play an instrument.

Gudrun explained that the people of Sweden had taken Uncle Sven closer to their hearts than any public figure who had come before him, and it seemed unlikely he would ever be replaced. He was the first man on the radio and his voice had reached out to the entire country. It was almost impossible to describe how loved he was by the population, how familiar he seemed to them. It was as if everyone thought of him as a dear old friend.

This was precisely what made Susso suspicious.

She found it hard to understand how such a person – in his time the most famous and perhaps most popular in Sweden – could be involved in the mystery surrounding the disappearance of Mattias Mickelsson. It was implausible, quite simply, that the trail should lead to him, of all people.

Somewhere along the line there had to be a misunderstanding.

Or a lie.

She just could not work out where.

They had been waiting for about half an hour when there was a clanking in the lift shaft and the cables started to move. Then the lift cage slowed down and shuddered to a halt, the gates slid apart with a rattle, the doors opened and an elderly woman wearing a beret and a mushroom-coloured poplin raincoat stepped out.

Gudrun immediately stood up.

'Barbro?'

Her voice echoed out harshly but the woman did not appear to be disturbed by it. She looked at Gudrun, taking stock of her with her clear light-blue eyes, which were tucked into the pockets of wrinkles covering her face. When she registered that two other people were sitting on the stairs, her face took on a more quizzical expression.

'We spoke earlier on the phone,' Gudrun said softly.

From her coat pocket the old woman drew out a bunch of keys and studied them intently. It looked as if she had forgotten what to do with them.

'You had better come in,' she said.

Radio personality Sven Jerring had been dead for a quarter of a century, but the strong smell of his tobacco smoke still lingered in the apartment. It was not particularly clean or tidy, either. The grey layer of dust on top of the television, the coffee cup on the windowsill and another perched precariously on the edge of the table, the trail of potting compost below the radiator, the shapeless pile of newspapers. Susso felt sorry for the old woman. Why was there no one to help her? Did she not have any children?

While Torbjörn and Gudrun stood at the windows looking out over the park, Susso examined a disorderly pile of carved wooden figures. She was standing looking at these when Barbro came out of the kitchen. In one hand she held a pair of reading glasses and in the other a black leather briefcase.

'Sven was an incorrigible collector,' she said, smiling at Susso.

Susso nodded. She carefully picked up one of the figures. It was wearing glasses.

'It's him, right?' she asked, and Barbro smiled.

She stood the briefcase on the floor beside an armchair and sat with her hands in her lap.

Susso, Torbjörn and Gudrun sat in a row on the sofa, and the old woman regarded her guests steadily, which soon made them feel uncomfortable. Susso grinned slightly as her eyes wandered around the room, looking for something to fix on. She settled for the decorative roller blind pulled down over one of the windows.

On the greyish-blue fabric was a painting of a castle with towers and spires and a drawbridge. The moat's wavy outline blended with the sea beyond, and the castle appeared to be floating, rather like a mirage.

'That's Vadstena Castle,' Barbro said.

'Oh yes!' exclaimed Gudrun, taking a look at the blind. 'I've been there, I think.'

Barbro twisted her head to look at the castle.

'That is not a particularly realistic impression,' she said, adding: 'My cousin painted it.'

'Oh, was he an artist?' Gudrun asked.

'I don't know if you could call him an artist,' Barbro replied. 'But he painted. And he painted that for Sven. Vadstena was where Sven grew up, of course. Erik thought he could look at the roller blind and take himself back in time, or something like that.'

Then she fell silent. Judging from the small movements of her thin lips she did not know how to continue.

'I have carried this story for such a long time,' she said. 'Now that I have the opportunity to unburden myself I hardly know where to start. It is all so incomprehensible and awful. And you will never believe me.'

'We'll believe you,' Susso said, nodding.

Gudrun agreed immediately and said:

'When it comes to the Myrén family, our belief is limitless. That goes for Torbjörn too.'

Barbro was wearing a gold bracelet around her right wrist which she twisted and turned and pushed up and down her arm. It was as if she could not decide where it fitted best.

'Limitless enough to believe in trolls?' she said.

Torbjörn gave a laugh, a snort of air through his nostrils, and when Susso heard the word it was as if a leak had sprung open inside her and was beginning to seep out. She pressed her upper lip between her teeth, tearing off a shred of skin, and glanced sideways at her mother's face, which had frozen in a serious expression. The corners of Gudrun's mouth drooped and lines ran down from them to her chin.

'Haven't you told her anything, Mum?'

'No. I didn't know quite how to put it . . .'

'My mother's father saw a troll,' said Susso. 'And he took a photo of it. That was in 1987, in Rapadalen. Up in Sarek.'

Barbro changed position in her chair, listening attentively as Susso went on:

'The troll, or whatever it was he saw, was riding on the back of a bear that was running across the marshland. So trolls are nothing to scoff at in our family. In fact, I have a website where I collect evidence and pictures people send me of trolls and shape-shifters or other things.'

'The troll was riding on a bear?'

'Yes.'

'And you have a photograph of it?'

'An aerial shot, so it's not very detailed. Have you got a computer?'

Barbro shook her head.

'You can see it isn't an animal, anyway,' Susso said, 'although I don't know what kind of animal would ride on a bear. So we call it a troll for lack of a better name.'

'And how much do you know about the stallo people?' Barbro asked. 'Since you come from up there.'

'Stallo?' answered Susso, hesitantly. 'It's . . . well, what can I say? In Sami mythology they are giants, a kind of troll. But people think there is some truth in the tales, or rather to the creatures in the tales, and that they were a kind of foreign tribe the Sami people often clashed with. There are various cultural relics – graves and dwelling sites and so on – that are known as stallo graves and stallo land. But no one really knows.'

'And they took Sami children too, didn't they?' said Barbro.

Susso nodded.

'Yes,' she said. 'That's the kind of thing trolls do, generally.'

It looked as if Barbro had drifted far away in her thoughts, but then suddenly she took a deep breath and rested her hand on her pearls.

'I think you know about Magnus Brodin? The boy who disappeared? Well, I would understand if you don't,' she said, turning to Susso and Torbjörn. 'You weren't even born then. Anyway, he was abducted. It happened when he was in a cabin with his mother, somewhere near Färnebofjärden, if you know where that is. It is a national park now.'

'I remember,' Gudrun said. 'It was frightening that a child could disappear like that in this country. Every time I saw a person in a trench coat I thought it was a kidnapper.'

Barbro reached for her glasses, but as soon as she had fitted them over the bridge of her nose she took them off again. Instead she picked up the black briefcase and rested it on her knees. The initials 'SJ' were engraved in the shiny leather.

'In this briefcase', she said, 'I keep everything relating to Magnus Brodin. You could say I have pushed him down inside here to allow myself to shut it all away.'

Her stick-thin fingers rested on the briefcase but she could not bring herself to open it. Instead she began to toy with the handle and the lock.

'Sven was given this briefcase by Nordenskiöld,' she said absently. 'His boss at the radio station. It comes from the railway, Statens Järnvägar, of course, but Nordenskiöld insisted the initials stood for Sven Jerring. It was impossible to prove otherwise, he said. He thought that in a metaphorical sense Sven was a lot like the railway. You know, in the way he brought the country together.'

She unclipped both fastenings, lifted the lid, reached inside and pulled out a thick wad of newspaper articles that rippled as she placed them on the table. Susso leaned forwards to see. She carefully moved a strip of paper and carried on looking through the pile until she came to a black and white photograph of a boy's face. Magnus's face.

'The police spent the entire summer searching for him,' Barbro said. 'With helicopters and orienteers and defence volunteers and goodness knows what else. They used all available resources. Sven and I watched it on the television news, and at first he didn't seem to react in any particular way. He read the daily papers and asked me to buy the evening papers as well, so naturally I realised he was interested in the story. But later, when he made his own enquiries, talking on the phone to journalists who had been there and so on, I started to think he was going too far. It was an unhealthy interest. I noticed that it affected him very deeply, that it was taking over. And it was actually here, in front of this roller blind, that I suddenly became aware just how deeply it touched him. How it was based on more than compassion.'

She sighed and rearranged her collar.

'He was ill. He'd been having problems with the circulation in his left foot for years. He had recorded his final episode of *Children's Letterbox*, and having to end the programme that he had devoted so much of his life to, well, that marked the end of more than just his career, of course. And when the autumn came and the papers had stopped writing about Magnus Brodin, he was in such a low frame of mind that all he wanted to do was sit by the window and look out at the park. When I asked him what was wrong, or what he was thinking about, he wouldn't even answer. He just sat here, staring out into the darkness. He was being tormented by something inside him, something I knew nothing about, and it was only when I parked his wheelchair in front of the roller blind one day that I realised it was connected to something that had happened a long time ago. When he woke up he was facing the image of Vadstena Castle. He flew into a rage, and it was especially awful because he so rarely got angry. Prickly, at the very most. But on this occasion he was irate. I asked him if he wanted to talk about what was upsetting him, but he absolutely refused. After that I left him in peace.

'It was the beginning of March when he said he wanted to go

to Gränna. Not to Vadstena? No, Gränna. So we took the car. And as we drew closer to his old home he became dizzy and started complaining, saying he had to rest for a few minutes. We stopped at Brahehus Castle. For a good hour he sat in the ruins with his spiked walking stick between his legs and his fur hat on his head, looking out over the ice down below while I tried to protect him from tourists who recognised Uncle Sven and wanted to say hello. It was quite cold and there were strong gusts of wind blowing up from the lake. I was afraid he would catch a chill.'

Barbro smiled at the memory and sat quietly for a moment. Through the open balcony door came the sound of traffic on Valhallavägen, rushing faintly like rapids in the distance. The wind had picked up and the chestnut trees were moving restlessly.

'When Sven saw Vättern again,' Barbro continued, 'the lake of his childhood, the vast lake of his youth, it was as if something opened up inside him, because once we were back in the car and on our way towards Gränna he began to talk. He asked me what I knew about Per Brahe, and I answered that I knew a little, that Per Brahe was a nobleman who built Brahehus . . . but then he interrupted me. "Not *that* Per Brahe," he said, "I mean the steamer, the one that sank." "Oh yes," I said. "I know John Bauer drowned." Then he nodded and looked out of the window with a sorrowful expression on his face. "His wife drowned too," he said. "And his son, who was only three years old." "Yes, it was awful," I said. "You know," he said, "it was all my fault. Not that the ship sank, but that the Bauer family were on board at the time."

'I found that difficult to believe but I did not interrupt him because I wanted to know what had caused his depression all winter. I wanted to hear what he had to say.'

Barbro smoothed her blouse before she continued:

'In the autumn of 1918 Sven was working at the *Vadstena Läns* newspaper. He was twenty-three and had recently returned from Petrograd, where he had a post with the Swedish consulate. He had watched as the Bolsheviks seized control of the city with extreme brutality. He began to work for the *Vadstena Läns* by writing stories about his experiences in Russia. Those articles were highly regarded and soon his pen name, Crayon, was appearing more and more often in the paper.

'One day he had an unexpected visitor. It was none other than Esther Bauer, the wife of John Bauer, the dearly loved illustrator of folk tales. She walked into the editorial offices holding her son's hand and asked to speak to Crayon in private. She had something dreadful that she wanted him to put in the newspaper. Naturally, Sven was curious.

'Her story began in the summer of 1904, when John was working on illustrations for a book called *Lapland – the Great Swedish Land of the Future*. He was living with the Sami people and was allowed to travel with them as if he were one of their own. One day, when they were on their way to a fell lake to fish, they saw a group of timber huts in the distance which attracted John's interest. He wanted to take a closer look, but the Laps refused, so John had to go alone. The people living there were walking around in strange fur clothes – wolf pelts and bear skins with the animals' heads still attached. Some of them were enormous and others were more like dwarves, you could say. They had a tame bear which walked among the huts like a dog. John had never seen anything like it and was absolutely mesmerised.'

Susso, who had been leafing through the newspaper cuttings on the table, looked up and caught her mother's eye, and she heard the sofa creak as Torbjörn shifted position and leaned forwards.

'There was a squirrel,' Barbro continued. 'They kept it as a pet and John took a liking to it because it was unusually sociable, and when one of the giants said he could have it, he took it gladly. When he returned to the Sami the first thing he did was show them the squirrel, but they did not share his delight and one of them, an old woman, even tried to beat it to death. They told John he had been among the stallo people and that the little animal was one of them and not to be trusted. They said that if John wanted to stay with them, he would have to get rid of the squirrel, but he was not prepared to do that so he left for home the following day.'

'Are you saying there were stallo around as late as the beginning of the twentieth century?' Susso said. 'It must have just been something they said, something the Sami people told him to scare him. Or maybe they were joking.'

'Yes,' said Barbro, 'that could have been the case. But he could find no other name for them. And fourteen years later, in the autumn of 1918, they came to his home on Björkudden.'

'Who did?' Susso asked. 'The stallo?'

Barbro nodded slowly.

'They turned up late one evening,' she said. 'And they were really very strange. One of them was gigantic. His head hit the ceiling, so he had to stoop, and the ceiling of the ground floor was two metres and seventy-five centimetres high. The second was a dwarf, hardly a metre tall. The third man was normal height, which, under the circumstances, looked quite amusing. He did all the talking while the other two, who were wearing floor-length capes with hoods to hide their hideous faces, stood quietly in the background. Esther assumed they belonged to a theatre where John had worked as a set designer, but when she asked if they were actors, they did not answer. They just stared at her in silence. John told her to take Bengt up to the studio, which she did, and when she came back down a moment later, John was sitting on a chair, his face completely ashen, with Humpe the squirrel on his lap. That was the name he had given it. He wouldn't say anything at first, but eventually he told her that the men had come to settle a debt. Esther and John had been in financial difficulty for some time, so she received that news with a sigh and asked how much money they wanted. And then John said it wasn't money they were interested in, but the boy. He told her about his meeting with the stallo and how they had given him the squirrel. In exchange they now demanded to adopt John's child. Naturally Esther was beside herself and asked John if they couldn't just give back the squirrel, but John only shook his head and said that was completely out of the question as far as the stallo were concerned. They wanted the boy, and if he was not given to them, they would take him.'

Barbro sighed deeply before she went on:

'John contacted the police but they practically laughed in his face, and so Esther had come to Sven, hoping he would be able to help them by writing something in the newspaper. She thought if it was brought into the open, if everyone knew that there was an isolated group of people in the Lapland wilderness who were about to kidnap the son of the famous artist John Bauer, then the police would take the family seriously and the stallo would not dare to carry out their threat. But of course Sven did not write a word about it. He was convinced that John Bauer had corrupted his wife, poisoned her with his fantasies about trolls, and that she, a woman of taste and considerable artistic talent herself, had more or less lost her mind in that isolated house on Björkudden.'

'Yes,' Gudrun said. 'It sounds like it. Stallo . . .'

'Only a few days later they were dead,' Barbro said. 'Swallowed up by the waters of Vättern. Esther, John and the little boy Bengt, who they called Putte. Along with twenty-two other people. It was a horrible business at a horrible time. The war was over and the old world lay in ruins. Spanish flu was raging, following invisibly in the footsteps of the war, and would not be stopped by peace treaties or boundaries. Sweden had kept out of the battles, but the country had not avoided emotional scars. They were like a rot, hidden and inaccessible. By the time the war ended no one knew how many people had lost their lives, but it was thought to be a considerable number. And the shortage of bread – that was certainly not unknown in this country. Not to mention the lack of coffee!'

'Speaking of coffee,' Gudrun said, stretching, 'shall we make some?'

'Shortly,' Barbro said, nodding. 'On the first of October, in the final stages of the war, a train came off the track in Getå. It was caused by a landslip and there were forty-two casualties. And only a couple of months later there was the terrible accident on Lake Vättern. Bauer, the guardian of everything the war would not be allowed to destroy. How could he, the man with the enchanted pen who had revealed the hidden recesses of the Swedish forests and fulfilled the longing for myths that was beating in the heart of the population – how could he, of all people, have drowned *by pure chance*? At that very time. And on Vättern, of all places, the country's oldest and most impenetrable lake? How could that have happened?'

'Yes. Good Lord,' Gudrun said.

'Gustaf Cederström,' Barbro said. 'Have you heard of him? He is best known for his painting of the funeral procession of Karl

XII, and he was Bauer's tutor at the Konstakademi. He came up with an answer to that question. Let me see if I can find it here.'

She moved her spectacles to the tip of her nose and searched among the articles.

'Here,' she said, holding up a cutting. 'It's an obituary, published in *Gammalt och Nytt,* and this is what he writes: "Bauer's life was full and spent alongside the enchanted lake which became the grave of his happiness. The many legends that surround Vättern, and its ever-changing mystical nature, left a profound impression. Perhaps in some way his rich imagination is a gift to the lake, and indeed we see in the legends how trolls reclaim their gifts. This dreadful year, has not the lake taken back what it once gave?"'

Barbro put down the obituary, straightened her glasses and carried on with her story:

'After the ship sank, Sven felt terrible and blamed himself to an extent that those around him thought was unreasonable. Everyone was talking about the *Per Brahe,* so he was given countless opportunities to pass on the strange tale told to him by Esther Bauer, but he never made it public. It was all behind closed doors, so to speak, and he did eventually manage to put the dreadful story behind him, exactly as he had done with Petrograd. He left the newspaper and went back to his studies in Uppsala. But everything surfaced again. Literally. In 1922 the *Per Brahe* was successfully salvaged. By then Sven was employed by the newspaper *Östgöta-Bladet,* and it was his job to cover the story. He was stationed in Hästholmen and sent daily reports, and when the steamer's bilges were pumped he was one of the first to go aboard. In the hold, directly below the ladder, he found a body undiscovered by the divers, understandably so because the corpse did not resemble a body. It looked more like a heap of mud, which is what it was, chemically speaking. It brought back memories of Petrograd and he felt faint and unsteady and left the ship. They were difficult days for him.

'By the end of August the salvage operation was completed and the deceased were laid to rest in Västra Tollstad's cemetery. Now there was talk of a shipwreck auction: sewing machines, cast-iron stoves, irons, bicycles, gold rings, clocks and brooches. Knick-knacks. The whole lot was going to be put up for sale. According to unconfirmed sources they had even found brand-new motorcycles from the Huskvarna munitions factory among the wreckage. But of course they had not. It was a dream. A dream of treasure on the lake bed! Sven was part of the newspaper's editorial team and he refused to write about it. He had had enough.

'But then something happened. An unusual find was made on the shore at Medhamra, just north of Vadstena: John Bauer's tail-coat had washed ashore. They knew it was his tail coat because his savings book was in one of the pockets. Naturally the name Bauer came up for discussion again and so Sven told the editor about his remarkable meeting with Esther Bauer four years earlier. The following day, when he walked into the office, his editor came up to him with a copy of the magazine *Idun*. I've got that copy here somewhere . . .'

Barbro rummaged in the briefcase and brought out a magazine that she laid on the table. It was dated 10 October 1915. The headline read: 'AT HOME WITH THE STORYTELLER OF BJÖRKUDDEN', and underneath were three pictures framed in entwined stems.

Susso, Gudrun and Torbjörn bent over the table to get a closer look. 'THE ARTIST IN HIS STUDIO' was written above the first picture of John, who was standing behind a table laden with paper and drawing tools. He was holding a pen and smiling into the camera.

In the second photo, which had the caption 'THE ARTIST AND HIS WIFE', John was standing next to Esther, who was wearing a white dress and a white lace hat. John was holding his pipe with the shaft pointing towards his stiff shirt collar.

In the third and largest photograph, which completely dominated the page, John was standing in profile, his head turned towards a fir tree, his pipe between his teeth and his hair combed over his forehead. His right hand was tugging gently at the foot of a small figure sitting on a branch level with the crown of the artist's head.

'What's that?' asked Susso, wrinkling her brow. 'Is that supposed to be the squirrel?'

'That is exactly what Sven wanted to know,' answered Barbro thoughtfully, as she tapped the flimsy paper. 'He and the editor agreed that it was probably a trick of photography, but trick or not, that little object aroused Sven's interest. Now, having seen that photograph, he was determined to write something about it. He would write with a light touch, creating an appendix to the idyllic photo reportage in *Idun*. From the right perspective it could be rewritten as a heart-warming story. The fact that Esther Bauer had believed that trolls from Lapland wanted to get their claws on her child was also a scoop, of course, but he held back from writing about that because he didn't want to bring shame on the family after they had died so tragically. But the squirrel – that was entirely different! He could write about that unhindered. He wanted to know what had happened to it. If John had not taken it with him onto the vessel, it could still be alive, perhaps even at Björkudden. Sven asked his father, who was the district vet, if he knew how long a Swedish squirrel could live. His guess was five or six years, up to fifteen in captivity. If Bauer had been given the squirrel in 1904, it couldn't possibly still be alive. But who knew? A couple of days later he took his bicycle and pedalled down to Gränna. It had already started to get dark when he arrived at the Bauers' old house on the promontory. There was no one home. In fact, the door was barred and the curtains closed. Sven walked around the house a few times and peered in through the windows, but he could see nothing. He caught sight of a boat on the lake and shouted from the shore to the man sitting in it, an old man, and asked if he knew the whereabouts of the house's owner and whether there had been a tame squirrel on their land. But the man knew nothing, so Sven left. And that was when it happened.'

After Barbro said this she fell silent.

'What happened?' Susso asked impatiently.

'As Sven was standing under a fir tree something hit the brim of his hat and he saw a pine cone fall to the path beside his feet. He stood still and a second cone landed beside the first. Baffled, he turned his gaze upwards. Thick, heavy branches hung down, and he could not see anything. He turned round and looked along the path because he thought he had heard footsteps behind him, but there was no one there, so he looked up into the branches again and there was the squirrel, sitting on a spruce twig. Its coat was grey and its black eyes looked at him searchingly. Sven was paralysed. All he could do was stare at the bedraggled animal. It was sitting so close he would have been able to touch it if he'd had the courage to reach out his hand. But he didn't. It was immediately apparent that this squirrel was no ordinary squirrel. Sven bolted and without looking back leapt onto his bicycle, and it would be almost sixty years before he summoned up the courage to return.'

'So he didn't write anything about it?' Gudrun asked.

'Not a word,' answered Barbro. 'He buried it under a layer of concrete inside him. But that summer, when he heard a little boy had been abducted in Dalarna, a crack appeared in the concrete, and the crack widened when he spoke about it to someone he worked with at the radio station. Earlier that day the colleague had discovered that the missing boy's mother had said that a giant had taken her child. Her account of what had happened was dismissed out of hand as a fantasy brought about by shock and triggered by medication abuse, but the circumstances were made more complicated by the fact that the police found huge footprints in the vicinity. There was no doubt that a larger than average man had been outside the cabin, but they could not establish the extent of his involvement in the kidnapping.

'Sven phoned Magnus's mother, Mona Brodin. She reluctantly agreed to talk about the giant. It had happened in the evening, so she had not been able to see him clearly. She estimated the giant to be between two and a half to three metres tall. He had not spoken. All he did was pick up the boy and disappear into the darkness of the forest. She had followed, but of course she had not been able to catch up with him.

'Between two and a half to three metres! That was the exact height of the kitchen ceiling in John Bauer's house in Småland. This indicated to Sven that there could be a connection between the mysterious disappearance of Magnus Brodin and Esther Bauer's harrowing story. After he had spoken with Mona Brodin and thought about everything she had said, he realised that he had the chance to do something about his betrayal of the Bauer family

– because to him it did feel like a betrayal. Bengt Bauer was gone for ever but he might be able to help Magnus Brodin – *save him*, in fact. Except he did not know how.

'If Magnus Brodin had been carried off by the stallo people, then Sven was obliged to discreetly point the police in the right direction. But Lapland is a vast region and Esther had never told him precisely where John had been when he found the stallo. And even if she had, it was doubtful it would have been of any help after so much time had passed. He made a few tentative phone calls to a couple of police officers he knew personally but they led nowhere, and eventually he began to doubt that there was anything he could do, and perhaps because it was a way of helping him endure this feeling of powerlessness he started questioning the truth of Esther Bauer's story again, and whether it was so far removed from reality that any further investigation was futile.

'But then there was the squirrel. The squirrel's eyes had begun to shine inside him. Two small black lamps that came on when he lay in bed at night. They would not leave him in peace. That is why we travelled down to Gränna.

'Of course, it was difficult for me to believe what he told me in the car that day, but I knew we did not have much time left together. I could hardly turn the car around and have his head examined. I didn't have the heart for it.

'We arrived at the place where Sven said he had seen the squirrel in 1922 and stood there for a while, but no squirrel appeared. Large areas of Björkudden were surprisingly unchanged, Sven said. The facade of the beautiful house was the same shade of red. We met the present owner of Björkudden, Fredrik Dahllöf, who you spoke to, and his daughter, a girl of about six or seven. Naturally Dahllöf was astonished when Uncle Sven stepped into his kitchen out of the blue, and he was no less bewildered when Sven asked about a special squirrel that had belonged to John Bauer. He thought it was some kind of joke. But Sven repeated his question and emphasised how vitally important it was that he told him everything he knew. To underline the gravity Sven explained that the squirrel was connected to the kidnapping of Magnus Brodin. Dahllöf knew about Magnus Brodin, he had read about him in the papers, but he had never heard anything about a squirrel. And what a squirrel from the turn of the century had to do with the kidnapped boy he really could not fathom. That was obvious from his expression.

'Sven started to walk around the room, scanning the walls, and it wasn't long before Dahllöf became curious and wanted to know what he was looking for. So Sven told him everything. He pointed his stick at the ceiling, and when he asked if it was two metres and seventy-five centimetres high, Dahllöf nodded in confirmation. Sven explained his suspicion: that Magnus Brodin had been stolen by the same person who in 1918 had come to Björkudden to take the three-year-old Bengt Bauer.'

Barbro placed her hands together and studied them. The nails were cut short and coated with clear varnish.

'We went back out to the car,' she continued, 'and I was about to turn the key in the ignition when we heard a small thud on the roof. I jumped and leaned forwards, wondering what could have landed so heavily. A bird? A pine cone? But then something started moving above us, tiny footsteps on the metal. I opened the door and got out. And there was the squirrel, right under my very nose. It was sitting on the roof, watching me, and I saw straight away that something was wrong with it. It looked ill. It was so thin and its fur was patchy and matted.

'Sven was sure this was the same squirrel that he had seen in 1922. It hadn't aged a day, he said. And when he reached out his hand and rested it on the car roof, his palm cupped like a bowl, the squirrel approached him. With a gentle movement he picked up the little animal in his large hand and pressed it to his chest, and after sitting down in the back seat he said it was Humpe, Bauer's squirrel, although I thought surely he knew it couldn't be. "What do you know about it?" he said, stroking the little animal's coat. "Squirrels don't live that long," I answered. "They live for fifteen years at the most. You know that's what your father said." "But between you and me," Sven said, "this is no squirrel. At least, not only a squirrel." "If you say so," I said. And then we drove home.'

'So he took it home with him?' Susso asked.

Barbro nodded.

'He kept it in his room.'

'Here?' Susso asked.

'Yes,' Barbro replied. 'At first I was against it, naturally, because in all honesty there is not much difference between a squirrel and a rat, but when I noticed how happy the squirrel made him, I relented. He often called me to come and look when it was doing something amusing or unexpected. It was as if it had breathed new life into Sven, and he seemed to have forgotten all about Magnus Brodin, which was just as well, I thought. But then one day Sven was suddenly taken ill. When the ambulance arrived and they put him on the stretcher, he clung onto my hand and made me promise to look after the squirrel.'

Barbro looked down at the swirling pattern on the Persian rug. It was so big that the parquet flooring was visible only as a thin frieze bordering the skirting boards.

'He was dead by the time we reached the hospital,' she said. 'I had to come home, to this empty flat. Which was not entirely empty. It was several days before I gathered enough strength to open the door to his room. In some way I hoped it had all been imagination, that the animal would not be there. But there it sat, of course, right in the middle of the bed, looking at me. I closed the door but I remembered my promise, so I put a bowl of water and some seeds in the room. And I thought: it can't be happy in there, surely it will die soon. Every time I opened the door, I hoped it would be lying dead in a corner.'

There was a creak as Barbro moved in the chair.

'After a few months had passed and it had still not died I went into the room and opened the window. I didn't think that was breaking my promise to Sven. If the squirrel wanted to go willingly, then I thought it should be allowed to do so. Later that day, when I looked into the room, it had gone. There are large trees outside, so I expect it jumped onto one of them.'

Quickly she stroked a curl of hair from her forehead.

'It was an enormous relief, I can tell you.'

Barbro stood up and looked at Gudrun.

'Shall we have that coffee now?'

While Barbro was in the kitchen, Susso and Gudrun sat looking through the cuttings. Torbjörn had got up from the sofa to take a closer look at the roller blind. He ran his fingers over the surface. Then he sank back down onto the sofa again, watching Susso, who had lifted the briefcase onto her lap so she could look at it more closely. She slid open the locks one at a time and lifted the lid.

She found a crumpled plastic bag with a small grey revolver

inside it. It looked like a piece of scrap metal. The handle was made of dark wood, almost black with a greasy shine. Scattered around the gun in the bag's many creases were cartridges, ten at least. She held up the bag so that first Torbjörn and then Gudrun could see what it contained.

'That's Sven's pistol,' Barbro said, walking in carrying a silver tray that rattled with small white porcelain cups. 'You see, when he was in Petrograd, which was practically a war zone, he asked his father to send him a gun so he would be able to protect himself. His father sent that little pistol by courier. And do you know who gave it to him? The author Verner von Heidenstam. Sven's father looked after Heidenstam's horses out at Naddö, so they were as good as friends.'

'But what happened to the boat?' asked Susso, replacing the plastic bag in the case. 'Why did it sink?'

'It was overloaded and Vättern was in a bad mood,' Barbro said, placing the tray on the table.

'So the stallo people had nothing to do with it?'

'That we will never know,' said Barbro, pouring the coffee.

'But what do you think then? About what he told you? About Bauer and the stallo people?'

'I don't think anything,' Barbro said, putting down the coffee pot. 'I am *convinced* it is all true.'

They waited for her to continue.

'You know I told you that the squirrel disappeared the day I left the window open?'

'Yes?'

'Well, it came back. That same evening. I had hung Sven's bedding to air on the balcony and there it was, sitting on the railing, staring at me. My first impulse was to rush inside and close the balcony door, but before I could reach the door, he had already slipped in.'

Barbro gestured towards the balcony door.

'I hunted around desperately looking for him, but it was pointless. You can't catch a squirrel with your bare hands. So there was nothing else I could do but let him into Sven's room again, and he hopped in there. It was our deal, if you can put it like that. And he knew it. He wanted nothing more than to be allowed to live in there. And now,' she said, staring blankly ahead, 'now, after twenty-five years, I can say with certainty that Sven was right.'

'Right in what way?' Susso asked.

Barbro gave her a blank look.

'That it was John Bauer's squirrel he brought back from Björkudden.'

'What do you mean?' said Susso, and when she did not get an answer straight away she cast an enquiring look at her mother, who was bending forwards with her elbows on her knees, rubbing her forehead and making her skin wrinkle.

'She means', said Gudrun, 'that the squirrel is still alive.'

'You're joking!' Susso said.

Barbro nodded.

'Not at all. He's in Sven's room.'

Seved was aware that the old-timers could know things, that they could infiltrate people's heads. At least Skabram could, if you got close. Ejvor had told him once that he should watch out for Skabram especially, that he should take care not to make eye contact with him. Things Skabram picked apart with his probing old troll fingers could never be repaired, and he did not care. Quite the reverse. The destruction amused him.

Funnily enough, it did not strike him that the old-timers would know what had happened to the lemmingshifter until after he had pulled off the road to get rid of the sleeping bag and its contents. He had not wanted to look inside the bag. He had simply hurled it out among the birches. But then he had changed his mind, waded through the snow and tipped out the little body. Not to see it, but so that the ravens would get to it as quickly as possible. He could not bear the thought of it shrivelling up inside the sleeping bag. He wanted it to disappear. Totally.

It had lain there in the snow, a mottled yellowish-brown. A little scrap.

What if it wasn't dead? What if it was only unconscious?

He had to be sure.

A lorry thundered past, followed by a cloud of snow, and Seved waited until it had settled and no other cars were in sight before striding out towards a broken roadside snow pole. In the fold where it had broken in two the orange plastic had faded. Holding the pole, he reached out and prodded the creature.

No blood, as far as he could see. But one eye had popped out and was hanging like a white marble on a thread against the swollen cheek. If it was pretending to be dead, then it was doing a bloody good job. It's not certain I'll get away with this, he thought.

Would even Lennart be able to defend him if the old-timers caught wind of what he had done? And what would Lennart even say? Not to mention Torsten Holmbom – it was his shape-shifter after all, and Seved knew how attached he was to his small friends.

Yet he did not regret it. Not for a moment. Trampling the little thing to death had felt right at the time and it felt right now.

It was nasty. It was *evil.*

An evil being.

It had harmed Cecilia Myrén. He wondered what had happened to her, whether she had recovered, but most of all whether she remembered what had happened. Whether she remembered *him.* Most likely she did, but only hazily. Like a memory after being drunk. She would never recognise him, and if she did, she would not remember where she had seen him before.

But was that why he had killed it? No. It was something more primitive. Instinct. He disliked it – he had never liked the little creatures. You never knew what they were up to.

He had done it simply because he could.

And because no one would ever find out.

He hoped.

And perhaps it was not so bad. He had seen Ejvor beat a shrewshifter to death with a log once, and her only explanation had been that the animal was ill. And there hadn't been any great fuss when Börje shot the hareshifter. Well, it had been an accident. He hadn't realised it was a shifter.

What Seved had done, on the other hand, was no accident.

He had not only done it deliberately. He had done it gladly.

It was that name.

At first he had dismissed it as imagination.

But he knew what he had heard.

The one the foxshifter had made him hear.

Signe and the boy were outside when he pulled into the yard, and he stiffened behind the wheel when he saw Skabram standing on Hyblett's veranda, motionless and wrapped in a grey-green tarpaulin with only his eyes and his hairy legs showing. But the covering did not help: the boy was scared anyway. He was sitting on a pile of snow, facing the opposite way and hacking at the snow with a tomato-red flat plastic sledge between his legs. And Signe looked cold. She was bobbing up and down on her toes.

Seved drew up, parking as far from Hybblet as he possibly could, and went straight into the toilet. He sat there, burying his head in his hands. Usually he could feel it if they got right inside his head, but he was so tired and tense he doubted he would notice. As long as Skabram was down in the hide there was no danger, but how long was he going to stand on the veranda, watching? If he could get Signe and the boy to come in, Skabram would probably go back down.

He pulled off his jeans and put them in the washing machine.

Hanging on a hook was a pair of grey tracksuit bottoms, and he took them out into the hall. As he was pulling them on he opened the door and called for the others to come in.

The boy instantly slid down and ran to the veranda, and Signe followed him. She asked him where he had been.

'Away,' he said, and opened the fridge.

Fortunately the window in Sven Jerring's old bedroom was slightly open. Susso could only imagine what it would have been like in there otherwise. The pungent smell of urine struck her nostrils immediately. This was something other than patches of dried piss and she could not help pulling a face.

Even Gudrun reacted strongly.

'Good grief!' she said, stopping in the doorway, her hand over her nose and mouth like a lid. Her face was contorted and the skin fell in folds below her chin. She rolled her eyes as she looked at the others. Wasn't the stench *awful*? It looked at first as if she was going to stay outside, but when Susso and Torbjörn entered the room she followed, her hand in nervous readiness in front of her face. Barbro said nothing. She waited until they had all stepped in through the door, then closed it gently behind her.

There were rings hanging from the curtain pole but no curtains, and no rugs on the floor. The light filtered in through the angled slats of the venetian blind, casting a striped pattern on the bed. A few pictures in glossy, dark-brown wooden frames hung above the bed. They were photographs of people, darkly dressed shapes. The gilded swirls of the wallpaper's medallion pattern shone faintly in the gloom. On the bedside table stood a portable radio with its telescopic antenna retracted.

There was a crunch under Susso's heel and she stopped to see what she had trodden on.

'It's a nutshell,' Barbro said, kicking the sole of her shoe over the vinyl flooring. 'And cornflakes. I haven't cleaned in here for years.'

She looked at the floor, annoyed.

'There's no point.'

They stood still, waiting. Torbjörn had folded his arms across his chest and cupped his hand under his chin. His eyes searched the walls inquisitively, examining every corner. While they had been listening to Barbro's story, he had sat without saying a word, looking down at his feet and not touching either his snus tin or his mobile. It seemed as if his disbelief was beginning to fray at the edges. As for Susso, she did not know what to think. She felt ill. It came and went but would not let go of her. And now she felt it drilling deeper and deeper inside.

She wanted to discuss everything that had come up during the day but there had been no suitable moment. They had only had time to glance briefly and enquiringly at each other when Barbro went to make the coffee. She could no longer judge what was realistic and what wasn't, and it was making her giddy.

'Hello,' said Barbro, in a soft sing-song tone. 'Is anyone home?'

Shards of nutshell were crushed under the heels of the old woman's flat shoes as she slowly walked towards the window, looking around falteringly. Bending her stiff legs she leaned down and checked under the bed, and also glanced up at the wardrobe.

'He stays out most of the day,' she said, loosening the latch that held the window in place. 'Luckily he sees to his bodily functions in the park. The smell in here is due to some kind of territorial behaviour, I think. I've found it is especially strong at this time of year. As if he becomes anxious or something, but I scarcely think about it now. At the beginning I put down newspaper, but he only tore it to shreds. He also went for the curtains, so I had to take them down. But otherwise you wouldn't know he was here. I hardly notice him.'

She opened the window wide.

'Hello!' she called out.

Susso walked up to the window and looked at the chestnut tree outside before scanning the park.

A car was driving slowly along the road below, and from the other direction a cyclist came down the pavement, which was dotted with partially melted patches of ice. The pedals squeaked.

'He sleeps in here every night, at least at this time of year. He lies here on the bed with his tail round his body looking like a small fur hat.'

'So you've had him in here ever since Sven died?' Susso said, looking at the messy floor.

Barbro nodded.

'But why haven't you shown him to anyone? Surely you must have? To someone who could examine him, I mean. A vet or someone.'

'What is there to show?' said Barbro, straightening up. 'That I have a squirrel, a tame squirrel? If the landlord found out, he would have me evicted, Sven Jerring's widow or not. You can't see from the outside how old he is. You can't see what . . . he is.'

'And what is he then?'

'A troll, I would think.'

'That looks like a squirrel?'

Barbro brushed her hair back with her hand and patted it down before answering.

'He has another side to him too. It's as if his fur covering shrinks back and you can see a tiny face. He looks like a sad old man. The first time I saw that side of him I screamed, and I think that upset him because it was several years before I saw his face again.'

'You mean he can change shape?' asked Gudrun, who had walked up to the window.

'"Shapeshifting" is the correct term. I have managed to find out that much at least. When he gets frightened or does not want to be seen he takes refuge in the form of a squirrel. It happens in a second. It takes considerably longer the other way round. I think he feels better as a squirrel. He seems so unhappy when he isn't one. But of course, he might always be unhappy. It's just that I can't see it.'

'But how often is he like that?' asked Susso. 'Not a squirrel, I mean?'

'In recent years it has happened less frequently. It's as if he hasn't got the strength. I've wondered if it is to do with his age. He is over a hundred, you know.'

'But are you sure this is the same squirrel? The one John Bauer brought back from his Lapland journey? Humpe?'

'He has lived in this room for twenty-five years. And if he can live to twenty-five, then he could just as easily live to a hundred, don't you think?'

Susso nodded. In some weird kind of way it seemed perfectly logical.

'If only you knew how many times I have come into this room and thought he had finally left,' Barbro said, 'and that it was all an awful dream. But he is never far away. All of a sudden there he is, sitting on the balcony railing, looking at me through the window. And so of course I have to let him in.'

'That's what I can't quite understand,' said Gudrun. 'If you don't open the window, well, he can't come in, can he?'

Smiling, Barbro brushed the windowsill with her fingertips, as if to feel whether the smooth surface had any uneven patches.

'I used to reason like that too,' she said. 'Many times I thought I let him live here because I promised Sven that he could, but that isn't what I cared about really. It was only an excuse. It's more that I don't dare to shut him out, because if I do he sits out there staring at me. From morning to night. Either on the balcony rail or in one of the chestnut trees. It is extremely stressful, I can tell you. Having those eyes following me the whole time. I can't bear it. He . . . he gets to you.'

'Why haven't you moved then?' Susso asked her.

'Move?' said Barbro, wearily. 'Where should I move to?'

'I don't know. Anywhere.'

'No,' she said, shaking her head. 'It's . . . I can't.'

'Why?'

The old woman's eyes narrowed and it looked as if she was going back in her mind, recalling all those times she had asked herself the same question.

'Because I *can't*. Because I have . . . responsibilities.'

'But you said just now that you didn't. That really you don't care about your promise.'

'Not to Sven. I mean to him.'

'To the squirrel?' Susso said.

'You haven't met him,' Barbro said, and looked down at her hands, which were clasped together and resting on her stomach. 'You don't understand.'

Torbjörn had left the room; Susso could hear his voice mumbling in the apartment, and when she went into the sitting room she found him sitting on the sofa with his mobile pressed to his ear, holding the tin of snus in his other hand and tapping it against his thigh. He was embarrassed and looked at her questioningly, and when he had ended the conversation he sat for a long time looking at Susso, who had seated herself in the wicker chair opposite him. His upper lip bulged from the snus pouch and there were dark circles under his eyes.

'I just can't stand the stink in there,' he said.

Susso held out her palm and caught the snus tin as it came flying through the air. She inserted a pouch under her lip, pressed the lid back on and threw the tin back to him.

'You get used to it,' she said. 'Our sense of smell is adaptable.'

'Not mine,' he answered, tapping the keys on his mobile. 'Obviously.'

'So, what do you think then?' Susso continued. 'About the squirrel?'

Torbjörn grinned and imperceptibly shook his head.

'I don't know,' he said, rolling the snus tin up and down his leg. 'I mean, I was there when we saw the film at that guy Mats's place, and I've seen the photo from your wildlife camera, but this, this is like . . . I just want to get out. That's how it feels.'

'We've got to stay a bit longer, until it comes back. If it comes back.'

He nodded.

'Then we'll see,' Susso added.

Torbjörn continued:

'I'm okay with the fact that the dwarf snatched Mattias, or that he's mixed up in it. I accept that. And I've never suggested your granddad's picture is a fake. But a squirrel that isn't a squirrel?'

He shook his head.

Susso did not answer. In speechless confusion she had asked herself the same question, but she could not take it in and was probably too scared to follow that train of thought to its logical conclusion. She waited for Torbjörn to say something else but he had picked up his mobile, so she walked off.

Barbro and Gudrun stayed where they were by the window when Susso walked in.

The chestnut tree swayed and from time to time the wind took hold of the open window so that Barbro had to hold onto it. Susso crossed her arms and was about to sit on the edge of the bed when she changed her mind, twisted her body and ran her hand over the bedspread. There was a thin carpet of hair covering the rough weave, bunches of soft greyish-brown strands between three and four centimetres long. Susso picked up a tuft and rubbed it between her finger and thumb.

'How long is he usually gone for?' she asked, flicking the hair away and rubbing the palms of her hands together.

'Not long,' replied Barbro, stretching to look at the top of the tree outside the window. 'He'll be back soon.'

'Can't you entice him in somehow?'

'There's no need. He knows you are here.'

'Does he?' Susso said.

'He's never gone for long,' Barbro repeated. 'He usually stays in one of the trees outside here. Or somewhere in the park where there happens to be a lot of people. People interest him tremendously. Especially children. There is a little pond and a playground with swings over there,' she said, pointing. 'He usually hops around and lets the children chase him. He finds that funny. But of course now, in the winter, when the park is practically deserted, I suppose you could say he gets depressed, because he sits in the chestnut tree staring at nothing all day. He can sit motionless for hours, waiting.'

'So he knows we're here?' Susso said, walking up to the window and looking out over the park, away to the playground that could be seen through the trees.

'I'm convinced of it,' Barbro said.

'Perhaps that's why he's not coming, because he knows who we are?'

'There is no point in trying to trick him,' Barbro said, giving Susso a stern look. 'If that is what you're thinking.'

'No, I only . . .'

Barbro stood up straight and said:

'He'll be here when he gets here.'

Torbjörn was out on the balcony, leaning over the railing. His shoulders were hunched and angular. There was the occasional clang as his knee or foot struck the metal. He had gone out to talk on his mobile. His tight-fitting jeans were creased in the crook of the knees and a corner of his T-shirt was visible below his black hooded sweatshirt.

In the sitting room Susso was looking at sturdy bookcases, varnished brown, that filled the walls all the way to the ceiling. She walked with her head tilted to one side, reading the spines.

She pulled out a book in German that had glossy prints folded between the pages, including a large map of Sweden. She had begun to open it out when there was a creak from the balcony door. She spun around and held up the book.

'Look, it's Nils Holgersson,' she said. 'In German.'

Torbjörn was standing stock still, and Susso looked from his transfixed expression to his arm, which he was holding out in front of him.

On it was a small bundle of grey fur with a pair of pointed ears.

Susso put the book back on the shelf behind her and stared.

The squirrel had wrapped its sinewy arms and legs around Torbjörn's trembling lower arm and it was clinging on tightly, as if it feared someone would try to force it off. Its gleaming brown curved claws were digging into Torbjörn's sweatshirt. Its eyes shone like small black beads and whiskers ten centimetres long sprouted from its nose. The teeth in the half-open mouth were like dark-yellow spokes.

'Mum!' she shouted. 'Barbro!'

The two women came into the room.

Susso pointed.

'It's here!' she called. 'Over here!'

Without so much as a glance at the squirrel Barbro walked over to the balcony door and pulled it shut. Gudrun stood with her mouth open in amazement. One of her hands plucked at her scarf.

'What's it doing?' she asked. 'Why is it sitting there?'

Torbjörn shrugged his shoulders and gave a wary smile. He had been holding his arm outstretched as he walked in through the balcony doorway, as if to keep the little squirrel as far away from him as possible, but now his arm was bent to give him a closer look at the animal. At its fur, matted all over, and its long bushy tail, brown and streaked with black.

'You wouldn't believe how fast it moved,' Torbjörn said.

'What happened?' asked Susso. 'Did it come from the tree?'

He shook his head.

'I don't think so. Suddenly, out of nowhere, there he was on the balcony railing. He jumped onto me before I had time to react.'

By this time Susso and Gudrun had drawn closer, but Barbro kept her distance. She was gripping her elbows and her head was tilted to one side.

'I was shit scared at first and tried to shake him off my arm. I thought it was going to bite me or something, but then it was . . . well, I don't know how to explain it. It was like my fear disappeared, like I *felt* he wasn't dangerous and that he didn't want to hurt me.'

'That's what he does,' Barbro said.

After bending forwards and listening to the animal's breathing – a rapid hiss coming from the little triangular mouth – Susso straightened up and looked at her searchingly.

'He plants thoughts in your head,' the old woman said, tapping her fingers against her forehead. 'It's a kind of telepathy.'

Susso studied her to see if she was being serious. It was clear that she was.

'You mean he can read people's thoughts?'

Barbro shook her head.

'No, I don't mean that. I don't really think he can *do* anything. He just pops up in your head, unexpectedly. And then you know exactly what he wants. It's not even words, it's only . . . thoughts. His thoughts. But you don't feel they are not your thoughts.'

'That sounds dangerous,' Gudrun said.

'But it isn't,' answered Barbro, shaking her head. 'It's not as if he can control you. He only wants to make you understand what he needs. He communicates with you. It's not as if he makes you do what he wants, or anything like that.'

'Are you completely sure about that?' Gudrun asked.

Barbro approached Torbjörn. His arm had begun to ache so he was supporting his right elbow in his left hand. The squirrel was crouching down with its tail stretched behind it along the sleeve.

'At the beginning he pestered me continually to let him out of the room,' she said. 'But I didn't do that because I didn't want him out here. I used to sit watching television, knowing what he wanted. It was just like having a cat scratching at a door when it wants to go out or come in. It took me a long time to realise that he was in fact trying to communicate with me. Not that he says very much. If he had been able to control me, naturally he would have made me let him out of the room, don't you think?'

The squirrel had lifted its head a little and appeared to be listening attentively. The tassels on the tips of its ears stood erect and its whiskers were vibrating.

'Does he understand what we are saying?' Susso asked.

'Oh yes,' replied Barbro. 'Every word. He understands Swedish.'

She reached out her hand, and the instant her fingers touched the straggly tail the squirrel rolled up into a dark knot.

'He really is quite fantastic,' she said. 'Don't you agree?'

Torbjörn's eyes glittered as he nodded. He moved his arm warily to get a closer look at the squirrel from the front, but every time he tried to make eye contact, it twisted its head away.

'How do you know he understands?' asked Susso, who had taken a step back and pushed her hands into the back pockets of her jeans.

A smile spread across Barbro's thin lips.

'Ask him something,' she said.

'I . . .' said Susso, then she fell silent and thought for a while before going on: 'I can't think of anything I want to ask.'

'No?' said Barbro.

Susso shook her head.

'If I remember correctly, you came here with a particular purpose in mind.'

Susso did not know what to say, and that must have shown on her face because Barbro immediately continued:

'You are here because of the boy, aren't you?'

'Yes.'

Gudrun wasted no time. She went out to the hall and returned with her handbag, taking out the rolled-up plastic folder with the printouts.

'Do you know who this is?' she asked, holding the photograph of the Vaikijaur man in front of the squirrel.

'Mum,' Susso said, but when she looked around she noticed Torbjörn and Barbro were not smiling at Gudrun's question. They were watching the squirrel expectantly.

'Do you?' said Gudrun.

Whether the squirrel was looking at the photograph was impossible to say, but it raised itself up slightly and its grip on Torbjörn's arm weakened. The dark eyes blinked and the upright ears slanted together, making it look as if the animal was wearing a tasselled hat.

'No,' Gudrun said, and slid the paper back into the plastic folder, which she then pushed into her bag. 'Well, at least we asked.'

The little animal sat on the dining table, an oval slab of highly polished wood. Its head tested new angles ceaselessly, as if the room was undergoing change and was a constant source of amazement. The squirrel seemed unable to decide whether to stand on all fours with its legs wide apart, or to sit up, with its tail upright behind it. It gave an impression of indecisiveness. Without taking his eyes off the squirrel Torbjörn had lowered himself onto a chair that stood with its back to the wall. There was a worried look in his eyes, but something else as well. A kind of manic concentration. Susso looked at him closely. He was not behaving like himself, and that worried her.

Barbro had gone to the kitchen to make some fresh coffee, and when she returned she had a Swiss roll with her as well. She unwrapped the cellophane wrapping and told them to help themselves. Susso threw herself at the sugary cylinder and Gudrun also took a slice. As she ate she nodded towards the squirrel and said:

'So you thought that was who the Vaikijaur man was looking for?'

Barbro nodded.

'But why?'

'It must have been connected with Magnus Brodin, one way or another, don't you think? Do you know how many children have disappeared without trace in Sweden in the past twenty-five years? Four,' she said, holding up four fingers. 'Johan Asplund in 1980, Amina Nyarko in '97, and then only a month later Saranda Ademaj. That was down in Småland. And then in '99, Henrik Jansson. But both Johan and Henrik were relatively big – eleven, twelve years old. The girls were six and eight. I have a feeling it might be something to do with them having family abroad. As I say, I'm only sure about the numbers from 1978 onwards, but I have discussed this with other people and no one remembers anything like this happening before. This kind of child abduction, the kind that remains unsolved, is exceptionally rare. So I don't think it was a coincidence that he made a visit to Björkudden so soon after Magnus disappeared.'

'But why?'

'No one knows what happened there after Esther contacted Sven at the newspaper. But something must have happened and you can presume the squirrel was involved in it because it was the squirrel that got John into trouble. But I don't suppose we will ever know anything about that.'

Gudrun nodded and helped herself to another slice of Swiss roll.

'You do wonder if it was him,' she reflected. 'If he was the dwarf who was at Bauer's house in 1918.'

'Well, of course he was,' Susso said.

'If there's one, there's bound to be more,' Gudrun said.

'Barbro,' said Susso, 'did it never occur to you it could be him when you saw the picture of the Vaikijaur man in the newspaper? That it was the same dwarf Sven had told you about?'

'Of course it did. But what was I supposed to do?'

'Have you spoken to Magnus's mother recently?' asked Gudrun.

'I have never spoken to her.'

'Oh, haven't you? I thought you had.'

Barbro shook her head. She was holding the tiny handle of the gilt-edged porcelain cup in one hand and the saucer in the other.

'Of course, there have been times when I thought I ought to,' she said. 'But I never got round to it. I wasn't sure, you know.'

'No, of course not,' Gudrun said.

Barbro pursed her lips and lowered her head, and it was clear she did not want to talk any more about Mona Brodin.

Unexpectedly Torbjörn stood up, staring intently at the squirrel.

'You know something?' he said hesitantly. 'He wants to help us. With Mattias.'

'With Mattias?' Susso repeated. 'How can he know who Mattias is?'

She folded her arms across her chest.

'His hearing is excellent,' Barbro said. 'I'm fairly convinced that he has been sitting in one of the trees outside, listening to everything we have been saying. He loves doing that. Listening to people in secret.'

'Does he know where Mattias is?' asked Susso, facing Barbro. Then she turned, directly facing the little animal. 'Do you know?' she asked it.

The squirrel sat motionless, watching her closely with one eye. Its rodent mouth was open and there inside was the tiny tongue, twitching in the darkness behind its teeth.

'Does he know?' she asked Torbjörn. He thought for a while, then shook his head.

'Well, does he know who has taken him, or what?' interrupted Gudrun.

Torbjörn shrugged.

'I don't know.'

There was a grunt of agreement from Barbro. She was standing up, straightening the thick fabric of her skirt.

'Sometimes he disappears, but he always comes back.'

'So we just sit here and wait?'

'You must take him with you.'

'*We* have to take him?' Susso said.

She looked in astonishment at Barbro.

'That's the best thing to do.'

'He'll help us,' Torbjörn said. 'He told me he will.'

'He *said* that?' Susso asked, giving Torbjörn an angry look.

'Well, not said exactly . . . I only know that's what he wants. To help us.'

Still with her arms folded Susso stared at the squirrel. It was standing up, practically on its toes. It stretched its body, thrust out its puny chest and lifted its nose as high as possible. The animal appeared to be trying to pick up a scent. The fur on its chest and stomach was white.

'All right,' Gudrun said. 'But we can't have it loose in the car. I had a kitten in the car once, when Cecilia was little. You never knew where it was. Sometimes it went under the pedals. It was absolutely lethal, not being able to press the brake pedal. Perhaps you've got a box we could put it in?'

'I'm sure I'll be able to find something,' Barbro replied.

'Otherwise I can keep him,' said Torbjörn. 'Inside my jacket.'

As soon as he reached out his hand the squirrel raced along his sleeve and up onto his shoulder, where it wrapped itself in its dark tail.

'He won't be any trouble,' said Torbjörn, who had turned his head and pulled his shoulder forwards to be able to look at the squirrel. 'So we won't be needing a box.'

Barbro walked over to the table beside the roller blind to pick up the briefcase.

'Take this too,' she said.

Susso reached out her arm to take it.

'But what about the pistol?'

'That's included.'

Börje had left the kitchen and stamped up the stairs. Seved usually left the table at the same time as Börje, and Signe was probably wondering why he was still sitting there looking at her occasionally.

'What is it?' she said hoarsely, scratching at the neck of the outsize jumper where it was irritating her.

Slowly Seved pushed his plate aside. Then he leaned forwards and looked at the boy, who was sitting with his head bowed, lost in his thoughts.

'Mattias?'

He did not react.

'Mattias?'

Then he looked up. Signe stared too, and Seved turned to face her.

'And what are you called?' he asked. 'Really?'

She could not answer. She looked terrified.

'Don't you know what you're called?'

'Amina, I think.'

'Amina?'

She nodded.

'And your second name?'

She did not know.

'Do you know what else you're called?' he said, turning to look at the boy. 'Apart from Mattias?'

He did.

'Mickelsson.'

'So now we know. Mattias Mickelsson. And Amina . . .'

'And Jim,' said the boy.

With his head still bowed he lifted up his cupped hands to show them the little being. He let it peep over the edge of the tablecloth. A wave of disgust swept through Seved when he saw the wrinkled face, no bigger than a thumbnail. The little creature stared straight back at him with its beady black eyes. It had been given a taste of the boy's lingonberry jam and its lips were dark red. A couple of its whiskers were stuck together.

'Do you want to go home, Mattias?' asked Seved.

He did.

'Then give Jim to me.'

The boy hesitated. He closed his hands around the thing as if to protect it. Then he slid his elbows across the table and handed the creature to Seved.

'Why don't we go there?' Gudrun suggested. 'To Magnus's mother?'

They were sitting in the car, Gudrun and Susso in the front and Torbjörn at the back, holding the squirrel. Susso had the briefcase on her lap. She was silent. The need to discuss everything that had happened, everything they had learned, was threatening to explode inside her, but as long as the squirrel was with them she preferred not to open her mouth. If everything really was true, it meant the animal could *understand.* She was also disturbed by the intense affection Torbjörn had shown for the squirrel from the very beginning and which seemed to be growing by the minute.

'Why should we do that?' she said eventually.

'It's possible she knows something.'

Gudrun squeezed the small leather key holder, and as she was considering her answer she zipped and unzipped it time and again.

'Remember how obsessed your dad was with trying to work it out?' she said. 'How much time he spent looking for an explanation? And not only has this woman, Mona Brodin, seen the giant, he took her child as well. And that was over twenty years ago. So we can assume she has spent hours searching for answers.'

'In that case she ought to have found my website,' Susso said.

Through the windscreen, streaked with dirty grey water, Gudrun looked at Valhallavägen and the cars moving past in a slow stream. Darkness was descending on the city. The street lights were glowing.

'Perhaps it never occurred to her that trolls might be involved,' she answered. 'Generally speaking it's not easy thinking along those lines.'

Then she glanced at Torbjörn's reflection in the rear-view mirror.

'Don't you think so, Torbjörn?'

She had said it loudly and not without a certain sharpness, with the intention of distracting his attention, which was entirely focused on the squirrel. But he appeared not to hear her. It was as if he was in another world.

'So what else would she have been looking for?' Susso said. 'Giants?'

She sounded sarcastic, she could tell, and she sighed.

'Not giants as such,' said Gudrun, 'but a giant. An unusually large person, in other words. Just like the Vaikijaur man is an unusually small person.'

After saying this she turned round and barked:

'Torbjörn!'

This time he looked up.

'Where does she live then?' he said quickly.

'Who?' asked Gudrun.

'Magnus's mum.'

'I don't know,' she said, resting her hands on the steering wheel. 'We'll just have to find out. Didn't Barbro say she lived on one of the Mälaren islands? It can't be far away.'

'If she's still there,' Susso said, leaning back against the headrest.

'Torbjörn,' Gudrun said, 'find the number.'

'So we're going to phone this time?' asked Susso.

'Yes, I think so. This is different.'

'Three Mona Brodins,' said Torbjörn after a while. 'One in Askim, one in Sundbyberg and one in Svartsjö.'

'Askim is to the south,' Gudrun said. 'Did you say Svartsjö?'

'Svartsjö, yes. It's got a Stockholm code.'

'Then that's probably the one.'

'You can ring,' Susso said.

'It's so close,' Gudrun said, moving the gear lever to check it was in neutral. 'We might as well go there.'

Its eyes shone like small peppercorns and its mouth was wide open, giving the little face a nervously curious look. Did the creature know what to expect? Seved felt the occasional movement of the tail against his hand. It was like being stroked, and there was something almost beseeching about it.

He tried to summon up the liberating feeling of disgust that had filled him when he had stamped that evil creature in the sleeping bag to death, but he did not succeed and for a few seconds he almost let the thing go. He opened his fingers slowly, thinking how tiny it looked. But then he checked himself and squeezed his hand shut again. The very fact that he felt that way could only mean that the thing had wormed its way into his consciousness to weaken him.

Shocked by this realisation, Seved walked over to the sink. He had to do it straight away. He scraped out the strands of spaghetti forming a slippery border around the plughole, pushed in the plug and turned on the tap. While the sink was filling with water he glanced at the creature. It was looking in curiosity at the running water. He turned off the tap. It had to be done faster. If the being possessed even a fraction of the persuasive power the other one had shown, it would probably resist in a way he could never imagine. And the smallest ones could be dangerous if they were caught in a tight situation. On one occasion Ejvor had been almost blinded in one eye after sitting on a mouseshifter that was sleeping underneath a cushion on the sofa. Her sight returned after a week or so but she had blurred vision in that eye for the rest of her life.

He considered hurling the thing onto the stone slab in front of the stove. It was so tempting that he actually walked over there and lifted his hand, but there was no certainty it would die or even be knocked unconscious, giving him the opportunity to stamp it to death. Especially if he missed the stone slab, which he might well do if he threw it as hard as he could.

He had no idea how much the little thing suspected, so he dared not loosen his grip and change hands because then it might seize its chance and wriggle free. Neither did he want to squeeze it to death in his hand. That would be messy and take too long.

It had to happen quickly. Without warning.

He pushed a chair aside and crouched down beside the kitchen table, pretending to look for something on the floor. When the creature began to show an interest in what he was doing, he slammed its protruding head against the underside of the table with all his strength. A glass fell over and there was a clatter as the cutlery jumped on the plates.

The little body seemed to crumple up in his hand. The blow had pushed it down and only a greyish-brown flap showed above his clenched fist. He saw no signs of life so he opened his hand a little. Immediately there was a jerking movement, and Seved wrapped his left hand around his right to tighten his hold.

He had not hit it hard enough, but the thing had probably made itself smaller. It had turned into a forest mouse, and he stared it straight in the eyes.

At least now they understood each other.

There was no going back. If the mouse slipped out of his grasp, he would never catch it and it would be only a matter of time before Skabram came lumbering across the yard. There were plenty of places where the mouse could hide in the cracks between the skirting board and the cork flooring, and around the stove, so it was pointless shutting the door to the hall. But he did anyway.

There was a knife in the sink, so he picked it up. It had a serrated edge and a black plastic handle. He was pretty sure the little being could no longer influence him. Generally forest shifters lost their persuasive powers when they shifted shape into animals. Still, he wanted it done as soon as possible.

A high-pitched wail escaped from its mouth as Seved pressed the mouse's head against the edge of the draining board, and one paw with outspread claws scratched desperately at the zinc surface. He raised the knife, but he could not use it. He could not bring himself to do it.

The boiler room. He would have to go down to the boiler room. Why had he not thought of that earlier?

His footsteps echoing with determination, Seved went into the hall and put on his boots. Then he ran outside and down the snow-covered concrete stairs to the cellar. When he pushed open the door he could hear the boiler burning at full force. Börje must have loaded more logs into it a short while ago. The ceiling was low, so he walked with his head bent towards the heat of the boiler.

He opened the iron lid and raised his hand to drop the mouse into the fire. He was not entirely sure what happened next. He threw, he knew that, but somehow the mouse did not leave his hand. Instead it shot up his sleeve and from there jumped down to the floor. In his haste to get the killing over with as quickly as possible Seved had not bothered to close the cellar door behind him, and he watched as the little creature ran over the high threshold and was gone.

Susso had pulled out the yellowing newspaper articles and spread them over the envelope to get them in order.

Gudrun gave her a quick glance.

'The fact that the squirrel exists and is sitting here in our car after all these years suggests that what Esther told Sven was true. It doesn't prove it but it *suggests* it. Doesn't it? In which case there is no reason to doubt Magnus's mother when she says a giant came out of the forest and took her child.'

'I want to know what happened to the Vaikijaur man,' Susso said. 'I mean, that's why we came down here. It was for Mattias's sake. I don't actually care about Magnus. That was twenty-five years ago.'

'But it could be the same kidnapper.'

Susso sighed and pulled off her hat.

'Are you sure Dahllöf's daughter doesn't know something else? Something she's not telling us?'

'Pretty sure.'

'But he can't have just disappeared!'

'What do you mean?'

Susso thumped her thigh with the side of her hand.

'Where did he go after he ran out onto Björkudden?'

'I don't know. But perhaps the squirrel does. Or Mona?'

✲

They had driven out of the city. The sky had sunk lower and sleet was striking the windscreen. In the ditches framing the farmland, rushes had sprung up in tight clumps and Susso thought it was weird seeing rushes growing like that in the middle of a field. She looked down at the mosaic of newspaper articles on her lap but had little desire to read them, and soon her eyes returned to the window. A feeling of nausea was building up inside her.

'Phone Cecilia again,' Gudrun said, pressing one nostril closed with a knuckle and blowing air out of the other one.

'I'm sure she's all right,' Susso said weakly.

'But why doesn't she answer then?'

'There are probably lots of customers. Maybe she hasn't got time.'

'She always answers her mobile.'

'Can you stop for a minute . . .'

Gudrun glanced at her and then took a second look. Immediately she slowed down and swung into a lay-by.

Susso gathered together the cuttings, pushed the envelope behind the briefcase, opened the door and climbed out. She filled her lungs with fresh, damp air. They had just driven across a bridge. There was open country on all sides and the pine forest was keeping its distance like a dark, watchful army. In the withered and flattened grass on the roadside lay a cracked hubcap, and an angelica plant looking like a charred spire had snared a plastic bag that was rustling in the wind.

Torbjörn also got out but he left the squirrel in the car. He zipped up his hooded sweatshirt and looked at her, his eyes narrowed in the wind.

'Not feeling so good?' he asked.

Susso shook her head and stepped aside to avoid being splashed by a large white car that roared past them.

'I don't know what it is.'

'Do you think it's the squirrel? Because I don't feel too good either.'

'Don't you?'

He shook his head as he swallowed. Then he leaned forwards and spat on the tarmac. Susso opened the car door and bent in to ask her mother if she was also feeling ill, but Gudrun was talking on the phone, and judging from her sharp, animated voice it was not a good time to interrupt her. No doubt she had got hold of Cecilia and had one or two things to tell her.

'I felt like this the night I was followed in the park, and when we were out with the snowmobile at Holmajärvi, right before those guys leapt on us. I thought it was a migraine or something.'

'You never told me.'

'I didn't know what it was, did I?'

Torbjörn took out his snus tin. He twisted off the lid, took out a pouch and lifted his upper lip in preparation, but then he stopped. A thought had occurred to him and he stood for a moment, holding the snus before finally inserting it in his mouth.

'The bat,' he said.

'Oh yes,' Susso said. 'That makes sense. But where did it come from?'

Torbjörn looked at her.

'Have you still got the film you took?'

He started hunting for his phone as the car door slammed. Gudrun came running round the bonnet of the car. She was holding the collar of her down jacket together to keep out the cold wind.

'The shop has been closed all day and Ella hasn't been to nursery! And Tommy hasn't been able to get hold of Cecilia either.'

'Do you feel ill?' asked Susso.

'Tommy's going round to her place now,' Gudrun said, and held up the phone as if to double check it was not ringing. 'Oh God, think if something's happened? And what about Ella!'

Susso folded her arms.

'She's probably just not well.'

'But why isn't she answering her phone!'

'What about you? How are you feeling?'

'Well, I'm worried of course!'

'Yes, but how *are* you? Have you got a headache? Do you feel sick? Because both me and Torbjörn feel ill, and we think it's because of the squirrel.'

'Oh yes, blame the squirrel. You've both just got hangovers.'

'Do you remember I asked you if you had ever had a migraine?' Susso said. 'After I had been followed in the park? This is something similar, and Torbjörn feels it too.'

'That's not so strange,' said Gudrun, 'if it's true what Torbjörn says about the squirrel talking inside his head.'

'He doesn't talk exactly . . .'

'Communicate then.'

'But haven't you noticed anything?' asked Susso. 'That it hurts?'

Gudrun shook her head.

'Oh, I don't know,' she said, turning out of the wind. 'Maybe a little. It's hard to say what's causing it, after everything that has happened. It gives me a headache just thinking of everything Barbro told us, and that the squirrel, that squirrel in our car, is supposed to be the same one John Bauer brought back with him from Lapland a hundred years ago.'

She took out her lip balm and rubbed it over her lips.

'It's not easy to take it all in. So of course my head aches.'

At first Seved thought it was the boy standing at the top of the steps, short and with narrow, sloping shoulders, legs pressed tight together. Then he saw the ancient face like a pale speck in the hood's opening. The sharp yellow eyes.

Seved stopped momentarily and then backed up and almost tripped over the threshold. He knew only too well what was being held in the hand hidden in the sleeve of the anorak and pressed up against the old man's chest. Now he was in trouble.

The old man stared at him. His grey lips were parted and the canine teeth of his lower jaw pointed upwards like two spikes. They looked worn. Between them protruded the tip of his tongue. He was wearing canvas shoes and he placed the old battered soles carefully in the snow that lay thick on the flight of steps.

'What do you want?' asked Seved from inside the gloom of the boiler room, where he had taken refuge. He tried to sound harsh but his fear of the foxshifter had a stranglehold on his vocal cords.

'Flee. You must flee.'

The cracked voice sounded so strange that it was impossible to tell if this was an accusation or an order. He had heard the forest folk talk, listened to their squeaky chattering, but it was only a lot of nonsense. Bits of words he hardly understood. But this was directed at him.

'You flee. And then he will destroy. He will tear down.'

The words had been spoken inside Seved's head and nowhere else, and that frightened him. He had never experienced forest folk talking like this before. The old man drilled deeper and deeper inside him, and he had nowhere to run.

'Kills. He kills.'

Seved backed up until his shoulder came up against the enamelled curve of the hot-water tank. He could go no further in the cluttered cellar.

The old foxshifter had come to a halt. He was standing motionless in the doorway, watching him. His tail had found its way out of the long jacket and was moving freely and furtively behind his legs. It was not red exactly, more a grey colour, but the tip was as white as if he had dipped it in a pot of paint.

'But we're not running away.'

'You flee. And he kills.'

Not until then did it occur to Seved that the old man might not have come to hurt him, or even rebuke him. If that was the case, he would have done it already. Instead it seemed as if he was trying to help. But it could be some kind of mischief. Skabram could have sent him.

'Then what shall we do?' he mumbled.

There was no answer. The old man had shuffled up to the boiler. He tilted his head to one side and knocked on the green-painted casing as if to test it, whispering something only the forest mouse could hear. It had dug its claws into the old man's shoulder and was hanging on, its tail dangling like a hook, and it was also looking at the boiler.

'There's burning.'

Seved took a step sideways. He was not thinking of escaping

exactly but he wanted to be in a position to do so if the old fox-shifter turned nasty. He knew how cunning they could be.

'See how it burns. When it burns.'

What did he mean?

'See how the fire bites at your fur. Biting, biting.'

I was scared to death of meeting Mona Brodin. I imagined a wreck, a person eaten up with guilt and suppressed grief. She must have had to distance herself from all her memories to be able to go on – buried them, more or less like Jerring had done. In one way it was surprising she was still alive. If it was true she had been abusing prescription drugs at the time of her son's disappearance, then it was not difficult to work out how she would have chosen to deal with his loss and the doubt in her own mind about what she had experienced.

What happens to you if you can no longer trust your own eyes? Dad had asked that question often, but at least he had his camera with him. What had Mona Brodin had? What proof did she have to challenge the disbelief she faced? The *suspicions* directed at her? With a burden like that there was only one thing to do, and that was to betray herself and try to create someone new.

How would she react when we appeared and raked it all up again?

However, my fear of meeting Mona Brodin was put aside when I found out the shop had been closed all day. Instead I sat there trying to work out what could have happened to Cecilia. What if the people who had attacked Susso were not driven by a hatred for her but for our whole family? Maybe they thought we were all involved in the website – which in a way we were. I was on the point of calling the police in Kiruna to make them aware of that when I heard my mobile's ring tone. It was Tommy, saying that Cecilia was at home watching a video with Ella and wanted to be left alone. She'd had all her hair cut off and Tommy thought she was unhappy about it and didn't want to show herself in public. My relief was so great that I wasn't at all nervous by the time we pulled up outside Mona Brodin's house.

It looked neat and very ordinary: painted red wood panelling, black concrete roofing tiles and house plants on the windowsills. Behind a fence were apple trees with bird feeders, a small greenhouse and a vegetable garden. There were two cars, one big and one small, a guest cottage, a flagpole with a faded pennant catching the wind, and a couple of bird boxes on an oak tree on the slope leading to the edge of the pine woods.

A man wearing blue overalls came out of the cellar door and stared at us.

Torbjörn wondered if he should bring the squirrel.

'I think we'll save that for later,' I said, and opened the door.

He greeted them by imperceptibly lifting his chin, and when Gudrun asked if Mona was home he walked slowly towards them on the gravel, wanting to know what it was about. He was in his fifties and had light-grey hair combed in a centre parting. He seemed more suspicious than hostile. He thrust his hands into the pockets of his fleece.

'We need to speak to her,' Susso said. 'About her son.'

The man stopped walking. His eyes moved between Gudrun and Susso.

'What about him?'

'We would really rather tell Mona,' Susso said. 'Is she at home?'

'She's down by the lake.'

'Is it far?'

'Just follow the road and then turn left. She's burning reeds,' he added, and it took a second or two for Susso to realise that he was telling them to keep a lookout for the flames.

They got into the car again and Gudrun reversed out of the drive and narrowly avoided a collision.

From behind a straggly hedge that edged the plot of land and hid the gravel road from view appeared the bonnet of a large motorhome, with six eyes and a Mercedes emblem in the middle. Gudrun braked so hard that the back of Susso's head was thrown against the headrest.

The motorhome rolled slowly past, and as they followed it on its way towards the ice-covered lake that soon came into view Gudrun became irritated that it was driving so slowly.

'Something's up with the squirrel,' Torbjörn said. 'There's some kind of danger. It's like it's warning me about something.'

The little animal was sitting on Torbjörn's chest, holding up its paws as if to show them it had no need to hold on. When Torbjörn tried to remove the squirrel his top went with it in four extended cones as the animal's claws dug into the material. He had to pull hard to loosen its grip, which the squirrel did not like. It struggled in Torbjörn's hands and made an angry chattering sound.

Torbjörn dropped the squirrel onto the seat, but it did not want to be there and instantly returned to his chest, resuming its strident chatter directly in his face.

'What do you want?' he said, concerned. 'What's so dangerous?'

'There she is,' said Gudrun.

Some distance along a small track a woman was standing looking at a pile of reeds. She was wearing a hat and a dark-blue padded waistcoat. In her hand she held a stick, pointed towards the ground. A white fog of smoke rising from the pile was the only sign that the reeds were burning, and every so often it hid the woman from view.

They drove up into the snow at the roadside and left the car there. Then they walked along the track. One side was lined with bushy spruces, their bark grey, and towards the water the ground was marshy, with alders and leaning willows in a tangle of undergrowth.

Susso had brought the briefcase with her but they had left the squirrel in the car. It might be too much all at once, especially given the way it was behaving: Torbjörn practically had to throw it down on the seat. He trudged along behind Gudrun and Susso, pulling at the neck of his sweatshirt and looking down at his chest to see if there were any scratch marks from the claws.

A floating jetty extended into the water. Under the elder trees were a couple of wooden trestles supporting a surfboard. It was patchy with green algae, and a thermos flask was balanced on the top. Mona looked at them searchingly. Her hair was tucked under her knitted hat, her complexion was tanned and downy, and her jaw line was slack. Small feathers protruded through her waistcoat and long, wavy strands of hair had attached themselves to her fleece-lined collar.

'We've come about . . .' Susso began, but she fell silent as Mona's gaze moved over her shoulder, and when she swung round she saw that the man they had been speaking to up at the house was walking along the track towards them. He had pulled on a woollen hat and clearly wanted to know what was going on.

'We would like to talk to you about what happened in 1978,' Gudrun said. 'When your son disappeared.'

Mona did not appear to be surprised. She did not even look at them. She was quiet for a long time, poking at the ground with her stick, which was scorched at the tip and left small grey holes in the snow.

'Why?'

'Have you read in the paper about the Vaikijaur man?'

She said she had.

'The person who took Mattias . . . we think . . .'

'We think he belongs to the stallo folk,' Gudrun interrupted. 'They are a kind of troll, you might say. Lapland trolls, which really do exist. And we think whoever took Magnus also belonged to the stallo folk. And that's what we want to talk to you about, Mona, because if they did take Magnus, then perhaps he is still alive.'

They had not expected Mona to be overjoyed by the news, but they had expected her to be astonished at the very least. Instead she continued prodding with the stick as if she were writing in the snow.

'Did you ever find out anything about the giant?' Gudrun continued. 'Anything at all? Whether anyone has seen him somewhere else?'

'I haven't wanted to talk about it,' Mona answered. 'Or rather, I haven't had anyone I wanted to talk about it with.'

'You can talk to us about it, if you like,' said Gudrun.

Suddenly Torbjörn leapt over the planks leading onto the jetty. Susso looked at him in surprise, but she had no time to wonder what had got into him because at the same time she heard a sound of smashing and crunching, followed immediately by a noisy crash.

It was a car window giving way.

Through the haze of smoke she saw someone standing over by the Passat.

Quite rationally she thought someone was trying to break into the car, but why the hell were they doing that in broad daylight? It had to be some druggie. It was not until she stepped to one side and had a clear view that she saw what it was, and the fear sliced open a freezing cold chasm in her chest.

In among the fir trees a stone's throw behind Hybblet there was a hatch cover in the ground. It was made of steel and hidden by a piece of carpet with a pattern that looked like moss. Now, however, the snow lay in such deep drifts between the tree trunks that Seved had to stamp around scraping it away for a good half-hour before the shovel uncovered the frozen remnant.

Twilight was starting to fall in the forest. The trees gradually melted together forming black shapes, and the snow became a grey mass. A raven cawed somewhere and away on the main road a lorry drove past.

When he saw the rusty-brown shades of the carpet below the layer of snow he stopped to think. There was so much that could go wrong and he had no idea where it would end. That was probably the worst thing. Where was he to go? He tried not to think about it. He would think about Mattias and Signe. Amina.

He had to do it now. There would never be a better opportunity. Both Karats and Lennart were far away, and so was Börje, in a sense. He was not himself, anyway, and he had been like that ever since he had returned from Kiruna.

He cleared the snow slowly, trying not to make a noise. If the shovel hit the hatch cover, the sound would be carried through the tunnel and into the hide. That was just over fifty metres away and the carpet would absorb the clang of metal, but there was no doubt it would be heard. Skabram was probably asleep but the little creatures never slept, at least not all at the same time, and not very deeply. If they heard an unfamiliar noise, they would wake the others immediately.

The only thing he knew about the tunnel was that Börje's father had made it with the intention of creating a rear exit for the hide. He had seen the hatch once, when he was about ten years old. Naturally, the hairy old-timers had not bothered to disguise it. Börje and Ejvor had gone to the trouble of doing so, but on that occasion they seemed not to notice that the carpet had been pushed aside. Or had the hatch not been hidden then? Seved could only remember the rectangular plate of steel in the moss and how it had alarmed him. Because of course he understood who would be coming in and out.

He did not uncover the carpet completely. Instead he cleared away enough to be able to cut it open and get at the handles, which he clearly recalled. Two lengths of reinforced steel that had been bent and welded in place on each of the double doors.

He dropped to his knees and removed his gloves. After thrusting them into his pockets he took out the Mora knife. His nose had started running and he wiped it on the back of his hand. He could feel the two raised handles below the frozen pile of the carpet. The blade was blunt and he had to saw hard to cut through the nylon backing. It was not easy to do and he had to take care in case the knife scraped against the metal below.

Once he had slashed open a hole big enough for him to insert his fingers, he tried to widen it by pulling the carpet apart, but it was tougher than he had expected. He had to make a few more cuts with the knife. Now at least he could get his hand inside and reach the handles. He tugged them. They seemed to be attached firmly enough.

The chain hanging on the stump of a branch of a nearby spruce tree glittered like a silver eye in the thickening darkness. Its oval links were not especially thick, but he planned to wrap it around the handles as many times as he could. Skabram was incredibly strong but this would hold. It had to hold. For a while he had considered taking the tractor and parking it with its back wheels on the cover, but he risked getting stuck in the deep snow, and anyway it would make too much noise.

He fed the chain through the handles as carefully as he could so that it would not clang against the reinforced steel. The chain formed a thick skein and he had to wrestle with stiff frozen fingers to get the bolt of the padlock in place. When he had fastened the lock he threw a few shovels of snow on top of the cover and then strode hurriedly away.

'But the door,' Amina said. 'He'll break down the door.'

She was sitting on the bed with her legs pulled up under her chin, and beside her Mattias was sitting with his head bowed and his face lit up by a twittering electronic game he was holding in both hands. He did not appear to be listening to them, and that was just as well.

Quietly Seved explained his plan. When Hybblet started to burn, Skabram would run down the tunnel but find he could not get out that way, and by the time he ran back the fire would have spread down the stairs and blocked his exit. Fear and anger would bring out the bear in him, and when he shifted shape the flames would set his fur alight. If he did not die from that, then Seved would be able to shoot him.

It showed on Amina's face that she did not like the idea. Why not just escape? Seved shook his head. Skabram would be demented when he discovered the boy was missing and he would take out his rage on Börje. And she didn't want that, did she? But the big old-timer had always been kind to her. It wasn't right to burn him alive.

'He wasn't so kind to Ejvor.'

'That was Karats, I'm sure it was.'

'But don't you understand? He'll kill Börje after we've gone.'

'Serve him right.'

Seved rubbed his thumb along the edge of his jacket sleeve where a ridge of frozen mucus had formed. He wanted to ask her why she had said that, but he knew why. She had every right to be angry with Börje. He was the one who had snatched her. She would never forget.

'And he'll kill me too, when I come back.'

Mattias shut down his game.

'Aren't you coming with us?'

'I'll drive you into town. Then I'll come back.'

They looked anxious and he realised he would have to give them an explanation.

'I've been away so long. Börje is all I've got.'

It was big. So big the Passat dipped as it leaned against it. It had begun backing away from the car as soon as it saw them. After taking a couple of unsteady steps to one side it put its hands down in the snow and stood there on all fours, glaring at them. It was about a hundred metres away and Susso could not make out any facial features, but she noticed the skin on the immense body was grey and that its flesh was partially covered in black fur.

Then suddenly it rushed towards them. Although its body was large and heavy, its footsteps were almost inaudible. The only indication it was coming closer was the sound of its panting.

Mona had already run out onto the ice beside the jetty and her partner had done the same. They collided with each other and he almost lost his footing.

Susso dropped the briefcase but stopped and lurched backwards. Bending down she clasped her fingers round the leather handle.

She ran with the case clutched to her chest, not out onto the jetty but further along the track. She shouted to Gudrun, who was hopping about with her arms spread wide like the wings of a penguin, clearly unsure what to do.

'Run, Mum!'

The trail sloped uphill before coming to an end at a rocky outcrop. Beyond that was a rotting steamboat jetty and then only pine forest on the other side of the ice. She heard a shriek behind her.

The rocks looked slithery so she ran straight out onto the ice, where she fell and hit her elbow hard. When she was up on her feet again she ran as fast as she could on the furrowed snow. It was hard work running with the briefcase in her arms, but she dared not slow down to open it.

There was a small island out in the middle of the frozen lake and she aimed for that, without really knowing why. She would never make it to the far side. It looked at least a kilometre away.

The fear gave her no extra strength. Instead she felt paralysed, but she forced her legs to move. Time and again she altered her grip on the case, first holding it by the handle, then bringing it up into her arms again. It was easiest like that, anyway.

By now she was so close to the little island that she was running in the shadow of the trees.

Behind her she heard a howl. It was no human sound. Instinctively she tried to look over her shoulder without slowing down, but that made her lose her balance and she fell. She scrambled quickly up onto her feet again and staggered a few paces backwards to see what was going on behind her. Torbjörn had already made his way to the other side of the bay. He was doubled over, his hands on his knees. Behind him Gudrun ran in shorter steps, her coat flapping. They were small dots in the distance but it looked as if they were safe.

The troll had stopped some distance from the shore. It had picked up Mona's partner and was holding him above its head on outstretched arms. A few metres away from them a dark, immobile bundle lay beside a patch of reeds. It was Mona. It did not look as if the man was struggling to get free. He was hanging in mid-air and may have lost consciousness.

A moment later the troll slammed him hard onto the ice.

Susso turned round, took the last few strides to the shore and dropped to her knees. She was utterly drained. She gasped for air. The briefcase lay in front of her on the snow. She grimaced in pain as she pressed the locks open.

How long did she have?

Sixty seconds? Thirty?

She tore open the plastic bag and groped around for the small revolver. Her hands were shaking and her nose was running like a tap. When she wiped it she noticed a red streak along her finger. She located the lever, pressed it hard with her thumb and the six-holed cylinder swung out.

How far away was it?

Should she stop to check?

No, not yet. Load first.

She thrust her hand into the plastic bag and found a cold cartridge and with shaking fingers inserted it into one of the chambers. A drop of blood from her nose landed on her hand and another on her sleeve before she managed to snap the cylinder closed.

Kneeling and holding the revolver with both hands she quickly turned round.

The troll was less than twenty metres away. But curiously enough it had stopped.

It was standing on its hind legs, its arms dangling by its sides. The hair on its sagging chest and heavy stomach was sparse and its skin was mottled with grey and cracked. The small eyes were set deep between the coarse creases in its thick-skinned forehead and the bridge of its nose, which protruded like a massive joist in its wrinkled, melancholy face. Its lower lip hung open and strings of saliva dangled in the wind.

The blood was streaming from Susso's nostrils now and the strong taste of iron filled her mouth. She spat weakly, wiped her nose and chin with the palm of her hand and sniffed.

Why was it standing there?

Then she noticed that its eyes were directed at something in the snow.

Something small and grey. The squirrel.

The little animal had positioned itself between her and the troll. It was standing on all fours with its legs wide apart, and its upright tail was jerking spasmodically, as if it was trying to work itself free from the body.

She was aware of the headache, the flashing lights in her skull. That would explain the nosebleed.

The troll took a step to one side, perhaps in an attempt to walk around the squirrel. But the animal was having none of it. In a flash it followed the troll, its gaze like a rod holding the beast at a distance.

He's protecting me, she thought. Protecting me.

And from nowhere a word came into her head: *beschermen.*

At a distance she saw Gudrun running over the ice towards her, with Torbjörn following behind. He was holding his phone in his outstretched hand.

Susso wanted to yell at them to stay where they were but she stopped herself, fearing the troll would spin round and turn on them instead.

At least for the moment she and the squirrel were keeping it at bay.

But for how long?

Had anyone seen what was happening out here on the ice?

Had Torbjörn or Gudrun phoned the police? It was possible, but how long would it take before help arrived? Too long.

Susso swallowed. When she lifted her right hand from the revolver to wipe her nose she found her skin had stuck to the barrel. She licked her lips, coughed and took a deep breath.

The squirrel was tense. She could see its hind legs trembling. Was it difficult for it to keep up the resistance? How long could it continue?

Should she just sit here?

She grabbed the bag and picked out a few cartridges. They were like ice in her hands. When she had filled the cylinder she slowly got to her feet and backed up a few steps. Her legs were shaking. The troll did not appear to notice. It was standing still, its head hanging, staring at the little animal.

Susso began walking around the squirrel in a semicircle, tentatively and with the revolver in both hands, thinking she could perhaps get past and continue towards land without the troll noticing.

But she must have overstepped some invisible barrier because all of a sudden the troll began to move, and its eyes were not directed at the squirrel. They were directed at her.

She panicked and began to run. It happened so fast she had no time to think. She should have taken cover behind the squirrel again, of course, but there was no protection there. Nothing she could see, at least.

So she ran. Straight towards Gudrun and Torbjörn.

The troll caught up with her in an instant. She did not see it coming. She only heard its wheezing breath at her side before she was knocked over. Daylight disappeared below the mighty body and her face was covered in blood and snow and her eyes were blurred and she screamed. She screamed in fear but also with the rage that suddenly poured out of her. She swore. She saw one staring yellow eye and four fangs in the dark interior of the troll's gaping jaws, and into that darkness she rammed the revolver.

When Seved carried the petrol can out of the barn and hurried towards the dog enclosure it was as if he was looking at himself from the outside and a screeching voice inside his head was demanding to know what he thought he was doing. The doubt assaulted him with such force that it paralysed him, and for a while he stood still with the can in one hand, staring at the house, while the dogs whined behind the chicken wire. It was impossible for him to work out if it was madness to set fire to Hybblet or madness not to. The motivation that had filled him on his return from Kiruna had evaporated. Although then, of course, he had only thought they would run away. Pile into a car one night and leave.

This was something else.

To make the fire spread fast enough he had to go inside the house, throw petrol on the walls and floor, and down the cellar staircase as well. Presumably he would be able to get in unnoticed but he had no idea how the little beings would react when they picked up the reek of petrol. It could make them agitated.

Perhaps it was better after all to set light to it from outside and hope for the best? No, the cement-fibre panels would probably not ignite.

He pulled a box of matches from his jacket pocket and clasped it in his hand.

Now.

You have got to do it now. It will only be worse if you wait.

He went up the veranda steps, opened the door and walked into the oppressive stench that coiled into his nostrils. He shut the door behind him, but changed his mind and left it open. It would let out some of the petrol fumes. Then he reached out for the handle and closed it anyway. The shapeshifters would probably feel the draught and wonder why it was open.

He stood still and listened. A washed-out grey light fell across the clawed wallpaper. The kitchen door stood ajar and from inside came a faint but unmistakable munching sound. Someone was in there, eating. Someone big. When he peered in the sound stopped immediately. In the shadows over by the sink, beside one of the plastic buckets of dry fodder, was a body, stooped and thin. It was one of the hareshifters, he could see that straight away from the outline of its ears. There was an oily shine in its staring eyes.

'You can eat later,' Seved said. 'I've got to clean up now.'

They normally cleaned in the mornings and the hareshifter looked as if it was wondering what it had done wrong. It shrank to a ball behind the bucket and stayed like that for a while, as if hoping to be forgotten, but eventually it came out and thumped past Seved in a couple of awkward leaps.

Relieved, he listened to the thuds continue up the stairs to the upper landing. He had been afraid he would never be able to get rid of it. There was something about cleaning that fascinated the hares. They hopped cheerfully behind the vacuum cleaner as if they were taking part in the job, and sometimes they would bring him rubbish that they wanted to throw away. He let them do it and some days their helpfulness even made him smile.

He walked to the jumping room and took a hasty look under

the bed before unscrewing the stopper of the petrol can. He sprinkled some drops on the floor and on the old foam rubber mattress. He knew he had to be sure that the stairs down to the hide would burn properly, so he returned to the hall and slowly opened the heavy door. A muffled murmuring came from below. He altered his grip on the can and was about to pour when someone down below began to mumble and complain in a gruff voice.

He froze.

The big one was awake.

Someone must have seen him and told the others! Unless it was the foxshifter itself that had tricked him. He cursed himself for allowing a shapeshifter to plant thoughts in his head. Should he take the petrol can with him or leave it? Confused, he tried to replace the stopper, but the hoarse voice below was getting more and more excited. Not until a roar of sudden rage filled the house did he throw down the can and run.

A terrible howl rose up the staircase and the steps creaked under the feet of the big old-timer as he made his way up. The instant Seved raced out of Hybblet, the cellar door was flung open behind him.

The terror made everything a blur.

Börje came running across the yard, his legs awkward and heavy, his shirt unbuttoned. His eyes were staring and he was shouting something Seved could not hear, but it was not aimed at him. He was firing words in the Sami language at the hunchbacked old bear, which was standing on all fours in the snow, swaying its broad, greying head from side to side and roaring, saliva spraying from its sagging lips. Its open mouth exposed red gums with gristly ridges like a row of white arcs, and out of them jutted the fangs.

Holding out one hand Börje walked towards the wildly snorting bear, talking constantly to it in a soft and gentle voice.

One after the other the little beings ventured out of Hybblet to see what was happening. All of them had taken refuge in animal shapes, petrified by the old-timer's irate bear form. Among the mice and shrews and lemmings that had lined up in a row of tiny tufts of fur on the veranda railing an ermine stood out like a white porcelain cat, and in the doorway the hares were hiding, liquid-eyed, their ears like antennae.

The bear's head was hanging so heavily that occasionally its shrivelled lower lip dipped into the snow. Air came in snorts from the enlarged nostrils.

'*Vuordil*,' said Börje gently. '*Vuordil*.'

Seved did not understand the word but even so he guessed its meaning.

It was meant to pacify.

And the bear seemed pacified. It rocked from side to side, managing only to pant.

But suddenly it lunged and its muscles quivered under the dingy brown fur. Snow flew up in an arc as it reared up. It was a warning to the man to back off, and Börje took a few steps backwards, flailing his arms to keep his balance.

A low but threatening growl came from Skabram's throat.

He had no intention of remaining calm.

It was obvious from Börje's back and his bent knees that he was terrified. He stood hunched and tense, ready to flee. Seved, who had stepped up onto the veranda, wondered if he should run in and get the air rifle, if only to persuade the bear to back off, but he decided against it because the sight of a rifle would likely provoke a new outburst of rage. One that could not be quelled with calming words.

Börje let out an astonished shout when the bear attacked again, and this time it was worse. Its solid frame rammed into Börje, who fell over and stayed on his back, silenced. Seved was sure the bear was going to bite him.

But the bear left Börje alone. After letting out a hideous roar it plodded off quickly behind the dog compound, its rump swaying, and disappeared among the pine trees.

When the troll threw itself at Susso, when it wrapped its long arms around her body and rolled her over and over on the ice, I screamed.

Then the shot rang out.

At first it was a muffled boom and I did not quite understand what it was. But it was followed directly by the crack of a second, third and fourth shot.

I had forgotten about the old revolver in Sven Jerring's briefcase, so I cried out as I ran:

'Who's shooting? Who's shooting?'

There was a moment's silence over the blinding, icy surface and I noticed that the huge body was not moving. It had collapsed. Then two more shots rang out, and by this time I had come close enough to see the spray on the ice and the long red streaks.

Susso lay on her side with half her arm inside the troll's mouth. Except it was no longer a troll. It was a bear.

Exhausted and confused, but at the same time filled with a paralysing gratitude, I sank to my knees beside her. Her mouth was smeared with dark blood that had coagulated in streaks, and that terrified me until I realised it had come from the bear. She had removed her arm from the bear's jaws and the hand that was holding the small dripping revolver was lying across her heaving chest. Her Inca hat had slipped off and the back of her head was resting on the ice, with her hair fanned out in the snow. Her eyes were closed but the tension showed in the furrow between her eyebrows.

'Have you seen?' I said. 'Have you seen what's happened to it?'

With a barely perceptible nod she indicated that she knew what had happened to the troll. It looked as if she was in pain and I asked her if she was hurt, but she shook her head, even though I could tell a mile off she was lying. I looked up at Torbjörn. He had picked up the brown envelope with the newspaper articles and was crouching down, holding one hand on Susso's heavy boot and rubbing it with his thumb. Not that she would have been able to feel it.

'Oh thank God!' I panted. 'And thank you, Sven!'

Torbjörn nodded.

'And Verner,' he said quietly, glancing at the bear.

Susso opened her eyes and squinted at me.

'It's the squirrel you should be thanking. He saved me.'

She tried to see what was behind her but only managed a partial turn of her head before grimacing and letting her head fall back on the snow.

'Where is it?' she asked weakly.

Torbjörn nodded towards the little island.

'It rushed up there when you fired. I expect it was scared.'

Mona got away with light concussion. Her partner Klas, on the other hand, was still unconscious when the ambulance arrived. The doctor at Sankt Göran's hospital said he had been lucky and would probably make a full recovery.

A couple of police inspectors had come from the Västerort police to talk to us all. They had recovered the bear's corpse and were going to send it to the National Veterinary Institute. One of the police officers told Susso that if she had not shot the bear in the mouth, she would probably never have stopped it.

Judging from the animal's ears, which were pierced in several places where presumably there had once been earrings, it must have been an imported circus bear that had gone crazy, or so one of the police officers said.

Where it had come from remained to be seen. It was a mystery.

That's what we thought too, of course, from our angle.

How had it found us?

The preferable choice of doubting the existence of trolls was no longer an option and I have to say I missed that alternative as I sat there in the brightly lit waiting room. It's not such a bad idea to doubt at times.

But we had been given an answer to the question of why trolls had never been found.

They hid themselves.

They took refuge in the shape of animals.

You would certainly have to look hard to find a better hiding place.

My restless fingers played with the glossy magazines on the side table but naturally I couldn't read them. I couldn't even look at the pictures. I looked at Mona from time to time. She was sitting with her arms folded, her head leaning against the wall and her eyes pinned to the floor, and I wondered what was going on in her mind.

What must she be thinking!

As I understood it, she had turned on the troll when it got hold of Klas, who had slipped on the ice. Was it pent-up rage, years of bottomless grief and all-consuming despair that had made her go on the attack?

The giant who had taken her child – was this the same one?

I badly wanted to know but didn't like to ask her. It didn't seem proper at a time like this, when I could hardly even bring myself to look at her. And what were we doing there, really? We knew the police would want to talk to us, naturally, but the real reason we had followed the ambulance to the hospital was that we didn't know where else to go. We were shocked, all three of us. Torbjörn had actually been shaking in the back seat. It was cold in the car because of the missing window but I'm pretty sure it wasn't only the temperature that was making him shake like that.

Susso, on the other hand, seemed calm, and for a while I was afraid she was damaged inside, paralysed somehow. But she wasn't. She drove the whole way to the hospital. I told her that her face was covered in blood, so she spat in her hand and rubbed at it, but that made little difference. Once inside the hospital she walked off briskly to fetch mugs of hot coffee for us and she answered the police officers' questions clearly and steadily. She was even sarcastic. Why had she had been carrying a revolver in her bag? To hunt bears. Was it her weapon? Yes. Did she have a licence? For hunting bears? No, a licence for the weapon. No. So who did the revolver belong to, then? Verner von Heidenstam. Heidenstam? Yes. The poet Heidenstam? Yes. Isn't he dead?

'Yes,' she had sighed, nodding. 'So now it's mine.'

I thought they were going to take the gun from her, but they didn't. They never mentioned it again and I got the impression those burly police officers thought Susso was a tough customer as she sat there slurping coffee, her face smeared with blood.

And that's what I thought too. I was amazed at the incredible strength she was showing and didn't know whether she had always been like that, or whether something inside her had changed as she lay under that troll, fighting for her life.

Later a crowd of visitors came into the waiting room – I never worked out who they were – and when they began talking in whispers to Mona I looked around for my bag, thinking it was time we were off.

Torbjörn was like a robot.

'Let's go,' I said, and he stood up without a word. He had put in some snus and was standing with his mouth open, very pale and with the hood of his top turned inside out. Susso was sleeping, so I shook her knee.

'We're going now,' I said.

'No!' Mona said. 'You're not going anywhere!'

A man with wide shoulders was standing in front of her and she had to lean to one side to be able to see us.

'I think it's best . . .' I stammered.

'You have to tell me . . . you've *got* to tell me what happened today.'

My first thought was that she was suffering from amnesia from the bump on her head, but then I saw it was corroboration she wanted.

'You're not leaving me here! Not again!'

Again? We had never met before. But then I understood exactly what she meant.

'Well,' I said, 'I don't know what to say . . . It wasn't a bear, I can tell you that. It was . . .'

'Oh, it was a bear all right,' Susso said. 'But not only a bear.'

What she said was incomprehensible, you could see that written on the faces turned towards her.

'He could mutate,' she said, waving her hands. 'Shapeshift.'

Her explanation did nothing to clarify things for them. Quite the reverse. Shapeshift?

'He was the one who took Magnus,' Mona said, looking at one of the women standing beside her, who I took to be her sister.

'Was that him?' I said, stepping forwards, clutching the strap of my bag. 'Are you sure it was the same one?'

'Do you understand now?' Mona said. 'Do you understand that what I saw was real?'

She looked entreatingly at the woman next to her, who was looking sad. She had spectacles with thick light-blue frames and her cheeks drooped in thick wads.

The man in the down jacket pointed at me.

'Who are these people, Mona?' he asked.

And then he said:

'Leave Mona alone! Do you hear?'

But Torbjörn had pulled his mobile out of his trouser pocket.

'I filmed him,' he said.

'Karats is dead,' Börje said.

He was sitting at the kitchen table holding the receiver in his hand. The coiled cord ran across the room and was so taut it had straightened out in places. The gravity of the news made him incapable of getting out of the chair and hanging up. Seved took the phone from him and replaced it in its base on the wall.

'Those Myréns have shot him. Down in Stockholm.'

Seved had nothing to say and clearly that irritated Börje.

'Don't you understand what that means!'

Seved continued to say nothing. Ever since Skabram left Hybblet he had felt as if something had come to a standstill inside him. He had no idea what it was, only that suddenly and unexpectedly everything stood still, like the hands of a clock that had stopped working. He swallowed hard.

'What about the one up at the Holmboms' then? Luttak.'

'I've phoned Torsten's mobile but he's not answering. But if Skabram has picked up on it, then you can bet he's taken off as well. And Urtas. Wherever he might be.'

'But where would they go?'

'I don't expect they even know that themselves. They'll wander about and, if worst comes to worst, they'll get shot. Otherwise they'll make their way back eventually.'

'But Urtas never came back.'

Börje snorted and said sneeringly:

'Those fellows are ancient. Luttak is almost certainly a thousand. Urtas has been gone twenty-five years but that's like an afternoon for them. He'll be back when he feels like it.'

Now, thought Seved, this is where I ought to tell him, tell him I know I haven't always been with them. That I know who took me and why – I just don't know why they chose me. Was it by chance? Who am I – *really*?

Then he looked at Börje, sitting at the kitchen table in his worn denim shirt, his hair hanging in greasy strands over his lined forehead and the palm of his hand pressed to his chest where the bear had sunk his claws in. He knew he would never be able to find the words.

'What the hell were you doing in there anyway?' Börje said, nodding towards the window.

They had not closed the door to Hybblet and the small shape-shifted creatures were still on the veranda and in the yard, milling about, unconcerned. The dogs had barked themselves hoarse and were too worn out now to make a sound.

'Nothing. I just thought I'd tidy up.'

It was Börje's job to draw up the rotas for cleaning and feeding, and to make sure they were followed, but presumably he was too weary to work out whose turn it was because all he said was:

'Tidy up? In the afternoon?'

'So what happened in Stockholm then?'

The question came fast and brought Börje's thoughts back to the phone call from Lennart, and that depressed him. All he could do was shake his head.

'She's nothing but trouble, that girl,' he said, and his yellow teeth flashed. 'She took the gun from Jola when we were up in

Kiruna. Pulled it right out of his hand. And now this.'

He leaned heavily across the table, staring vacantly to one side for a few moments, lost in thought, before saying:

'Lennart thinks someone helped her.'

'Who would that be?'

'That's what we don't know. She was down in Småland, that's for sure, and it's possible she met up with someone who contacted her through that website.'

'Well, what are we going to do now?'

'We'll have to wait and see. The old-timer will come back tonight, I'm sure.'

'You think so?'

'They always come back. Sooner or later.'

Compact flurries of snow swept in columns across the yard and were illuminated in the lamplight as Seved hurried back to the house. He had been in the barn looking for the foxshifter but there was no sign of him. Maybe he had taken the opportunity to slip away now that the hide was empty?

Börje had said it might get a bit out of hand while Skabram was gone, and it turned out he was right. After shapeshifting into animals the majority of the woodland beings naturally shied away from daylight, or were reticent to say the least, but in the absence of the old-timers many of them appeared to have forgotten that.

When he had entered the barn he had noticed a pair of squirrels perched on the antlers decorating the wall, and a pine marten had been stretched out on the netting of the dog compound for hours. The dogs were disturbed by those black eyes staring down at them but had made only a half-hearted attempt to bark at the inaccessible spectator. Seved had told Börje about the pine marten because he was surprised there had been one in Hybblet, but Börje told him it usually stayed in the fir trees behind the house, and so did the squirrels. They wanted to be close to the bearshifters but not too close, and now that the big old-timers were gone, they were worried.

Amina and Mattias were playing Connect Four on the floor when Seved barged in through the cellar door. They were still extremely frightened, especially the boy, and jumped when the door flew open. When Seved had gone down to them after Skabram's attack of rage he had found them curled up and terrified at the top of the bed, and Amina said they thought he had been bitten and killed. Now Mattias did not want to go out, and that was a problem. Seved could always carry the boy out to the car at night but he was afraid he would call out, and Börje woke at the slightest sound. He had slept half-awake all his life and could only get a good night's sleep when he was drunk, but he would not be drinking that night.

This was one of the reasons Seved had been looking for the foxshifter. A mouseshifter would probably have been able to calm the boy down, at least enough to keep him from getting hysterical. He had gone into Hybblet to try and catch one but had failed. They would not come out, let alone allow themselves to be caught. They were always much more fearful when they were camouflaged in fur.

Some of them even forgot they could be anything other than mice.

Now he crouched down and watched Mattias and Amina playing. Amina sat cross-legged and hunched, and Mattias was kneeling. He had filled his hand with discs and picked one out each time it was his turn. The red discs, which were Amina's, had already made one vertical and one horizontal row, but they carried on playing anyway.

Seved waited for Amina to look at him, and when she did he said:

'I can't find him, so it's best we wait.'

Torbjörn turned on his phone and held the screen towards them. Everyone in the waiting room, apart from Mona and Gudrun, pressed forwards to see.

The picture was poor quality and shaky, but there was the troll, standing stock still far away on the ice beside Susso. The squirrel could not be seen, naturally, and from a distance the troll looked a lot like a bear. The man in the grey jacket was quick to point that out. He sighed and pulled a face to show he had seen enough but still he could not tear himself away from the film.

Suddenly the camera zoomed in, precisely when the troll threw itself at Susso. The picture had stabilised and Gudrun came running into it, shrieking. The man in the grey jacket – Göran, Mona had called him – frowned.

All of a sudden he said:

'There was a letter, Mona.'

He seemed as if he wanted to avoid eye contact with the others while he was speaking. This was clearly difficult for him, something he had been carrying for a long time.

'A letter came and I never told you about it. It was four, five years after Magnus disappeared, and you were starting to feel better. I didn't want to make it worse by dragging up the past . . .'

There was silence in the room. Everyone was waiting for him to continue, which he did after twisting the rod of the venetian blind a couple of times. A flap of checked shirt was sticking out from below his jumper.

'The letter came from a woman in Kramfors who had read about you in the paper, read what you had said about the giant and all that. She said there was a giant living at her neighbour's, and that she had seen it. With her own eyes. It was living in their guest cabin. There was a rumour that the couple's son had died, and when the woman saw the giant she remembered what she'd read in the paper. She thought they might be the ones who had taken Magnus, to replace the child they had lost.

'So she looked in the cabin window. The curtains were drawn, so she couldn't see anything, but the neighbours must have seen her because a couple of weeks later they moved. I thought it was nonsense and I wanted to protect you from it. So I didn't say anything.'

Mona sat staring at his back. Her fingers were resting in her lap, not moving. It was impossible to tell if she had understood what he had told her. She looked completely blank.

'What was her name?' Gudrun asked. 'Have you still got the letter?'

He shook his head, his gaze directed at the windowsill.

'But I remember what the family was called,' he said. 'The name has stayed with me for some reason, I don't know why. It was a fairly unusual name, so perhaps that's why . . .'

He turned round.

'Skarf,' he said. 'Skarf was the name.'

There was no reason for Mona to sit and wait. Klas would not be coming round for a long time and his condition was stable, so she ought to go home and get some sleep. But she just shook her head, and when Göran said naturally he would go with her, she shouted that she did not want to go home.

That she never wanted to go home again. That she did not dare!

Susso stood with a plastic mug of water raised to her mouth and looked at Mona.

'If it's a troll you're afraid of, then it's more dangerous sitting here in the waiting room,' she said. 'It was me it was looking for, not you.'

Torbjörn had done a search on his mobile for Skarf. There were about thirty people with that name in the whole country, but none of them lived north of Stockholm, oddly enough. It seemed to be a family name in Småland, in the south.

'We'll have to phone round and ask if any of them have ever lived in Kramfors,' he said. 'I'm sure it's possible to find out, if we do it carefully.'

He went out to phone straight away.

'They live in Boden now,' he said, when he returned. 'Inger Skarf has remarried someone called Yngve Fredén. I spoke to one of Inger's cousins, but he didn't have an address or telephone number. I searched but I couldn't find anything, but I'm sure we can find out somehow.'

'Did they have a son? An adult son?'

Torbjörn looked up.

'I don't know,' he said. 'Perhaps I should have asked that . . .'

Then he added:

'He would be . . . how old?'

'Thirty-two this year,' said Mona. 'So thirty-one.'

'I'll check,' he said.

He sat down to write a text but then changed his mind and

went out to phone instead, and when he came back he said in a low voice to Susso:

'I spoke to Matti Alkberg. He's going to see if anyone knows someone called Fredén. Or Skarf. And who is that age.'

'Okay, but it's important we get an address for Inger and Yngve.'

'What would you like to do?' Gudrun asked, unscrewing the top of her lip salve as she looked at Mona. 'We'll find those people, don't you worry. Boden is on our way home. Would you like to come with us? I would understand if you did.'

'I don't know. I really don't. I'd like to sleep on it.'

Susso, Gudrun and Torbjörn checked into a hotel in Kristineberg, a pink building right next to an underground station. The standard was poor. The furnishings were shabby, the venetian blind was broken and there was an unpleasant smell in the bathroom. They decided to share a room because no one wanted to sleep alone.

Susso sat for a while on the toilet lid before turning on the tap and washing around her mouth. Then she wetted a wad of paper and used it to clean out her nostrils. Torbjörn and Gudrun were watching television when she came out. She found it impossible to relax and paced the floor until finally saying she had decided to drive out to Färingsö and look for the squirrel. Gudrun thought she should wait, at least until it was light, but that upset Susso. The squirrel had saved her. She would be *dead* had it not been for the squirrel.

In a bin outside the hotel's delivery entrance Susso found a cardboard box, which she flattened and taped to the damaged car window. It flapped in the wind as she and Torbjörn drove out to the islands.

It was half past midnight when they arrived. They parked in the same place as before. The ambulance tyres had left deep furrows in the snow. Torbjörn used the torch on his mobile to guide them. Susso had inserted the two remaining cartridges in the revolver and was holding it tightly.

The troll's blood was a black shadow in the churned-up snow. Both of them saw it but neither said anything. They walked around the tiny island several times, calling softly in all directions. It was pointless trying to climb up onto the rocks. Susso made a half-hearted attempt but got no further ashore than a few metres. The trees were crowded together, their branches intertwined, and there was nowhere secure to put her feet down among the shingle and the sheer rocks.

At last they heard a cracking sound among the trees and soon something small scampered towards them through the snow.

'Here he is!' said Torbjörn.

Susso crouched down in front of the squirrel as it sat upright. Then she held out her hand.

She held the squirrel on her lap all the way back to the hotel and was amazed at how calm it was. She stroked its white breast with her finger.

'Have you felt how soft he is?' she said

'Yes,' Torbjörn replied. 'Like cotton wool.'

They padded into the room. Gudrun was lying on her side, snoring loudly. Susso went into the bathroom and took her toothbrush from her toilet bag, and as she was brushing her teeth the squirrel sat on the edge of the basin, watching her intently. The ceiling lights were reflected as distinct dots of light in the animal's black eyes.

Torbjörn's pale face appeared in the doorway. He was standing a few metres from the door, looking at Susso's reflection.

Then he slipped into the bathroom and suddenly there he was, behind her. A cold hand rested on her right hip, which was indented slightly at the lacy waistband of her knickers. When Susso felt his touch, she took out the toothbrush and supported herself with her other hand on the handbasin. He had already placed his other hand on her left hip.

'You've got blood in your hair,' he said.

'What?'

'You've got blood here,' he said, taking hold of a lock of her hair. The end was stiff with coagulated blood and he showed it to her in the mirror. 'Is it yours?'

She shook her head.

'I don't know . . .'

She watched as he lifted the strand of hair first to his nose and then to his mouth. He put the rust-red tip between his lips and sucked, not taking his eyes from hers. Then he nodded slowly.

'It tastes of Susso.'

A puff of air came from her nose as she laughed. She smiled. He had not pressed up close to her yet. All he did was stand there, holding her hips in a tight grip, as if they were ice dancers preparing to leap.

Very slowly he leaned forwards, and as his mouth touched her neck she closed her eyes. She did not want to see herself in the mirror, to see how she was transforming. She drifted away, breathing between parted lips. But he saw. Only he saw. His mouth blew warm air against her throat, and like a cautious animal the tip of his tongue appeared and brushed against her skin. She knew he would push his hips against hers at any moment, knew how rough the denim of his jeans would feel against her skin. But he took his time. The lips left her neck as slowly as they had arrived and he released his hold on her hips. She opened her eyes. This was not what she had expected.

Torbjörn stood with his back to the wall, and when she saw his frozen expression she raised her eyebrows.

'It's no good,' he said.

And then she noticed the squirrel. She had completely forgotten about it. It had climbed onto the rim of the handbasin and was standing there on all fours, staring at Torbjörn as its tail jerked from side to side. It was as if the little animal had nailed Torbjörn with its eyes. Susso waited a few seconds before reaching out her hand and prodding the squirrel with her toothbrush. It did not move from the spot.

'You know,' she said, 'I think he's jealous.'

Tracks from paws of various shapes and sizes criss-crossed the snow that had fallen during the night. Necklaces of patterns from the smallest animals meandered haphazardly, crossing the wider and more prominent prints the hares had left over the yard and around the buildings.

Something had crept up onto the roof of the Volvo and left behind a twisted black strand, and Seved thought it must have been one of the weasels. That would be typical of them. 'The kind ones', Ejvor had called them, and Seved had believed her until he realised that 'kind' really meant 'quick', and that the weasels were anything but kind as he understood the word.

With his hands in his pockets he stopped a few metres in front of Hybblet and checked to make sure there were no bear footprints there. He had not heard anything during the night but he knew the big old-timers had no trouble making themselves inconspicuous when they chose to. As a child he had more than once been startled to find they had crept up close to him while he was playing. It was always their heavy breathing that gave them away. That and their stench.

The worry that Skabram would return had kept Seved awake most of the night. It was the chain he was mainly concerned about. What if the old troll decided to go in that way for some reason? The hatch was bolted from the inside, so he would not be able to get in while there was no one inside the hide to open it for him. Even if he knew Karats was not waiting for him it must still be something he desperately desired – so desperately perhaps that he let himself be controlled by his desire. Besides, Seved had no idea what went on in the big troll's head. Rage had driven him to shapeshift, but what had triggered the rage? Was it as if someone had suddenly ripped a tooth from his jaw? Did he know Karats was dead or had he only felt the pain of it?

Börje was in the dog compound, crouching down and patting the Lapphund cross, digging his fingers into the thick, curly coat on its neck and murmuring a stream of questions one after the other.

Seved opened the shaky gate and stepped in.

'They've crapped on the car,' he said, holding out his hand so the little Laika could come forwards to sniff it. It ran its rough tongue over his little finger, making it wet and warm.

'Better that than tipping it over,' Börje said.

They sat back to back, stroking the dogs.

'Has he come home?'

Börje shook his head, sniffing the mucus back into his nose.

'But Lennart will be here tomorrow, you'll see.'

'Has he given up on that now?'

'What?'

'Hunting down that girl Myrén.'

'Oh no. He'll never do that.'

He stood for a few moments in Hybblet's kitchen, waiting for something to flit past the corner of his eye, but it was totally still. In the pallid daylight he saw how filthy the floor was.

He imagined most of them were down in the hide but he

certainly did not want to go there, so he walked upstairs instead. In one of the lofts he found a solitary batshifter hanging with its claws attached to the edge of a sheet of plywood. It was old and grey and had a tiny, compressed, dog-like head. The sight of it would probably scare the boy, so he left it alone.

When he came down from the loft a mouse was sitting on a chair, looking at him. It was a birch mouse and he thought it was one of the shapeshifters Torsten had given them to bring back. Seved squatted down and chatted kindly to the creature until it was brave enough to walk up to his outstretched hand.

He allowed the mouse to crawl onto his hand and get used to him before carefully putting it into his jacket pocket, where it scratched around for a while and then settled down.

Mattias was sitting on the bed playing a video game. He was frenetically tapping the buttons on the controller. Seved stood with his hands in his pockets, looking at him.

'Are you winning?'

The boy was engrossed in the game and did not answer.

'Look,' Seved said. 'I've got a new mouse for you.'

He took out the creature and released it onto the bed. It scrabbled against the duvet cover and almost disappeared among the billowing folds.

The boy put down the controller. It looked as if he had forgotten about the game.

Mona had been staying the night with friends in Sundbyberg and early the next morning she phoned to ask if they could all meet up in the hospital cafeteria.

They went directly after breakfast.

The squirrel lay in the front pocket of Susso's jacket like a hot-water bottle and it made her feel more secure than the weapon she was carrying. During the night the little animal had sat immobile, watching the lights from the trains as they swayed past immediately outside the window.

Now it was sleeping soundly – or at least, it was completely still.

On the table in front of Mona was a coffee cup and a plate with a cake still in its cellophane wrapper. The coffee looked cold. Subdued and seldom looking them in the eye, she told them she was in two minds about finding the Skarf family. She knew, of course, that the chance of them being involved in Magnus's disappearance was very small, and the chance that he was still with them even smaller, but, oddly enough, the thought of seeing him again filled her with mixed emotions. She was worried about what it would do to her. How it would affect her.

He had been gone half her life and she had become used to the hole he had left. She had grown around it. And however it turned out she would never get him back. She would be fooling herself to think otherwise. All she knew of him was the way he had been back then.

'A little boy. The most wonderful little boy in the world.'

Now he would be a man and they would be strangers to each other. There was no guarantee he would even remember her. And what if it all went wrong between them!

Then he would be gone for ever and she was afraid all the precious memories she had of him would be tainted.

She dreaded the thought of it.

'You'd think this was something I longed for, after all these years,' she said. 'Getting him back. But now that the opportunity has come I don't know what I want. I'm ashamed to admit it.'

Gudrun shook her head.

'No need to be.'

Susso agreed, muttering something about it being only natural to think like that. What Mona had gone through was so awful that she could think of nothing helpful to say. She thought about Carina Mickelsson and Edit and wondered whether she should mention them, but was not sure if it was suitable to move the focus from Magnus at a time like this.

'Have you seen the films of the tsunami?' Mona asked. 'From Thailand?'

They nodded.

'There were children on those beaches,' Mona said. 'Little children. The wave came in and took them, as if it was collecting them. I think it was the same with Magnus. The person who took him was like that flood wave, the same kind of indifferent force.'

She moved her fingers across the surface of the table to show how the wave had swept in.

'It has been explained to me that my shock formed an image of the person who took him,' she went on. 'That the pain inside me took on a physical shape, the shape of a giant. And in the end you believe it was like that because it's the only reasonable explanation. And it wasn't only the giant. The day Magnus disappeared I saw a fox and a hare as well outside the cabin. Perhaps you know about that?'

'Yes, Barbro said Sven had told her.'

Mona shook her head and gave a half smile.

'Do you know, I thought I dreamt that he phoned. Uncle Sven! It was so unreal, that *he* of all people should phone. When I told people about it afterwards they said I must have imagined it just because he was so kind to children. Perhaps I thought he would care about Magnus and would help him, which was why I dreamt it. But he did ring, didn't he? He really did?'

Gudrun nodded.

'He did want to help. That was exactly what he wanted. It wasn't a dream.'

'How strange,' Mona said. 'It all feels so strange.'

'Yes,' said Gudrun. 'You can imagine how surprised we were when it turned out he was involved in all this. And John Bauer too.'

'So those animals were real. And the bat too.'

Torbjörn looked up but he said nothing. He only looked at Susso, passing the question on to her.

'What bat?' she asked.

'I killed a bat,' Mona said. 'By mistake. And then, after we had been shopping, we found it in the fridge. I thought someone was playing a trick on us. But I have wondered about that since, whether it was a kind of message, and if that was why the giant took Magnus. In exchange, or something. Perhaps it was his bat I killed, because it had a little ring in its ear.'

'I don't think so,' Gudrun said. 'I expect they took Magnus because they wanted him. They wanted to have a child, a human child. It seems to be something these stallo folk do.'

'And those animals I saw, were they like the bear, do you think?'

Susso nodded.

'That's the secret,' she said. 'They are animals. And that is why they are so hard to find.'

'The bat as well?'

'Presumably.'

Without thinking, she had put her hand on her stomach. She wondered whether she should show Mona the squirrel but decided to wait for another occasion. She did not want to wake the animal and it felt wrong to open her pocket while it was sleeping. And after all, they were in a hospital. It would cause quite a stir if someone discovered she had smuggled in an animal – a rat, more or less.

By now Mona had broken open the cellophane around the cake and gone back in time. She told them what it been like for her afterwards. How furious she had been with the police.

'A giant can't hide himself very easily, but they didn't want to listen to any of that. It was as if their minds were made up, and eventually they didn't listen to anything I had to say. To be treated like that . . . in the end you doubt yourself, your own sanity, and there is nothing worse. I began to wonder if I really had seen what I thought I had seen. And then I got a letter from the prosecutor, I think that's who it was, where it said 'Mona Bodin'. Bodin! How would they ever be able to find Magnus if they couldn't even get his name right!'

She dipped her cake in the coffee cup so forcefully it struck the bottom. She let it drip before putting it down on a napkin.

'They needed help checking the details and everything, so they were in touch quite often, and every time I went from hope to despair. Once they came to my house and showed me a pair of underpants they had found under some trees and I had to tell them if they were Magnus's underpants. You can imagine what that felt like. And another time they phoned to ask if Magnus had any holes in his teeth, because they had found a body. Just like that! He was four years old. Do four-year-olds usually have holes in their teeth?'

She shook her head.

'Of course, I know they have to do the job their way and they can't always be wrapping things up in nice words, but they were so horribly insensitive. And there was *no one* to talk to. All that about counselling and support and so on – that only came later. There was nothing like that then. I was completely alone.'

'What about now?' Gudrun asked. 'What would you like to do now?'

'What do you mean?'

'As we said, we are going to try and find those people. See what kind of people they are. It might not lead to anything but you're welcome to come with us.'

'I think I'll stay, what with Klas and everything . . .'

Gudrun stood up.

'We'll keep in touch,' she said, giving Mona a brief hug. 'As soon as we have spoken to those Skarf people we'll let you know. Then we'll take it from there.'

Seved was lying in bed fully dressed, and he could hardly breathe. His nervousness manifested itself in long waves of nausea that radiated from somewhere below his ribs. His body told him to wait, to stay where he was and stare at the wall looming over his bed, and let the night pass. This night like every other night.

He was hoping to make it back before Börje woke up so that he would have time to talk to him in peace and quiet. It was impossible to say what would happen after that, but he vaguely thought they could move somewhere. He did not know where but he had a wad of 100,000- and 50,000-kronor notes in his jacket pocket, and he guessed Börje also had some money stashed away. It might take them a while but eventually the police would be able to work out where Amina and Mattias had been staying.

He doubted he had the courage to tell Börje the truth, so he had a story prepared at the back of his mind: that Signe must have taken the car and escaped with the boy. Once, Börje had sat beside her in the Volvo and shown her how the gears worked and which pedal to use to brake and which to accelerate. The engine had roared and cut out alternately as she searched for the right gear. So in a way it would be his own fault. He had given her the knowledge she needed to get away, and maybe, Seved thought, maybe that was just what Börje wanted. He was the one who had snatched her, and as far as he could tell that act had tormented him for many years. Was it so strange, then, that he wanted to let her go?

The television droned softly on the upstairs landing and it was almost 2 a.m. before it fell silent. The remote thudded onto the coffee table. A glass knocked against a plate and the sofa springs groaned. The floorboards creaked and then the stairs. There was the sound of running water in the handbasin, the flush of the toilet. Then, with heavy steps, he came upstairs again. It would not be long before he fell asleep. Seved listened carefully but instead of Börje's heavy breathing he heard the front door close.

Someone had come into the house. He lay there anxiously, listening. He had made sure the door was locked, so it could only be one person.

Fully dressed in their outdoor clothes, complete with hats and scarves, Amina and Mattias stood squashed together in the small entrance hall, alert and wide-eyed with fear as he came stealthily down the stairs.

'Shit!' he hissed as he shoved them into the kitchen and shut the door behind him. 'I was going to come down to you! He isn't asleep yet.'

'We thought you had forgotten us,' said Mattias.

Slowly Seved opened the door and listened in the direction of the staircase. If Börje had been awake, he would probably have heard the door by now and come down to see what was going on.

The boy pressed his mittens to his chest and Seved knew what was inside them. He was not sure how much the mouseshifter understood but he did not want it to realise they were doing something forbidden. It could very easily run off and tell the others, just to make mischief. So he said in as loud a voice as he dared:

'Are you hungry? Do you want something to eat before we go?'

The key to the Isuzu would have to be hidden. Börje might be able to start the car anyway but that would take a long time – he would never be able to catch up with them.

A deep silence met them as they stepped out onto the veranda and hurried towards the Volvo. The sky was starry and it was bitterly cold. A low yelp came from the dog enclosure but as long as the dogs didn't start barking too loudly there was no danger. The car windows were covered in a crystalline layer of frost but he would have to scrape it off later.

Seved unplugged the engine-heater cable and opened the back door. Mattias was allowed to jump in and sit down, but Amina had to help push.

'You'll have to push from the back,' he said softly to Amina, who nodded. She was wearing Ejvor's old knitted mittens and a woollen hat which was so loose she had to keep pushing it up her forehead.

He put the engine into neutral and with one hand on the wheel pushed the frozen car. Sluggishly it moved forwards, its tyres creaking in the dry snow. He changed his grip and grimaced. The Volvo rolled unwillingly.

Behind him he heard Amina mutter something.

'It'll get easier soon,' he said over his shoulder.

But she went on muttering.

It was a while before Seved caught sight of it because it was small and its coat was as white as the snow. A weaselshifter. It was crouching on the rear of the car roof, watching the girl's dark face with interest while also keeping an eye on its surroundings. No doubt it was the first time it had ever ridden on anything.

Releasing his grip and chasing the shifter away was not an option for Seved because then they would lose momentum.

Instead he increased his speed, thinking that would make the weasel nervous and it would jump off. But it stayed where it was and rose up on its hind legs, looking around. Then it ran to the front and slid down the windscreen onto the bonnet.

In his eagerness to get the weasel off the bonnet Seved had not noticed that the car was moving of its own accord over the brow of the slope, and now everything was starting to go wrong. He had to make the car stop. As he pushed his elbows back against the doorframe and dug in his heels, he called to Amina to stop pushing. When he realised that was pointless he tried instead to leap onto the seat and grab the wheel, but tripped and almost fell.

The car rammed into the wall of ploughed snow where the road went round a bend. The chassis squealed and the snow grated as the radiator grill slid along it, but otherwise it was a silent collision. The door was still open.

Panting, Seved and Amina stood looking at the rear of the car. It was shining faintly in the darkness. Neither of them said anything. After a second or two a back door opened and the boy climbed out slowly, his hands clasped to his chest.

The right front wheel had ridden up the ridge of snow but not too far for Seved to be able to reverse it out, he thought. It might wake Börje, but he had no choice. He glanced back at the house, sat down behind the wheel and put the key in the ignition.

As usual the Volvo spluttered a few times before starting. He put the engine in reverse and gently depressed the accelerator. The beam from the headlights struck the compacted snow and made it glow. They were on a slope, so he would have to accelerate quite hard, but not too much otherwise the wheels would skid, and it would be as slippery as glass beneath them. The car moved slowly but steadily backwards, and when the front wheels had noisily freed themselves from the snow and he had turned the wheel he waved to Amina and Mattias that they should leap into the car. They both sat in the back.

Seved bent over the wheel and tried to calm himself.

'The weasel,' he said to Amina. 'Did you see where it went?'

She shook her head and he could hear her hat rubbing against the hood of her jacket.

'That bloody weasel,' he said. 'I only hope it doesn't tell.'

'Who would it tell?' she said quietly.

She was right. The hide was empty, of course, and it would hardly be able to get into the house and Börje's bedroom. Even so, he could not shake off the anxiety. It had begun badly and that did not bode well.

The road to the barrier had never felt so long. It was as if it had found new bends in the forest. He dared not put the headlights on full beam, so he could see only a few metres ahead. In his thoughts he was still inside the house. Had Börje woken up by now? Was he running around looking for the keys to the Isuzu?

He stopped at the barrier, got out, and after pulling his glove off with his teeth he unlocked the padlock. He moved the barrier to the side and jogged back to the car. He sat down, shut the door and looked at the clock. Almost two thirty. That meant they would arrive in Sorsele at 3 a.m.

He had thought he would just drop Amina and Mattias off at the first house they saw, knock on the door and leave, but when they got to Sorsele and saw the dark frozen buildings he felt unsure. The cold was intense and it would be a few hours before anyone was up and about. If no one let them in, they could very easily freeze to death.

He drove up to the hotel on the river bank but carried on slowly past. There were too many eyes in there. Someone would see the Volvo and he wanted to avoid that, even though the number plates were covered in snow. After driving around aimlessly without catching sight of a single person, he finally turned into Strandvägen, where he pulled up by the bus station. It felt safe somehow and he needed to think. To wait. Amina and Mattias sat in absolute silence on the back seat, wide awake and staring.

'Someone will come along soon,' he murmured.

The waiting room was not open at this time of night, he knew that, otherwise they would have been able to sit inside until someone found them.

Mattias whispered something in the back and he heard the mouse moving about, scratching at the child's snowsuit. That mouseshifter was clearly harmless. He had been lucky there. But he would still have to get rid of it.

He looked at the clock. It was four.

He had to drop them off somewhere. But where? It would have to be the hotel. There was surely someone awake in there. It was the safest option as far as Mattias and Amina were concerned.

He started the car and drove slowly along the riverside and over the bridge to the Norra Esplanade. The snowdrifts shimmered from within and in the darkness the lamp posts looked like columns of light. He passed the hotel and parked about fifty metres from the entrance.

'You'll have to go in here,' he said, nodding towards the illuminated building. 'It's a hotel. Tell them it's Mattias, the one who . . . who went missing. They'll look after you.'

Then he reached into the darkness of the back seat.

'You'd better give that to me now.'

But Mattias did not want to hand over the mouseshifter, wherever it was. He was quiet and sitting still, looking down at his hands.

'You have to!'

'He's not like them. He's just a mouse.'

'No, he isn't. He looks like it, but he's not.'

'Mattias,' said Amina hoarsely.

The boy raised his hand to his shoulder and then held it out to Seved, who took hold of the wriggling object. It liked the boy and had no doubt lodged itself deep inside him.

'Amina,' he said, 'no one is going to believe you, you know that, right?'

There was no answer so he went on:

'They will think you're making it all up, that you're lying. So there's no point in saying anything, at least not straight away. Then you can tell someone you trust. But be prepared for no one to believe you.'

She nodded.

'You've got to go in,' he said.

Amina opened the door and climbed out. She turned and reached for Mattias, who had scrambled across the seat. Without saying a word she shut the door and in the rear-view mirror he saw them cut across the street and disappear round the corner of the hotel.

The mouseshifter would not stop squirming in Seved's fist, so he dropped it onto the seat and it darted off instantly. It was impossible to know where it had gone. He drove on for a short distance before turning left, and as he passed the hotel on his way back he slowed down. Hopefully they had already been let in.

Mattias was standing inside the entrance doors and someone

was crouching down in front of him. But it wasn't Amina, because she came running straight up to the car with her hat in her hand. Seved stopped and wound down the window.

'What's up?' he asked. 'What's happening?'

'I don't want to go in there!'

It took time to find a garage that could repair the car window while we waited, so it was Tuesday before we got away, and we were at the Statoil filling station in Gävle Bro when Roland phoned to ask if we had heard. Heard what? I wondered. That Mattias had been found. In Sorsele.

Naturally I wanted to know where he had been and if he had been taken by the Vaikijaur man. But Roland didn't know and eventually he tired of my questions.

I had immediately gestured to Susso and passed on the news. She put the car radio on but was unable to find a news bulletin. Torbjörn sat with his head bent over his mobile but for some reason he couldn't find anything either.

Susso phoned Edit but no one answered.

'Ring his parents then,' I suggested.

But she didn't want to do that. She thought it would be an intrusion.

A few miles north of Sundsvall Susso finally got hold of Edit Mickelsson, but she had no more to add to what Roland had already told us. She had not seen Mattias yet, she had only spoken to Per-Erik, and the only thing the boy had said was that he had been given a TV game and no one had been unkind to him. As far as the Vaikijaur man was concerned, Per-Erik was unclear, but as Edit understood it he was not the one who had taken the boy.

After hearing that news we were quiet in the car for a long time.

If all that was true, there was nothing that clearly indicated that Mattias had been held captive by trolls. The attack in Holmajärvi and the bear troll that came out of nowhere on Färingsö could be related to the fuss surrounding Susso's website. It stunned us into silence.

A few kilometres further along the motorway the yellow bear logo of the Preem service station shone in the darkness through the snow.

'Let's stop here for coffee,' I said. 'I'm feeling a bit tired.'

I diluted my coffee with three mini Tetra Paks of milk, stirred, tasted it and opened a fourth.

I was the only one drinking. Torbjörn was standing chewing a wooden stirrer and Susso had bought a bag of nuts for the squirrel and an evening paper, which she spread out so that we could all see. It said Mattias had knocked on the door of the River Hotel in Sorsele at four o'clock in the morning. He was cold but in good spirits. His parents were overjoyed. The police were satisfied. A huge relief, said head of investigations Kjell-Åke Andersson.

Torbjörn's mobile buzzed.

'Rackvattnet,' he said, reading the display. 'The Skarfs live in Rackvattnet.'

Susso looked up and straightened her glasses.

'Where's that?' she asked.

'Don't know. Just got the address from Matti.'

He tapped the keys and soon a new text came in.

'It's between Boden and Älvsbyn.'

'Have they got a son?' I asked, without looking up from the paper.

Torbjörn held out the phone.

'All I've got is the address. Rackvattnet 4.'

He trudged on through the thin light of daybreak. The snow had forced its way into the shafts of his boots and lay there like cuffs of ice around his ankles, stinging his skin. Amina walked a few metres behind him, with snow up to her thighs. When he turned round she looked away because she thought he was angry with her. She might as well think that, though in actual fact he wasn't. He was grateful she had returned. It meant he did not have to be alone in the forest.

He knew the snowdrifts would become shallower as they came down into the valley, and they would also be able to hide there. But for now they were on a slope covered with spruce trees. Visible between the trees were the contours of the mountains, like immovable clouds on the lower rim of the sky. He thought he could make out Varåive.

With Amina in the back seat he had driven towards Jillesnåle at breakneck speed. If Börje was still asleep, they could pretend they had forgotten to lock the cellar door. It would not have been impossible for the boy to escape and make his way to the main road, not now the hide was empty. Or else they could blame the foxshifter.

At the top of the hill after Grannäs a pair of tail lights had appeared out of the darkness and he had stamped on the accelerator to pass, but it was not until he had swung out into the oncoming lane that the glint of the aluminium ladder caught his eye. Now there was no going back. His only hope was to pass the camper van so quickly that Lennart would not be able make out the model of the car in the cloud of snow. The old man's eyesight was not the best, so it might work.

He had driven past the road to the house and not until he reached Kraddsele had he dared to stop. He had pulled into a lay-by and waited, convinced the headlights would appear in his rear-view mirror any minute. But they had not and that meant Lennart had not seen him. He had stared into the mirror for ten minutes before finally switching off the engine. His breathing had been quick and shallow and he had not been able to think clearly. For a brief moment he had thought about returning to the hotel and saying he was responsible for taking the boy. But who knew where that might lead? He realised he would be hated and the thought of all those hostile looks scared him more than anything. And what would happen to Börje?

He hoped Lennart would set off the minute he found out what had happened. When he discovered they were gone he would be fuming, but also afraid, inasmuch as he could be afraid. Sooner or later the police would turn up, and Seved was sure they wouldn't just take a quick look around as they had done at Torsten and Elna's. That ought to force Lennart to flee pretty much straight away. But Seved had no desire to sit in the car and wait. He wanted to get off the road, so he decided to walk to the house, hide nearby and wait until Lennart had left.

But it was further than he thought. They had been walking for two hours, much of it uphill. Luckily there was no wind. They had scooped up snow and eaten it. That made them cold on the inside, of course, but they had no choice. Amina lagged behind, standing still for long periods, and he could see she wanted to sit down. But it was too cold. There was a risk he would never get her back on her feet. They could rest when they reached the forest. He told her that and she struggled on with drooping shoulders and mittens that ploughed furrows in the snow.

He should have parked closer to the road leading to the house and walked from there. Or they could have simply sat on the other side of the road, hidden among the trees, and waited for Lennart to leave. In agony from all the effort he reproached himself for the way he had rushed up into the trees, full of the energy the fear had pumped around his body and the desire to get far away from the road as quickly as possible.

Now they had to rest for a while. He broke off some spruce branches, snapped them into pieces and made a lining for a crater they had trampled in the snow. They sat down. He scraped with the heel of his boot and uncovered a frozen black crowberry bush in the powdery snow. He uprooted the bedraggled little bush and stripped it of its berries.

'Here,' he said, tipping a few black globes into Amina's glove, which was covered in clumps of snow.

When he dug in his pocket for his gloves he found something warm and soft. Alarmed, he pulled back his hand, and in the split second before he realised what it was the mouseshifter emerged. After sticking out its nose and looking around, it crawled out and sat on his knee, where it turned round a few times, its long tail whipping around behind it. Irritated, Seved brushed it aside and watched as it sat perfectly still on the spruce branches, as tiny and grey as a pine cone.

'What's the matter with it?' Amina said after a while. 'Is it cold?'

'I don't think it likes the needles,' Seved said. 'They're sticking into it.'

Together they watched the mouseshifter.

'Why has it got such a long tail?' she asked.

'It's a birch mouse. That's what they look like.'

Unexpectedly the little creature started to make a sound, an intermittent razor-sharp squeak. Seved kicked the branches to make it stop but that had no effect. It carried on squeaking with increasing strength.

'Cut it out,' he said.

'Perhaps he's wondering where Mattias is?' Amina said.

Seved nodded distractedly, looking towards the trees. It was light now and he knew more or less where they were. The Råvojaure shack was only a few hundred metres away.

Soon the forest thickened on all sides. It was as if the spruce trees were coming forwards to greet them. Before long the shack came into view, a section of a greying timber wall not enveloped in snow. Grimacing with exertion, Seved turned round and watched Amina labouring towards him, followed by her shadow. Her lips were moving silently.

The door opened inwards so getting into the shack was no problem, but of course it was freezing inside. The frost had etched so many white roses on the windowpane that it was impossible to look out except through a thin strip around the edges.

There were whisky bottles on the table, holding candles. A radio hung from a beam, its antenna extended. The battery compartment was empty and its lid was missing.

Seved looked at the logs and wondered if he could risk it. The smoke would be noticed from far away, and the smell too, but sometimes trekkers stayed overnight in the shack. Mainly in the summer, of course, but even so. They needed to get warm. Amina had found an old blanket and wrapped it around herself, but still she looked blue with cold and was slow to reply when he spoke to her. He picked up the axe, gripping it high on the shaft, and kneeled down to split a few smaller logs, then rolled up some sheets of newspaper, pink ones from the sports supplement, and pushed them into the stove. Beside the log basket was a box of matches, and he took out a match, struck it and put it to the paper. Then he sank down and felt the warmth from the stove spread across his face.

He must have fallen asleep because all of a sudden he threw out his arm and shouted something. He did not know what, only that he had shouted out loud because he was afraid. The fire had almost gone out and Amina was sleeping. Her eyelids were swollen and her mouth looked cross. The birch mouse was running around in the wan light that filtered through the frosty window onto the tabletop, its long tail trailing behind it. It looked demented and Seved did not understand how it had so much energy. He put more logs in the stove and looked at his watch.

He did not feel thirsty but he knew he ought to drink, so he found a blackened saucepan and opened the door. After he had filled it to the top with snow he stayed where he was, bent over.

The wolverine was standing between the branches of a fallen spruce. At first Seved thought it was a bear because of its shaggy pelt, but then he saw the wide bushy tail, the greying, almost white forehead and the curved claws buried in the bark.

He had never seen a wolverine before, but Ejvor had once shown him a chain of tracks outside Hybblet. She had spread her fingers and laid her hand over one of the prints, but had only just been able to cover it.

But this one was smaller than a real wolverine, and because it was in animal disguise they still had a chance to escape. But Seved wanted to know why it had come. Perhaps the mouse had led it here?

He soon found out.

The splutter of an engine reached him from behind the shack. He peered around the corner and saw that a snowmobile had cut a line in the slope on the fell and was on its way down to them. It was his own snowmobile and in front of it ran a cluster of hares. He counted five. But it was not Börje coming towards him. It was Jola.

It was pointless trying to run away, so Seved waited with the saucepan in his hand.

The mobile came up to the shack, and when Jola stopped he immediately shrugged off the rifle he had been carrying over his back. He rested the butt over his thighs, switched off the engine and looked at Seved. His cheeks and the edges of his ears were bright red, and he was breathing heavily through his open mouth. A snus pouch, damp and dark, was showing beneath his lip.

'Bring the boy out,' he said.

Seved did not answer.

The hares had spread out in front of the shack, round-eyed and silent, and Seved felt all his resistance leave him, to be replaced by a paralysing nausea. All he wanted to do was lie down. Numbly he backed to the door and spotted two other shapes detaching themselves from the darkness surrounding the fallen spruce tree.

One of them sat partly concealed by the tree. It was an owl. At least, that is what Seved thought until it occurred to him that the wolverine shapeshifter had taken the head of an eagle owl and made it into a mask. The hooked beak hung down like a claw in the wide-open jaws of the predator, and the tufts projecting from the crown of its head looked frozen and rigid.

The other one was standing upright on bowed, dark furry legs and was jutting out the bony lines of his ribs as if it wanted to flaunt its unnatural manifestation. The slimy lump of gristle that bulged above the groove that was its mouth was not a nose or even a snout, and with every breath a fleshy flap of skin on each side of it flapped. It was trembling and panting with excitement. Around its neck was a strap with something metallic dangling from it that clinked as the creature expanded, and Seved realised they were ring pulls from old aluminium cans.

'Bring him out!' Jola roared.

By now he had raised the barrel and was aiming the black dot of its mouth directly at Seved.

'He's not here . . .'

'Bollocks!'

'He's in Sorsele,' Seved blurted out. He took a step backwards and one leg sank into the snow, forcing him to sit. 'We dropped him off there. At the hotel.'

Jola spat. Then he climbed off the snowmobile and lowered his head to walk into the shack and take a look. Amina was sitting up and staring at him, still half asleep. There were not many places to hide so he soon came out again and asked when they had left the boy.

'Early this morning,' Seved mumbled. 'About four, I think. I'm not sure . . .'

Jola put down the rifle and rooted around under his jacket. There was a rasping sound as he ripped open the cover of his mobile. He pressed the keys hard with his left thumb and it was clear he was agitated. Through his tight little mouth he drew sharp intakes of breath, and when the call went through he turned his back and in a tense voice said he had found them but they had let the boy go.

'In Sorsele,' he said. 'This morning.'

Jola pointed the rifle at them and ordered them to start walking, and Seved thought, Now, now he is going to shoot us. He even closed his eyes and stopped breathing for a few seconds, to prepare himself. I'll hear a bang, he thought, or I'll hear nothing, and everything will go black.

But there was no shot. They tramped through the snow, its surface rippled from the tread of the snowmobile. The engine spluttered at a low speed behind them. Amina walked in front, wrapped in the blanket she had taken from the shack. Occasionally one of her legs sank deep into the snow and a couple of times she fell over. The hares kept disappearing behind the trees but they never strayed too far from the procession.

Seved wondered what had happened to the wolverines and whether they were following at a distance, padding on their large paws. But he did not turn round to look. He did not want to know.

They had left the E4 at Luleå and driven in the direction of Boden, travelling south along the 356 towards Älvsbyn. The road was a narrow corridor through forests made dim by clouds of snow sweeping off the fir trees. Up ahead glowed the rear lights of a car and every time there was a bend in the road the red dots disappeared from view only to reappear almost immediately.

They were travelling on a straight stretch when Torbjörn braked so violently the seat belts jerked and Gudrun, now sitting in the back, cried out.

The car in front of them was stationary.

As they drew closer they saw it was inching forwards and then stopping again.

'What's going on . . .?' Susso sighed.

Torbjörn was craning his neck.

'A reindeer,' he said.

In the headlights they saw the animal's pale-grey rump as it ran in front of the car, its legs pumping and its hoofs slipping.

'You can't just bloody well stop like that!' Susso said, leaning across and honking the horn. 'You'd think they'd use their hazard lights!'

The reindeer had bounded into the deep snow at the side of the road and was leaping off into the birch trees, but the car in front didn't pick up speed. Instead, the engine was switched off.

The exhaust fumes drifted like a veil through the headlights of the Passat. Torbjörn was about to pull out and pass it when the driver's door opened and a man stepped out. His dark beard circled his mouth and he was squinting. The next second the door on the passenger side flashed as a second man got out. He was older and also had a beard, but his was longer and stuck out in a wiry grey frizz.

'Thanks for that,' Torbjörn said to Susso through gritted teeth.

The driver stood for a while looking in at them, before knocking on the window with the knuckle of his index finger. Torbjörn pressed the button and lowered the window. The man bent forwards but before he could open his mouth Susso leaned across Torbjörn's legs.

'You know that button with the red triangle?' she said. 'If you've got to stop on a road with a ninety speed limit, you might like to use it!'

The man said nothing. Taken aback by Susso's angry tone he had straightened up and stepped away from the car. Now he was slowly stroking his beard.

'We almost ran into you!' she went on. 'Don't you realise that?'

'I braked. You saw the brake lights . . .'

'Yeah, well, because you drive like a little old lady your brake lights have been on more than they've been off for the last few miles, so *that* was no help.'

'It's because of the reindeer,' the man muttered. 'You've got to take it easy.'

The older man was standing with his hands in his pockets and his shoulders raised. He was carrying a small knife with a horn handle on his belt. He said something but it did not carry into the car, and his friend shook his head and spread his hand across his chest. Then he walked swiftly off without looking back, the second man following him, but more slowly. They both got in the car but did not drive off, so Torbjörn swung out and overtook them.

The squirrel was awake and lively and clung to Susso's hand. Playfully she tried to shake it off but it hung on tenaciously. She inspected its front paws, stroking its claws with her thumb, bending them and feeling how sharp they were.

'What the fuck was that all about?' Torbjörn said.

'Two stupid hillbillies, that's what,' Susso said, without looking up.

'But don't you think they were a bit suspicious?'

'Hillbillies are suspicious. That's what hillbillies are all about.'

'But it was almost as if they were afraid. Of me.'

He held out his arms.

'And I'm not exactly a big guy.'

'There are four of us in this car,' Gudrun said hoarsely from the back seat. 'Don't forget that.'

'Yes,' replied Torbjörn, glancing at the squirrel, which was sitting on Susso's lap with its head on one side. 'But he's not very big either.'

'You saw what he did with the troll out there on the ice,' Susso said.

Torbjörn was quiet.

'He held it back just by looking at it,' she continued.

'But I thought that was something between them,' he said. 'Because of what they are. If he can also affect people, then it's like Gudrun said – he's dangerous.'

'So what shall we do?' said Susso. 'Throw him out?'

'No, but . . .'

'But what?'

'He's dangerous, that's all. So you've got to watch out.'

Susso nodded, looking out of the window.

'But he's nice as well,' Torbjörn added, grinning. 'Isn't he?'

Shortly before six that evening they arrived at the village of Rackvattnet. It consisted of a few weather-beaten houses clustered together on each side of the road. A boarded-up shop with lining paper taped over the windows slipped past in the car headlights and on a gentle slope they came across a man pushing a kick sledge. He walked with small shuffling steps and in the rear-view mirror Susso saw that he had stopped and was watching the car go by.

Susso studied the map in the dim light of her mobile's screen. She told Torbjörn to carry on and then pointed at a building standing behind a row of young birches.

'There,' she said. 'It has to be that one.'

As they approached the solitary house, a red brick single-storey building, they saw a tarpaulin stretched across the garage doors. The wind blew small waves in the sea-green plastic covering, and when Torbjörn pulled up and put on the handbrake they caught sight of a face through a gap.

'There's someone there,' Gudrun said.

A door swung open in the side wall of the garage and a tall, older man in a fleece jacket came out. The front door of the house had also opened and the man exchanged a few brief words through the crack with whoever had opened the door before walking up to them. Judging from the look on the face that peered through the car window he was not pleased to see them.

Susso stepped out. Black pine forest towered behind the

house, and from the treetops came a faint whispering. The wind tugged at the tassels on her hat as she asked if the man was Yngve Fredén.

He said he was.

By this time Gudrun and Torbjörn had climbed out of the car, and Susso stared up at Yngve.

'What do you want?' he asked.

'Do you happen to know a giant, Yngve?'

Yngve did not answer but neither did he look away, and Susso thought a look of sadness spread across his face. There was a tension in it that quickly disappeared. He had a strong, sculpted nose and the shadow it cast lay like a black fin over his cheek. Underneath his jacket she could see the collar of a checked shirt.

'A giant . . .' he said.

Gudrun was standing behind the car on the road, stamping her heels against the hard packed snow. She was holding her coat collar closed and hiding her mouth behind it.

'Oh, it's so cold,' she said. 'Can we go in and talk?'

'Well, I still don't know what you want,' Yngve said.

Still stamping her feet, Gudrun nodded towards the house.

'We wonder if you've had a giant living with you, because if you have, that giant is now lying in the freezer at the National Veterinary Institute. As a bear.'

A rectangle of light fell on the snow as the front door opened and then closed.

A woman walked towards them, and Susso realised it was Yngve's wife, Inger. Her down jacket was hanging crookedly from her shoulders and on her head she was wearing a cap. Her glasses glinted under the flat peak. With her hands in her pockets and without greeting them, she stood half a metre behind Yngve, who threw a look over his shoulder when he heard the snow crunch under her boots.

'And why', he said, 'would you think we have had a giant . . .'

'Because your neighbour saw him,' Susso said. 'When you lived in Kramfors.'

Yngve muttered something to his wife about going in and they began to walk. Susso ran after them with her hand on her stomach.

'Wait!' she said, and they both stopped immediately. The squirrel that was weighing down her front pocket was very still but she was sure it was not asleep.

'It's important,' she said.

'I think we want to go inside now.'

'Do you know anything about Magnus Brodin? The boy who vanished in 1978? Down in Dalarna?'

They shook their heads and she knew they were telling the truth.

'I presume you have heard about Mattias Mickelsson,' she said. 'The boy who disappeared at Christmas. The one they found in Sorsele today.'

'Yes,' Inger said. 'We saw it on the news.'

'We think the stallo folk might have taken him. And that they took Magnus too. Some of them are big, big as giants, and we have been told you had a giant living with you.'

'We've never kidnapped anyone.'

'But what about the giant? Did you have one staying with you?'

They exchanged a look, as if to agree on an answer.

'He's not here any more,' Inger said. 'He . . . he turned into something else and left.'

'A bear?'

She nodded.

'Yes,' she said. 'How did you know?'

'Because I shot him. He attacked me and so I shot him. But what I don't understand is how he could have found me.'

'We've been waiting to hear this,' Inger said. 'That he's been shot or something like that. But we haven't seen anything on the news yet.'

'It happened further south, outside Stockholm.'

Yngve looked puzzled.

'How would he have taken himself all the way down to Stockholm? That's impossible.'

'They can wander long distances,' Susso said, but Yngve found that hard to believe.

'He left, when was it, Sunday? Sunday afternoon, two days ago. So you're saying he travelled almost a thousand kilometres in two days? And when did he get shot, did you say? Today?'

Susso slowly shook her head.

'On Sunday,' she said. 'In the afternoon.'

'Then it can't be him,' Inger said. 'Because he was here then. He was at home. Yes, that was when he went berserk, or whatever it was.'

Susso looked over her shoulder and wondered if she ought to call the others, but she was afraid Yngve and Inger would clam up.

'What happened?' she asked.

'Well, you can see what the garage looks like,' Yngve said. 'I was standing there, clearing the snow, when suddenly he started growling and banging on the door. We had never seen him get angry before.'

'Oh yes we had,' Inger said.

'But not like that,' Yngve said. 'He was wild with rage. And for no reason at all. Before I knew what was happening he made firewood of the door and stormed out. And then I saw what he had turned into, although just at that moment I didn't realise it was him. I only saw a bear and I thought, This is it, I'm going to die. But he paid no attention to me. He didn't even seem to see me. His eyes were almost white and he ran past me and into the forest over there. And since then we've been waiting for them to say on the news that a bear had been shot. Of course, we didn't understand any of it . . .'

'But then it can't have been him,' Inger said.

By this time Gudrun had walked up to them. She had let go of her collar and her arms were crossed as she jumped from one foot to the other, surveying the red brick house.

'You might as well come in for a while,' Yngve said. 'So we can talk.'

It took them almost an hour to get down to the house and it was dark by the time they reached it. The walls looked black and the Advent lights were shining between the open curtains of Ejvor's room. Lennart was standing inside his camper van, watching the procession as it came out of the trees. He was bareheaded and his mobile was pressed to his cheek. There was no sign of Börje. On the other hand, the Volvo was there, parked beside the Isuzu, and when Seved saw it he was filled with an overwhelming sense of guilt.

The snowmobile fell silent and Jola climbed off and turned his cap round. He walked towards Lennart, dragging his feet in his heavy boots, and spoke softly to him. He had slung his rifle over his shoulder like a moose hunter. Lennart nodded, pulled out a handkerchief and began wiping his mouth, and after replacing it in his pocket he nodded again. He looked tired. White streaks of stubble fell into folds as he lowered his chin to his chest, where his dark glasses hung from a cord.

'Makes no difference,' he said loudly, and then he disappeared into the camper van, which swayed under his weight.

'Go in,' Jola said. He waved the rifle barrel. Towards Hybblet. Seved walked a few steps before asking over his shoulder what they were going to do in there, his voice trembling.

Jola told them to empty their pockets. Only the tip of his

blond stubbly chin showed below the peak of his cap as he spoke. Seved placed the keys to the Volvo and his torch on the veranda railing, which was dotted with footprints. Amina said she had nothing in hers.

'Jola,' Seved said. 'He's not down there, is he?'

'You'll have to wait and see.'

The staircase dropped steeply down into a dense darkness. The hide lay deep underground to maintain the correct temperature. Seved listened for any sounds but heard none, and he was not sure if that was a good sign or a bad one. There was no bannister so he went slowly with his knees bent, feeling his way with his fingers along the cold, damp concrete lining. Amina was close behind him. Her breathing hissed against his neck and she was gripping his shoulder tightly.

'Down!' commanded Jola, standing in the doorway.

At first Seved held his breath, a reflex action, but when he had come halfway down the stairs he had to take a breath. The fermenting, acidic stench of decay and excrement that filled his nostrils was so sickening that he threw himself backwards and retched violently, emptying his stomach of its contents. The vomit splashed down the steps and his eyes stung with tears. He had one hand on Amina's boot and the other on the rough wood. Then it went dark around them. Jola had shut the door, and when the lock was turned it felt as if the darkness itself was being locked.

'Watch out,' gasped Seved, wiping his lips. 'Mind you don't slip where I puked . . .'

There was no answer and that made him irritated, but also afraid.

'You've got to answer me, Signe!' he said, tugging at her boot. 'Otherwise I won't know where you are.'

She mumbled something inaudible.

When he had found his feet he stood rubbing his mouth to get rid of the remains that had fastened to his beard.

'We'll sit here,' he whispered, climbing back up.

He sat on the top step, leaning his shoulder against the door, and soon he felt Amina's fingers touching his face. He took hold of her hand and helped her.

'Sit here,' he said.

The smell of vomit lingered and he regretted wiping his mouth because the smell of his digestive juices was preferable to the hideous fumes that came from below. They sat still, listening, and Seved was convinced that any shapeshifters that were in the hide were doing the same thing. He did not believe Skabram was down there. They would have heard him by now, especially if he was angry. So that left only the little ones. He knew there was a badger in the hide, he had even seen it bolt past in the darkness early one morning, but no one really knew whether it was a shapeshifter or a normal badger that one of the big fellows had taken a liking to.

We're supposed to sit here and feel scared, he thought. That's all. Börje would never allow anything to happen to us. We're his children, almost.

'Seved.'

'Yes?'

'I think I've got to pee.'

'You'll have to go down a few steps and sit there. But watch out you don't slip.'

He heard her make her way down, very slowly, her thick-soled boots scraping on the stairs. Then she swore sharply through gritted teeth and he knew what she had put her hand on.

'Seved!' she hissed.

'What is it?'

'Something's shining down here.'

Surely not. Or was there a source of light down there he knew nothing about? Mystified, he stood up and crept down the stairs.

'Where are you?' he whispered.

'Here,' she said, and soon he caught hold of her thin, cold hand.

Seved stared out into the darkness. A light flashed. Once. Twice. He twisted his head and could hear that each flash was followed by a faint clicking sound.

Someone was playing with a light, switching it on and off every few seconds. And it was far away. Clearly the hide was not nearly as confined as he had thought and the unanticipated size of the cellar frightened him more than the strange light signals in its depths.

'Let's go up,' he said, grabbing Amina's jacket.

'But I've got to pee,' she said.

'Do it then, but come up afterwards. We'll sit up there, it's safest.'

'I can't! I'm scared! You've got to stay here!'

'Well, hurry up then.'

He heard her fumbling with her clothes.

'Promise you won't go!'

'I promise.'

'You mustn't go!'

'Here,' he said.

She felt for his hand and grasped it hard, and shortly afterwards he heard a splashing against the wood. When she had finished they crawled up to the door and sat down. Seved looked at his watch. The hands were pale but he thought it was seven fifteen. He shut his eyes. Then the stench returned. It had been lying there, in wait.

Inger and Yngve Fredén told them the troll had been with them since 1982.

'And during all that time you never saw the bear in him?' Susso asked.

She was standing in the garage, waiting for her eyes to get used to the gloom. There was a sofa covered in grey floral fabric, and blankets and fir-tree branches on the concrete floor, which was brown with old pine needles. Empty plastic bottles lay everywhere. Sheets of cardboard were tacked over the window and there was a smell of dog and rotting food.

Yngve shook his head.

'It came as a complete surprise. I mean, he was like a bear, I admit that, but we never imagined he could *turn into* a bear. I know it sounds strange. And I think it's strange, now he's no longer with us, that we never really talked about him.'

After sitting down in the kitchen Inger explained in a trembling voice that they had lost their son. They had moved to Kramfors to start again, and that is when the troll came to them. He had been sitting naked in the forest beyond their garden, looking at their house with small moist eyes. In his hand he held a birch twig that he slowly waved about him to keep the mosquitoes away, but also perhaps to wave at them. They had never been afraid of him, despite his appearance. It had seemed obvious from the very beginning that they would look after him. There had been no discussion about it either, and as the years passed they hardly mentioned him. He had simply been there, and they accepted him as he was. They had given him food and cleaned up after him, but never even tried to talk to him. It was not until now, after he had gone, that they realised how peculiar that was. They had not even given him a name!

'Can you understand that? Over twenty years and not even a name!'

They had no idea what he did all day because the windows were always covered. Presumably he slept a lot, on the floor on top of a heap of blankets and branches that he carried in. Roughly every third day he came out and lumbered up to the forest to answer a call of nature, leaving behind a huge stinking pile of faeces, and they were only too grateful he was house-trained, so to speak. Sometimes the radio would be on for an hour or so, always very quietly. They heard him sing sometimes too, but never any words, only a low humming as if he was trying to lull himself to sleep.

Occasionally he came into the house and sat for a while on the sofa and fell asleep, but they were never very comfortable with that because he smelled, and even if they were not exactly afraid of him, they never dared get too close. Some days he wanted to play. Couronne, for example. At those times he would appear at the window and tap on the glass with a stick that looked so tiny in his hand. They used to take turns playing with him. He knew he had to get the rings into the holes in the corners, but he never realised he had to shoot with the red ring, or that the rings had to be knocked into the holes. Instead he either pushed them with the stick or threaded them onto the stick and moved them slowly to the holes. Taking turns did not seem to bother him and it was never clear who had won, nor was it important. That is what he was like: quiet, sleepy and incomprehensible.

'Are you sure it wasn't him who took Magnus Brodin?' Gudrun asked.

No, they knew nothing about what he had done before he came to them. He had never said a word.

'We know for certain there are at least two of these giants,' Gudrun said. 'And there might be even more. So it wasn't necessarily him.'

'Have you got a picture of him?' Susso asked.

Inger shook her head.

'Take a photo of him? That was out of the question.'

Yngve agreed.

'The very thought of getting out a camera would never have occurred to us. That's probably hard to understand unless you have met him.'

Yngve asked about the giant they had shot in Stockholm and the circumstances surrounding his death. Gudrun explained what had happened on Färingsö and she told them about her father and the website and the photograph of the Vaikijaur man, about John Bauer's Lapland journey and his meeting with the stallo folk. Finally Susso was obliged to show them the squirrel. The sight of the animal curled up in Susso's pocket left them speechless and Yngve had to stand and walk up and down the kitchen because he did not know what to do with himself.

'All this,' he said. 'All this . . .'

They had let Torbjörn use their laptop and he sat with it at a kidney-shaped coffee table in the sitting room. He clicked on the trackpad and stared intently at the screen.

'Here,' he said suddenly, and started reading: '"The police are giving out a warning about an aggressive bear. A man was attacked by a bear when he was out walking in Storuman on Tuesday morning. He was scratched and bitten and now the police are warning the public not to go out in that area. The thirty-nine-year-old man was alone when, according to the information he has provided, he was subject to an unprovoked attack by a bear in Stensele, south of Storuman. The bear hit the man and bit him before he could get free, run away and climb a tree. The bear chased him as far as the tree but then ran off. The man climbed down, went home and raised the alarm, says Tomas Wretling of the Västerbotten police's communication centre."'

Susso and Gudrun had walked up behind him and were reading over his shoulder.

Torbjörn continued: '"Västerbotten police have sent a specially trained bear-tracking unit to the area. They advise the public not to go out of doors in Stensele for the time being. The man was taken to hospital to receive treatment for his wounds, which are not life threatening. Are they shooting to kill? 'Yes, they will destroy the bear,' says Wretling. 'That decision was made by the police authority and is based on the fact that the bear has injured someone and therefore constitutes a danger to the general public. We are presently waiting for our dog handlers and then we will set off.' When asked how common it is for a human to be attacked unprovoked, Wretling explained: 'This bear has quite literally woken up on the wrong side of bed. And you don't mess around with a fractious bear.'"'

'Where does it say that?' asked Inger. 'In *Västerbottens-Kuriren*?'

Torbjörn shook his head.

'*Dagens Nyheter*. Posted two hours ago.'

They carried on searching and it was not long before Gudrun

placed a hand on Torbjörn's shoulder and pointed. In the 'LATEST LOCAL NEWS' column on the *Norrbottens-Kuriren* site was an item with the heading: 'Let Sleeping Bears Lie? Not in Glottje.'

Torbjörn clicked on it and read:

'"A roused bear" – that's what it says – "has been sighted in a forest clearing beside the Västra Kikkejaure lake about five kilometres northwest of the village of Glottje in the municipality of Arvidsjaur."'

'Glottje,' Susso said. 'How far away is that?'

'It's just over a hundred and twenty kilometres to Arvidsjaur,' Yngve replied.

'And to Storuman?'

'I don't know. Maybe three hundred, by car. But the 94 runs in a straight line westwards and so does the 45, so it is more or less the same for a bear. Say two hundred and fifty then, as a bear travels.'

'The *Kuriren* article was posted at 15.09,' said Torbjörn, 'so it can't possibly be the same bear.'

'There are more of them, Torbjörn,' Susso said. 'I *know* there are more.'

Torbjörn kept his mouth shut when he saw the look Susso gave him.

'Right,' was all he said.

'There are four,' Susso said, looking down at the floor. 'Or rather, there *were* four.'

'Four?' said Yngve. 'How do you know there are four?'

Susso looked down at her pocket.

'Four bears,' she said slowly, looking the squirrel in the eyes. 'There have always been four bears, but now there are only three. And . . . that's not good.'

He could not sleep, of course, but it was not the fear of being woken by hefty footsteps on the veranda that kept him awake. It was the painful position he was sitting in and the fear that he would tumble down the steep staircase in his sleep. And then there was the cold. It was so cold he was shivering. Amina was not asleep either, he could tell, because from time to time she sniffed loudly.

She had asked him if he thought that Mattias was with his parents by now, and he had nodded and said yes. She had more questions but he was too tired to answer. Or rather, he did not want to, because he had picked up muted whisperings from down in the darkness. It was a shifter of some kind that could form words and was imitating them in a thin, hollow pitch.

Promise. Prrromise. We'll sit up there. It's safest. Promise you won't go. Promise, promise, promise. It's safest. Pee. I've got to pee. Pee, pee, pee. Where are you, where are you. Where aaare you.

After it had gone on for a couple of minutes Seved had been close to shouting at it to shut up, but he controlled himself. Shouting was guaranteed to make things worse, and it could also be dangerous. He had no idea who was down there. The little creatures mainly, he thought, but he could not be sure. At least one of them was big enough to use a torch.

They had been sitting in the darkness for several hours and he thought it was odd that Börje had not persuaded Lennart to let them out. Börje went along with most things but Seved knew he could refuse orders if he had to.

They must have locked them in the hide because they had discovered that Seved had chained the escape hatch shut.

There was a certain psychology to it. He had locked himself in. What he did not know was whether they had detected the smell of petrol he had poured on the floor of the jumping room, or whether they had worked out why he had blocked the emergency exit. There could not have been many reasons for doing that. Lennart had understood what was going on, without a doubt, and that was a double betrayal by Seved. He had not only let the boy go, he had also been working on a plan to burn Skabram to death. Attacking the old-timers was like attacking Lennart himself, or even worse. He must be beside himself with fury, and the more Seved thought about it, the more intense the fear inside him grew as he sat blinking in the darkness.

Finally he could not sit still any longer.

'We've got to get out,' he said, standing up.

Amina only sniffed in answer. He knew she was playing with the little mouseshifter she had slipped into her pocket unnoticed when Jola had fetched them from the shack.

'Can I borrow your scarf?'

She passed him the scarf, and after he had tied it over his nose and mouth he went slowly down. He used his hand to feel his way on the rough steps. The wool soon became warm and damp over his lips.

The entrance to the hide was a heavy fire door and he knew it would be almost impossible to break it down. Unless against all expectations he found a crowbar down there he did not stand a chance of getting it open.

He did not want to fumble around blindly but he thought he might start by borrowing the torch from whoever was playing with it. With the help of the torch he would be able to find his way to the tunnel.

In his pocket he had the key to the padlock. He had been sitting holding it so tightly in his hand that it had cut into his palm. It had probably not even occurred to Lennart that he might have the key on him. With a little luck he might be able to push up the two halves of the hatch enough to reach the padlock. And if that failed he could at least get an iron bar or something similar through the gap and manipulate it until the chain or the hinges gave way. It was certain to be impossible but he had to try. He could no longer sit there and wait. Too much time had passed and with every minute his suspicion was growing that Lennart and Jola had not locked them in simply to scare them.

When he reached the bottom and had taken a few steps along the cluttered concrete floor, hunched over, he stopped. It was a strain not being able to see anything. His eyes almost hurt. It was all the staring, he supposed.

He waited. Presumably the thing that had been holding the torch had fallen asleep. But he had a rough idea where the light had been coming from so he moved in that direction with one hand held out in front of him like an antenna.

Things crunched and scraped under his boots but he did not want to know what he was treading on. All he could do was try to breathe through his mouth, but it was as if his nose was curious because occasionally it drew in a breath of its own accord. Instantly the convulsions rose up and he had to turn his head away and cough into the scarf. It was the sweet, pungent smell of bloated, maggot-filled decomposition.

The small shifters were there. He heard them scurry off and then sit down.

He had moved about ten metres, he guessed, when his foot struck something solid but soft, something that did not crumble under his boot or move. He squatted down, reached out and his hand felt . . . a shoe. The tread of a rubber sole. His fingers continued upwards and he found himself stroking bristly reindeer skin and then a furry rim.

Ejvor's boot.

It was Ejvor lying here.

Horrified, he gasped for breath, drawing in the stench that surrounded the corpse like a dense film. He slapped his hand to his mouth, which he had uncovered, but his stomach was empty and he retched into his glove. He threw himself to one side and began to crawl away, overwhelmed by the feeling of revulsion.

But then he stopped.

The head torch. It must have been her head torch he had seen.

Whether some little being had taken it or whether it was still around her neck, he did not know. There was only one way of finding out.

With his chin pressed down on his chest, he crawled back. He waved one hand ahead of him and finally came into contact with Ejvor's denim-covered lower leg. When he had worked out which way was up he shuffled on his knees to get closer to her head. He turned his face away and took a deep breath. His hand fumbled around, sweeping hesitantly in circles. If they had been eating her, they would probably have started on her upper body, where it was softest, and the last thing he wanted was to put his hand into the mess of a crushed and gouged-out chest cavity. But he thought it was her cardigan he could feel under his glove, so perhaps they had not touched her after all.

He had to think about taking a breath again, but before he turned away he searched more urgently. And there it was, lying on her chest. As soon as his fingers had grasped the little head torch he began to pull it up towards her chin. The elastic band fastened onto something and he tugged as hard as he could. He felt her heavy head lift from the floor. Her neck cracked like broken wood.

When he had freed the torch he edged a short distance away and fumbled with the buttons. The light clicked on and in a dull, tight circle of light he saw the concrete floor, the cracks in it, and the carpet of brown pine needles. The battery would probably not last much longer.

He backed away to avoid the worst of the smell and because he did not want to accidentally see the state of Ejvor's corpse. He did not want to see what had happened to her face.

He walked with his knees bent, sweeping the lamp across the floor and the walls, which were lined with concrete blocks. He saw an upturned freezer that someone had filled with twigs and leaves and moss, a blue or perhaps grey child-sized rocking chair, a barrel used as a toilet and a rusty floor drain. There was an armchair that sloped because the legs on one side were missing, and a twisted woollen blanket on a bed of brown spruce branches. Was this where the big trolls slept?

Every so often he caught a glittering pair of eyes that slid away, but they belonged to the small creatures. The largest thing he saw was a vole with its stumpy tail running past in a straight line as if it was on a tightrope.

Close to the staircase was a sink. It was made of stainless steel and reflected the beam of light as the head torch found it.

Above it was a mixer tap with a long, flattened handle, and the water pipe ran alongside the wall and disappeared into an ugly hole. He hurried up to it, pulled up the handle and drank. The water was so icy cold it made his teeth ache.

'Signe,' he hissed up the stairs. 'There's water here if you're thirsty.'

Inger and Yngve Fredén said they were relieved the giant had gone and they had no plans to look for him. They did not even want to know what had happened to him. Now that the garage was empty they could not understand how they had managed to take care of him for so many years: cleaned him, given him food and guarded him. They had felt no affection for him, they realised that now. It had been something else, as if he had planted their fear inside them.

We were weary. At least, I was. I was tired of staying in hotels, and it was not exactly cheap. That is why I suggested with a long-drawn-out yawn that we ought to go home. It was only three hundred kilometres and we could manage that if we drove for an hour each. Then we would be able to sleep in our own beds and think about what we were going to do in peace and quiet. It might also be a good idea to talk to the police and find out what their thoughts were concerning the attack at Holmajärvi and the kidnapping of Mattias Mickelsson.

'Home,' Susso said, glaring at me coldly as she sat in the car with the squirrel in her arms. 'You mean home where there are people who want to kill me, Mum?'

Yes, '*Mum*,' she said, emphasising the word. How could I be longing for my own bed and my dog and my man when my own daughter's life was in danger? I was ashamed of how selfish and stupid I was. For some reason I had thought the threat to Susso had vanished now that Mattias had been found, but clearly I knew nothing about it. It was like Susso said under those copper pans and Sami boots at Vippabacken. The people who had gone for her had probably done so because of her website.

It wasn't about the boy. It was about her.

And the only thing we could do was track down the bear. With a little luck that would lead us to Mattias's kidnappers, as well as the people who wanted Susso dead. And that might also give us an answer to what had happened to Mona's son.

So we drove to a hotel in Älvsbyn.

Next morning, after I had showered and taken my last clean blouse out of the case, I went down to breakfast, where Susso was sitting with a bowed head, dropping pinches of muesli into the front pocket of her jacket.

'Are you mad?' I said, standing right in front of her. 'Think if someone sees you! We'll be thrown out!'

But the thought of being discovered with a rodent in her pocket in a restaurant didn't seem to worry her in the slightest. It was as if she hadn't heard me.

Torbjörn was slouched opposite her, drinking coffee and reading the *Kuriren*, so I turned to him and asked if there was anything new in the papers. He told me Susso had spoken to a man called Eskilsson at the council's environmental protection agency. He was a forest ranger in northern Västerbotten, and that morning he had received a phone call from a church warden who had found fresh bear tracks in the area around Lake Storavan. They ran in a westerly direction over the ice just north of the headland where

Bergnäs was situated, and according to Eskilsson, who had already been to the site and checked the tracks, there was no doubt it was the same bear that had been observed in the forest clearing north of Glottje. He thought it seemed strange that it had not found a new place to hibernate yet. Bears that wake in the middle of winter usually curl up under the first available fir tree or simply dig themselves down in the snow, but because this one had done neither they were keeping an eye on it. If it was feeling stressed for some reason, or sick, it could be dangerous.

'If only he knew,' I said, looking over at the breakfast buffet. People were queuing there, helping themselves, and that was making me feel stressed.

'So we thought we should head in that direction,' he said. 'Because it seems he knows where he's going, and it isn't far from Sorsele. So that might be something, considering that was where Mattias turned up.'

'But what have you told that forest ranger, Eskilsson? What is he going to think?'

'He just thinks I'm interested in bears,' Susso said.

'Interested in bears?'

She nodded.

'And, of course, I am.'

'You look tired. Couldn't you sleep?'

'Not really.'

'Are you having nightmares? Because I am.'

'I've got a headache,' she said.

I found a girl in a white blouse who worked at the hotel, and she soon returned carrying a plate with two tablets: one paracetamol and one ibuprofen. Susso took the tablets and washed them down with a glass of water that I fetched for her.

*

Some kilometres east of Arvidsjaur is a village called Deppis, and I couldn't help joking about that as we drove past the sign, and then at a villager who was shuffling along the roadside. Didn't he look awfully depressed? But I was the only one who thought so. Torbjörn was rustling a map he had taken from the hotel and Susso was talking on the phone to Ulf Eskilsson.

'Granmyrheden,' she said after the call had ended. 'There's an old guy there who has seen tracks that lead under a tree but don't come out. So that's probably where he is. It's by the Laisälven river and Ulf is on his way there now. If we're lucky, we'll be there before they . . . before they disturb him. I told him we know things about that bear that he doesn't know, but he didn't seem to be listening. He didn't seem too happy.'

'Hardly surprising,' I said.

'Here it is,' said Torbjörn, with his index finger on the map. 'Just over twenty kilometres on this minor road that runs north from the 45. Where are we now? Have we passed Arvidsjaur?

'Deppis,' I said with a sigh.

'A hundred kilometres,' Torbjörn said. 'You'll manage that in an hour, Gudrun.'

'Easy.'

The tunnel was a black rectangle in the far wall and Seved thought it looked small. He would only be able to get in if he bent down. Could the big old-timers really get through there? He lowered his head and held up the lamp. The walls were damp and it was impossible to see where they ended. Something was lying there in the circle of light – was it a shoe? Yes, a man's shoe, an old one. And further along there was a rock. It looked natural, a rock in these cavernous surroundings, but still it seemed odd. Someone must have carried it in. But why?

The passageway smelled musty and old, but it was a relief to be rid of that putrid stench of decay. He walked slowly, keeping an eye out for concrete blocks that had been displaced by the heavy ground frost. After he had gone a few metres he switched off the torch and in the darkness saw a fuzzy strip of light from the ventilation system, which consisted of a pipe that rose up out of the ground behind Hybblet and was topped with a cone-shaped steel hat.

The handle of the hatch grated as Seved slowly turned it. There could very easily be someone sitting up there guarding them, so he did not want to make a noise if he could help it. He noticed immediately that it would be impossible to get at the chain. The gap that appeared when he put all his weight against the hatch doors was less than a centimetre wide.

He crawled out of the tunnel and heard the tap running. It was bloody lucky there was water at least. He thought Jola could have mentioned it, but then again perhaps he thought Seved knew what was inside the hide. Either that or he didn't give a shit about them.

To save the fading batteries he switched off the light and inched his way back with his hands in front of him like a sleepwalker.

The blackness seemed to have paled imperceptibly, as if daylight was breaking through, but he was sure that was only his imagination. Or perhaps his eyes had adjusted somehow. The hide door was left open fairly often but even so he thought it was surprising that the old-timers did not go blind from spending so much time in the dark. But their eyes were different, of course.

When he thought he was close to the sink he flashed the light to orientate himself. He had not come as far as he had expected. Amina was standing with the blanket round her shoulders and he could hear she was moving her lips. She was talking to the little creature. During the night it had shapeshifted. 'Feel here,' she had said, but Seved had not really wanted to. He thought she should let the thing go. 'I'm not holding it,' she had said. 'It wants to be with me.'

He sank down on the bottom step and buried his face in his arms. They had been in the hide for over twelve hours and the hunger was gnawing at his insides. He had kicked over one or two tin cans on the floor but the thought of eating from them turned his stomach.

What would be waiting for them if they managed to get out? The hares would be waiting, that was for sure, spread out in the forest, quick to pass on the news. And the weasels. But mainly he thought about the wolverines. Jola must have had them with him.

They had frightened Seved and he did not want to think about them, but he could not help it. They appeared as soon as he shut his eyes. The one with the owl mask especially. It had stepped right out of a nightmare and frozen its imprint inside him.

Ulf Eskilsson sat in his car with his elbows resting heavily on his knees and his boots in the snow. His thin hair was sticking up in tufts that were damp with sweat and he was holding his woollen hat in his hand. He nodded silently at an older man in a green trapper hat who was leaning his hand against the door, talking. Beside the Volvo Eskilsson was sitting in stood a snowmobile, an old Ockelbo with a wide track and a trailer. Gudrun pulled up behind it.

'You know, the red fox kills the Arctic fox and they are both carrying scabies,' the older man said before clamping his mouth shut and glancing sideways at Susso, who was walking quickly towards them.

She could tell by looking at the men that they were shaken. It was obvious something had happened, something they had not bargained for. The snow was falling in large flakes across the narrow road, and Susso ran her eyes over the white, solidified forest.

'Well,' Gudrun said, slamming the car door shut, 'where's the bear then?'

There was a pause before Ulf Eskilsson answered:

'I don't know what it was, but it certainly wasn't a bear.'

'Have you seen him?' Susso asked.

They said they had.

'And he wasn't a bear?'

'Well,' said the older man, 'he was, partly. But not all of him, I can tell you that for sure.'

Susso gave Gudrun a worried look, and Gudrun's eyes narrowed.

The other man's name was Randolf Hedman. At about ten o'clock that morning he had been driving his snowmobile over the frozen river when he found tracks that crossed the ice and led into the forest. The previous day he had travelled the same route and there hadn't been any tracks then. He would be seventy-four in the summer and he had never come across a bear, so out of pure curiosity he had followed the trail for a couple of kilometres.

'I knew it wasn't sensible, considering what had happened in Jokkmokk in the autumn when that hunter was killed, but I wanted to see what Bruno was up to in the depths of winter. I just wanted to get a glimpse of him, of his back, I thought, from a distance. And on the other side of the marshes up here I saw that he had gone under a large spruce tree and hadn't come out. That was when I phoned the forest ranger. And when we got there, well . . .'

Randolf fell quiet and was waiting for confirmation, but none came. Ulf Eskilsson stared straight ahead with unseeing eyes behind the misty lenses of his glasses.

So Randolf continued:

'That's when he came out. I expect he heard the snowmobile. They don't sleep as deeply as people think and this one had just been up and about, of course, so he probably hadn't slept properly. But yes, it's like he says, it wasn't a bear. It was more like a troll, I would say. If I can use that word.'

'Yes, that's all right,' Gudrun said.

'He roared at us and we . . . well, we fell over, both of us. Sat down in the snow, like this.' Randolf bent his knees and flung out his arms.

'And there we sat. Pretty shaken, I can tell you. It was as if we were paralysed. And it must have been five, ten minutes before we got to our feet, and just as long again before we could say a word. By that time he was long gone. He set off in the direction of that mountain, Stor-Gidna, I noticed that. And we've been discussing whether scabies has made him like that, but we don't know. It has to be something else . . .'

Ulf looked up at Susso.

'What was that you said you knew?' he asked. 'About that bear . . .?'

'What?'

'You said on the phone you knew something.'

'Oh,' she said. 'Just that he could mutate like that.'

'Mutate?'

'How long has it been since you saw him?' she asked.

'It's twelve fifteen now,' he said. 'And I got here just after ten. But I can't say for sure how long we've been sitting here.'

'So two hours, max?'

He nodded uncertainly.

'It's no more than an hour,' Randolf said, 'since we saw him.'

Susso walked over to the car and took out her bag. She pulled a tangle of clothes out onto the seat and from the pile dug out a pair of blue thermal leggings and a thick jumper.

'Randolf,' she said, carefully removing her jacket and giving it to Torbjörn, 'we need to borrow your snowmobile. How much fuel is left?'

'What do you mean by *mutate*?' Ulf said, standing up unsteadily.

'I don't know about borrowing it,' said Randolf. 'But I could consider letting you hire it.'

Swiftly Susso undressed down to her bra and pants. She felt

the goosebumps spread over her thighs and upper arms. Gudrun protested, but mainly because Susso was stamping barefoot in the snow.

'How much do you want?' asked Susso, pulling a thermal T-shirt over her head.

'Well, that depends, of course, on how long you want it for,' said Randolf, who was polite enough to turn his head away and inspect the snow-covered treetops. 'But we could say a thousand kronor for twenty-four hours. Fuel included. And the tank is almost full.'

Susso turned to face Gudrun, who immediately shook her head.

'I've got no cash on me,' she said.

After Susso had picked up her jacket and put it back on Torbjörn opened his wallet.

'I've got twenty,' he said.

'You'll get the money when we bring it back,' Susso called as she walked over to the boot of the car to get Torbjörn's backpack. She pushed the plastic bag containing the revolver into the top section.

'I'll want a deposit then.'

By now Susso was fully dressed and carrying the backpack. She fastened the top straps and put her mitten to her Inca hat to straighten it.

'Okay, Randolf,' she said. 'I don't think we want to hire it after all.'

'Oh, right.'

'We would really prefer to borrow it.'

The old man frowned and then nodded.

'I suppose that's a possibility,' he said slowly.

'It's going to be very cold, you know,' Torbjörn said.

'And we want to borrow your ski pants as well,' she went on.

'My trousers . . .'

'Borrow. Not hire.'

'Oh,' he said, looking down. 'Well, I'm sure that will be all right.'

Slowly he undid his jacket, shrugged off the shoulder straps and pulled down his bright-yellow ski pants. When Susso saw that he was wearing only long johns underneath, she felt sorry for him.

'Mum,' she said, 'you'll have to drive Randolf home.'

Gudrun threw a look at the trouserless man and tightened her lips to prevent a smile breaking out.

'Ask the warden if we can borrow the GPS he's got in the car,' Torbjörn said in a low voice as he took off his jacket.

'Ulf!' Susso said. 'We're borrowing this!'

'That,' he said, without opening his mouth properly, 'that is a GPS receiver.'

'I know that, Ulf,' Susso replied with a smile. 'You haven't got a torch as well, have you?'

They were sitting leaning against the wall on either side of the sink when they heard determined footsteps on the porch above. It had been silent for over twelve hours and the sound terrified them. Seved grabbed hold of Amina and moved her to the side. They positioned themselves so that they would not be seen from the door as it opened.

'It's time now.'

It was Jola.

Amina did not move, but even so Seved held her tightly.

'Can you hear me? Come up now!'

They stood waiting in silence, hearing his panting and his impatience.

Eventually the door was shut. And locked.

'Come on,' Seved said. He switched on the torch and they hurried towards the tunnel. He pushed Amina ahead of him. She crept inside a short way and crouched down, looking at him.

There was the sound of heavy feet up above again. Light poured down the staircase and then they heard Lennart's voice:

'If you don't want to burn to death, you'd better come up now!'

Burn? Had he said burn?

'Seved! I'm setting fire to it whether you come up or not.'

Seved took a step towards the staircase.

'I want to talk to Börje,' he shouted.

There was silence for a few seconds and then Lennart said:

'Are you coming up or not?'

'Not until I've talked to Börje, I said!'

He waited for an answer but none came, and Lennart left. But the door was left open. The flight of stairs was illuminated and the sink was shining.

Seved wondered why they did not come down and get them if they were so keen on them coming out. Were there shapeshifters in the hide that they wanted to avoid?

An hour or so later Seved thought he heard a car engine. A diesel engine, idling. The camper van probably. He walked closer to the stairs but he wasn't sure. He asked Amina if she had heard anything, but she only shook her head.

Had they left? He wondered whether he dared go up and look. But just then there were heavy footsteps above and Jola came and stood halfway down the staircase.

'Seved,' he said quietly, 'he's serious. We're setting light to the house. We've got to leave here, and quickly. So you've got to come up now.'

Seved had become trapped in his silence but now he was beginning to feel uncertain. It actually sounded as if Jola was telling the truth. But why could he not talk to Börje? That could only mean they had hurt him, and if that was the case it was highly likely he and Amina would meet the same fate.

'Why can't I talk to Börje?'

'He and Lennart have gone. It's only me left.'

'If I can't talk to Börje, then we're not coming up!'

Jola had bent down and was staring into the darkness. He muttered something and then ran back up the stairs. Seved turned towards Amina. She sat curled up with her arms wrapped around her legs in the opening of the tunnel. She was still holding the creature. Shit, that shifter! Could it have somehow managed to make its fear stick to them? He squatted down below her, leaned his back against the wall and waited.

About five minutes later Jola returned.

'Are you coming?' he shouted from the doorway.

Seved did not bother answering.

The next moment something bounced down the stairs with a hollow sound and landed on the concrete floor. It was the petrol container, green with a yellow label. Seved stood up and watched as a blue snake with a fin of flames shot down the stairs.

It was as fast as lightning and it found the container in no time.

The flames that leapt up in the darkness forced Seved backwards.

The rubbish on the floor caught alight and the flames crackled on the wooden staircase. Billows of blue-grey smoke surged forwards under the roof. There was a rustling of small feet as the animalshifters fled up the stairs. Petrified, Amina had vanished into the tunnel, and he followed after her. She crawled ahead of him, her boots scraping against the concrete, and he soon caught up with her. He almost wanted to fling her out of the way to get past. Panic was snapping at his heels. We're going to die here, he thought. The smoke will suffocate us.

Then it struck him that Jola might have taken off the chain. Perhaps they only wanted to smoke them out, to teach them a lesson. Yes, that must be it.

But the hatch doors would not open.

The chain rattled and a crack of watery light opened up. With all his strength he rammed his shoulder against the steel plate. He lay down and kicked wildly with his right foot, then stood up and pushed and thumped powerlessly.

'Open!' he screamed. 'For God's sake!'

Were they standing out there, grinning? Or did they mean business? Had they left already? He pounded and pounded and then sank down and leaned his head against the frozen concrete wall at the end of the tunnel. His eyes were stinging already and he knew there was nothing they could do. He heard Amina's hand patting weakly but unceasingly against the hatch, heard her cracked voice and her coughing.

The snow fell thicker and thicker, and they drove as fast as they could, but the machine was heavy and difficult to manoeuvre. When Torbjörn revved the engine as far as it would go it began to complain and splutter, and he swore loudly.

They followed the track Randolf had made and without any difficulty found the tree where the large creature had found shelter. It was pitch dark underneath so they decided not to look there and rattled on past. Time was short and the tracks left behind by the bear would soon be snowed over. For a long way it had lumbered along the edge of the marshes, where the snow was packed down hard by the wind, but after a few kilometres the tracks veered off into the forest. It was considerably harder for them to make progress in there, but at least the snow was not falling as heavily.

Torbjörn rested one knee on the seat and tugged the handlebars hard, and they leapt forwards over the deep snow. Susso lifted her backside to counteract the jolting as best she could. Slowly but surely the old Ockelbo covered the ground. Periodically Torbjörn twisted the throttle as he steered the skis to the side, zigzagging between the overhanging birch branches and stooping fir trees.

The shadows had deepened and Susso worried about the encroaching darkness. When night fell it would be practically impossible to follow the trail.

She supported the GPS against Torbjörn's back and tried to zoom out to see what kind of terrain lay ahead, but her fingers froze and it was hard to use the navigation buttons with her gloves on. They had driven through a hollow filled with stunted birches but now the ground sloped steadily upwards. Susso jumped off and ran beside the snowmobile as Torbjörn made his way diagonally upwards. If it continued like this, it would be faster to go on foot. But they would be able to make up for lost time on the marshes, where they could get up some speed. The only question was what the troll would do when he heard the sound of the approaching snowmobile. Attack them, probably. The squirrel had shielded her on the ice and she supposed it would shield her again. There were only two cartridges left in the revolver, and she had not forgotten what the police officer told her at the hospital: she had been lucky to bring down the bear with such a feeble old weapon. Yes, hunting down a troll like this without stopping to think was like putting your life on the line, but as she had told Gudrun with a grin when she had seen her anxious face, they could not stop now.

It was doubtful she would ever get as close again. The troll was maybe a kilometre or two ahead of them, and anyway the danger she was facing now by following the troll had to be weighed against the danger she was already facing and would continue to face until she found the people who had tried to get her in Kiruna. She unzipped the pocket on the front of her jacket to let the squirrel out. It sat on her shoulder and settled down, and she felt safe with it there.

They had juddered down a hillside and there in front of them was the wide expanse of marshland the troll had crossed. They were going fast now, trailing a cloud of snow behind them. Torbjörn lowered his head below the frosty windscreen and Susso hid her head behind his back, feeling the squirrel's long whiskers sticking into her cheek like nails.

The revs slowed and they glided gently down a ridge of snow to find themselves on a forest road lined with snow poles. Torbjörn drove alongside the ploughed wall of snow, craning his neck. There were no footprints on the other side and the trees were growing so tightly together it was impossible to see where one began and the other ended.

'We'll have to go up and look and then come down again,' Susso said, pointing. Torbjörn nodded and swung the snowmobile round.

They went so slowly that the exhaust fumes caught up with them. Torbjörn stood looking for tracks, while Susso read the GPS screen. Giertsbäcken and Giertsjaure. Gångstig. Jippmotje. Further on there should be a church. She thought that was odd because they seemed to be in the middle of nowhere. The squirrel clawed around on her shoulder and then hopped down onto the road. It sat still for a moment or two and then darted forwards, only to stop again. Then it carried on a few metres before running up the wall of snow and vanishing in among the trees.

'He's off,' said Torbjörn.

Susso nodded.

Further on there was a sign. It was covered in snow but the blue paint was visible. That meant they were approaching a village.

'There are a few houses here,' Susso said, studying the GPS map. 'And a church.'

'Shall we go up there then,' Torbjörn yelled over his shoulder, 'and find out if anyone's seen anything?'

'Seen anything?' she said. 'That could very easily be the place he's run off to.'

Torbjörn sat down in his seat. Then he turned the handlebars and began carefully swinging the snowmobile round.

'What shall we do then?'

There was no need for Susso to answer. The squirrel had run out into the road a few hundred metres away, and when they drove in its direction it scrambled up a ridge of snow and raced backwards and forwards. Susso climbed off, and a few metres in among the trees she found deep holes in the snow.

Pulling together they managed to get the old machine to the side of the road and then waded into the forest on foot. Branches tore at their jackets, and here and there sharp sticks protruded from the snow, trying to stab them. They caused slabs of snow to slip from the heavily laden spruce trees and it soon became such an effort to move that neither of them had the energy to speak. They stopped frequently. The squirrel was ahead of them the whole time. They had been trudging for about half an hour when Torbjörn's mobile started ringing. It was Gudrun, wanting to know how it was going and where they were. Susso told her they were close to a hill called Varåive, and Torbjörn repeated the name several times.

'It's almost impossible to get lost with one of these,' Susso said, holding up the GPS. Then she added, as an afterthought: 'As long as the battery's charged, of course.'

'How much is left?'

'More than half.'

Torbjörn glanced at his mobile.

'Mine's almost run out. I should have charged it before we left.'

They were both worn out and neither of them felt like struggling on straight away so they stood where they were, surrounded by towering spruce trees wrapped in utter silence. Susso's legs were very cold. She looked up at the treetops and the sky, where the lower layer of clouds was constantly moving. It was rapidly getting darker and she thought it had felt better when they were sitting on the snowmobile. Now the giant could emerge from anywhere and they would have no chance to get away.

The squirrel seemed eager. It had hopped down into the snow and was leaping from one of the bear's deep footprints to another as if to show them which way to go.

Susso scratched herself with the GPS, the solid antenna against her cheek.

'Okay, we get it,' she said. 'But you'll have to wait for us. We can't run in the tracks like you can.'

But the squirrel did not seem to realise that they understood. Torbjörn inserted some snus, clicked the tin closed and looked at the little animal in amusement. It was embroidering the snow with its impatient circling.

They trudged on with the squirrel in front, at times so far ahead it was out of sight. Sometimes it ran into the trees, seldom visible, but branches dipped and snow came crashing down. They heard it rustling inside a fir tree, and as they strode past it chattered. It seemed to be excited. Susso waited for it to come up to her, but when there was no sign of it she walked under the tree and looked up among the branches. She could see the squirrel sitting upright with its claws embedded in the trunk. Then she almost lost her balance.

High up in the shadowy gloom hovered a pale, gaunt face.

'Torbjörn,' she said softly.

'What is it?'

'Come and see.'

The snow crunched as he bent over to get under the tree.

He jerked back when he saw it, but he said nothing.

'Isn't that him?' Susso said.

Torbjörn nodded, the hard bulge of snus disfiguring his lip.

It was a man's head, wedged in the fork of two branches. The blood on his shredded neck was almost black. His mouth was gaping open and his teeth and tongue were grey. One of his eyes was staring, the other was out of sight behind the branch. But it was still possible to recognise him. It was the man with the axe. The man Torbjörn had wrestled to the ground and punched on the jaw in Holmajärvi.

'Oh shit. What's he doing here?' Torbjörn said.

It was not intended as a question.

Susso removed the backpack. She opened the top section, pulled out the plastic bag and unfolded it. She took out the revolver, tugged off her glove with her teeth, released the cylinder and checked that the cartridges were in the right place.

'Fuck it, we've got to call the cops now,' Torbjörn said, striding up to her. He was frowning and wiping the snot from under his nose. His voice was tense and she thought he looked like his father. It was a resemblance she had never noticed before.

Susso pushed in the cylinder with a click and put her glove back on.

'All we have to do is give them the GPS coordinates,' he went on. 'They'll be here immediately. It's murder! He's been murdered!'

'What, you think a human has done this?' she said, nodding towards the tree. 'Ripped off his head and climbed up into a tree with it?'

Torbjörn stared intently at her, and even the squirrel had come out onto a swaying branch.

'We've got to phone.'

'Then we'll never get them. And you know it.'

She started walking. The squirrel was already ten metres ahead of her.

They made their way down a slope and crossed a small lake. The bear's tracks had divided the frozen surface in two. Susso slipped a few times and dropped the revolver in the snow. She brushed some of it off with her glove, blowing the rest away. She asked Torbjörn if he thought the mechanism had frozen, but he did not answer. His eyes were fixed on the GPS, which is why he almost collided with Susso when she stopped.

'Can you smell it?'

'What?' he said, pulling his hat straight.

'I can smell smoke.'

He sniffed and then nodded.

'Yes. And that's some fire.'

They raised their eyes and soon saw the smoke drifting over the treetops in thick black billowing clouds. They walked faster, almost running. They were on a hill and down below, between the trees, they saw the fire.

The whole place was going up in flames.

Susso noticed the squirrel had huddled down and its whiskers were trembling. Its head was jerking up and down repeatedly and it was hard to tell whether it was afraid or excited. Torbjörn had phoned Gudrun to tell her where they were, and for a moment they stood there staring at the fire filling the sky with driving clouds that looked as if they were illuminated from within.

They walked closer and soon a facade of fibre cement slabs appeared between the trees. It was covered in black scorch marks.

There was the sound of explosions and crackling, tongues of fire shot up and Susso heard a window shatter into pieces. Flakes of soot floated down, dotting the snowdrifts with black.

Then suddenly the squirrel, which had been riding on Susso's shoulder, leapt down. Susso did not want to lose sight of it, so she ran after the bushy tail as it wove through the trees. It was not easy to see it in the strange atmosphere created by the powerful, glowing flames unfurling in the smoky night-time darkness. Wading through the snow she broke through the trees, hearing Torbjörn behind her. He was yelling at her to stop.

The squirrel sat in the snow, and there was a fox too, watching her. Its ears were erect, its breast white. Her first thought was to scare it away in case it went for the squirrel. But then she realised it was not a normal fox. When she came closer it trotted off in a semicircle, and the squirrel moved in the opposite direction.

And then she heard it.

A sound like someone banging. Under the ground.

Confused, she looked at the snowdrift.

It was moving.

There was someone underneath.

Or something.

She took a step back and looked at Torbjörn, who had caught up with her. He had also heard the sound. His mouth was hidden below his collar and he gave her a dark look as he slowly shook his head.

Susso clutched the revolver indecisively.

He was right. It could be anything down there.

But surely the squirrel would not risk putting her in danger?

She cleared away the snow with her boot until a pair of iron handles appeared, wrapped with a glinting silver chain. A metal hatch cover. Right in the middle of the forest.

She took a step forwards and stamped on it.

She heard screaming from below. It was impossible to make out the words but there was no doubt that there were people down there screaming for their lives. Susso tugged at the handles and shouted that she would help them. Then she ripped off her glove and put the revolver to the chain, but the sudden fear of the bullet ricocheting off the metal made her turn away as she squeezed the trigger. She was unclear whether she had missed or whether the chain was too strong, but the shot had no effect apart from making the fox run off and the squirrel scurry up the nearest tree. Now she had only one cartridge left, and because she did not want to waste it she began kicking the padlock as hard as she could.

'We've got to find something to break it with!' Torbjörn said.

'Run and find it then!'

She yelled at him to hurry but instead he stood rooted to the spot. She realised he was afraid.

'Ring Mum!' she called over her shoulder as she raced towards the house. 'Tell her where we are and that it's burning like hell! And there are people here!'

She was racing towards the blinding heat of the fire, with the squirrel running in front of her. She had dropped her glove, so she drew the hand holding the revolver back inside her jacket sleeve. She had very little energy left and soon slowed down to walking pace. That was probably sensible because she did not have a clue what to expect. Was the bear here?

The trees thinned out.

Apart from the building they had seen from the forest there was a two-storey house that was in flames and a large barn spewing out smoke through its doors. In the yard stood an all-terrain vehicle, but there was no sign of any people. The squirrel climbed up onto her shoulder. The fire roared and crackled around them and the smoke surged in dense clouds. Susso blinked. A stinging feeling penetrated deep behind her eyes. She persevered onwards and then the squirrel jumped down.

'Come on,' she said.

But it refused. It sat in the snow, panting.

Inside the dog compound lay a few grey furry bodies. They were still. Susso saw the white underside of a curled tail and stayed where she was, her hands resting on her knees. Had they died from the heat? Or the smoke? She squeezed her eyes shut and spat, then carried on towards the barn, bent double in the heat.

The smoke had intensified in the tunnel and now their eyes were stinging so badly they could hardly keep them open. They coughed violently and helplessly, and Seved had to keep his mouth open. All he could do was try to bury his face in the crook of his sleeve, which had become soaking wet with his saliva. He could not understand why the fire had spread so fast in the hide; after all, it was mostly made of concrete. Had Lennart and Börje prepared the room in some way?

Amina had been banging constantly on the hatch, and when they realised there was someone on the other side Seved rose up and joined in. He banged as hard as he could with his fist and yelled and shoved and tugged at the handle.

He thought it had to be Börje. That he had kept himself hidden until Lennart and Jola had set off and now he had come to let them out.

But it was a woman shouting hoarsely through the gap into the smoke-filled darkness, and Seved, confused, thought it must be Kicki Hedman from Storsjö, their nearest neighbour, or someone from over Bergnäs way. Naturally, the flames would be seen from a distance.

They did not have much time left, he knew that. The fumes would poison them and they would probably not even be aware of it. Their lungs would burn. It would not take many breaths.

'Hurry!' he and Amina screamed together.

Then Seved shouted in a cracked voice:

'I've got the key!'

He leaned his shoulder heavily against one half of the hatch, while Amina wedged her fingertips under the metal rim and pulled the other half inwards as Seved tried to push the key out through the gap. It did not work. The gap was too narrow. If only he had a piece of wire!

'The mouse!' he yelled. 'Where's the mouseshifter?'

They searched about clumsily in the light from the head torch and called the little being. Amina found it and Seved felt her cold hands pressed to his as she gave him the squirming little body.

'Here,' he said, holding the key towards the little mouseshifter. 'Take this key. You can get out. And then you can give it to the woman outside.'

The key was big for the shifter. It held it like a shining guitar and it was impossible to tell if it had understood the instructions. Its mouth hung open. Seved shouted that they were going to try and get the key out. Then he thrust himself towards the hatch and pressed his fingers into the gap to widen it.

'You've got to get out through there,' he said.

'It's too narrow,' Amina said. 'He can't.'

'He has to!' bellowed Seved, ripping off the head torch and giving it to Amina so that she could direct it at the gap and show the creature the way out. But the little thing did not seem to understand.

'I think he's afraid.'

'What the hell has he got to be afraid of? We've got to get out, for God's sake!'

'He is afraid,' she said, coughing. 'He's afraid of dropping the key.'

She was exhausted and leaned against the wall, breathing with short, sharp breaths. Under her filthy jacket her chest heaved constantly. They did not have much time left.

Seved crawled into the tunnel in the direction of the ventilation pipe.

'Come here!' he called. 'You can get out this way!'

It was hard work for the mouseshifter to make its way while holding the key, so Amina picked it up and crept along the tunnel towards Seved. Seved held it up to the mouth of the pipe in the roof of the tunnel. But Amina told him to wait.

'Take off your necklace,' she said to him. 'So we can tie the key to him.'

Out of habit he pushed his hand behind his hair, but then he ripped off the necklace. It consisted of a leather thong holding a medallion that Börje had given him. Amina gnawed at the thong and then pulled it in two. Seved crouched down to illuminate her hands and in between coughing told her to hurry.

After she had threaded the key onto the strip of leather and fastened it around the mouseshifter's delicate neck she lifted the little thing up so it could get into the pipe. They heard its claws rapidly scrambling upwards. But it did not get far. There was a scraping sound and it came sliding back.

Amina had taken off her jacket and rolled up one of her sleeves. She took hold of the mouseshifter and pushed it up the pipe. Her arm was so skinny she could push it in all the way up to her shoulder.

'Is it working?' Seved asked, his mouth pressed to the sleeve of his jacket. His eyes were blinking frantically in the caustic smoke.

'We'll see,' Amina answered, pulling a face.

Amid the smoke from the blaze Susso went through corridors that ballooned towards her and shrank back as she made her way forwards, but it was impossible for her to get close to the flames inside the barn. The heat was like a wall, and when she tried to break through it felt as if the skin on her face was scorching. So she turned and ran back to where the squirrel had left her. It was still sitting there, and when she came running out of the grey haze it ran up her arm and sat on her shoulder again.

After looking about she ran to the jeep and tried the door. It was unlocked, and after checking the seat to see if there was anything she could use to break the chain she ran round the vehicle and opened the tailgate. She foraged among the various items but there was nothing there either that she could use, so she ran back.

'I couldn't find a bloody thing,' she panted as she came up to Torbjörn. He was kneeling deep in the snow beside the hatch as the roaring blaze in the building closest to them made the shadows of the trees dance around him.

'They've got a key,' he said. 'They shouted that they've got a key and they're trying to get it out. But the crack is too narrow so they can't.'

A furious chattering made Susso look up, and then she bent down under the branches and switched on the torch. The squirrel was running in circles around a pipe that was protruding from the white ground. It was a steel pipe with a cone-shaped hat topped with snow. Susso squatted down and shone the torch onto the pipe.

Torbjörn walked up heavily behind her. He leaned forwards, his hands on his knees, and sniffed loudly. Susso knocked the torch against the pipe and heard shouting from below.

'Wait! He's coming up.'

'What?' Susso shouted. She could not work out what they meant.

'He's coming now!'

A few seconds later a small grey ball fell into the snow below the pipe, and when Susso shone the torch on it she saw it was a mouse. She was amazed and almost fell backwards because the mouse was standing upright. The head turned as the wrinkled face of a little old man shrank back from the powerful beam of the torch.

Around its neck was a leather strip with a key hanging from it, and as soon as Susso saw it she put the torch down in the snow, where it sank in an eerie ball of light. She reached out her hands to the little object, which stiffened as she gently worked the knot loose with her frozen fingers and took off the key.

When they had opened the padlock and unwound the chain from the handles the hatch doors flew up, and in the smoke that billowed out and turned Susso's eyes into two watery slits someone came crawling out. It was a thin girl with black hair hanging down in frizzy strands. She crawled a few paces before collapsing. Susso helped her up because she was only wearing a sweatshirt and the snow was deep. For a moment the girl stood bending over and coughing violently, before staggering a few steps to one side and sinking down on all fours.

'You've got to stand up,' Susso said, tugging at her. 'It's better for you. You'll get more air in that way.'

Then Torbjörn called out, and when Susso turned round she saw that he had climbed down into the smoke-filled opening. She hurried over and grabbed hold of a bearded man who Torbjörn was trying to get to stand up but who seemed barely conscious. His face was grey and his mouth gaped open. Together they pulled and pushed him up through the hatch. When they got him out they were not sure what to do with him, so they laid him down in the snow. Within seconds he came round and tried to stand up. With lumps of snow on his back and his neck, he bent over, slurring the same words over and over again, and they realised he was probably asking about the girl, who by now had picked up the strange mouse and was holding it to her hot cheek as she shivered in the cold.

'She's here,' Susso said. 'She's okay.'

The squirrel sat at her feet and she picked it up. She started brushing away the snow that had gathered in its tail as she studied the man.

'I have to ask,' she said. 'Are you Magnus?'

I had parked outside Randolf Hedman's house in Sorsele, but Randolf seemed unwilling to get out of the car. He sat there, picking at the loose threads of his long johns and looking at me with tired eyes. He wanted to know more and more about our strange journey, and that was lucky really because when Torbjörn phoned telling us about the fire and that they were at a farm somewhere between the Råvojaure and Jumovaure rivers, Randolf said he thought the place was in the direction of Ammarnäs, so we headed that way. There was no trace of any smoke, but it had become overcast with heavy grey clouds and it wasn't easy to tell if we were on the right road, but I trusted Randolf because he had lived in the area all his life.

We drove up into the forest on a narrow road. Just as the fire became visible as a golden-brown glow in the sky, we met a man stumbling along the roadside.

He tugged the rear door handle open hard and threw himself onto the back seat, shouting at me to reverse. Of course, I wanted to know why, but I soon found out.

Two bears came lumbering towards us along the road, looking grey in the darkness. It seemed the headlights were keeping them back because they stopped directly beyond the beams of light. Randolf pushed down the door lock on his side and I did the same. I suppose that's the kind of thing you do in drastic, life-threatening situations – you react instinctively, so stupidly that it makes you embarrassed afterwards. We sat there for ages, staring at the huge animals wandering backwards and forwards in the dark. Occasionally we saw their small eyes like shiny buttons.

The man in the back seat panted and whimpered. He wheezed as he breathed and it seemed he could not decide whether to lie down on the seat or sit up. Between gasps he said he had wounded one of the bears and they were dangerous.

'Drive!' he said. 'Drive, for God's sake!'

I expect the bears had worked out that the headlights were not as dangerous as they thought, and soon they were so close I could see their nostrils.

'Perhaps you ought to reverse,' Randolf said.

But I shook my head.

'Susso is up there.'

'There's no one there!' the man said. 'I promise you, there's no one there.'

Flashing the headlights at full beam was no good, so I tried hooting. That made one of the bears stop and tilt its head to one side. It annoyed the other and it ran towards the car, hitting a wing mirror with such force it snapped off. The man shouted from the back seat:

'If you don't back out of here, they'll tip the car over!'

It looked as if he was right, so I put the car into reverse and rolled slowly backwards. The bears followed, of course. I increased speed but drove carefully because the road was winding and in the dark it wasn't easy to see where the bends were. But soon I managed to put thirty metres between me and the bears.

'Randolf,' I said.

'Yes?'

'Hold on!' I said, putting it into first.

I pressed the accelerator so hard that the tyres skidded. Randolf clutched the handle above the door, taking my advice literally. I hooted again and flashed the headlights.

The bears waited for a long time and I thought they were never going to move. But finally they did. They lurched off on opposite sides of the road. The one on my side of the car had his jaws wide open as I drove past.

After that I floored it because naturally they came after us, and this time they were running, so Randolf informed me.

A little further along the road was an upturned car, and as we passed it we saw flames shooting up behind the trees. It wasn't until then that I remembered that Torbjörn had told me to phone the fire service. But at that moment all I could think about was Susso. And the bears, of course. I got out my phone and tried to ring Torbjörn, but the driving took all my concentration, so I threw the phone to Randolf.

'Redial the last number!'

Randolf tapped with his thumb, and when the call was answered he introduced himself by his first and second name and even added that he was the owner of the ski trousers Torbjörn had borrowed.

'Ask where they are!'

'She is wondering', he said ponderously, 'where you are.'

With my hand pumping the horn I drove right into the fire. That's how it felt, anyway, as if we were hurtling ourselves straight into a sea of fire. Every building was alight and the sky was flickering yellow with all the smoke that had gathered like an enormous ceiling over everything. The barn walls were bulging out and the roof of one of the buildings had fallen in. But the yard was big, so I was brave enough to park in the middle. Randolf informed me that it was dangerous, but I told him I was not going to drive away without Susso. The bloke in the back seat didn't say a word. He seemed happy as long as the bears were not around.

They came running up in a line, first Torbjörn and then two people I didn't know, a man and a girl. Susso came last, with the squirrel on her shoulder.

Randolf opened the door. 'Jump in!' he shouted.

When we had driven out of the smoke, I turned to look at Susso and Torbjörn, who were lying in the luggage compartment at the back, coughing.

'What the fuck is he doing here!' Susso exclaimed when she saw who was sitting in the back seat. It surprised me that she knew who the man was, and I told her we had picked him up along the way, with two bears breathing down his neck. Practically shouting she explained that he was one of the two men who had attacked her and Torbjörn in Holmajärvi. The man in question sat immobile, staring out of the window. He had nothing to say.

We drove back past the upturned car, and further along we came across the bears.

'Well, Susso,' I said, slowing down, 'there they are. I don't think we'll get any closer than this.'

The man we had rescued broke his silence.

'Drive,' he said. 'There are three of them. The third one's keeping out of sight but he's much more dangerous than the others, and if he gets close, we're done for, all of us. So drive!'

It sounded as if he knew what he was talking about, so I drove on, but after we had travelled a short distance in silence Susso shouted at me to stop.

'You're getting out of this car,' she said to the man.

The man did not move, and I assumed he was going to refuse. But then I heard him fumbling for the handle and opening the door. Randolf protested. It was like murder, he said.

'Perhaps you would like to get out as well, Randolf?' Susso said. 'There are six of us in the car, after all, and that is illegal.'

'No,' he said, considering the prospect. 'I'd prefer not to.'

'That's all right then.'

I drove on and I could see the man's back in the rear-view mirror as he stiffly climbed down into the snow at the side of the road, and I remember I felt dreadfully sorry for him and that I was already ashamed of what I had done.

Jola Haapaniemi was his name and nobody knows what happened to him after he stepped out of my car that evening at the end of January 2005, when the Öbrells' farmstead was burning. The police found Ejvor Öbrell's charred remains in a cellar and subsequently her younger brother, Börje Öbrell. Parts of him, at least. I think it was a lower leg and lower arm the dogs unearthed from the snow. The police never located the actual head, even though Susso had given them the GPS coordinates. Whoever had put it in the tree had moved it, maybe to keep it as a trophy or to have as dessert. The wolverines, perhaps. It's the kind of thing they do, decorate trees with the ripped-off heads of their prey, and no one really knows why they do it. Perhaps they don't even know themselves.

But, as I say, nobody found a trace of Jola Haapaniemi, apart from his car, and when the guilt makes me break out in a cold sweat at night I try to persuade myself that he got away somehow. That the bears left him alone. Because Randolf's words, when he said it was like murder throwing him out, they come back to haunt me, I can tell you.

I know I should have put a stop to it, but at the time it seemed reasonable, even the right thing to do, to throw him out. Susso explained afterwards that she wouldn't have had any rest until he had ended up the same way as the man in the tree.

It was not until later that we found out there was someone called Lennart Brösth, and if there was anyone Susso should have been afraid of, it was him. It was Mona who phoned and told us that. She had been to Umeå to talk to Magnus, who was in prison there. When we were driving away from the farm neither Magnus nor Amina had said a word. They were so overwhelmed that I had chosen not to bother them with questions. We had gone our separate ways, more or less without saying a word, after we had managed to stop the ambulance that came racing along Ammarnäsvägen after the fire and rescue vehicles. In his conversation with the police Magnus had admitted to abducting Mattias Mickelsson, but the police also suspected he had killed Börje and Ejvor Öbrell. He was in custody now, awaiting his hearing.

Mona had assured him that he could tell her absolutely everything, but he had remained silent anyway, and she completely respected that. So he had said little about the trolls.

But he had told the police about Jola Haapaniemi.

And Lennart Brösth.

Susso sat holding the squirrel and I could see she was tense as she heard what I had to say about Lennart Brösth, but I don't think she was afraid of him. And she didn't have to worry for long about him tracking her down – the police actually nabbed him a week or so later. Then she drove down to Luleå to talk to Kjell-Åke Andersson, who told her about the arrest. He shared every detail with her, and that was thanks to what she had in her pocket – which, of course, he knew absolutely nothing about. She even found out that DCI Ivan Wikström had been removed from the investigation and transferred to other duties because of the difficulty he had in cooperating.

The only Lennart Brösth in the national register was born in 1914 in Gällivare, and the police doubted very much that a ninety-one-year-old could have murdered and dismembered Börje Öbrell and then climbed up a fir tree in the middle of nowhere with his head. At the same time Magnus had given them a detailed description of Lennart Brösth and described both his cars. It was the cars that eventually put the police on the right trail.

According to the registration documents the cars were owned by a partnership called the Tjautjas Tourism and Transport Consultancy. The police contacted both of the owners, two brothers, and managed to get a phone number. With the help of this they managed to track down Lennart Brösth – don't ask me how. They found him in a cabin in Gällivare, one belonging to a hostel in the Other Side, as that part of town south of the Vassaraälv river is known.

The police had knocked, and when no one answered they had walked in and there he was on the sofa, in his underpants. A big man with a swelling gut, dripping with sweat. At first glance the officers thought he was under the influence of drugs because he had a belt tied tightly round his left arm, just like an addict. His left hand had been severed and was nowhere to be found. He had lost an enormous amount of blood and was taken to the hospital.

The police wanted to know what had happened to his hand but they never got a squeak out of him. Kjell-Åke Andersson said that Lennart Brösth was a mystery. No way was he over ninety. He was seventy, max, and it would not be easy to connect him to any crime. Everything depended on Magnus Brodin's testimony, and they could not rule out that he had identified Lennart Brösth in order to cover himself.

It was lovely to come home but there was a lot to do because the shop had been closed for several days. Cecilia was still off sick and would only stay at home with her cropped hair, watching television and not doing much else. The dog was happy and so was Roland. I knew he had planned to go to Thailand at the end of the month, though I really thought he would cancel his trip after everything that had happened, but he didn't. He had to go, he said. Wasn't he covered for cancellations? Yes, but he would need a doctor's certificate, and did I want him to commit fraud? Fourteen days later he returned with a tanned forehead and a sun-streaked moustache that had grown longer. It was hanging down over his lip in a most unattractive way.

There was a shower fitting in the room and a brittle, plastic shower curtain, but nothing else. Not even a hook to hang a towel on. Magnus wondered if that was for the same reason his cell had no door. Suicide risk, the lawyer had said. And because the door to the shower room had no handle he couldn't hang it on there, so he was forced to drop it on the floor beside his slippers. He pushed the curtain aside and turned on the tap. The water was icy cold to start with and he let it gush against the palm of his hand until it became slightly warmer. Then he stepped under the shower head. At home the water had trickled out slowly and it took time to get wet all over. Here he was wet in a second. After working the soap into a lather he washed under his arms, over his stomach and around his cock. Then he dropped the soap and began scratching his beard with both hands. He did not want to be dirty when she arrived. Not this time. He had felt ashamed during her first visit. She had cried so much she had dark circles under her eyes, but he had hardly said a word or lifted his head. The tears had come afterwards, as he lay in bed watching TV. His body had shuddered with the crying. It had felt good, howling like that. And no one could hear him.

After he had dried himself with the towel he wrapped it round his waist and then thumped his fist on the door, which opened almost immediately. The prison warden, a woman in a navy-blue uniform, stepped aside and followed him back to his cell. The door was locked behind him as he pulled on his underpants, and as he stepped into his jogging bottoms he glanced at the red digits on the clock radio. She would not be here for over an hour, and he thought that was a long wait.

She was sitting in the armchair, and when he came in through the door she half stood up. He gave her a quick look before shuffling over and sinking down on the bunk, which was covered in the same oxblood red plastic as the sofa. He thought she had cut her hair since last time but he did not like to ask. The police officer had folded his arms and was leaning against the wall. In the door behind him was an oblong window covered in paper. Magnus knew why. It was a room for shagging.

She cleared her throat hesitantly and asked in a low voice what the prison was like, and he shrugged and tugged at his green fleece jacket and then they fell silent. He looked out beyond the bars on the window. There was a car park outside. Snow-covered birches. A white sky. From his cell he could just see an inner courtyard. The only things that moved there were the snowflakes and the shadows from the roof.

Mona sat with her hands clasped, also looking out of the window. There was not much else they could do. On the wall behind her was a long row of red streaks, probably marks from the back of the armchair. Down on the floor, with its speckled surface, was an alarm button.

'I've got to go to the toilet,' she said, standing up.

She opened the tall narrow door and shut and locked it behind her.

Magnus sat for a while staring at the police officer's black shoes before turning his eyes to the window again. Far in the distance a huge crane towered above the rooftops, and on the white window-frame surrounding the bars someone had etched some words in spidery letters. There were names and messages scrawled all over the prison. The mirror in the toilet in Magnus's cell was made of polished steel riveted to the wall and there was hardly a patch free of graffiti.

'Excuse me, but could you leave us a minute?'

She had come out of the toilet and was standing with her back to him. Magnus looked at the police officer, who naturally shook his head.

But she did not give up.

'It would be very kind of you,' she said.

'There are restrictions,' the officer said tersely.

'Just for a little while.'

'It isn't allowed.'

'I'm sure you can make an exception.'

The police officer had been standing all the time with his arms tightly crossed over his chest, but when Mona took a short step towards him he let them fall.

'If you want . . .' he said in a mouth that had turned dry. 'If you want to go out . . .'

'No,' she said. 'You're the one who should go out. You've got to make an exception and go outside.'

He looked at his watch, a digital one with steel links.

'All right,' he said. 'But only for a short while.'

There was a beeping sound as he pressed the button on the intercom.

'You can open it yourself,' he said, and when the door was unlocked he went outside.

Magnus watched his mother as she returned to the armchair. She sat down again and immediately pulled one arm inside her tunic top, so the sleeve hung empty. She looked up at the ceiling.

'There's got to be a camera in here, hasn't there?' she said.

He shook his head.

In her hand, which she struggled to get out of her tunic, she held a little object with a grey strip of fur on its forehead, and Magnus saw immediately that it was the birch mouse that had been with him and Signe in the tunnel when Hybblet was burning. He could not for the life of him understand how it had come to be here, in his mother's hand. It must have shown in his face because she began instantly to explain.

'Amina gave it to me. Or Signe.'

'Signe?' he said. 'You've met Signe?'

She nodded without looking up from the little animal.

'She's with her parents in Växjö. I went down to talk to her. She said you were to have it so it could help you get out. Like it did last time you were locked in.'

'But I haven't done anything,' he said. 'I didn't murder them.'

'I know that, Magnus. But there will be a trial anyway, and I presume you can't explain exactly what happened. This Lennart Bröst isn't likely to say much, is he? And you have admitted you were there when the boy was taken.'

'It wasn't me, it was Börje.'

'But you were with him, weren't you?'

He nodded and looked down at his slippers.

'Well, it can't hurt, can it, having him in the court with you?'

He continued nodding.

'No.'

He lifted his eyes and looked at the little object lying completely still in Mona's cupped hands. Its eyes were closed and it looked as if it was trying to sleep. The long fluffy tail lay coiled around its huddled body.

'Take him,' she said, and Magnus held out his hands.

'I don't get it,' he said. 'How did you manage to bring him in here?'

She sat up straight and held back a smile.

From his closed fingers it looked as if Lars Nilsson wondered whether he had the right to touch the squirrel's tail. Trembling, he moved them closer to the bushy tail, but no further. Susso had said he could pat him, but the old man refused. He did not feel brave enough. When she had told him there was another face concealed behind the fur he had looked scared. She might just as well have said that the squirrel would bite.

How could there be another . . .

Susso picked a snus pouch from the tin and held it to her lips.

'He's stallo,' she explained. 'That means he can shapeshift.'

After saying this she inserted the snus, and when her tongue had pushed it under her upper lip she added:

'It's the best hiding place in the world.'

Towards the end of February we decided to arrange a presentation. We advertised in *Kuriren* and *Norrländskan* and the Kiruna free ads, and there wasn't an empty seat in the Nåjden hall. There was not enough room for everyone, even though the hall holds almost four hundred.

Of course, people came because they wanted to hear about the Vaikijaur man and Mattias Mickelsson's miraculous reappearance. I had asked her how much she was actually going to tell – surely nothing about the squirrel or the bears, or what had happened to Jola Haapaniemi? – but she hadn't actually said, so I assumed she would be speaking about her website and the photo Dad took.

Cecilia introduced the presentation. I thought she ought to let me or Susso do it because she was still unbalanced. She had been off sick for over a month, and Tommy and I had been helping her look after Ella. It was as if Cecilia looked right through her. But she insisted on holding the microphone. It all went wrong, of course. She repeated herself and lost her thread and then started telling everyone about how Dad had forgotten her on a beach once when she was a little girl and how they had flown to an inland lake in the fells to go fishing. Over and over she scratched her scalp hard – it was a kind of nervous tic – and I more or less had to lead her off the stage so that we could start the presentation.

Afterwards Susso got up on stage and took the microphone.

She explained about her website and how she had taken the photo of the Vaikijaur man. She put in a joke here and there and that made people laugh, but otherwise they sat in absolute silence. We would never really know who the Vaikijaur man was, she predicted. However, the police had confirmed he had nothing to do with the disappearance of Mattias Mickelsson. In conclusion she said she now knew there was no such thing as trolls and that she had decided to close down her website.

I was gobsmacked, while Roland took out his snus and sat there with it in his hand. I looked at Torbjörn, who was standing to the side of the stage, but his expression didn't change, so I expect he had known exactly what she was going to say.

Someone asked what had made her stop believing in trolls, since it said on the website that she had believed in them all her life.

She could not answer that question. She was embarrassed and jangled her earrings and said it was simply that she didn't believe any more, and when the questioner insisted she asked him if he believed in trolls himself. That shut him up.

There was a bit of a rush in the shop after that. There always is after a presentation, that's why we have them. Susso and I were at the counter and Roland helped too, although mostly by yapping with the customers. Torbjörn was also there, standing with Susso's backpack over one shoulder. He was a little pale and I asked him how he was feeling, but all he did was look at me.

Edit Mickelsson and her son Per-Erik had watched the presentation, looking deadly serious in their seats at the end of the front row, but Carina and Mattias had not been with them. They all came to the shop, though. Edit was wearing a small fur hat and came up to the counter to shake hands, but the others stayed by the shop door, content to say hello from a distance. Susso crouched down to look into the boy's eyes. She held out her hand and tugged gently at his jacket as she spoke to him. He smiled and nodded, with the tip of his little nose tucked into his collar. Before they left, Mattias's mother gave Susso a tight hug and I noticed tears in her eyes.

As it started to empty out at around four-thirty Susso and Torbjörn went home, and I was just about to switch off the till when a girl came into the shop pushing an elderly woman in a wheelchair. I had noticed them before the slideshow because they stood out from everyone else. The lady in the wheelchair had large dark glasses like a film star and was wearing a fur-trimmed poncho in an expensive-looking fabric. Cashmere, I thought. The girl pushing the wheelchair was about fifteen and looked foreign. Her hair was short and raven black and she said nothing.

I said hello and the woman in the wheelchair replied, asking very graciously if we were about to close. Not at all, I assured her. She thanked me for the presentation, praised Dad's outstanding photographs, especially the ones from Lofoten, where she came from. She asked if I was his child, and when I nodded she asked if I was his only child. No, I said, I also have a sister. And I told her how we had moved with Mum from Riksgränsen to Kiruna when we were children and that Dad had stayed up there on his own.

'You must have longed for him very much,' the woman said.

'Dreadfully.'

'Isn't it remarkable how very strong our love for our parents is, despite all their faults?'

I agreed. It was an infinite love. Unconditional.

'As a child you are prepared to do *anything* for them.'

'Yes,' I said. 'Anything at all.'

'You forgive them everything.'

'Everything.'

The woman sighed and turned her face to the ceiling. The spotlights were reflected in her glasses. It looked like she had white pupils in a pair of black eyes.

'That must be the worst thing that could happen to a child,' she said. 'Losing its mother or father.'

'No child should have to go through that,' I said.

'Just as no parent should have to lose a child.'

'No, that's awful,' I said. 'I've come close to that, so I know.'

'Which is why we have to look *after* them,' she said, looking at me. 'Make sure they don't come to any harm. We have to *watch over* them. Like a *binne*, a she-bear!'

'Yes, of course,' I said. 'It is our responsibility. Our duty.'

'Our duty,' she repeated, nodding in agreement.

Then she pulled off her glove and extended her right hand, which was thin and a little crooked, so I held it gently. As I shook it she looked at me and said once again: 'Our duty.'

Then she withdrew her hand, remarkably slowly.

That was when I felt the claw, lightly scratching my palm, and when I looked down I saw that two of her fingers were hairy and deformed.

Slowly she pulled on her glove, nodded at me and smiled, and then the girl wheeled her out of the shop. I stood there speechless, with my hand still outstretched. Roland pushed his glasses onto his forehead and asked what was wrong.

'Didn't you see?' I said. 'Didn't you see her hand?'

He had not seen it. So I described how her little finger and index finger were covered in tufts of fur, how instead of nails she had claws!

He didn't believe me, I could see that. But we had spent a long time talking about what had happened and how the troll on Färingsö had turned into a bear, and Roland had even met the squirrel, which Susso had agreed to extremely unwillingly, so he dared not say anything.

I slumped down on the stool at the end of the counter. I could still feel the touch of her soft fur and hard claw in my hand. It felt as if she had taken my hand away from me. Or as if it was no longer my hand.

'But that was definitely a threat,' he said. 'She threatened Susso. In that case we've got to phone the police. It was a death threat. I'm a witness.'

'But don't you understand, Roland? They're the same creatures John Bauer was dealing with. The stallo. They're not human. The police can't do a thing.'

'That was an eccentric woman, I'll give you that, but no way is she a troll. The police *can* arrest her. For threatening behaviour. That's a prison offence.'

'It wasn't even a threat . . .'

'It was a veiled threat, no doubt about it.'

I was shaken and tired so we said no more. We got a Thai take-away and walked home in silence. Was it going to begin again, I wondered? And here was me thinking it was all over. On the way up I rang Susso's bell. I had to press the button several times and even knock before she shouted for me to come in. The venetian blinds were closed and the TV was on. She was sitting on her bed in her knickers and a T-shirt. Her hair was unwashed and she was wearing her glasses. I looked at her briefly before my eyes were led to the ceiling. I knew where the squirrel usually sat, and just as I thought, there it was on the curtain rail, looking down at me watchfully. Despite everything it had done for us I had really started to dislike it, but that was not something I could say out loud or even really *think* about in its presence, so I tried looking in another direction.

When I told her about the woman who had come into the shop all she did was nod.

'Trolls can have children with humans,' she said. 'But then the children turn out like that. Deformed. So it's not surprising they take fully human children instead.'

'How do you know that?'

'Skrotta told me.'

'Who?' I asked.

'Skrotta.'

'Who, him?' I said, nodding in the direction of the squirrel. 'Isn't his name Humpe?'

'He's called Skrotta. That's what he said.'

'He *said something*?'

Susso shook her head. 'He didn't need to.'

She thought everything would be all right now that she had taken down her website. So I had no need to worry. She got up and walked towards the door, more or less pushing me out.

But what about the bear? Had she forgotten that she had shot one of them? It was in self-defence, she said. She was sure he understood that. If she left the trolls alone now, they would leave her alone too. It was as easy as that.

She guided me out to the stairwell, where Roland was waiting patiently with our takeaway.

'Has the squirrel told you that as well? That they're going to leave you alone now?'

But she didn't answer. She just closed the door.